Strangers in the Dreamtime

Bruce PENNEY

STRANGERS
IN THE
DREAMTIME

Strangers in the Dreamtime by Bruce Penney
Published by Australian eBook Publisher
www.AustralianEbookPublisher.com.au
© Bruce Penney

This is a work of fiction. Names, characters, businesses, places, events, locales, and incidents are either the products of the author's imagination or used in a fictitious manner. Any resemblance to actual persons, living or dead, or actual events is purely coincidental.

1st Edition 2019, pbk.
ISBN: 978-0-6485505-7-0
Designer: Australian eBook Publisher

National Library of Australia Cataloguing-in-Publication entry:
Creator: Bruce Penney, author.
Title: Strangers in the Dreamtime / Bruce Penney.
ISBN: 978-0-6485505-7-0 (paperback)
           978-0-6485505-9-4 (ebook : mobi)
           978-0-6485505-8-7 (ebook : epub)

Also available as an ebook from major ebook vendors.

Contents

Contents...

FOREWORD

During almost two decades living in the Northern Territory, I had the privilege of meeting and interacting with many Aboriginal people, including many of whom still maintained their traditional lifestyles. I hope that this time has given me some insight to their way of thinking and, out of respect for their culture and beliefs, I have invented all of the Aboriginal names used in this book to ensure that no disrespect is accidentally shown to a deceased person. None of the Aboriginal characters or their names represent real persons, historical or present day. I have attempted to show proper respect for our original Australians, their way of thinking and their lifestyle, while maintaining a realistic interpretation of how they might have acted if they had met white people in the situation I have created. Most of the Dutch names that I have used as characters in the book were real persons, in the area and at the time period that this book is set. Similarly, some of the Indonesian names were actual persons of the time but this is a book of fiction and as with the Dutch, I do not infer that any persons named actually did the deeds that I have attributed to them.

Bruce Penney, July 2019.

PROLOGUE

Dark shadows thrown by the small fire danced around the cave as the man led the two young children to the flat rock. He was as black as midnight, his hair and beard stiff with white clay and with ornately decorated arcane patterns all over his body in blue and white clay, blood and ochre.

He was dressed in only a cape made of kangaroo skins. Sweat ran over his well-fed belly as he pushed the bound and terrified children onto the rock.

He looked up at the artwork on the ceiling and took in the paintings he had completed earlier. One of the children, the girl, whimpered in fear, staring up at him with dread-filled eyes. He stroked her head reassuringly, his eyes bright with what he was about to accomplish.

'It's alright little one. This will all be over soon.'

He could almost taste the utter terror in the two children as they stared up at him in wordless dread. He was well aware that this was the worst of nightmares that their mothers and aunties had warned them of to make them obedient; suddenly and terrifyingly come true.

The man took powders from pouches inside his cape and began chanting as he fed first one powder, then another and another into the flames. They changed colours and sent forth pungent and acrid odours as the powders trickled over them. He inhaled deeply, feeling the power of the magical powders seep through his body.

The chanting went on, rising in pitch as he chanted faster and faster. He went to the little girl, pulling her upright as his flint knife pressed against her throat. His eyes were now wide and protruding, white spittle flying from his lips as he continued the incantation.

The girl let out a short scream and them a gurgling sound as the knife sliced hotly across her throat. The boy saw what had been done to his cousin and his scream was so long and loud that he was almost hoarse when the knife sliced across his throat, his blood mingling with hers as it flowed into the flames.

The man reached the end of his incantation and let out a final shout of glee as he watched the figures on the wall almost come to life. Then the paintings shimmered and disappeared from the ceiling of the cave.

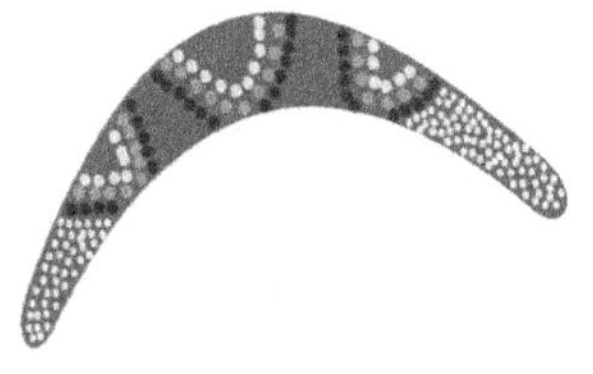

CHAPTER ONE

Tourists

Kakadu in Arnhem Land, at the top end of Australia is one of the most spectacular places on Earth. It was towards the end of the monsoonal wet season in late February and the rains had been plentiful, bringing the top end of the Northern Territory alive with luxuriant flora and teeming wildlife. There were countless thousands of birds of hundreds of species; kangaroos, wallabies, wild buffaloes and feral pigs roaming everywhere; abundant rivers and billabongs covered in water plants in full flower and brimming with millions of barramundi; and lots and lots of big, ugly crocodiles.

It was a trip months in the planning and longer in anticipation for William Wasley before he finally convinced his girlfriend Laura to come with him from dreary Melbourne up to the Territory to explore one of Australia's last frontiers.

Someone looking at him would see a big man, standing almost two meters tall, with wide shoulders, big arms that had done a lot of work and strong legs that had covered a lot of miles. Neatly trimmed, thick black hair showed that baldness was never going to be a problem for him and piercing green eyes set off a ruggedly handsome face.

After five years as a young infantryman in the army,

during which he rose to the dizzy height of Corporal, he'd decided that policing was for him. He was a uniformed beat cop, a team Sergeant working in the rough Melbourne Ports precinct, one of the toughest and most crime ridden areas in Victoria. A good work shift was one where neither he nor any of the ten men and women in his team were injured during their ten hours of attempting to control the organised crime, drunken brawls, ugly domestic violence and drug induced mayhem that was their usual serving for a shift.

He loved his work and knew that he and his team were making a difference but it was very, very wearying both on the body and the mind. In the last year alone one of his team members, a very capable young cop who would have gone onto a brilliant career, had been diagnosed with PTSD – post traumatic stress disorder after being called to a particularly nasty murder-suicide. The sight of a young mother with her throat cut in one room and her two children bludgeoned to death in another, the coward of a father taking the easy way out with a quick bullet to his head was more horrific than anyone should have to see.

It had been too much for the young Constable. He was still undergoing therapy and was now pushing paperwork in the property office because he could no longer cope with what he had been facing on a day-to-day basis on the streets. Even if he recovered from the PTSD, he would never be a front-line police officer again. Another team member, this one a female officer was still on sick leave, recovering from the broken collar bone she'd incurred in taking down and cuffing an offender.

As their Sergeant, William felt their pain and anguish, more so in some ways, because he knew that it was his job to protect them from that sort of harm. After graduating as a police officer, he'd gone back to school and as a result, had a Diploma in Psychology, very common among police and very handy in dealing with human nature. With the benefit of his diploma, he understood how the stresses of work in any of the armed forces or emergency services could get to a person. William hoped that he was mentally strong enough not to succumb to PSTD and he'd been a cop long enough to have effective strategies in coping with the traumas of his work. He loved karate and his martial arts provided an excellent outlet for the aggression and anger that incrementally built up inside of himself. A lot of running helped too but they were only short-term fixes. The most effective of all was in having complete breaks for extended periods and a long way from Melbourne. This seven-week trip to the Northern Territory was going to be just what the doctor ordered. The tropical North of Australia was as far removed from the squalor of Melbourne's wharves as he could possibly imagine.

For a while it was a toss-up whether or not Laura would come at all. Aside from the fact that he didn't like being alone, he wasn't too sure that he would have been disappointed if she'd stayed in Melbourne. Laura had consented to come with him only after carefully checking that he had booked nothing but first-class travel and five-star accommodations for the whole trip. It took a huge chunk out of his holiday pay from the Victorian Police Force but at last they were here.

They'd driven their hire car to a place called Obiri Rock, which was a couple of hundred kilometres from Darwin, the Territory's capital. It afforded the most incredible views of the wetlands around them, as well as an abundance of

Aboriginal art sites and signs of indigenous occupation of the area dating back many thousands of years. The site had been used in a number of movies, including one of the *Crocodile Dundee* films.

He glanced at Laura, and while he and dozens of other tourists looked at the magnificence of nature. She was working her smartphone, oblivious to everything else.

William sighed at her lack of interest, although he wasn't particularly surprised by it, given her general attitude to anything that was of interest to him. As he turned away, he noticed a young woman walking past Laura, and was struck by how lovely she was. She had a pretty face set off nicely by stylish short blonde hair visible under a broad brimmed hat. She had the broad shoulders of a swimmer and a lovely figure that would have set her out in any crowd. Someone from the other side of the rock called out to her, and he realised that she was with a group of six males and females, probably university students. They had that look about them although they were collectively a little too old to be under-grads. He figured that they were post-grad students or perhaps work colleagues. He wondered which of the lucky young guys was with her.

One young bloke called out something that William didn't quite catch but the woman laughed and shook her head.

'I'll catch you in a while. I want to explore a bit more first,' she called.

Disappointment stretched over the young man's face. William felt sorry for him. It looked like any romantic aspirations that he had towards the blonde were falling a little short.

William watched the woman heading off to the edge

of the rock and was intrigued as she peered down over the edge and then began to climb down over the side. He convinced himself that he was simply concerned that she might fall and started towards where she had disappeared. The girl had found a pathway from the edge of the rock leading towards a shadowed depression in the side of the monolith.

He stopped and glanced back at Laura but she still had her universe centered firmly around her phone. 'Laura, I want to have a look over the other side. Do you want to come with me?'

She looked up from her phone and rolled her eyes. 'Seriously? We'll miss happy hour at the hotel if we don't leave soon. Haven't you seen enough?'

William wondered why he wanted to follow the blonde woman so much but the thought of two hours driving back to Darwin with Laura as she sighed and moaned about the desolation and heat, just so that she could cosy up to the drunks around the hotel swimming pool was enough to convince him.

'Wait here then, I'll only be ten minutes.'

'Whatever!' and the phone was back in front of her face.

As he climbed down the pathway, he caught a glimpse of bright yellow blouse when the woman rounded an outcrop of granite and then passed from sight.

He hesitated, realising how it would look to her to be followed so obviously by a stranger. He shook his head and turned back but then stopped and turned again. For some reason, he realised that he really wanted to go after her. He frowned and tried to rationalise the urge. It was like a compulsion and yet he knew it wasn't for any sinister reasons; he just felt a need to follow her.

He shook his head once more. What the hell was wrong with him? He realised that he had starting walking towards her again before he consciously took a step. What the hell—he just wanted to make sure that she was okay.

Cathy.

Cathy Johnson loved the rock and had done so ever since her parents had first brought her here as a little girl. The attraction that she felt to the rock was almost weird and seemed to get stronger every time that she came here. Quite aside from the affinity that she seemed to have with Obiri, the ancient feel of the place and the incredible views over the Kakadu wet-lands made it so special.

When some the other guys from NT Uni mentioned that they wanted to check the place out she had jumped at the chance to come back again.

A Darwin girl born and bred, she was right at home in the heat and humidity with the sights and sounds of the tropics all around her. She felt a little guilty at leaving her friends up at the top, but one of the guys was being a little too obvious that he fancied his chances with her. Not only was he a little young for her – he was barely out of his teens, but he had bad breath and insisted on talking to her inches from her face! She wasn't at all looking forward to the trip back in the mini-bus.

She hadn't known that this cave existed and was glad of the urge that had led her to explore over the side of the rock. She looked around in fascination. She pulled a small torch out of the survival pouch that she and her friends all carried and shone it up towards the ceiling, her eyes widening with delight as the beam of light revealed Aboriginal paintings. She made out a running figure with a spear and a fleeing kangaroo bounding away in front of him. The circular image in front of the kangaroo puzzled her though. It was unlike any Aboriginal art that she'd ever seen and looked like a big round target that archers used, yet it was wavy.

She heard footsteps behind her and felt a moment of alarm as she recognised a guy she had spotted earlier from up top. She shone the torch on him, wondering for a moment if she needed to run past him. Her feelings eased when he stopped abruptly on spotting her and saw the expression on her face.

He raised his hands in apology. 'Sorry! I didn't mean to um... I was just curious about where you were going. Just wanted to make sure you were okay.'

She left the torch on his face for a moment but was satisfied at his open, friendly features, reading the guilt he was obviously feeling for intruding on her. He was a good-looking guy, dark hair, very tall and well built, like a rugby player. He was definitely a few years older than her but … nice. Deciding that he was no threat, she smiled, and remembered seeing him earlier with a tall, gorgeous woman. She'd thought he looked cute then.

'No, it's okay. Thanks. I heard that there was some more artwork down here; I found it.' It was lie. She hadn't heard anything about these paintings—or the cave. Somehow, she had suddenly just known that they were there and she knew she had to get to them. It was as though they'd been calling to her.

William watched the artwork illuminated as Cathy's torch lit up the ancient paintings. 'Wow, it looks like it was painted yesterday!' he said.

They followed the beam of the torch in silence for

several minutes, finding other animals in the background that appeared to be staring at the warrior as he chased the kangaroo towards the round object.

Cathy noted that he had deliberately stayed back near the entrance to the small cave. She realised he'd probably done so as to not invade her space. It was a nice gesture. To his surprise she beckoned him closer. 'Look at this one!'

The small torch revealed a second male figure in the background. Whereas the first person was clearly a warrior, being virtually naked and with a lean, almost stick-like body, this other figure was clearly not. For a start, his body was fully covered in furs of some kind—presumably kangaroo furs—and his face and arms were decorated with intricate patterns of ochre and white. It was his eyes though that set him apart from the other. They were opened very wide and had a strange, almost mad look, glowing as though the artist had used luminescent paint just for the eyes.

The painting of this figure was in a lower portion of the ceiling than the rest of the painting and Cathy suddenly realised that she could reach it.

'What are you doing?' William said. 'You're not supposed to touch them! You'll damage the painting.'

Cathy froze, her hand just centimetres from the mysterious painted figure. She found that he was staring at the eyes of the figure and found herself moving part of her body without volition. She barely noticed that William's hand too reached for the painting.

Their fingertips just brushed the eyes…

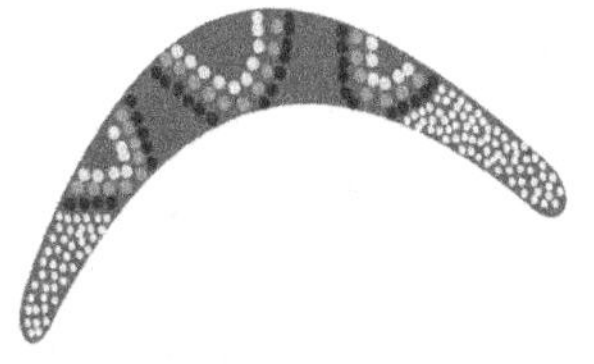

CHAPTER TWO

Lost in time

William

As his fingertips touched the painting, William felt something happen. He turned to the woman and it was like the air between them was frozen into something best described as cold soup, while his stomach threatened to erupt in protest at a sudden feeling of extreme nausea.

Whether it lasted for a moment or an hour, William had no idea. When it was over, he looked at the woman, who seemed just as bewildered as he was. They both breathed a huge sigh of relief.

William attempted a laugh even though his heart was pounding. 'Well that was...'

'Weird?' she offered. 'It felt weird.'

William didn't, as a rule, swear in front of women, particularly ones that he didn't know. It was a habit he'd developed in dealing with members of the public, although the language that he shared with other police officers – male or female, was a different matter. But such was the reaction to what had just happened that now he nodded and exclaimed, 'Fuck yes!' When his heart rate returned to normal, he realised what he'd said. 'Sorry. Excuse the language.'

The woman managed a smile. 'What language? Don't worry. I think it was called for.'

They left the cave and climbed from the pathway back up onto the top of the rock. William froze. Seconds later, the woman spun to face him in confusion. There had been more than twenty people there only a few minutes ago and now there were none.

'Where's everyone gone?' she asked.

He looked around and shrugged. He looked at his watch, frowning when he realised it wasn't working. He took out his mobile phone. It wasn't working either; the screen was black. What the hell?

'It must be later than we think,' he tried to convince himself. 'They've gone.'

The woman checked her own mobile phone with a similar frown. She looked doubtfully at him. 'My friends wouldn't have gone without me.'

William thought of Laura; he wasn't so sure that she wouldn't have left without him! He and Laura had been together for almost a year but it had been a long and difficult year at best, at least from his point of view. In the last few months, he had begun to realise that their time together was just about over. This trip was, in his mind, a sort of farewell gift to her, even if he'd had to effectively bribe her to get her to come along.

She was from 'old money' and, where he wanted adventure and travel, Laura wanted to show off her big tough police sergeant like a pet attack dog at dinner parties and on the cocktail circuit of Melbourne's so-called social elite—a bunch of snobs and would-be intellectuals who William found insufferable and who, he had overheard in turn, considered him a 'Neanderthal'. For the rest of that one particular night, William had taken great delight in glowering and grunting every time the ignoramus who'd made the comment came anywhere near him; much to the twit's obvious alarm. He didn't show up at any function that William attended for quite some time after that.

Laura was a stunning looking tall brunette with a face and figure that could have earned her big money as a model for Victoria's Secret and since he was tall and dark-haired himself, he supposed that they made a fairly impressive couple. However, he realised more and more that he and the beautiful Laura had very little in common outside of the bedroom. Where William wanted to spend time in the great outdoors, Laura wanted to attend stuffy art shows and theatre premiers. Where he was into physical fitness and martial arts, Laura was more interested in meditation and going to protest rallies in support of whatever cause was in vogue with her friends. Neither of them had ever suggested that they move in together and they were mutually happy to keep their relationship on a casual basis.

He put the thoughts of his problems with Laura to the side. 'It's okay. Let's get back to the carpark.' He faked a grin and pulled out his car keys. 'My girlfriend can't leave without me.'

'I'll catch a lift with you then if they've deserted me—if that's okay?'

'Yeah, of course,' he shrugged.

'I'm Cathy, by the way.' She extended her hand. 'I figure you'd better know my name if we're lost in the wilderness together.' She laughed nervously.

He realised his bad manners. 'I'm William … Don't worry we'll be right.'

It was about five hundred metres back to the carpark along a well-marked path and it should have taken them only ten to fifteen minutes to reach it. Part of being a cop was to be a trained observer and he frowned as he noticed that there were no longer any cigarette butts or discarded cans along where the path should be. The white painted marker stones that defined the path had also somehow disappeared, but William knew that they were heading in the right direction as the carpark was in a direct line towards a corresponding rock outcrop; there was no other way to go. The only problem was that after an hour, with numerous turns and pauses, doubling back and retracing their steps, they realised that the carpark simply wasn't there!

William stood where he *knew* he had parked his Jeep Cherokee rental. Everything was wrong though. Instead of bitumen there was dirt, mud and grass; instead of treated pine fencing there were hundreds of native trees and instead of a sealed road leading out towards the Kakadu Highway… there was nothing but bush and ground that had never seen a vehicle's tyre.

Cathy looked at him with tears brimming in her eyes. 'I don't suppose that you know what's going on here do you? I mean I know that maybe people can disappear and cars can be driven off but where's the road? Tell me that please; where is the bloody road?'

He shook his head, unable to explain the unfathomable. 'I don't know.'

She grabbed his arm almost angrily. 'Why not? Where are my friends? They wouldn't have abandoned me.'

He tried not to show the growing sense of panic that he too was feeling. 'The cave... The painting...' He shook his head. 'I can't believe I'm actually considering this but... something happened there when I touched it. It has to be that.'

'I told you not to touch it!' she barked.

'No, actually I told you not to touch it. Anyway you touched it too!' he reminded her. 'But... it was like it wasn't me. You must have felt it too. It was like it was... calling me to do it. I couldn't stop myself.'

Cathy's jaw clenched. 'I don't even remember touching it.'

He couldn't decide if this was an obvious lie, or that she was blocking the event out. He had to admit it had been pretty freaky back there in the cave.

'Let's go back there—to the cave,' William insisted. 'We'll touch it again and maybe it'll be like Dorothy clicking her heels.'

She stared accusingly at him, as though looking for other words to punish him but then her shoulders sagged. 'Okay,' she said. Suddenly, she looked down at her hands, inspected her clothing and felt along the curve of her hips.

'What are you doing?' William asked.

'Just making sure this is a *Wizard of Oz* thing and not a *Freaky Friday* thing.'

William looked around at where the carpark was supposed to be. 'It's not like we have much of a choice.'

She took a long breath. 'Yeah. I'll settle for Kansas. Let's go back there then.'

It felt strange to cross the rock again with no one else there. William noticed for the first time that even the National Parks interpretive signs that explained the features of the location and the surrounding wetlands were no longer there. Further evidence that something— something really big—was not right with this situation. He glanced at Cathy but didn't mention anything about the missing signage—she was worried enough already. They climbed down towards the cave.

Cathy brought out her torch and shone it into the cave. 'Come on then, let's touch the bloody thing. I need to get back to my friends.'

He paused, giving her a look. Finally, she followed him in. They looked up as the small but powerful beam illuminated the ceiling of the cave. William felt a nasty feeling in the pit of his stomach. The paintings were not there.

Panic rose. 'Give me the torch please,' he instructed, as he pried it from her grip.

'Where is it? It has to be here! It has to be here,' she said again, her voice much louder with each word. 'Where did it bloody go?'

William shone the torch all around the cave. There were no paintings at all. He went back outside and made sure that they were in the same cave. He went back in and used the torch once more, then sat down on a flat rock, almost in shock. His mind was in a whirl of confusion. It was definitely the right cave. But the paintings were gone, the signs were gone, the people were gone, the carpark and the cars were gone. Even the road was gone. It was fucking crazy!

He forced himself to think it through logically and went through the possibilities of how this could have happened but nothing made sense. Ten minutes of mental torture came up with absolutely nothing. Then, he remembered one of the famous quotes from Arthur Conan Doyle's Sherlock Holmes books—'*When you have eliminated the impossible, whatever remains, however improbable, must be the truth.*'

He knew that it was impossible for all the people from the rock to simply disappear. He knew that it was impossible for the paintings, the signs, the path, the road, the carpark and the cars all to just disappear. If all of these things were impossible, it meant that they were all still there - except that they weren't. What was left was completely improbable but there were no other possible explanations and so it had to be the truth! With a lurch of fear, he suddenly realised what must have somehow, inexplicably happened.

He looked up at Cathy with a pang in his gut. 'I'm sorry. I wish I'd never touched the damned thing.' She was distraught enough as it was. No need to acknowledge her part in the situation just yet. He'd need her to be as level-headed as possible—if that were possible, given their circumstances. 'I'm so sorry to have dragged you back here with me!'

She looked confused. 'Back where?'

He had to force the words out. 'I don't think those paintings have been done yet. I think that we've somehow gone back in time!'

She shook her head, a half smile on her face. 'Bullshit! That's impossible and you know it! What is this—some kind of a joke? Have my friends put you up to this?' Even as she said it, William could see that she too was getting that terrible cold feeling in the pit of her stomach. This was no joke.

William shook his head grimly. 'I know it's ridiculous. It's just that there's no other explanation that fits the facts— at least not one that I can think of.'

She shook her head. 'Nope. Sorry. Travelling though time is just impossible. My dad is a physicist and he even knows Stephen Hawking. If you could travel through time—especially just by touching a stupid painting—then he would have told me so!'

He saw the fear that was lurking just below her anger and stubborn rejection of his theory and didn't blame her in the least.

'Yeah. Well I'm sorry, but I'm damned if I can come up with a better theory. I dunno a different dimension maybe. Pretty sure that's in the realm of quantum bloody physics somewhere.' He felt immediately guilty when he realised that his pragmatism wasn't helping her in the least.

'There has to be another explanation,' she pleaded, clearly fighting back the tears.

They returned to where the carpark should have been. Neither had spoken since the cave. He was lost for words, his mind a blank. Finally, Cathy looked at him.

She took a deep breath and rubbed her temples as though that would allow her to think more clearly. 'Okay, it looks like we're stuck here together—wherever "here" is.'

'Looks like it,' William said, trying to force the cloudiness out of his head.

'Well? All I know about you is your first name.'

'Wasley,' he said. 'William Wasley. I'm thirty-five. I'm a police officer from Melbourne. We're… up here on holidays.'

Cathy nodded. 'You and your "friend"—the girl on the phone?'

'Yep. That's her—and her lifeline.'

'It's everyone's lifeline. Wish my phone had signal right about now. She's very beautiful, your friend.'

'With some people, beauty is very definitely only skin deep, I have a feeling that your loveliness extends a lot deeper that Laura's does.' He immediately regretted the words, even if he thought that they were probably very true and turned bright red. Shit she must think him a heel of the first order! He couldn't tell if she took the comment as a compliment or wanted to cringe as much as he did at his words and mentally kicked his own arse.

.   She apparently, and to his relief, chose to ignore his idiotic comment. 'I'm Cathy Johnson. Um... I'm twenty-four. I'm a Territory girl. I'm at the NT University trying for my Masters in Australian History... or at least I was.' At the last second, she threw in, 'And I'm single.' She made a gesture with her hands, drawing circles in the air back towards the rock. 'Those people I was with, they're friends from my under-grad days, or some of them are.'

William nodded to acknowledge what she said, then cleared his throat. 'Look I guess we'd best face up to our predicament. It looks like we're stranded here without food, water or transport. I reckon that I'm pretty fit. You um, seem to be not totally unfit too, so I guess we can walk out of here.'

She looked back at him, a raised eyebrow a sign of her spirit. 'I can walk you into the ground buster!' Her face brightened. 'Hey, even if we have gone "back in time" there will be Aboriginal people around here. They can help us!'

He looked around them at the dense, virgin bush, thinking hard. 'If we have gone back in time—and it's the only thing that makes sense to me ... even though we both know that it's impossible—who knows how far we've gone back? Any Aboriginals in the area might not have even seen people with white skin like us. For all we know, they'll think we're just some kind of monsters. At best they'll run from us and at worst they could try to kill us!'

'Hey! Some of my best friends are Aboriginal, in fact according to family stories my great, great grandmother was an Aboriginal lady. I'm sure that they wouldn't try to kill us without reason.' she protested.

He looked at her but really couldn't see any native Australian in her features. 'You may be right but we just don't know how far we've come back and we can't take chances until we know better. I don't see any civilisation around here, do you?'

'Civilisation is just a matter of—'

'I didn't mean it like that,' he cut her off. 'No roads, no cars, no hospitals, no tour guide. You get the picture. Anyone we run into around here is likely to be a warrior, much like the Apache or the Kiowa were in America or the Maoris were in New Zealand when the British arrived. If we run into anyone it's quite likely to be someone who only knows of one way to deal with strangers!'

'Okay, that's a little bit dramatic,' Cathy rolled her eyes. 'But I suppose we should err on the side of caution. I mean, if we were dropped in the middle of medieval England we'd be just as likely to be savaged by Romans right, or Vikings?'

'*You're* the history student.'

'I never specialised in medieval England,' she said with a sigh. 'So, what can we do?'

William walked over to a flat stone. 'Let's empty our pockets; take inventory of what we've got.'

He had a clasp knife in a pouch on his belt that opened to a ten-centimetre blade. Laura had laughed at him when he'd bought it for the trip but he thought that—along with his Akubra—it made him look more of a 'bushman' and less of a tourist for their trip to the Top End. That went onto the stone, followed by his car keys adorned by an

Avis key tag; his mobile phone—no signal of course; his Rolex—a present from his parents on graduating from the academy and still not working; his wallet, full of useless currency and credit cards; and an empty zip lock plastic bag that he had always carried out of habit from being a cop, in case he needed to pick up an item of evidence.

Cathy had a small pouch attached to her belt on each hip. One revealed some lipstick and a small compact mirror, some keys, a card holder, a mobile phone that was as useful as his was, a muesli bar and some chewing gum. The other was a gold mine.

She took obvious satisfaction from the look on his face when she took out the torch; a compact little metal prismatic compass; a small but very solid pocket knife with two different sized blades and with both a toothpick and tiny pair of tweezers in slots at the end; a dozen waterproof matches; a brand new ferrocerium rod and striker, the modern survivalist's answer to a steel and flint; fishing line and hooks; and a mini first aid kit containing Band-Aids, a lancet and a roll bandage.

'It's my survival kit. We all got one in case we got separated while we were hiking.'

'You and your friends are pretty damned smart then!' He looked at it all like it was priceless. 'Okay, we can now navigate and we can catch fish. There's lots of water around so we won't die of starvation or thirst and hopefully we can find our way out of here.'

He glanced at her footwear and nodded in satisfaction at her sturdy hiking boots. They were both wearing good, broad-brimmed hats. Their clothing was more of an issue; his short-sleeved shirt and shorts weren't going to be much protection from vegetation or insects and Cathy's flimsy yellow top and denim shorts, while looking fantastic on her, were going to offer even less protection.

'Shelter first though, right?' she said.

William nodded. 'You're the Territory girl. Ever built a humpy?'

She looked offended. 'Of course I have. We used to use them for school camps instead of tents. So ... we're staying here tonight?'

'I don't think that we have a choice. I guess we could go back and sleep in the cave. Maybe it'd be better there in case this thing changes back."

Cathy shook her head emphatically. "To be perfectly honest, that place gives me the creeps now, I vote for the humpy.'

He agreed. 'It's getting late, too late to try and walk out of here now and I don't want to leave this area yet anyway. Whatever happened to us might... I don't know, reverse itself and everything might return to normal. Let's get some shelter in case it rains again and if I can use that fishing line, I'll see about catching our dinner.'

'Do you really think it might all just... go back to normal?' she asked hopefully.

He shrugged, unable to generate any real enthusiasm for his suggestion. 'Who knows? Shit, it's impossible for this to have happened in the first damn place so I suppose it's not impossible for everything to go back to how it was!'

She looked at him for a few moments and then reached down to pick up his larger knife. 'Don't hold my breath though, right?' She looked up at the gathering clouds. 'It'll rain, alright. I'll need this for the humpy. Watch out for crocs.'

He watched as she walked towards a stand of young

trees, admiring her spirit as she set about building their shelter despite the odds against them returning to their own time. At least he could do his bit too.

He followed a creek for a couple of hundred metres until it emptied into a small billabong. Using a stick, he dug up some long, fat worms from the muddy ground and stuck them in his pocket. The mud and worms in his shorts would have driven Laura insane, which gave him a weird sense of rebellion. A fallen tree enabled him to walk out for a short distance over the water and he cast out the fishing line, the first of the worms writhing in bitter complaint as they did their bit to lure dinner.

It took him longer than he'd hoped and it was almost dark when he got back to Cathy. His admiration of her grew again when he saw that she had bent and tied saplings into a rough dome, before weaving pandanus leaves and slender gum tree branches through the frame work so that there was an excellent roof to protect them from the elements. He puzzled at the yellow cord binding the branches until he noticed that the bottom of her blouse was now about an inch shorter, leaving her mid-riff bare. He looked away and tried not to look again.

She had even torn sheets of paperbark from Melaleuca trees to provide a ground covering of sorts and he noted that she had gathered a good supply of firewood, including a separate pile that she had prudently placed to the side inside the shelter to keep it dry from rain.

Cathy was facing away from him and he saw smoke rising as she started a campfire. She turned towards him when she heard his footsteps and looked with delight at the two nice sized black bream that he held by the gills.

'Oh they look so good! I'm famished!' She grinned and

held out half a muesli bar. 'I had my entrée already, here's your bit.'

He took the sweet bar and chewed. He was feeling pleased with himself. 'Yeah, well unless everything goes back to normal, this is how we're going to have to feed ourselves from now on.'

'From now on?' she repeated. 'Don't say it like that.'

'Like what?'

'Like this is it. Like we're stuck here for good.'

He cursed his thoughtless words. 'Yeah. I just meant I'm guessing that there aren't too many supermarkets around anymore.'

A couple of lily pads became their plates and their fingers were their utensils. The fish only took ten minutes to cook in the glowering coals but it seemed like hours. When they lifted them off the coals, the bream were charred on the outside and slightly undercooked in the middle but tasted heavenly.

William and Cathy were quiet as they sat around the fire after eating, listening to the insects and animals in the bush around them. William was lost in thoughts of his home, friends and loved ones and he was sure she was thinking the same, neither wanting to impose on the other's reflections.

The fire was burning down when William felt a few drops of rain and guessed that it would be pouring in moments. He knew enough about monsoonal rain to know that it didn't do things by halves; when it rained up here in the tropics, it came down in buckets!

'We'd best test out your humpy. It's about to get wet,' he said.

Cathy glanced at the shelter and then looked nervously

at him. 'I guess we'll both have to sleep in there then…'

He saw how nervous she was and realised why. 'I'll sleep out here. Let me have a sheet of that paperbark; I'll find a bush to keep the rain off.'

She thought about accepting his offer but then shook her head. 'Don't be silly, you'll get saturated. Besides, I can trust you… can't I?'

'Absolutely Cathy.' He was a decent man. She couldn't have been safer than with him. 'It'll be like sharing a tent with your brother.'

She snorted with a laugh. 'I hope not! My brother is a prolific farter!'

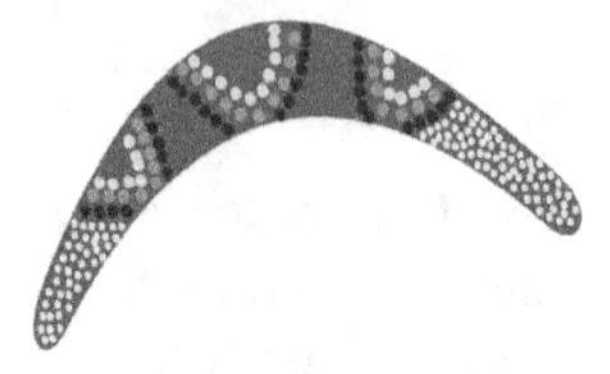

CHAPTER THREE

Reality sets in

To William's surprise, they both slept well. He put it down to the emotional trauma of what had happened to them. It took a wallaby thumping past their shelter to wake them and, aside from the aches and pains of sleeping on nothing but bark, they both emerged from the humpy feeling reasonably well rested.

The first thing they both did was to check out where the car park should have been. Virgin bush still confronted them and with sinking hearts they saw that nothing had changed and that they hadn't magically gone back to where they belonged overnight. There were still no tourists, no cars, no roads and no carpark.

Without much optimism they made the climb back up to Obiri Rock and to the cave on the other side. Nothing had changed there either and they hardly spoke on the way back to the 'missing' carpark.

It was sinking in, to him and he could see to Cathy as well, that were just the two of them and the immensity of the wild tropical bush. He saw that the desolation he felt was mirrored in Cathy's face.

William tried to take stock of the situation. He could just imagine the furore that would be going on back in their own time. They were probably using search helicopters by now and all available police and emergency services search parties would be out in droves looking for them. It would be the biggest mystery in years.

He felt sorry for every one of them. As a police officer, he'd been involved in and organised enough search parties to know how exhaustively they would be searching the whole area around Obiri Rock, which included lots and lots of very rough, very wet bushland. They would be crawling through every bit of dense bush; divers would be checking the bottom of every body of water for miles around; and teams would be looking into every crevice, every cave. Probably hundreds of thousands of dollars would be wasted and an awful lot of people were going to get extremely weary looking for two people who were no longer there to be found.

Plenty of people would have seen him following Cathy down over the side of the rock. Statements would have been taken from every one of them and no doubt the worst assumptions would have been made about his intentions when he'd followed her. He doubted that anyone would assume he'd followed her just to see what she was up to. Hell, he still couldn't understand the compulsion that he'd felt himself! He could just imagine the theories that would be flying around. No doubt there would be salacious theories about the 'sex crazed police officer' who had abducted a young woman and disappeared into the bush to have his way with her'!

By now, his bosses back in the Victorian Police would be liaising with the NT Police guys and he could imagine the carefully worded lines of enquiry. *'So, this Sergeant Wasley—do you feel he's the type to abduct a young woman? Has he ever given indication that he'd do something like this before?'*

He couldn't even blame them for thinking along those lines. If he was the investigating officer instead of the missing person then he would have thought the same bloody thing! He liked to think that at least his police colleagues were standing up for his character; he wasn't at all sure that Laura would, and he knew for sure that none of her friends would! He was comfortable that his parents and family, as well as the people who really knew him would all give him the benefit of the doubt and would give short shift to anyone who tried to slander him.

Then, he thought about all the other people who had inexplicably disappeared into the Australian bush over the years. It was an intriguing thought that what had happened to them might have also happened to others. He recalled that the book, 'Picnic at Hanging Rock' was supposed to have been based on a real event. Maybe they would stumble over a group of nineteenth century schoolgirls in their travels! It would have been half amusing if it wasn't so fucking serious!

Breakfast was leftover fish and then William admitted that they needed some sort of practical plan. 'I can't see any sense in hanging around here indefinitely in the hope that search parties find us,' he said. 'If I'm right, then we're not even in the same bloody time as the people who are out looking for us'

'I think we should head towards Darwin.' Cathy suggested. 'Even if we are back in time, maybe we're not so far back that Darwin hasn't been settled yet. It was called Palmerston in the beginning. HMS Beagle went there in 1839, so maybe we'll get lucky and we'll find a British ship!'

'The Beagle... that was Charles Darwin's ship wasn't it?'

'Yes—not that many people know that.' She seemed impressed. 'But he never actually came to Darwin; he'd left the ship before then. They just named Darwin Harbour after him.'

He nodded. 'I can tell that it's *Australian* history that you're majoring in.' He almost laughed. 'Lucky for us.' He thought about her suggestion. 'It's worth a try... and anyway we've got nothing to lose. I reckon that we're about two hundred clicks from Darwin...'

'Closer to three hundred, and that's as the crow flies.' she offered.

He thought about his normal rate of walking and then halved it to allow for being in the bush. 'Okay, so say we can walk ten clicks a day, maybe even more if we push it. We should be able to get there in about three and a half, four weeks.'

Cathy shook her head. 'You're talking about walking along a nice bush track. I've done my share of orienteering and I know that we're not going to make ten kays a day, not if it's all unbroken bush between us and Darwin. If your theory's right, then we're not going to stumble across some handy horses to ride, so on foot I'd say it's going to be more like two months to get there and maybe longer. Don't forget we've got at least four major rivers to cross and lots of smaller ones—in the middle of the wet season. On top of that, we've got crocs to watch out for and *maybe* hostile people to avoid.'

William looked at the bush, feeling like an idiot. He should have remembered from his army days the difficulties in crossing virgin bush. They would have to stop to hunt for food as well. This woman was thinking much more clearly than he was. He saw that he was going to have to adjust his thinking very quickly. 'Stuff it! You're right, I should know better.' Then he realised his choice of words again. "Sorry …"

'Oh come on!' she laughed. '"Stuff it" isn't anything, and besides, you said much worse yesterday when we ended up in this... shit-storm. And just in case you weren't aware, I'm not some naïve little girl! I bet that I know some swear words that you don't!'

'What—more than "shit-storm"?' he grinned. 'I'm sure you do.' He realised that he was treating her like a little girl, not the woman that she was. It was a habit of his to assume the big paternal role with younger people. He'd done the same thing over and over again with young police rookies straight out of college and for the most part it was an effective way to keep an eye on them as they slowly learned the ropes but he sensed that Cathy was at least as tough as some of the police graduates that he'd had the privilege of easing into the harsh world of being a cop.

William was amazed at how Cathy was adapting to their situation. She was clearly very intelligent and level-headed. Her borderline hysteria of the day before had disappeared and, at least on the surface, it looked like she wasn't blaming him entirely for their predicament. 'You should hear some of the language that comes out of the police officers I work with.'

'How long have you been a walloper?'

He laughed at the term. 'Where the hell did you ever hear that word?'

She grinned. 'That's what my dad calls police officers. I love it.'

He chuckled. 'It's a bloody old term for a cop and I'm guessing that your dad isn't exactly a fan of the police service if that's what he calls us.' He thought for a moment. 'I've been a *walloper* for about thirteen years now. I picked up my sergeant's stripes a couple of years ago … not that they're much use to us out here!'

'Do you like it—being a … policeman?'

'It's one of the best jobs around. I was in the army for a few years before that, straight out of school, so I'm used to being in uniform, but being a copper is so much better than the army. You actually get to think for yourself and there's a lot of satisfaction when you nab a bad guy, plus I enjoy the responsibility of having a team of good coppers to supervise. You'd be amazed at some of the funny stuff they come up with in the middle of all the crap we had to put up with. I had a great team.'

'I bet they loved having you for a boss.'

'Yeah, well they knew that I had their backs, so I guess they didn't mind me.'

Cathy looked wistful. 'I thought about joining the Northern Territory Police but my mum and dad talked me into finishing my degree first and then I took a couple of jobs for a couple of years before going back to uni for my masters and sort of forgot about the idea. Mum and dad are both academics—Mum is actually one of my lecturers at NTU and Dad is working on his third doctorate, just because he can. He's pretty well known in academic circles. Even my older brother is an academic—or trying to be. He's working on his Masters at Oxford.'

William was impressed. 'Wow! Intelligence obviously runs in your family. If I'm going to be marooned in the past then at least I'm here with someone who's a damn sight smarter than I am!'

She turned a lovely shade of pink. 'I don't think I'm as

smart as my parents... anyway you don't seem to be too much of a dummy either.'

It was hot and humid forcing their way through the thick bush. They were soon dripping with sweat as they picked their way around the thickest bush and rocky outcrops and dodged and weaved a route that more or less followed the course they needed. Water was very quickly an issue and, lacking the ability to carry their own supply, the location of streams and billabongs soon dictated their route. Their hats were a blessing but with the temperature in the thirties and the humidity sky high, heat exhaustion was a real threat so they made sure to drink as often as they could.

William dredged up most of his bush skills from his army days and knew how to follow a compass heading by lining up on a feature in the direction they needed and then onto the next feature when they reached it. Cathy's orienteering experience supplemented his skills nicely, so they were able to maintain a fairly constant direction even with the denseness of the overgrown tropical flora.

Cathy demonstrated her local knowledge of the bush on a number of occasions as she identified two brown snakes and a big taipan in their path that William hadn't even spotted and would have walked straight over. With forewarning, they gave the reptiles a very respectful distance in each case and thankfully the snakes had other game in mind rather than them.

Wallabies fled in their dozens as William and Cathy made their way through the bush and twice they saw much bigger kangaroos that stood up at their full impressive height as they looked to see who was invading their territory. William looked at one belligerent male that looked like he was considering making an issue of it. At full stretch, the red kangaroo stood almost seven feet tall and his shoulders and arms bulged with muscle that would have made a weightlifter envious. He took a couple of aggressive bounds towards them that quickly convinced the travellers that discretion was the better part of valour.

William had memories of seeing footage of big roos latching onto an opponent with their forearms and then sitting back on their tails and ripping them open with their huge toe-claws.

'I didn't know there were any big reds in the Top End,' he said.

She rubbed her chin. 'Well there certainly weren't when I was growing up; there were only wallabies around in the Top End. Maybe they were just hunted out by our time.'

'Yeah. Well I wouldn't want to take on that bugger armed with nothing more than a bloody pocket knife!'

'You're right,' Cathy said. 'We should have weapons. We don't know how far back we've come and what dangers we're going to face. Big kangaroos are unlikely to be our worst hazards. What if we get attacked by a croc or something?'

'Then we run like bloody rabbits!' William said. 'And as far as people go, we should probably steer clear of them until we can check them out properly, until we can be sure they'll be okay with us and convince them that we're not an enemy.'

He saw Cathy's nervous shiver. 'We'll be okay. It would be good to have some weapons aside from the two knives though. Keep your eyes open for some decent lengths of wood and we can at least make spears.'

Her eyes grew wide with excitement. 'Make me a bow and some arrows! I was the women's club champion of the Arafura Archery Club for two years in a row!'

'I thought you must have been a swimmer but that explains those broad shoulders! What sort of bow do you use?'

She glanced at her shoulders in turn and then looked strangely at him. 'Do I look weird or something?'

'Ah shit, I keep putting my foot in it don't I? No, really you look fine!'

'Fine?'

In a small voice he said. 'Can we just forget I spoke?'

She took pity on him. 'I've got two compound bows—one for competition and one for hunting. I've dropped wild pigs with my hunting bow too. It's quite powerful.'

He was grateful for the reprieve and so hurried on. 'I don't reckon that we'll be able to manage a compound bow but if we can find the right type of wood, I think I'd be able to make a decent long bow. I'll tell you what, let's make a spear that will hopefully allow us to pot a wallaby or a pig.'

She was thoughtful for a moment. 'Pigs were only brought to the top end by trepang gatherers in the seventeenth century. What if we've gone back even further than that?'

'Yeah, well I guess we aren't going to know the "when" of it for some time.' He stopped himself from adding, '...if ever.' He looked at her. 'What's a trepang gatherer?'

She seemed pleased to be able to share her knowledge. 'Trepang—they're sea cucumbers. I did a paper on them last term. The top of Australia was visited by people from the Indonesian islands from around the beginning of the seventeenth century, except of course it wasn't called Indonesia back then; each different island was a nation in itself. Abel Tasman encountered some of the trepang gatherers when he sailed through the area in 1644 and recorded it in his log. Later on, Matthew Flinders met some as well.'

'So maybe we could meet some Dutchmen if we get to the coast? Can you imagine what it'd be like to actually meet historic figures from our past?' Then he thought about what he said and chuckled. 'Mind you, everyone we meet is probably a historic figure from our past!'

Cathy didn't share his humour. 'Just as long as we're not too far back—for all we know it could be 1066 and they're about to fight the Battle of Hastings!'

He shrugged. 'Well, we should be cautious of all people - black, white or brindle, at least at first.'

'Yeah, yeah, I know—at least until we figure out who they are and *when* we are.'

'Anyway, back to the spear. If we can kill an animal, not only will we eat but we can use the gut for lots of things… including a bow string. We just have to find the right wood to use for the bow staff and then some other material for the arrows.'

The thought gave her some enthusiasm. 'It'd be great to have a bow. I could use it to hunt and I'd feel a bit safer at least.'

At around noon, Cathy spotted a bush with small, green fruit hanging from it. She excitedly ran over and began stuffing the fruit into her pockets and when they were full, she hungrily ate more.

She must have seen William's doubtful expression.

'Come and get some!' she said. 'They're Kakadu plums—taste so good and they're full of vitamin C!'

He looked warily at the small ovoid fruit. 'Maybe I should wait for a couple of hours and see what effect they have on you.'

'Typical Southerner!' she laughed as she bit into another fruit. 'Kakadu plums,' she said again. 'The locals call them "Woial" and have been eating them for thousands of years. Don't be such a big wuss!'

William tried one, finding the flesh creamy and tangy. 'You're sure these won't kill me? They don't look like anything I ate during boot camp!'

'Eat too many and you might poop yourself to death, otherwise they're nutritious and tasty.'

He ate several more. 'You Territory girls are pretty handy, aren't you?'

William regained some masculine pride by catching a good-sized barramundi for that night's meal. They cooked it wrapped in leaves and buried under coals and dirt, agonising as the wonderful aroma of cooking fish wafted up to them. Washed down with crystal clear and un-polluted water, the flakes of succulent white flesh was the finest feast imaginable to the two temporal-castaways.

The fish was big enough that they were able to keep some of the larger bones for carving into fishing hooks. William remembered from his army boot camp survival course that they made excellent hooks if shaped correctly. He knew that the hooks in Cathy's survival kit wouldn't last them long.

Tonight's humpy had been a joint effort and William learned much from watching Cathy's building skills as she shaped and bullied the saplings into a useful shape.

Pandanus leaves and gum branches again provided a roof and rushes provided a mattress. Exhausted from the long trek, sleep claimed them long before the fire died down.

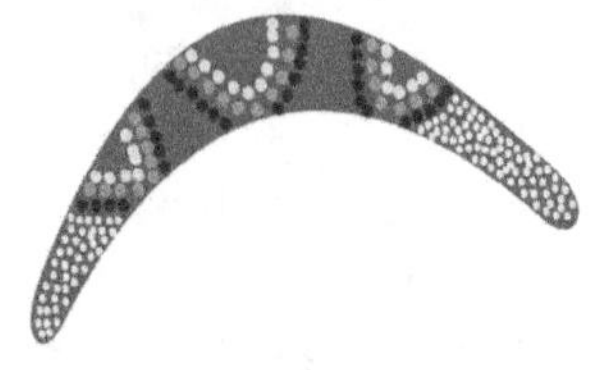

CHAPTER FOUR

Contact with the locals

They met other people a week later.

Progress that day had been slow due to several small rivers that they had to cross. They were drying off after the last crossing and both looked up when they heard the distinctive sounds of shouts of anger coming from nearby.

William had fashioned a rough spear from a eucalyptus branch to which he'd tied his opened knife and he instinctively brought the spear up now as the shouts continued, followed soon after by a long, drawn out scream.

Cathy darted into a stand of wild bamboo and he quickly followed her. She held a smaller spear tipped with her knife but it suddenly felt very inadequate as shouts and screams continued and seemed to be coming closer.

Suddenly, a middle-aged Aboriginal man, naked except for a woven loincloth and carrying a long spear and throwing stick, came bursting out of the bush and ran straight towards them.

William was sure that the man had seen them and was attacking. He brought up his spear to defend himself but just as the man was about to reach them, a spear hurtled out from the bush behind him and flew into his back, the barbed tip erupting out through his belly in a shower of blood.

The man's spear flew from his hand and landed almost at Cathy's feet as he let out a piercing scream of anger and pain and then crashed to the hard ground, his screams soon reducing to whimpers of agony.

Cathy almost let out a scream as well at the sight of someone being murdered right in front of her but she bit down hard on her hand and managed to suppress the sound. She and William shuffled back into the bamboo when they realised that other people were coming out towards the dead man.

Three tall, very black skinned warriors, their chests covered in a latticework of deep scars, were laughing among themselves as they approached their victim. Through the bamboo, William could see that they were all armed, two with spears and throwing sticks and the third with a heavy, vicious looking club as well as his throwing stick, which he'd obviously just put to use.

Their victim looked up weakly as they approached him but was too badly injured to defend himself as the man with the club happily used it to smash against his victim's head with a wet 'thud' that carried easily to where William and Cathy hid. A spray of blood and grey matter flew out over the ground and almost reached their hiding place. Even William, who had seen his share of blood and gore in his time as a police officer, had to look away at the callous execution. He'd never seen another person killed in such a brutal manner and so close up.

The killer seemed overjoyed with the damage he'd caused as he stood looking down at the dead man. Then he retrieved his spear by pushing it right out through his victim's torso, holding up the blood-soaked spear in triumph to his companions. The killer reached down to take his victim's spear thrower but then there were more excited shouts from the direction they had come from and the three all called out in answer before running excitedly back into the bush, the dead man forgotten for the moment in their zeal for further victims.

William realised he was shaking as he and Cathy finally emerged from the bamboo. Cathy too was trembling with scarcely contained shock and horror.

She stared down at the dead man, tears cascading down her face. 'They killed him. They just killed him!'

William held her to his chest, finding it hard to control his own shock and fear—fear because he reasoned that for all he knew, they too might have been lying on the ground if the three warriors had found them!

He took a deep breath. 'I'm guessing that this poor bugger was obviously from an enemy tribe. They're probably still chasing some of his mates.'

Cathy kept her face buried in his chest. 'It was horrible!'

He stroked her back to try and soothe her. The two of them had been travelling together for several weeks and despite the fact that he found Cathy to be completely lovely, he had been very careful not to make any moves that might make her feel threatened or offended. After all, he was a decade older than her and he felt that it was up to him to be responsible and a gentleman. Their situation was hardly given to romance in any case with the constant need to keep moving while at the same time provide their own food and shelter, but it took more and more effort all the time to convince himself that he was right in adopting the role of a 'big brother' to his beautiful young companion. Not to mention, he still technically had a girlfriend. Laura. She seemed like a lifetime ago now, not just in a different time.

Despite what they had just witnessed, he suddenly realised that the way Cathy clung to him brought forth a welling surge of a deep emotion within himself that he had never felt for another woman. The weak and purely physical relationship that he and Laura had shared was absolutely nothing compared to what he was feeling now. Of course the feel of Cathy's body as she clung to him now was incredibly nice on an entirely different level and he had to force himself to let her go.

Cathy

She had calmed herself within the first few moments as she leant into William's chest with her arms around him. It was a good feeling as he lightly stroked her back and she could have happily stayed in his arms if it were a different situation. She lingered there for long moments as she enjoyed the feel of his broad chest against her face and his strong arms around her body. It felt safe and wonderful. There had been moments when she thought he would make a move on her over the past weeks and she had been both disappointed and relieved when nothing had transpired.

She wasn't an inexperienced maiden by any means but sensed that if anything was going to happen between her and William it was going to have to wait at least until they knew each other better. She still wasn't sure about his relationship with his beautiful girl friend from 'back then' either and so once again experienced the same conflicting emotions when he let her go. Even so she knew that she would long for the next time he held her.

William

He saw that Cathy was okay now and, keeping an eye out in case the others returned, moved towards the battered corpse. 'It looks like we'd best get used to this sort of thing—and it's bloody obvious that we're going to have to be even more careful from now on!'

She looked once more at the dead man. 'Should we bury him?'

William considered it but then shook his head. 'They might come back. It'd be too dangerous to stick around.'

She didn't need much convincing. 'Please, let's just get away from here then!'

He nodded. There was clearly nothing that they could do for the dead man and William wanted to put as much space between themselves and the warriors as possible. He quickly retrieved the man's spear and picked up the throwing stick. The spear was far superior to his own crude effort; it was longer and beautifully balanced, with a long, wicked point that had tiny barbs of flint embedded along the sides to make it almost impossible to pull the spear back out. He knew enough about Aboriginal weapons to know that the throwing stick or *woomera*, enabled the user to get much more power and range from the spear. It was a talent that he might well have to learn.

He unfastened his folding knife from his crude spear and threw the remains into the bush. 'Let's get going.'

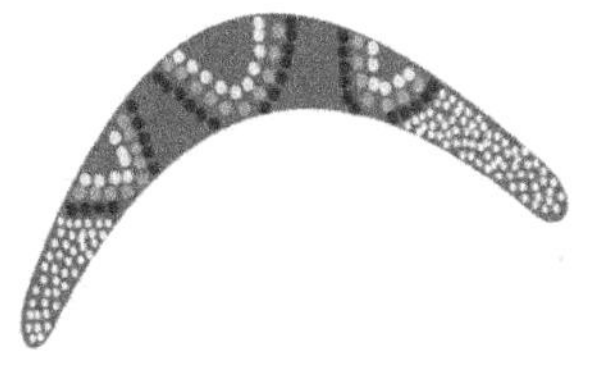

CHAPTER FIVE

A brief sojourn

They picked a route that took them well clear of the war party and headed up towards an outcrop of granite that they hoped would provide them with some shelter and cover in case the warriors returned. Threading their way through a maze of smaller granite boulders, they climbed up to a high circle of huge rocks that formed a natural citadel with an open area at the top covered in soft green grass.

It was a good defensive position and William knew they could stay there until it was safe to go on towards Darwin. A nearby stream would provide them with water and probably fish. The experience with the hostile locals had left him shaken and even more aware of how vulnerable the two of them were in this era—whenever they were. He and Cathy needed to stay somewhere like this at least for the time being

A gap between two rocks made perfect walls for their shelter and the grass made a lovely mattress. He caught a barramundi and Cathy found a patch of wild garlic near the stream so they ate well that night, though both were very quiet, with thoughts of the violence that they had witnessed still weighing in their minds.

They had a good fire going and leant side by side against

a log. Intimacy was the furthest thing from William's mind after the traumatic day, but when Cathy leant briefly against his chest again, his arms just naturally enclosed her against him. She looked up at him with glistening eyes and her inviting lips were just too perfect to ignore.

They kissed for the first time, continuing for long, sweet minutes as they held each other lightly. He sensed that Cathy was as reluctant as he was to break the kiss as they finally moved apart and he knew it would have taken very little for things to progress a lot further, very fast.

They just looked at each other for a few moments, then William cleared his throat. 'Um, sorry that just sort of happened.'

A momentary smile flickered across her lovely features. 'Yes it did … didn't it.'

He struggled for the right words. 'Not that it wasn't nice.' He said lamely.

'It was very nice.' She whispered back.

For a moment he almost reached out for her again but then held back. She just looked so vulnerable and lovely! His heart was pounding as he looked yearningly at her lovely lips, then he tore his eyes away from her impossibly lovely face and forced himself to look around their redoubt.

'This place seems a pretty good place to hold up for a while.'

He thought she was going to say something else but she seemed to change her mind. 'Yes, a nice place.' Was all she said as she looked up at him.

Later William wondered at his self-restraint and cursed himself for it at the same time as he tried getting to sleep, incredibly conscious of how close Cathy was as she lay near to him.

When they woke up the next morning, William worked up the courage to greet her with a fleeting kiss on the lips. 'Good morning, how did you sleep?'

She looked a little surprised at the kiss and smiled shyly. 'I slept well thank you.' She paused and smiled. 'Aside from the times that your snoring woke me that is.'

He was horrified. 'Shit I snore? I'm so sorry!'

She looked searchingly at him for a moment. 'Didn't your girlfriend ever tell you?'

He reddened. 'We didn't um, spend the nights together aside from a couple of times early on.'

'I thought you lived with her.'

'No!' he quickly replied. 'Look Cathy, I want you to understand that me and Laura weren't ... we weren't close. It was just ...' he paused, lost for words.

'Just sex?' she suggested.

He went even redder but then thought about it for a moment before looking into her eyes. 'I think it was just convenience on both of our parts. I didn't love her and I'm sure that she never loved me. With the pressures of my work I had to have a social life and she and I, well it was nice to have a good-looking woman to go out with. I'm sure that she felt the same way towards me.'

'You brought her up to the NT with you.'

He tried to explain it. 'Yes I did, but I knew that this was going to be our last time together and I reckon she knew and wasn't too perturbed about it. We fought more and more in the last couple of months in Melbourne. We both knew that what we had wasn't the real thing. Our differences were just too great for there to be anything meaningful between us.'

He stood awkwardly, lost for more words for the moment.

She looked up at him, waiting for him to continue. 'And?'

There was silence and finally he whispered. 'And I think that I am in love with you.'

Cathy stared into his eyes. 'Why would you think that?' she whispered back.

William knew that he couldn't stuff this up. 'It's not just that we're stuck back here together. It's more than that. I think about you all the time and not just since we kissed. I love watching you walk, talk, sit, smile.'

He waited with a racing heart as she took in his words, her eyes a mirror of the depth of her thoughts. She started to say something but then stopped herself and shook her head. 'Please William, I need time to think.'

He felt better that at least he had gotten it off his chest and offered a reassuring look. 'Hey, there is absolutely no reason to say anything. I just wanted to let you know … how I feel.'

She was obviously struggling for words as well and he thought that she was close to tears as she looked at him. 'Thank you, it's just that …'

He held up a hand. 'No explanations needed. There is no reason on earth that you should feel the same way towards me. Shit I'm almost old enough to be your dad to start with!'

She giggled at that. 'Hardly!' she looked earnestly at him. 'It has nothing to do with your age William. God you're only what, ten years older than me? No, I … I have strong feelings towards you and, like you, I'm sure it isn't just because we're stuck here together. I just need time William.'

Cathy

She knew how much she wanted to be with him and how much she wanted to believe that he loved her. Cathy had been in relationships before of course, one or two of them quite serious for a while too but she had never truly given herself to a man. She had never felt that hot spark that told her that it was love. With William it was different and it felt so right with him.

She knew that part of it had to be that they were marooned together like they were. Perhaps in the 21st Century she wouldn't have given him a second look, or vice versa! Then she remembered seeing him for the first time on the rock and knew she had been instantly attracted to him. She had even felt a moment of envy for the tall, beautiful woman that was with him.

She absolutely believed what he had said about his relationship with his girl-friend. God, anyone that beautiful just had to be a complete bitch!

Her parents had brought up a cautious and slightly sceptical daughter but try as she might, she was unable to find a single reason to deny the intense feelings that she had towards William. Now she just hoped that her reticence hadn't put him off!

She noticed how distracted he was all that day and wanted to reassure him, to tell him how she felt as she watched him gathering food and fuel to keep them warm and full, with only an occasional glance or word towards her. A tiny bit of girlish pride allowed her to enjoy the insecurities he was feeling towards her though. Men were such simple creatures sometimes!

It was only when the sun had set and they sat around the fire after eating that she finally spoke about the issue that hung so heavily between them. She realised how much she wanted things to happen between them … and soon.

'I'm sorry that I've been so out of it today William. It was wonderful that you told me how you feel towards me and I feel silly that I couldn't respond the way that you deserved.'

He shook his head vehemently. 'No way Cathy! Shit I hit you with some heavy stuff. I had no right to unload on you like that.'

Tears unexpectedly brimmed in her eyes. 'You had every right and I'm glad that you did.'

He looked hopefully at her. 'So ….'

'So are you going to kiss me again?'

The look of relief on his face was intense as he took her into his arms and their kiss seemed to sear their lips. He held her as tightly as she held him. This time their kiss didn't end. Their lips still tasting each other as they rolled together into the soft, green grass.

Their clothing just seemed to disappear as the soft light of the camp-fire washed over them and only the cicadas witnessed their intensity as their bodies seemed to blend into one being.

The second time was drawn out, their pleasure heightened as they began to learn what pleased each other. Afterwards they lay in each other's arms, a sheet of paperbark over them as they slept as a couple for the first time.

Both of them were feeling worn out from weeks of struggling through the bush. Each had lost weight too, although the body fat that they had lost had been replaced by firm muscle. They used the hiatus provided by their haven to rebuild their bodies while they explored their new physical relationship.

William quickly discovered that Cathy was an inventive and energetic lover who perfectly complemented his own desires.

Making a bow for Cathy was at the fore of his mind and on a food gathering trip, William found some long thick branches from stringy bark trees that had come down in a storm and had been seasoning nicely against lower branches and off the ground. He began carefully whittling and trimming the first of the timbers in the shape of a bow stave. Several rejects and some hours later he believed that he was on the right track.

He had watched enough documentaries to know that a good long bow got its power both from a dense central core that stored energy and then released it through the long, more flexible wings of the stave. Dragging up what he had garnered from the documentaries and from the innumerable Robin Hood movies of his youth, he took his time in shaping his final length of stringy bark until he had an almost two metre long stave, with a hand grip that he carved to fit Cathy's left hand. He loved working with wood and it was a real pleasure to see the stave come to life in his hands.

She had been busy making cord out of fibres from pandanus leaves and William used this to wrap tightly around the centre of the bow to both add to its strength and allow for a more secure grip. He carved notches at each end to fit a cord onto and the bow was almost there.

His newly acquired spear proved its worth when he managed to trap and then spear a wallaby that he surprised one morning at the stream. That night, they tasted their first red meat since their marooning, cooking a whole rump in glowing embers until the aroma of the cooked meat had them both salivating.

The unpleasant job of cleaning out the wallaby's intestine and then stretching, twisting and drying the slimy tube was shared between them. It took several days to get it right, rubbing fat onto it as it dried to keep it pliable but in the end they had a good length of usable gut cord with the strength of the cord in a tennis racquet. They cut it into lengths and then he knotted and tied a cord onto one end of the bow.

Cathy insisted on finishing the stringing process. 'If I can't bend the stave to fit the cord then I shouldn't have it.'

The bow was powerful and almost beat her, but she succeeded finally in fitting the cord by stepping inside the stave and then bending it around her leg. With a shaking hand she was finally able to loop the other end of the cord onto the bow and then to her relief she found that she could draw the bow cord back to her ear and when she released it, it made a satisfying thrumming sound that spoke of energy and power. Now the bow was done.

While he had been whittling and shaping, Cathy had been far from idle. She found another stand of bamboo from which she cut dozens of slim shafts, each one half again as long as her arm. A couple of dead and rotting magpie geese provided plentiful feathers and resin from a gum tree enabled her to fix the feathers to small slits in the end of each shaft. It wasn't the best fletching job that she'd ever seen but the flights of feathers were straight and should guide the arrows truly. The arrows were still too light to do any real damage and attempts to sharpen and harden the bamboo tips were hopeless. The arrows needed heads of some kind but bits of bone, granite, even shards of quartz proved useless. He actually found a use for his car keys though and ground them down on rocks to form points and then fitted them to the arrows. They were effective to a degree but had no balance, so he knew that he had to find a better solution.

William was stalking another wallaby some distance from their haven when he literally stumbled across an outcrop of flint. He was concentrating on the wallaby and didn't realise that he was about to step onto loose rock until the last second. He tripped with a loud curse and landed on his hands. A shard of rock cut his palm as cleanly as a razor blade, leaving a small but stinging cut that bled freely until he bound it with a piece of his shirt.

He picked up the offending piece of rock and was about to throw it away in annoyance but then realised what he was holding. Flint had been in use for thousands of years in making tools and weapons; it was used for spear tips like on the one he had taken from the slain warrior, as well as knives, axes and most importantly, as arrow heads!

As it turned out, producing arrowheads from the raw flint was easier said than done. It was a very good thing that the deposit of flint was extensive for it was three days of trial and error before they managed to produce a useable arrowhead, with a pile of discarded and ruined flint produced in the process. The heads were large and heavy but at least they gave the arrows some punch.

In their fumbling efforts with the flint, William and Cathy did however manage to accidentally produce a rudimentary axe head and a couple of handy and razor-sharp knives as by-products. It was astonishing how sharp the flint edges were and when William compare it against his stainless-steel knife he was amazed to find that a flint knife cut through wallaby flesh almost as easily as its modern replacement.

Fixing the arrow heads was almost as problematic and only by gluing the heads with resin into slots at the end of the bamboo shafts, binding them with pandanus cord and then using more resin to glue them again, did they finally succeed in keeping the flint in place as it penetrated a target.

Then they discovered that with the flint arrowheads, the arrows were front heavy and unstable in flight. They had to balance the shafts using a big wad of resin back near the flights.

When she dropped a wallaby from thirty metres away with her bow, William decided that he needed one too. Cathy's ability to protect herself and hunt with the bow was so superior to his ability with the spear that he realised that bows would be a game changer if he and Cathy were threatened by anyone armed with spears, clubs or boomerangs. The war-party—if that is what they'd been—and their attack on that poor Aboriginal man had stayed fixed in his mind.

Another down side to the flint arrowheads lay in the fact that they were single use only. The bow was so powerful and the arrows flew so fast that the flint shattered as soon as it entered a target.

William smiled wryly when he saw how the flint had shattered and penetrated through a large area from where it had entered the wallaby. 'You know in the police force, we use hollow point bullets in place of solid heads so that if we hit someone, the round won't pass right through them and hit someone else. The other advantage lies in the fact that the hollow point disintegrates inside the target and causes maximum damage. These damned flint arrowheads do the same bloody thing!'

His bow, when he finished it, was longer and thicker at the centre than Cathy's weapon and was even harder to draw back, but it out-ranged the other bow by a good twenty metres when they tested them side by side. He had to swallow his pride when his initial ineptitude with the bow resulted in a spray of arrows around the target that was just embarrassing. Cathy was very gentle with him as she taught him how to use the bow properly.

Even though William's bow could outshoot hers, he could see that Cathy took some satisfaction from the fact she was a much better shot than he was. He happily acknowledged her skill but, always up for a challenge, he determined to at least match her level of skill as soon as possible.

It was the work of several more days to make another thirty arrows. Their final touch was to scrape out some more wallaby skins and sew them with pandanus cord to make two rudimentary quivers to hold their arrows.

They had no idea that they would be using their new weapons so soon.

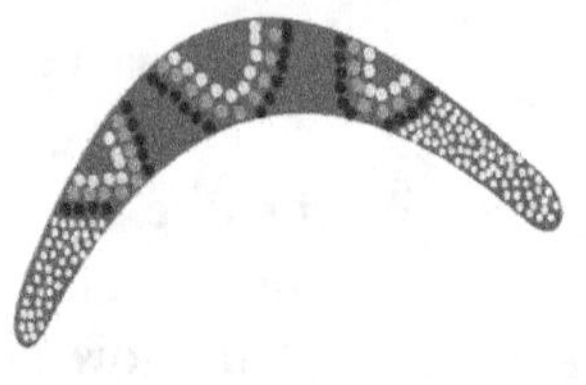

CHAPTER SIX

Jimmy's arrival

As much as he was enjoying the idyll of being here with Cathy, and as tempting as it was to remain in their haven as though the rest of the world didn't exist, he knew that if they were going to find out what had happened to them, and perhaps find a way back to their own time, then they had to keep going.

The sighting of some wild pigs in the bush caused real excitement, for it meant that the time period they were in was as least beyond the beginning of the seventeenth century. It somehow made them feel better that they were within only a few hundred years from their own time and not literally back in the real stone age, at least as far as the rest of the world was concerned.

It also meant that Europeans had by now had had some contact with Australia. William and Cathy might be able to make contact with civilisation—even if it was not civilisation as they knew it.

His feelings towards Cathy just grew and grew. He had thought he was in love on a couple of occasions before, but now he knew that those previous women in his life were just preparing him for the real thing. A part of him, the insecure 'little boy' in most men, made him wonder if Cathy felt the same about him. While their sex was incredibly good , it wasn't unheard of for people to simply enjoy sex for its own sake and without emotional commitment. Hell, there were plenty of his friends back in Melbourne who felt the same way! He knew though that for his part, the attraction that he felt towards Cathy was far more than just physical. It was ironic that back in the twenty-first century, she probably wouldn't have even looked twice at him and it had taken this freakish event to throw them together and alone.

Cathy

She saw William looking at her and must have read something from his expression. 'What's going on behind those big green eyes?' she asked. 'You look like someone gave you a puppy for Christmas and then wanted it back.'

He laughed. 'That's not too far off the track. I'm just feeling incredibly fortunate that I'm here with you and that you don't seem to mind me too much.'

She was genuinely surprised at his choice of words but recognised a fishing expedition when she heard one and realised that she had not actually reciprocated when he'd declared his feelings for her. She found his insecurity very sweet and thought that she should put him out of his misery. 'I don't mind you too much? You idiot; I'm bloody madly in love with you!'

His grin threatened to split his face in two. 'You are?'

She leant towards him and kissed him deeply. 'Of course I am and I know that you feel the same about me.'

She watched as he began to unbutton her blouse, the look in his eyes leaving no doubt that he was about to give her a significant display of his feelings towards her.

She sighed. 'There is one thing though.'

He stopped what he was doing. 'What thing?'

She hesitated, not wanting to spoil the mood but knowing she had to get this off her chest. 'William I was on the pill … back in our time. I had my last pill on the morning of when I went to Obiri with my friends but that's it. The bloody pills are back in my bathroom at home.' She looked into his eyes. 'I know that I love you but … I think maybe we should be a little more careful. I don't know how I'd feel bringing a baby into this world when we don't even know what date it is, much less what's going to happen to us from now on.'

She watched as he sat back with a dawning look of realisation on his face. 'Shit … I'm a thoughtless prick aren't I!'

She actually thought that was funny choice of words. 'It's always been my impression that most men's private parts tend to be kind of single minded!'

He had the good grace to redden a little at that. 'Point taken. I'll practice 'strategic withdrawals' from now on.' A thought occurred to him. 'What if you're already …'

She pointed to a pimple on her chin and gave a resigned look. 'Not an issue my darling.'

William

They'd built up a good supply of dried wallaby meat and smoked fish and they now knew several types of bush fruit that they found to be tasty and safe, including the fruit from Pandanus bushes that they had been ignoring up until now, so they were confident they were never going to starve on their journey. They once more set out.

Several weeks had now passed since they had encountered the warring Aboriginal people and they hadn't seen any sign of them since. He estimated that they must be roughly half way to Darwin. William hoped that it was now safe to continue onwards without running into any more trouble.

He was slightly ahead of Cathy as they threaded their way through some particularly dense bushland, walking alongside a raging river that they suspected would one day be erroneously called, 'The Alligator River' by an early explorer who didn't know the difference between alligators and the big saltwater crocodiles that were the undisputed rulers of Top End water ways.

Twice already they had attempted to ford the river only to be chased away by monster-sized crocs that thought they might make nice snacks. The big salties were much bigger than either of them had seen in their own time. William had seen enough natural history shows to know that without any natural predators aside from their own kind, they just kept on growing, sometimes living for more than a hundred years and were fearsomely efficient killers of anything that came into their territory.

They came across a lot of fresh water crocodiles as well, but these smaller, narrow snouted reptiles were no danger to them and even made up one of the main food items for their larger cousins.

William and Cathy finally found a narrow bend in the river with no crocs in the immediate vicinity and were about to make the crossing when they were startled by shouts in an Aboriginal dialect from what sounded like another angry group of warriors about three hundred metres away.

As the warriors grew nearer, William saw that they were all armed with spears and woomeras and, at first, he feared that they were being attacked, for the warriors were running directly towards where they stood near the edge of the river.

One of the Aboriginals was slightly in front of the others. William saw that he was young, little more than a boy in his mid to late teens and almost naked but for a woven loincloth. When William saw the terror on the boy's face, he realised that he and Cathy weren't the target, it was the boy that the group of warriors were after and he was unarmed. There were eight warriors chasing him and even as they watched, one of them paused to launch a spear from long distance that struck the boy a glancing blow to his leg, knocking him to the ground.

There was no thought of them not intervening. After watching one person being murdered in front of their eyes, neither William nor Cathy was willing to watch this boy being butchered when they could do something to stop it.

They quickly strung their bows and knocked arrows, using a couple of gum trees for cover.

The spear had left a long and bloody gash, with blood pouring from the wound. It had failed to lodge in his flesh though and to his credit, the boy struggled back to his feet and took five more paces towards where they hid behind the trees.

He was clearly not aware of them until the last second and when he finally caught sight of the two of them—two white people—he stopped in his tracks and even turned to run back towards his pursuers, more in terror of the white skinned apparitions than his enemies. He'd clearly never seen white people before in his life.

The pursuing Aboriginals were still fifty metres away but their excited shouts as they saw that their prey had stopped brought them on even faster.

William could see that the youth regarded the two of them in complete terror as they stepped clear of the trees. There was no time to consider his feelings just yet though and both he and Cathy loosed at the same time, the arrows flying past the youth and striking down two of the approaching warriors.

Neither man was dead but one had an arrow that had gone into his shoulder and the other with an arrow transfixing his foot. William later admitted this one was his and that he had been aiming at the man's torso!

It was then that the war-party became aware of William and Cathy. No further arrows were necessary after that, for with eyes wide open with fright, they collected their wounded tribesman and made a very rapid withdrawal in the direction they had come from, all the while shouting out to each other in their language, no doubt about the 'devils' that had appeared out of nowhere.

The boy was swaying on his feet, blood from his leg wound flowing much too freely. He was in complete terror still and would have turned to flee as well but then his eyes rolled in his head and he collapsed in front of them.

William's tattered shirt shrank once more as he tore off a wide strip as a binding over another wad of his shirt that acted as a pressure bandage. The boy was out to it but his pulse was strong and steady. If they could prevent more blood loss, he might be alright.

They still had to cross the river. It was more imperative than ever now. They wanted the river between themselves and the band of warriors, who at some point were likely to regain their courage and return to extract revenge against them for depriving them of their prey.

The last thing they wanted however was to drag a bleeding and wounded person through the water to attract every crocodile within a mile! They had intended to simply swim the river, and had already thrown together a light weight raft to hold their food and possessions. It was obvious now though, that they needed a much bigger raft on which they could float the boy across with them.

The flint axe made short work of some thick bamboo poles. It took longer to find some green vines that enabled them to bind the poles together but by the end of the afternoon they had constructed a raft that was just big enough to hold the unconscious boy and all of their gear.

They were almost across when Cathy cried out and pointed to where a tell-tale wake in the water marked a big salty swimming towards them. It was still some distance away but by now they were aware of how fast the big reptiles could move through the water. They both found an unsurprising burst of energy and just made the other side before the big salty could reach them. A few days before, William had watched a big croc chasing a kangaroo from the edge of the water for twenty metres into some bush before bringing it down and dragging it back to the water. He knew that the animal wouldn't necessarily quit just because they'd reached the bank and so he made sure that they hurriedly retreated well away from the water's edge. William carried the boy while Cathy brought up the rear as they hastened out of the croc's territory.

With the last light of the day they set up camp in the shelter of a huge hollow tree. Wallaby meat and some fruit managed to quieten their rumbling stomachs and a small fire provided warmth and a sense of security against the encroaching darkness.

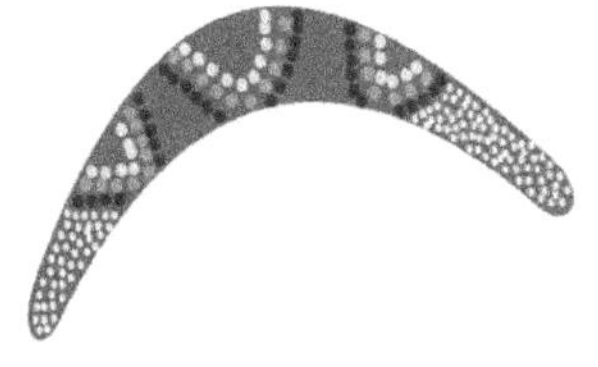

CHAPTER SEVEN

Two different cultures meet

Njimiti

Njimiti woke up in the middle of the night. He tried to sit up but a wave of pain from his leg caused him to cry out and collapse back on the ground. He tried to remember what had happened. He recalled being chased by warriors from the Ngurruku tribe, his tribe's traditional enemies.

He had passed his first initiation test the previous year, when one of the tribal elders had used a piece of flint to cut off the skin at the end of his manhood. He had been in agony for weeks after that but all boys had to go through the ordeal to prove that they were stoic in the face of pain. His final initiation test was to steal into the Ngurruku camp and take one of their weapons. The test had to be passed to be accepted as a man and fully-fledged warrior. He had succeeded in the test to a degree, stealing into the enemy camp in the middle of the night and taking a warrior's boomerang right from under his sleeping nose. All he had to do then was to make it back to his own tribe with the enemy weapon and he could be fully initiated into manhood!

An old woman's bladder had been his undoing when she got up from her wirra-wirra to make water. She saw him and let out a loud scream that had every warrior in the camp on their feet, armed and soon chasing him with every intention of killing him for invading their territory.

He'd almost escaped several times, for they might be bigger and stronger than he was, but he was fast and clever! The Ngurruku were persistent though and didn't give up easily. Frustratingly, they used their numbers and spread out to overcome each of the false trails that he left; no matter how clever the double-backs and dead ends were, they were right there. They had been hot on his heels for hours and had been getting closer all the time when he finally began to slow up from exhaustion.

He remembered then that a spear had hit his leg. Things started to come back to him and he looked down to see some strange cloth around his wound. Then he remembered the white demons!

He saw that one of them, the female had only been lightly sleeping and he cursed his cry of pain, for now she sat up.

Njimiti saw the female white demon coming towards him, speaking some incomprehensible incantation as she bared her teeth to eat him! It was too much for his blood loss weakened body and he sank back to the ground. His last conscious thought was that at least he wouldn't know about it when she ate him.

William

William and Cathy knew that it wouldn't be wise to move the boy for some time. With the right facilities, William knew that his type O Negative blood—the 'universal blood type'—would have been safe to give to the boy. Stuck here in the middle of the bush though, there was simply no way for a transfusion. The lad was going to have to replace his blood loss by himself.

While Cathy watched over the unconscious boy, William went out and caught a good sized barramundi. He'd become pretty good at filleting the barra and took the two big fillets and the wings off the fish and threw the remains into the river. The fillets were easily enough for the three of them and the 'wings' would make their next meal.

Njimiti

The next time Njimiti woke up it was to the smell of cooking fish. He looked in panic at his captors but saw that they were only looking at him as they ate some of the fish. Then he realised that a big portion of the fish was on a lily leaf at his elbow.

He was very hungry and decided that if they were fattening him up to eat him later, at least he could die with a full stomach.

The female demon offered him some water that she carried in a bark dish. He noted the shocking workmanship in the dish but drank the water thirstily. Maybe they weren't going to eat him after all.

When he'd eaten and drunk his fill, Njimiti found himself very sleepy. This time it was sleep rather than unconsciousness.

William

He watched as Cathy checked at the sleeping boy. 'He's terrified of us. What are we going to do with him?' she asked.

'We don't have any friends around here. Maybe saving this lad is going to turn out to be a Godsend for us. If we can get him back on his feet and then make sure he knows that we're friends, we might have found ourselves a valuable ally. I know it's not why we stopped those guys from killing him, but if he feels gratitude towards us then he can be bloody helpful with his local knowledge and maybe even a friendly intro to his tribe.'

Cathy looked at the sleeping youth. 'I like him. There was no way I was going to let those bastards kill him.'

William chuckled. 'Those blokes don't know how lucky they were. I noticed that you had your second arrow ready to go before your first one had even hit your guy!'

She thought about it. 'I expected to feel terrible about shooting a person. I've been shooting at targets and pigs half my life but it's so different to shoot at a living person. You know what though? I would have shot them all if I'd had to!'

He kissed her lightly on the cheek. 'When I watched you in action, for a moment there I thought you must be Diana, Goddess of the Hunt! You were magnificent.'

Cathy went a delightful shade of pink at the compliment.

Njimiti

Njimiti woke again mid-morning and saw that the female demon was oblivious to him and that the male demon was just returning with an armful of firewood. He looked down at his leg and saw that it was not bleeding at all. The cloth on his leg was different now though and he realised that it was the same colour as the female demon's torn clothing. She had used her covering to help him!

He sat up and she turned to smile at him. He decided that perhaps she wasn't a demon after all. Whoever or whatever they were, it seemed that they were trying to help him just as they had stopped the Ngurruku from killing him with their strange sticks.

Alright then, he would thank them. He looked towards them and spoke for the first time. 'Hello, er nice demons. You have saved my life and I am in your debt!'

Cathy

Cathy could tell that the youth was trying to be friendly but even with the smattering of Aboriginal words that she remembered from some of her friends in Darwin, his dialect was just a machine gun of meaningless sound to her ears.

She brought him some more water and simply smiled. 'Hello,' she pointed to her chest. 'I am Cathy. Cathy.'

William came over and she pointed to him. 'William. That is William.'

The boy looked from one to the other and then slowly smiled and pointed to himself. 'Njimiti.'

He spoke so quickly that Cathy had trouble catching his name correctly. She thought she had an approximation though. 'Jimmy! It's very nice to meet you!'

He shook his head. 'Nee… Njimiti!'

Cathy realised that she was mispronouncing his name but still couldn't understand him. 'Jimmy?'

She saw the look on his face as he shrugged at her pronunciation but at least they were communicating!

CHAPTER EIGHT

Jimmy returns to his tribe

Njimiti

Four days later, Njimiti's leg had healed sufficiently for him to leave. He badly wanted to return to his tribe, for his family would by now believe him to be dead. The trouble with this was that in his culture, when someone saved your life, they in effect 'owned' your life until the debt could be repaid. He had no idea how he would repay this life debt to 'Willem and Catty', but knew that he was honour-bound to help them, at least until he was able to repay them for what they had done for him. If he just left them without repaying the huge debt then his spirit would be seriously harmed.

So too the discovery of the spear and throwing stick in their possession had increased the debt. As soon as he saw it, Njimiti immediately recognised his uncle's spear and throwing stick. Survivors of the Ngurruku raid had reported his uncle's death and for the enemy to have his weapons was a terrible insult to his uncle's spirit.

Willem had readily given the spear back to him when he managed to communicate its importance to him, so now he would be able to return the spear to his auntie. Uncle's spirit would be much happier.

Njimiti had a big problem though. It would be

impossible to take his new friends back to his people. After all, he was still an uninitiated boy and nothing he would be able to say would stop the warriors of his tribe from attacking Willem and Catty if he just walked in with them. He wasn't only concerned for the two whites' safety either. He remembered the little sticks that they had fired at the Ngurruku and didn't want any of his people laying on the ground with the sticks in them!

Warriors practiced at dodging spears and boomerangs. It was called 'the blaantityi dance', or 'sway the body' and a trained warrior could usually avoid being hit if they were ready for an oncoming spear, but Njimiti remembered how blurringly fast the deadly sticks had moved and knew that no warrior would be able to dodge them.

Willem and Catty had allowed him to examine their strange weapons closely but they simply made no sense to him. How could such puny string make the sticks go so fast and so far? The spear and boomerang were the weapons that his spirit ancestors had invented and were what he was meant to use. He would leave the strange weapons to his friends and rely on weapons that he knew.

Njimiti knew of a good camp that was close enough to his tribe for him to go to them by himself but far enough distant so that Willem and Catty should be safe from his own people. He would take them there until he could work out what to do.

William

They spent much of their time trying to teach each other words of their respective languages while they waited for Jimmy to get well enough to travel. He and Cathy were slowly picking up some words as they followed the Aboriginal youth to where ever he was taking them. As a result, William and Cathy were able to carry out rudimentary conversations with him, using a mixture of English words and the handful of words in his dialect that they had been able to learn and lots of signing. They realised from what he managed to get through to them, that he was taking them to a safe camp but had to guess at the politics of why he wasn't taking them directly to his tribe.

'Jimmy seems like a nice lad and he trusts us but I suppose it's a bit too much to expect his people to feel likewise towards us.' William said.

Cathy nodded. 'I know it's safer by ourselves when everyone we meet is likely to try and kill us but it would be nice to find some friendly people!'

The spot that he led them to was a brilliant campsite, with a grassy clearing alongside a bubbling stream. There was even an old but easily renovated grass hut that was still there from the last time the spot had been used.

They realised that Jimmy waited until he was sure that they were happy with the place he had picked out for them before he took his uncle's spear and throwing stick and disappeared into the bush with a few apparently reassuring words towards them.

William put an arm around Cathy's shoulders as they watched him go with a sense of sadness.

'Will we see him again?' she asked.

William shrugged. 'I have a feeling that our fates and Jimmy's are intertwined. The whole sequence of events from watching his uncle being killed to being in the perfect spot to stop those other fellas from also killing him makes it seem like it was all meant to be.'

Njimiti

Njimiti's arrival back at his tribe caused a sensation. His parents and auntie were overjoyed to see him alive and when his people saw that he had recovered his deceased uncle's weapons there was much joyous shouting and slapping on the back. Everyone wanted to examine the healing leg wound and all were full of praise for his courage and endurance in making it back alive.

The Bilambi, the council made up of his tribal elders, announced that bringing back his uncle's weapons was an even greater feat than bringing back an enemy weapon and that he had indeed passed the test for initiation.

Njimiti was sorely tempted to claim all the credit for the feat but knew that he couldn't do it. 'It wasn't really me… some friends of mine got the spear and woomera and they gave them to me.'

One of the elders looked at him in surprise. 'What friends? We don't have any friends out there… unless you mean one of our cousins from the Djinjiki mob, but they're a long way away now.'

Njimiti shook his head. This was where it was going to get interesting. 'No, it wasn't them. It was the white demons that helped me. Their names are Willem and Catty and they saved me from the Ngurruku mob and then they healed my wound. They gave me Uncle's weapons so that I could bring them back here.'

The elder just stared at him. 'White demons did this?'

He nodded. 'Willem and Catty.'

Their medicine man was standing nearby. As far as medicine men went, he was fairly harmless, unlike a lot of medicine men who were also Kadijah or magic users, but he was always trying to make himself seem knowledgeable and important. 'Describe these white demons to me.'

'Well, they seem like nice people. They're not really demons, they are just like us only their skin is all white and Catty has yellow hair. They have funny coverings all over them and they tore off bits of her covering to stop my bleeding. Oh and they use funny sticks to kill with. This big stick shoots out these little sticks so fast that the eye can't follow them.'

The medicine man considered Njimiti's words and then nodded sagely before turning to the awed people around them. 'It seems obvious to me that Njimiti has been helped by Dreamtime spirits. I believe that his spirit called out to them and they have come down to this place to save him!'

Njimiti tried to correct the medicine man. He really knew that Willem and Catty were not actually demons or spirits but had lacked the words to otherwise describe them.

'Nee, I only thought they are demons at first. Now I know they are not.'

The medicine man looked almost pityingly at him. 'You are much too young to know what is a demon and what is not.'

Before he could argue further, his parents and his auntie swept him away in triumph and the elders all agreed that he could be initiated in a big corroboree that very night.

Everyone accepted the medicine man's verdict about what had taken place, except for Jimmy's best friend Marinja.

Although she was a few years older than him, Njimiti had been good friends with her since childhood. They were of the wrong totems to ever be a couple. His was the crocodile and Marinja belonged to the owl totem and so mating between them was strictly forbidden upon pain of death. Everyone knew who they could mate with and who they couldn't as soon as they could walk. The complicated system of who could marry who was how Aboriginal tribes prevented inbreeding. As a result, their friendship had been able to develop along strongly platonic lines so that they were closer than brother and sister.

Njimiti was over the moon at the prospect of becoming a warrior that night and fervently hoped that his initiation would not affect his close relationship with Marinja. Traditionally, warriors formed a close-knit group within themselves that enabled them to fight and hunt as a cohesive unit but generally speaking, this cohesiveness was usually to the exclusion of female childhood friends.

He didn't want that to happen between himself and Marinja. She didn't have a lot of friends in the tribe in the first place because her mother, who was now dead, had at one time lived with one of the boat people from the islands just across the sea.

As a result, when Marinja was born she had much lighter skin than the rest of the tribe, all of whom had skin so black that it was almost purple. As she grew up it was with differently shaped eyes, a slightly narrower nose and differently shaped lips that set her apart from all the other girls. Her father must have been a tall man as well for she kept shooting up as she approached womanhood. Marinja became taller than all except for some of the largest warriors.

She was way over the usual marriage age too, having reached womanhood with her first red flower four turns of the seasons ago. None of the eligible men in the tribe wanted anything to do with the strange looking Marinja and unlike every other girl in the tribe, she was not promised in marriage to anyone. He had heard some of the men quietly describe her between themselves as being 'that big ugly girl'.

Njimiti was proud of the fact that Marinja was also highly intelligent and was the first to question anything that didn't make any sense to her. This was another reason that none of the tribesmen wanted her. Who needed a woman who thought she was as smart as a man and argued over every little thing? He often had to swallow his pride when his friend figured out something that made him feel stupid but she was always nice about it… sort of.

Marinja

For her part, Marinja knew Njimiti all too well and knew that there was something he was keeping to himself. In addition, the medicine man's interpretation of what had happened to her friend made no sense at all to her and she was sure that the old windbag had made his dramatic announcement just to impress the tribe. Well, she wasn't impressed.

She came up to Njimiti as he was getting his white clay and ochre ready for when he painted himself that night for the all-male ceremony.

'Tell me about these so-called white demons Njimiti. I've never heard of such a thing in the Dreamtime stories and I reckon you're just making it up!'

He looked guiltily around. 'I didn't make it up at all! But I know they aren't demons; they are people just like you and me, only they are so strange in a lot of ways and not just their white skin and Catty's yellow hair! They can't even talk properly and call me a funny name like "Jimmy"!'

She seemed surprised. 'They really exist then? You didn't make the whole thing up?'

He shook his head. 'They are real! They really did save me and help me get better.' He looked around to ensure they were not overheard. 'They are nearby at the camp that we used two years ago!'

She stared at him. 'They are?'

CHAPTER NINE

Mary finds out

William and Cathy spent their time exploring the area, making more arrows and extra bow cords as well as the attending to the never-ending need for hunting and gathering food, which took up an astonishing amount of their time in itself.

He had agonised over whether to stay and see if Jimmy would return or leave by themselves and make do without him. He realised that it was a gamble but his gut told him that if the Aboriginal boy came through for them, it would be of inestimable help. He had the same debate with himself everyday as they waited.

Fortunately, the constant need to keep 'doing' helped take their minds off their situation for much of the time … but not all.

William came back from the never-ending job of gathering firewood to find Cathy staring into the stream with tears running down her face. 'What is it honey?'

She sniffled loudly and look up with a sad smile on her face. 'Oh, I'm just being silly. I was thinking about my mum and dad and how dreadful it must be for them, not knowing what happened to me. I suppose they think I'm dead.'

He put an arm around her. 'Yeah, my parents would

be in the same situation and it's kind of worse for them in a way because a lot of people will still be accusing me of being responsible for kidnapping you … or whatever.'

She shook her head at that. 'No they won't, at least only the dick-heads might and they don't count. Most people will know that you're not the type to do anything like that.'

He smiled ruefully. 'You know my folks would be over the moon if they knew that I was a married man at last. I think they've given up on it ever happening.'

She looked at him in shock. 'We're not married!'

The look that he returned her was intense. 'We are in every sense other than a church ceremony. Perhaps we're not going to find a priest to marry us officially but I certainly consider myself married to you.'

Suddenly the tears, which had dried right up, were back with a vengeance. She nodded tearfully at him. 'I think that's the nicest thing I've ever heard!'

He took her into his arms. 'I'm sorry we can't have a nice church wedding Cathy but I love you with all of my heart and I am so happy that you're mine.'

She sniffled loudly and pulled his head to hers, kissing him hard and long. 'Perhaps you could demonstrate just how much you love me then.'

He smiled as she pulled him down onto the grass with her. 'That would be my pleasure wife of mine!'

During their hunting forays, they had discovered that the bamboo arrows, while relatively easy to make, were too light to penetrate a big roo for a quick kill.

They were great for shooting small animals and even birds but nothing larger. Cathy had made an amazing shot and succeeded in shooting a big grey Cape Barren goose in flight but they were useless against larger prey. William was a realist and strongly suspected that large animals might not be all that their bows might be needed against too. He realised that the light arrows simply wouldn't be up to the task against humans if they wanted to inflict more than flesh wounds.

Their only attempt to shoot a pig had seen the feral animal charging towards Cathy with the bamboo arrow dangling mockingly from his shoulder. It was only the proximity of a very tall tree that saved her from the animal's tusks until William arrived on the scene making maximum noise and throwing a lot of rocks. The irate but lightly wounded boar eventually made his contemptuous exit into the bush and after that close call he was determined to improve the hitting power of their bows.

After a lot of trial and error, they finally found that young branches from blue gum trees made excellent arrow shafts once they were smoothed off and straightened. They were relatively straight to begin with and had enough weight to give the arrows good penetration. The extra effort to fledge them with goose feathers and to fit arrowheads was well worth it for the extra punch they now had.

Jimmy had found them a great location and they were drying and smoking wallaby meat and barramundi fillets until they had all that they could possibly carry. William discovered a pepper tree that added a fine flavour to the meat and Cathy found reeds in the stream that provided fat juicy bulbs that, when sliced up and cooked, tasted like garlic and onion combined.

Because they had no idea what Jimmy's reception was going to be back with his people when he told them about the two of them, William was a little undecided as to whether they should stay and wait until he returned or continue on towards Darwin. The last thing that they needed was for his tribe to decide that they were a danger to them and had to be killed or driven off.

It was late afternoon and William was starting a fire using the ferrocerium rod and striker. For once they'd let their fire go right out when they'd been too busy to keep an eye on it. He'd become quite adept at the task by now and had a shower of sparks cascading down onto the filings of bark that he had shredded with his knife. He got a tiny flame and carefully nursed it into a fire, adding twigs until it was strong enough to begin adding bigger pieces.

He went to the woodpile to get more sticks and suddenly had the feeling of being watched. The hair on the back of his neck went up and he backed away towards where his bow was stored.

'Cathy… I think we've got company!'

They grabbed their bows and stood back to back, ready for any danger.

No attack was forthcoming and they were more than a little shocked to hear, instead of shouts of angry warriors attacking, the sound of giggling coming from the bush near where he had been lighting the fire.

They looked at each other.

'What the hell?' William muttered.

Cathy looked into the bush and a sudden movement allowed her to make out the shape of a young woman squatting behind a shrub.

She eased the pressure on her bow string. 'I think it's just a girl!' she whispered.

William warily eased his bowstring back but was ready on an instant to redraw and release towards a threat.

There was another giggle and suddenly the woman stood up and surprised them with a wide, very white smile as she stepped out from concealment. She said something to them, a torrent of words of which they picked out perhaps two or three that they'd learned from Jimmy.

Cathy

Cathy laid her bow down and smiled in return as the girl walked towards them. 'Hello there… Are you a friend of Jimmy?'

The girl laughed then, her laughter light and delightful. 'Njimiti … Jimmy!' She laughed again, obviously thinking it was a huge joke.

Cathy fought the urge to be irritated at being mocked, apparently over her mis-pronunciation of Jimmy's name. Something about the girl made her feel that there was absolutely no malice in her mockery though. She looked at her anew. She really didn't look like any 'average' female Aboriginal that she had ever met back in Darwin and she knew many Aboriginal people who had unbroken blood-lines going back to the days of pre-European settlement of the Top End.

She appeared to be in her late teens and was practically naked, with high firm breasts on open display and only a flap of kangaroo skin tied around her hips and hanging in front to preserve her modesty and with nothing else on except for a necklace of shells around her neck. She was also taller and more light skinned that she would have thought, certainly of lighter skin than Jimmy. So too her facial features had almost an Asian aspect that combined in a very nice way with her Aboriginal features.

Cathy realised that William was staring wide eyed

at the near naked woman and felt a moment of jealousy. Then she admitted to herself that she was doing exactly the same thing. The girl was really quite lovely.

The girl came right into their camp, not in the least afraid or nervous. She pointed to where William had put the ferrocerium rod and striker in his pocket and made a striking motion with her hands, while asking something in her language.

Cathy caught the word for fire. She knew enough about traditional Aboriginal way of life through her studies to know that they either carried embers with them from one camp to the next to start fires or else used friction between hard and soft wood to start a fire from scratch. The hi-tech rod would have been a lot faster method than she had ever seen.

'You want to see how he started the fire?'

William took the rod and striker out and handed them to her. He and Cathy watched as the girl examined the two pieces and then glanced up at him, obviously remembering what he had done. She squatted and then impressed them both by striking the striker against the rod, showers of sparks falling onto the ground.

She grinned widely and said something in rapid dialect before handing them back to William. Then she stood and walked around their camp, examining everything including the bows and pulling out one of their new arrows, which she looked at in detail.

Cathy's mobile phone appeared to intrigue her. They both realised how useless the phones were to them without a network but couldn't bring themselves to just dump them. William's phone had an almost full charge and Cathy's was three quarters charged so they had preserved the irreplaceable battery power by turning the phones off from the start and removing the batteries, wrapping them all separately in the plastic bag from William's pocket.

The phones might be useless to talk to anyone but they were still powerful little machines with calculators and good cameras that might come in handy one day. Both had galleries containing photos from their past lives as well and it had been with great effort that they hadn't used up lots of battery power pining over the photos of their families and friends from back in the twenty-first century.

Cathy decided a little bit of battery power could be spared for this curious visitor and she replaced her battery and powered it up. The girl watched closely as the phone came on with a big 'no service' message.

Cathy selected the camera and set it for a selfie before walking to stand beside the girl and taking a picture of the two of them.

She went to the gallery in the phone and brought up the photo of the two of them. She expected the Aboriginal girl to be at least surprised at seeing the image of the two of them and possibly even terrified at seeing such a modern miracle. She surprised her again, however.

Marinja

Marinja fought hard not to show her amazement as well as her emotions. She knew that these new friends of Njimiti were complete strangers to everything that she knew. It quickly became obvious that they were different to anyone that she or any of her people had ever met.

She remembered her father and his people from the boats, who were so completely different to her tribe and the way that they lived. It was only very rarely that her tribe had contact with these boat people, for her tribe's territory only briefly touched the ocean. She was told that it was on one of these occasions that her mother had been taken away.

She was only brought back to the tribe in her mother's arms as a baby. Her father had only made a couple of guilty visits over the years until her mother's spirit had gone to the Dreamtime, but she had been fascinated at the exotic man who had carried her mother away and she remembered a lot of their ways and customs from observing him during these visits. Certainly, they had been radically different to her tribe but different in ways that were understandable. For instance, their language was different... Well, okay these new white people couldn't speak properly either. Their skin was different but then even her own skin was different from everyone else in her own tribe due to her mixed heritage. Clothing was the same story, weapons the same again, all different but explainable as being things from a different culture to her own.

The stick that they used to start fires though, and now this strange little box that captured a perfect image of herself and the white girl, were very clearly different on a whole new magnitude and one that was in no way explicable in terms of being simply from a different culture. She knew instinctively that this smoothly surfaced, shiny little box with such amazing capabilities was not right in some way that she simply couldn't comprehend. Marinja fingered the smooth surface and stared at the screen, finding it very disturbing to see herself looking back out at her. She reasoned that it couldn't be magic because they hadn't made any of the gibbering incantations that she had heard the magic men use and anyway, they didn't look like magicians! She turned the box over in her hands, sniffed it, shook it and stared at it but there was simply no way to explain it.

As intriguing as the mystery was, her pragmatic nature made her realise that it was a thing beyond her capacity to really understand… yet. She handed the box back to the white skinned woman and simply shrugged. 'White person trick box… very clever!'

Now Marinja got to the main reason for her visit to Jimmy's friends. He had received a new special name from these people and anything that was good enough for her best friend was good enough for her.

She had an excellent memory and pointed a finger at Cathy and said, 'Catty', then at William and said, 'Willem'. Then she indicated herself. 'Marinja!'

Cathy

She looked expectantly at them and Cathy thought she understood. 'Oh Jimmy told you our names! Yes I'm Cathy. This is William. It's very nice to meet you Marinja.'

The girl shook her head. 'Nee! Njimiti… Jimmy. Marinja…'

Cathy finally clicked as to what the girl wanted and laughed with delight. 'You want a name from us just because we got Jimmy's name wrong!' She thought about it and then touched the girl on the arm. 'Marinja… Mary!'

Marinja tossed the name around in her mind and then grinned and touched her chest. 'Mary!' Then she further surprised then by getting the pronunciation of their names almost perfect. 'Willeeam… Cathy!'

Their brief guest disappeared not long afterwards, leaving the two of them bemused but with a nice feeling at having met the unusual but delightful young Aboriginal woman.

Cathy gave him a playful dig in the ribs. 'I saw you looking at her boobs!'

He tried to look the picture of innocence. 'Well maybe I noticed them … a little. It was kind of hard not to. She's not exactly shy.'

Cathy really couldn't blame William and wasn't in the least offended, given her own admiration of Marinja. She gave a soft chuckle. 'I don't think stupid modesty and morals have infected Marinja's people yet. We're going to have to get used to it, I suppose.'

William reached for the buttons of Cathy's tattered shirt. 'So, you won't mind going around topless too then?'

She laughed and slapped his hand. 'Watch it, buster! I might be a modern girl but I'm not about to burn the only bra within two hundred years just yet!' She looked down at her shirt ruefully. 'If I don't find a replacement for this rag before too long though, I might not have a choice. This poor old thing was great for a day out with friends but I don't think Target intended it to be the only item in my wardrobe! My shorts are in just as much trouble.'

William nodded thoughtfully. 'How about the next roo we manage to get, we put a bit of extra work into the skin and see if we can't make something for you.'

'That sounds good. I won't even mind wearing a flap thing like Mary had on as long as I can wear knickers underneath!'

He raised a playful eyebrow. 'Until they disintegrate too … Ow! That hurt!'

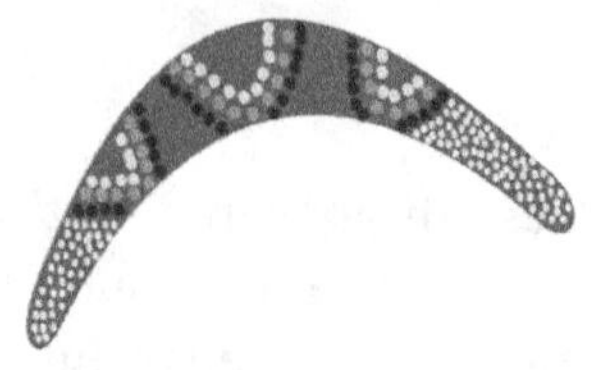

The group grows

Marinja

Marinja returned the next morning and to Willem and Catty's obvious amazement, she was carrying a large bundle containing wooden bowls and dishes, a digging stick, a stone knife, an assortment of beads and shells and two big kangaroo skin blankets.

Marinja had returned to her tribal camp the previous evening with the realisation that her life had just irrevocably changed. Even though she had hidden her excitement from them at the time, she had found the two white skinned people utterly fascinating on too many levels to not want to be with them a lot more.

She knew that her future with the tribe was never going to be a happy one. It was doubtful that she would ever marry within the tribe and in her heart of hearts, really didn't think that she wanted to marry one of the men from the tribe anyway. All that tribal life offered her were endless years of drudgery, hardship, brutality and unhappiness. On the other hand, being with the two white people was so exciting! She felt drawn to them very strongly and knew deep in her heart that her destiny was tied to theirs.

Tribal law only said who a person could and couldn't marry and how they should conduct themselves within the tribe. It didn't stop a person from leaving the tribe if they wanted to. On rare occasions, a tribal member would be expelled from the tribe for a serious crime that didn't quite warrant death, but it was unheard of for someone to actually want to leave the protection of their tribe, so there were no laws against it. She knew with a calm certainty that she wanted to leave right now. Because of her heritage, her uncles and aunties in the tribe made little effort to pretend that they really loved her and they treated her as a burden. Her one and only problem in leaving her tribe lay in the fact that she would also be leaving Njimiti behind. She would give that matter a lot of thought!

She had no idea if Willeeam and Cathy would even allow her to stay and so decided that the best way to overcome the possibility of them denying her was simply not to ask. There was another deserted and partially standing wirra-wirra on the opposite side of the clearing to the white people's, so she deposited her belongings there and stood back to assess what needed doing to make it liveable.

Cathy came to stand beside her and said something to her in her outlandish tongue but she guessed what she was asking. She was really going to have to learn their strange language in a hurry if she was going to live with them.

She gestured towards the old wirra-wirra. 'I'll fix this one up. Old Gdagaji and his woman used to live here. Don't worry; I'm not going to live on top of you and Willeeam.' She saw that Cathy hadn't understood her and patted the white girl on the arm. 'It's okay, I'm pretty damned smart. We'll be able to talk soon enough!'

William
William came over. 'So what's going on?'

Cathy shrugged. 'It looks like we have a new neighbour!' She watched as Mary began to work on her shelter. 'I suppose I'd best help her then!'

Mary began picking up English with astonishing speed. William and Cathy soon got used to the sight of the semi naked girl around their camp as she helped out with work, showed them some of her cooking techniques and continually pestered them for the English words for everything and anything she could think of.

It never ceased to amaze either of them that once Mary learned a word, she almost never forgot it and was stringing sentences together after only a couple of days. In the process, the two of them picked up a lot of Mary's dialect but neither of them had her rapidly growing fluency or vocabulary.

She was a delight to have in their camp but it was only at night that her presence was not quite as appreciated, at least from William's point of view, for the very simple reason that Cathy decided that they couldn't possibly make love with Mary only a few metres away. William did his best to reassure Cathy of how quiet they could be but it made no difference; he was on short rations until further notice.

During the next few days, Mary took an interest in the bows. Cathy showed her how to use her bow and wasn't in the least surprised that she was able to draw it fully back with ease. She set up a target of matting that Mary wove for her and allowed her new friend to practise with the bamboo arrows.

Mary cast a critical eye over the flint arrowheads. 'These ones not much good, break too easy and too heavy. See break lines in rock? That is why they break up when they hit. We go make gooder ones.'

'Fault lines and better ones.' Cathy corrected.

Mary nodded. 'Fault lines, better ones.' It was clearly locked away. 'William come too?'

William walked over. He wasn't at all surprised that Mary now pronounce his name correctly. 'Sure, I'm always happy to learn. You don't need to tell me how crappy my arrowheads are!'

Mary led them to a flint deposit about half a kilometre from their camp and went immediately to where her tribe had cached tools for working the flint. She selected a square, hand-sized square piece of quartz and then picked out a dozen likely pieces of flint, sitting down at a large flat stone that had been used over many generations for just this purpose. She glanced once at the single arrow that she'd brought from the camp and then set to work.

Cathy and William watched as she expertly used the square stone to flake away minute amounts of flint as she formed the shape of arrowheads. Where William had chipped away half a dozen bits of flint to shape his heads, Mary chipped and flaked hundreds of tiny flint bits until she was satisfied with the result.

She handed two of the finished products to William, who turned them over in his hands. The flint tips were much smaller than the ones he had crudely made but being more compact and with a narrower tip were going to penetrate much easier and be less likely to shatter on impact.

'I've seen North American flint arrowheads in museums that look exactly like this one. This is incredible! Look how sharp the edges and the points are.'

Mary glanced up. 'I made you happy? Good. But later you can tell me what is museum. Now I'm busy.'

She produced thirty arrow-heads during the morning and then showed them how to secure them a lot more solidly to the shafts.

William looked at the finished product and had to ask. 'Mary, these are very, very good arrows. How did you know how to do it? Have you seen some of these before?'

The girl was delighted to have pleased her big new friend. 'No, I never see little sticks… arrows before.'

'Then how did you know how to fix them up like you've done?'

She shrugged. 'Fixing arrows is same as fixing spear, just smaller and with feathers! It is all the same otherwise. Men from my tribe say that females shouldn't even know how to make weapons. They say that it is only for men to do, but that is rubbish and I just ignore them. I can make better spears than any of them. Arrows are just the same. They must have balance and must be made proper… properly.'

Cathy was listening and interrupted. 'Honey, why don't you make a bow for Mary?'

The Aboriginal girl grinned at the suggestion but William had a sudden worrying thought and shook his head. 'I'm not sure that's such a good idea.' He said with a cautious look on his face.

He drew her to the side and lowered his voice. 'Cathy, if we're actually in the sixteenth or seventeenth century, we have to be very careful not to 'change' things too much. I didn't think it through properly before and feel really stupid now that I think about it. We shouldn't have even let Mary improve the arrows like she's done. What if her tribe is suddenly armed with long-bows that out-shoot anything that their enemies have? In a few years they would control this whole area and then who knows what effect that will have on the future. For all we know, it could spark a stone-age version of an arms race, and the use of bows and arrows could spread like wild-fire. Can you imagine if the first fleet lands in 1788 only to be met by a shower of arrows fired by hundreds of black fellas armed like English long-bowmen?'

He paused but then went on. 'Just the fact that we're here might change the future. Shit, it probably already has in some way and who knows what the ramifications will be for the future? I think that we need to start thinking about ways that we can minimalize any changes that we cause.'

He glanced at Mary regretfully. He really liked her. She was a breath of fresh air after the trials that they'd been through and she and Cathy got on like a house on fire, so his next words were hard for him to say. 'As a matter of fact, we probably shouldn't even let Mary stay here with us any longer. We're probably ruining her life by the effect that we're having on her already through her contact with us.'

Either he was talking more loudly than he thought or Mary's hearing was better than he expected for now she stormed over to them, her voice angry for the first time since they'd known her. She walked right up to him until they were almost touching and looked defiantly up at him.

'Don't you talk about sending me away because I'm not going! I'm here because it's the best place for me. It is not good for me with my people. This is my place... with Cathy and with you! I don't belong with my tribe anymore; this is where I belong and this is my tribe now!'

Cathy

Cathy felt close to tears. She knew that what William said was right and yet the thought of making Mary leave them tore her heart out. She knew that she had to be strong though, to think of what was best for Mary, no matter how much she would have liked to keep her with them.

She put an arm around Mary's shoulders and walked a short distance away. She could tell that Mary was still angry and didn't blame her. 'I don't want you to go either Mary, but maybe William has a point. Don't you want to get married and have babies?'

Mary's anger seemed to disappear in an instant as she had a sudden inspiration. She looked briefly at Cathy and then back to William as it all clicked into place. Her eyes sparkled as she smiled and whispered. 'Sure I will have babies. You are going to have to share your man with me!'

Cathy was speechless and actually took a step backwards. 'Wh… what?'

Mary suddenly felt much happier. The solution to their problem was so simple that she wondered it hadn't occurred to her immediately. She smiled to herself and nodded. The matter was all settled as far as she was concerned. 'Sure Cathy… not hurries but we will share William. I think he is enough man for two wives!'

Cathy just stared at her with an open mouth and a stunned look on her face.

William

William looked across and was worried about that look that Mary had given him before she and Cathy started whispering. He wondered why Mary was smiling with such a strange, almost triumphant look while Cathy looked like she was standing in front of an on-coming train. He came over to them. 'What's going on? What's she saying? Did you explain why she has to leave us?'

Cathy just stared at him for a moment, then back at Mary before she finally replied and even then, her voice was unnaturally high, almost with an edge of hysteria to it.

'Um, she doesn't want to go. I'm sure we can sort something out but Mary is apparently not leaving us just at the moment.'

He looked at her, waiting for her to explain further but she could only offer him a weak smile, a helpless shrug and nothing else.

Mary looked at him with that disconcerting smile that made him distinctly nervous. 'I reckon I might be with you for long time!' she said.

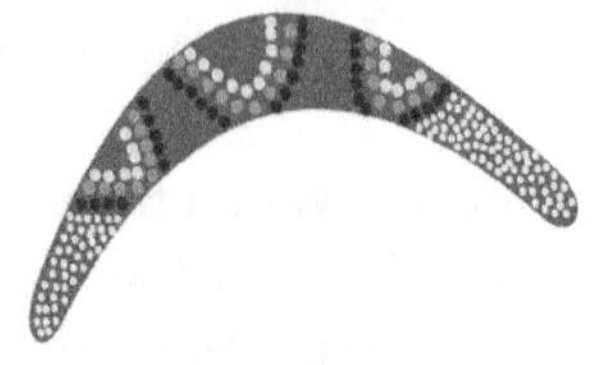

A Sapphic encounter

Njimiti

Njimiti visited them a couple of days later and proudly displayed his new initiation scars.

Cathy came over to him with a look of horror on her face, appalled at what had been done to him. Two parallel cuts had been made across his chest and then some sort of black mixture forced into the cuts. The result was deeply ridged black lines across his chest that stood out starkly like thin black sausages under his skin. They didn't look to be infected at all but tiny bits of blood still seeped along the cut lines through what appeared to be ashes and some other substance that had been rubbed into the raw wounds

Cathy surprised him in his own language. 'Oh Jimmy, that must have hurt very much!'

He was immensely proud of his initiation cuts. He had stood and endured them without any reaction whatsoever as his elder had slashed twice slowly across his chest with a flint knife, before taking a mixture of ashes and goanna fat and rubbing it into the cuts. Following so closely to his leg wound, he had nearly passed out with the incredible pain but had managed to stand stoically throughout. To have shown any of the pain he was feeling would have diminished him immensely in front of the men of his tribe.

Afterwards and out of sight of anyone else, his mother and auntie had soothed a paste of bush medicine onto his cuts that had gloriously numbed the pain. It had all been worth it though for now he was a warrior.

He blinked at hearing his language, however badly pronounced, coming from the yellow haired white girl. He looked toward Mary. 'Marinja, you've taught her to speak the language!'

She smiled smugly. 'Not only that but I can speak English!'

'What's 'English'?

'It's what smart people speak… do you mean that you can't?' This said with a cheeky grin. 'And by the way, my new name is Mary!'

The young warrior was now seriously aggrieved. 'Hey I'm just as smart as you and I learned some of their 'English' too before you even came here to annoy me. Why do you have a white fella name? I'm the only one with one of those!'

Mary grinned. 'Well that's too bad because I'm going to stay with them from now on and if you were as smart as you think you are then you'd find a nice girl and come and live with us too!'

Now he looked at her with alarm. 'Marinja, you can't just leave the tribe, they will punish you!'

She looked back at him challengingly. 'Why should I stay there? No man of the tribe wants me and I certainly don't want any of them! Everyone except you treat me like I'm an outcast anyway just because my mother was with a man from the boats. You're my only friend in the whole tribe so damn them! William and Cathy are wonderful and my life is now tied to theirs.'

Now she seemed to feel a wave of sadness. 'Njimiti, I will feel bad if I can't see you anymore but can't you see how I feel? William and Cathy saved your life; don't you feel a connection to them too? Cathy is such a wonderful person and William is a strong leader! It will be good with them.'

Njimiti worried for his friend. 'The elders won't let you just go and if I go too, they will lose a warrior! They won't let it happen.'

'Yes they will. They will be happy to see the back of me and you are only just initiated so they won't lose a proven warrior, just a boy whose scars haven't stopped bleeding yet! Why don't you go and steal a bride and come with us too?'

That made him pause. It was true that now he was a warrior, if an untried one and as such was able to take a wife if he could find one. He was a man in his body and he had passed the tests of manhood, so there was nothing to stop him. There was a girl from the tribe who was promised to him but she was only four years old and so he would have to wait at least until the year after her first red flowering. His manhood could shrivel up and die by that time! The most efficient and time-honoured way to find a wife was to literally steal one. If he could go to another tribe and kidnap a girl… He remembered a sweet girl he had seen at the last tribal gathering.

She was from the Djinjiki people, who were related to his tribe. They had spoken and he thought she was the prettiest girl he had ever met. If he could go to where they were camped and steal Ajunda, then he could be a real man with a woman! The idea appealed to his sense of daring. Of course, if his cousins the Djinjiki caught him trying to steal Ajunda they would kill him but she would be worth the risk.

What Mary said about him being tied to the white people was also true. He owed them his life and if they went away with his friend then how would he ever be able to repay the debt?

He grabbed his spear from where he had laid it down and nodded. 'I must go and think about these things. I will decide and then come back.'

Marinja

William and Cathy's grasp of their language hadn't had a hope of keeping up with the rapid-fire conversation between Njimiti and Marinja so as Cathy watched him wave to them before walking back into the bush, she had to ask. 'Where is Jimmy going?'

Marinja threw her a confident look. 'He's going to find out if he is a man yet. Don't worry though, Njimiti will come back. He's going to join our tribe.'

Cathy's eyes widened. 'We have a tribe?'

She smiled back at her. 'When William gives me and you beautiful babies, we will have the start of one!'

Cathy was grateful that William hadn't heard that bit. She sighed, completely lost for a reply.

Marinja came up to her the following day. 'Come on, I'll show you a really nice place to wash with water that falls on you.'

'You mean a waterfall? That sounds marvellous. I'll tell William.'

'No, just us. It is time for girl talk.'

Cathy

For some reason, Mary appeared to be in a hurry and Cathy had trouble keeping up with the Aboriginal woman as she loped along in an effortless, ground eating pace. This was a direction that she and William hadn't hunted in and she hadn't even known there was a stream this way, let alone a waterfall. After fifteen minutes, she heard the distinctive sound of a waterfall or cascade from up ahead. The thought of washing off the sweat and grime of the last day under lovely cool water was enough to lend wings to her feet so that she actually drew closer to Mary as they finally reached their destination.

It was only a small pool at the base of a delightful little waterfall that fell from about ten metres but it was crystal clear and so inviting, with a white, sandy floor.

Cathy had taken to wearing a kangaroo skin 'bikini' for the lack of a better word as her old clothing had finally given up the ghost and had been consigned to the rag pile along with William's shirt. Her inspiration for the garments had been what Raquel Welch had worn in the movie, *One Million Years BC*. She loved watching old movies and that had been one of her favourites. Her new wardrobe had won William's absolute approval for how much of her was now on display.

Mary however still wore only a loincloth and this came straight off as she dived into the cool, clear pool, surfacing half way out and grinning back at Cathy. 'It is really nice, come on Cathy. What are you waiting for?'

Cathy hesitated and was about to jump in fully clothed, or in as much as she had on at any rate, but then chided herself for her self-consciousness and dropped the newest items in her not-so-extensive wardrobe onto the grass.

Her attempts to appear unconcerned at her nudity was hardly rewarded however, for Mary immediately started giggling and pointing to her groin area. 'You are yellow hair there too!'

Cathy reddened and dived as quickly as she could into the water, hoping the cool water would soothe her burning face. Being blonde helped of course, but since coming back to this time, she had done her best to groom her bodily hair, even finding a type of pumice stone that, together with a curved, razor sharp flint had enabled her to keep her leg hair under control but hair in other parts of her body was much more problematic. William had it much easier of course, only needing to use his knife to keep his beard trimmed and hair at a reasonable length.

If Mary had any idea of the embarrassment she had caused then she gave no sign of it, instead swimming over to stop within inches of her. She looked boldly down into the clear water at Cathy's body and sighed. 'You are so pretty. I don't reckon William will want ugly girl like me when he has you.'

This only brought up the subject that Cathy had been very anxious to avoid altogether but she knew that she had to clear the air.

'Look Mary, in the first place you are not ugly at all; in fact, you're very pretty. The problem isn't whether you are pretty or not. The problem is that I don't know how William is going to feel about this idea of yours. I don't even know how I feel about it! William is my man, after all. The idea of sharing him isn't one I've ever contemplated!'

'What is 'contemplated'?'

'It means thought about… In my society once a man and a woman are married, they have each other and that's it.

We don't generally go sleeping around or sharing our partners with other people.'

Then she thought about the rampant infidelity and instance of divorces in the 21st Century and realised how inaccurate her statement had been and amended what she'd said. 'Well I guess some people don't really stick to the rules, but most people do. My point is Mary, I think of William as my man, my husband. I'm not sure that I can share him with you.'

Marinja put a hand on her arm and stared at her for a moment. 'I am your friend Cathy, aren't I?'

'Of course you are my friend Mary, in fact you are my only female friend in the entire universe at the moment!'

'Well then I don't understand. Our people's way is to share with friends. If I have too much kangaroo then I share with my friend and my friend's family. The same if I have too many witchety grubs, or too many woial. We share.'

Cathy scoffed. 'That's hardly the same as sharing my man with you!'

'Oh but it is! If Auntie's man is killed in battle then my Auntie will share her sister's man. It wouldn't be fair for her to go without sex after all! It is the way of things. I think we are more than friends Cathy. I think that we are sisters.'

Cathy was feeling more and more hemmed in by Mary's homespun logic. She knew of course that Aboriginal people shared just about everything with family. In her own time, whenever any of her Aboriginal friends came into a lot of money it was very quickly distributed about until nothing was left. A mining royalty cheque of a million dollars could dissipate within weeks once all the family members put their hands out for their share. There was no such thing as a traditional Aboriginal millionaire in the twenty first century.

She realised that to Mary, her argument was perfectly logical and correct. How was she to refute it by applying the moral standards of her own time? She wasn't about to deny that Mary was her friend, for she treasured her friendship, conversation and companionship and indeed, even her description of themselves as 'sisters' wasn't inaccurate, so strong was the bond that she felt for her.

In the end, she took the coward's way out. 'I'll think about it Mary, honestly I will.'

The other girl grinned and leant forward. 'I think about it all the time and it makes me hot in my pussy!'

Cathy burst out laughing. 'It makes you what!'

'Hot… you know, down there… It is called my pussy isn't it?'

The conversation was very rapidly becoming very uncomfortable. She vaguely recalled making a reference to 'her pussy' during an earlier conversation about how Aboriginal women handled their menstrual cycle and shouldn't have been surprised that Mary had picked up on the word. 'Well… that's one of the names for it.'

The conversation had come up when she had enquired how old Mary was.

She had shrugged. 'I don't know. I had my first bleeding four turns of the seasons ago. I have heard you and William talk of years but I am now sure if that is a year or not.'

Cathy calculated that if Mary had begun menstruating four years ago, that must make her somewhere between fifteen and eighteen. She certainly looked physically older than a fifteen-year-old so she was confident that the latter would be closer to the mark. She was still so young, but then she realised that the 'legal age of consent' didn't exist back in these times.

Now she snapped back to the present as Mary moved even closer to her and casually cupped Cathy's breasts in her hands. 'Your breasts are very firm and very nice. They will be good for feeding your babies. They feel so good.'

Cathy was startled at her breasts being touched and yet she realised that this sort of physical contact was perfectly normal for Mary. She reddened a little bit but did nothing to move away. She felt her heart-rate increasing as the long, soft fingers soothed over her sensitive nipples. She had to look up slightly at the taller woman. 'Um thank you, I guess yours are pretty nice too.'

Mary looked into her eyes with a smile. 'Black girls touch each other for pleasure. Do white girls do the same?'

Cathy went a little redder as memories of experimenting with one of her friends from high school came to mind. 'Well, sometimes…'

Mary was now toying with the very erect nipples, sending jolts of pleasure radiating from Cathy's breasts and through her body. She continued to look into her eyes. 'Am I giving you pleasure now?'

Cathy was about to answer but then her breath caught in her throat as one of Mary's hands slid through the cool water and down her body to between her legs. She bit her lip and suddenly found herself leaning onto Mary's shoulder as the girl's agile fingers found her centre.

'Am I giving you pleasure now Cathy?'

She moaned against Mary's shoulder and slid her hands down Mary's sleek back as waves of pleasure flooded her senses.

Afterwards, Mary acted as though nothing had happened between them. Only an occasional smile as she looked at Cathy giving a hint to what she was thinking about. For her part, Cathy felt even closer to Mary and didn't feel any of the guilt she would have expected after her foray into sapphic sex. What had happened had seemed so natural and so nice that she simply couldn't find a reason for feeling guilty about it and to the contrary, looked forward to more or the same some other time.

They chatted happily on the way back to their camp. Then Mary spotted a bee land on a gum blossom and got immediately got very excited, dashing forward to catch the little insect, taking care not to injure it as she cupped it in her hands.

'What are you doing?'

Mary grinned at her and went to a wild cotton shrub, taking a very small tuft of cotton and daubing it with a tiny bit of tree resin before sticking the cotton onto the bee's rear.

'This is a honey bee. It is going to take us back to where it keeps its lovely sweet honey!'

'Why didn't the bee sting you?'

Mary frowned. 'Bees don't sting… Do you have different bees in your home?'

Cathy mentally kicked herself. Of course native bees didn't have stingers. It was only after bees were brought from Europe that they could sting you.

'My mistake. But how is it going to take us to the honey?'

'You'll see!' was the reply.

With that, she released the bee, which shot away from her and took an immediate flight path back towards its hive. With a shout of glee, Mary began to run after it through the bush, able to keep sight of the bee because of the tiny tuft of white cotton dangling from its rear.

Cathy ran after her but Mary quickly left her behind as she sped lithely through the bush in pursuit of the insect. She was only able to keep following her by pushing her lungs to the limit but still almost lost her completely.

Finally, she came to where Mary stood at the base of a very big old gum tree, staring up with satisfaction at the busy line of bees coming to and fro from a dark opening high up on the tree.

Cathy gasped for breath, noting with dismay that Mary was hardly breathing heavily at all. 'I thought I'd lost you. I thought I was completely lost in the bush for a minute there!'

Mary seemed surprised at her concern; 'How can anyone get lost in the bush? No worries Cathy, I'd have found you; we are sisters don't forget. Now I'm going to go get honey for us!'

Cathy sank to the ground. 'Good, because I wouldn't have the strength to help you in any case!'

She watched as Mary leapt up and seized a low branch and then agilely worked her way up the tall tree, her hands and feet moving with a sureness that spoke of much experience. Mary came to the opening and ignored the loudly humming bees that indignantly swarmed around her head as she reached into the hive and brought out three big combs dripping with honey.

She came back down with the same deftness with which she had ascended and offered one of the combs to Cathy. 'Here sister, this is a wonderful and special day for us. We have agreed on sharing your man, we have given each other pleasure and now we have honey!'

'That looks so delicious but isn't there more honey up there?'

'Of course there is but this is all that the bees can spare at the moment. I don't want to leave them short.'

Cathy marvelled at the common-sense approach to consumerism. How the twenty-first century could learn from Mary! She sucked on the sweet honeycomb with delight. She hadn't realised just how much she had missed the pure pleasure of tasting something so sweet. She realised that by now Mary had made the assumption that she was in accord to sharing William and couldn't find it within herself to disillusion her; especially since she really didn't know herself whether she agreed or not! After what had happened in the water though, she was certainly much more inclined towards Mary's idea!

Mary wrapped the remaining piece of honeycomb in a large leaf and they finished off their sweet treat and returned to the camp.

CHAPTER TWELVE

Jimmy brings trouble

William was delighted at the big piece of honeycomb that the girls brought back to him but really thought his luck had changed when Cathy cuddled up amorously to him later that night. It had been weeks since she had been amenable to his advances and what followed was hot, fast and very, very nice. He had no way of knowing what had prompted his woman's sudden enthusiasm or change of heart and didn't really care. He loved Cathy deeply and their love making was a wonderful escape from their harsh new reality.

As time went on, he realised that he was more and more making the mental adjustment that he and Cathy were stuck in this time and that the likelihood of ever getting back to their time was remote in the extreme.

Time and again he had agonised over the wisdom of leaving Obiri Rock and trying to find Darwin. Would it have made a difference if they'd stayed there? Try as he might, he couldn't think of a way back even if they'd stayed near the cave. The paintings were gone and that was that.

He and Cathy had talked about it and he knew that she agreed. Their best hope lay in making a home for themselves in the time that they were trapped in.

Another very good reason to keep moving away from

Kakadu were Jimmy's old enemy, the Ngurruku. He had no doubt that they were still very keen of killing the lot of them!

Njimiti

He ran fleetingly through the bush, checking back all the time to make sure that his new wife was keeping up with him. He gave her encouraging smiles as he saw that she was staying close behind him despite the pace that he was setting and despite the load that she was carrying.

He knew that he had chosen well when he stole into her camp and cut his way through the back of her wirra-wirra. Rather than scream like a little girl when he clamped his hand over her mouth, Ajunda had simply opened her eyes and, once she saw who it was, her eyes had gleamed with excitement.

He'd put his mouth to her ear, conscious of her mother and father only feet away. 'I want you for my woman.' He whispered.

She insistently pushed his hand from her mouth and nodded. 'I am promised to one of the elders.' She whispered back. 'I remember you from the last time. I like you and think that you will be much nicer than the old one!'

He grinned hugely in the darkness. 'I will make you happy! Come, gather your things quietly. We leave straight away.'

He guided her out of the back of her parent's wirra-wirra and watched as she crept around, gathering the things that she wanted. He knew that her parents as well as her uncle and auntie would be happy when they read his sign and realised that a young warrior had taken Ajunda.

Maybe they would even recognise his sign and remember him from the last gathering.

They left the camp without a sound and only stopped when he felt it was safe. He pulled her close and kissed her lips. 'You are my wife!'

She looked shyly to the ground for a moment but then smiled and nodded. 'I think it is a good thing! You are Njimiti are you not?'

He was inordinately pleased that she had remembered his name from their one meeting. It only made him feel more confident that he had made the right choice.

It had surprised him at how readily he had given into Marinja's reasoning that he should come with her and with Willem and Cathy. He loved his tribe and he loved the thought of being a warrior in his tribe, but he also acknowledged the debt, and the bond that he had towards the two whites, as well as the deep connection that he had to Marinja. He felt that Marinja was right when she said he should be with them and it excited him as to what lay ahead of them.

He grinned and kissed her again. 'Yes. I am, and I am your man!'

She smiled shyly again but threw one worried look at him. 'Will you beat me if I am not a good wife?'

The mere question made him feel so grown up! He was aware that men of the tribes beat their wives if they displeased them but he had never been comfortable with the practice. His own father had only beaten his mother once and that one occasion had resulted in his father laying on the ground with a big lump on his head from the length of wood that his mother had retaliated with!

He knew that Ajunda had nothing to worry about in any case. If he tried to beat her, he knew fully well that Marinja would make his life a misery!

He shook his head. 'No I won't. We will be the happiest husband and wife ever!'

It was only when they were an hour into their journey that he realised that they were being followed. He back-tracked a little and made out the form of a warrior moving stealthily through the bush, his eyes cast down as he sought out their sign.

Fear surged through him as he realised that it was not one of Ajunda's relations tracking them to take her back to her tribe, but rather it was one of the elders from the Ngurruku! He knew immediately that he was in bad trouble. If Ajunda's father or uncle had found them, then perhaps he could have talked his way out of it. Perhaps he could have even kept Ajunda if he promised to pay her family enough in meat and weapons!

Not so with this Ngurruku warrior though. He knew immediately that for an older warrior to be out by himself, hunting like he was, he must be on a *Ngunndita – a blood hunt.* It happened when a warrior reached the end of his days, when he felt that he had to reaffirm his status by hunting and killing his enemies, or be killed himself, without assistance from his tribal warriors. Njimiti knew that it was rare and only happened when a warrior went a little bit funny in the head but that didn't make it any less serious for him and for Ajunda!

Then he remembered when one of the elders from his own tribe had left to go on a *Ngunndita*. He had not been allowed to just wander off by himself and some of the warriors from his tribe, his father among them, had followed him at a distance to ensure his safe return. Njimiti felt the fear increase within himself at the thought. Would the Ngurruku do less for one of their elders?

It was only a short time later that Njimiti stopped abruptly. They were about to enter a clearing in the bush and something was not right ahead of them. He sniffed the air, his eyes narrowed as he minutely searched the foliage in front of them.

He knew that Ajunda felt it too when she grasped his arm hard. Her eyes were very good though and when she silently pointed, he made out the tip of a spear protruding from a bush on the other side of the clearing.

Njimiti immediately realised that the Ngurruku warrior had circled around them. It explained why he had not heard the signs of pursuit for some time. This was a cunning and experienced warrior who wanted to kill him!

Fear made his heart race, but his pride as a warrior and his belief in himself made him nock his spear into its thrower and step defiantly into the opening.

William

Jimmy's arrival back at their camp came just as they were considering moving on without him. When he arrived, he had in tow a very pretty young girl, wearing only a loin covering and some beads and carrying a large oval shaped wooden dish and an ornate digging stick. The girl clung to Jimmy's arm and her eyes were wide with terror when she spied William and Cathy.

William noted that Jimmy was carrying two extra spears, aside from the one he usually had, plus a boomerang tucked into the waist band of his loin cloth. The spears were quite different compared to his usual spear, which simply had barbs carved into the hardwood head. The two new spears had wicked shards of small, sharp stones of differing colours glued into each side of the head so that they would rip through organs as they entered the victim and then prevent the spear from being pulled back out. He shuddered to think of the damage that they would do to a body.

'Hey Jimmy, you have new weapons?'

Njimiti smiled at William's improved use of the language and nodded proudly. 'I killed one of those Ngurruku fellas. Showed my woman what a great warrior I am! Got pay back for my uncle!'

Marinja looked from the girl back to her friend in sudden alarm. 'Njimiti, you killed a Ngurruku?'

'Got him right in the guts. He tracked me after I took Ajunda from her tribe and I reckon he was going to kill me and then take Ajunda for himself. I dodged his spear though and he was too old and slow to dodge mine! I reckon he was an Elder too… he had all the scars and look at his spears and boomerang—aren't they wonderful?'

Mary took in the superb workmanship in all of the weapons and knew that Njimiti was right. Only a tribal elder could produce such fine weapons. She looked worriedly into the bush. She knew all too well how their enemy would react to one of their elders being killed.

'Where was this?' she asked.

He looked uncomfortable. 'Half a day from here; Ajunda and I had to run like scared wombats to get away from those other fellas!'

William caught the alarm in her voice and now she appeared to be even more worried. 'How many of them were there?' she asked.

William caught the guilty look that he threw his and Cathy's way before he replied to Mary. 'Only two. There were three but I reckon the other one went back to bring more of those fellas. Um, William and Catty will be able to use those little sticks to send them on their way though eh?'

Mary closed her eyes in exasperation. 'Oh you idiot, you've led them right here haven't you?'

In a small, nervous voice he replied. 'Maybe it's a good time to move on eh?'

William had only followed some of the conversation between the two. 'So what's going on Mary?'

She rolled her eyes. 'This idiot friend of mine has killed one of the elders and led a Ngurruku *girravul*—that's a war party—right here. We've got to get out pretty damned quick. They could get here at any time and they will kill us all!'

William didn't bother asking any further questions. He'd had the sense that they should have moved from this spot weeks ago and was now kicking himself that he'd let himself get talked into waiting for Jimmy. The relative comfort of the camp, with plentiful hunting and fresh water at their doorstep had lulled him stupidly into a false sense of security. As much as he liked the lad, it looked like now he was endangering them all.

Their camp, while comfortable, was also indefensible. They were surrounded by thick bush and if the Ngurruku attacked them here it could be from any and all directions. They wouldn't stand a chance, even with the bows. He vowed never to make the same mistake again.

He was surprised that Cathy didn't feel the urgency too but rather decided that Jimmy's new woman couldn't be left standing terrified and alone while they all ran around preparing to depart. He looked on with growing impatience as she approached Jimmy and the girl.

'Jimmy, isn't it about time that you introduced your new lady friend to us?' From his look of incomprehension, she realised that she had become so used to speaking to Mary in English that she'd spoken to Jimmy using the same. 'Mary, tell Jimmy to introduce us please.'

Marinja looked at her best friend with distain. 'You men are all the same! Look how scared she is; if you want to keep her, start treating her good! Tell her who we all are.'

Njimiti looked guilty once again. 'Oh yeah this is Ajunda, she is my woman. This is Marinja and that big fella is William and that lady with yellow hair is Catty.'

'Her name is "Cathy", you idiot.'

'Stop calling me an idiot!' he complained.

She ignored him and went over to the young girl, who couldn't have been more than fourteen or fifteen years old, a marriageable age according to their ways but still very young. She hugged the confused girl to her chest.

'Hello Ajunda, we are going to be sisters and Cathy is our other sister. You will like it with us and I will help you put up with your idiot man.'

The young girl threw a worried look at William and Cathy. 'They are white like spirits and he is so big! Will they eat me?'

Marinja laughed. 'They are just like you and me except their skin is different. William is big but he is kind. I am going to be his woman like Cathy is!'

Cathy came over and gave the girl a hug. In her best effort at their language, she said, 'We welcome you Ajunda… welcome to our family.'

Ajunda clung to Jimmy's arm as she looked nervously around at them. 'I am Njimiti's woman so I have to be with him. Maybe it will be good with you.'

William wasn't at all comfortable with the thought that Jimmy had abducted this young girl from her tribe either, but reasoned that this sort of thing must be the norm for these times and it wasn't for him to tell them different. In any case, William had endured enough of the social niceties. He looked with a growing feeling of danger towards the bush. It was way past time to get things moving.

He offered their new arrival a reassuring smile but then turned to Cathy and Mary. 'Sorry ladies, but getting to know Ajunda is going to have to wait. I don't want to be here when the bad guys arrive, so let's get moving shall we?'

They all looked at him for a moment before scurrying to collect everything they needed.

Mary led a fast pace to the northwest, which was figured to be opposite to where the Ngurruku would come from and generally towards Darwin. She had long legs and was completely fit in a way that only a person who lives a wholly physical way of life could be. Jimmy and Ajunda had no issues in keeping up, even though Mary and Ajunda were carrying more than their share of their belongings. William and Cathy both considered themselves very fit people but still had trouble with the pace. Only with judicious and thoughtful stops on Jimmy and Mary's part did they manage to keep up until they reached a big river.

Cathy informed him that it must have been another branch of the South Alligator, but so soon after the end of the wet season it could have been anything. It was a barrier though and one that they vitally had to cross if the hornet's nest that Jimmy had stirred up was indeed on their tail.

They all knew the urgency and worked with a will to build a large enough platform to get them across the crocodile infested river, but while they all worked urgently on a raft, they had confirmation of pursuit when they began to hear faint but excited shouts along the back trail. Jimmy looked up from where he was lashing branches together and shouted out urgently in his Alawa language.

Mary nodded and turned to William. 'Jimmy thinks they are only five hundred paces away. I think he is right!'

William looked at the raft. It was almost done and should be sufficient to get them across the river, so long as a croc didn't decide to argue their right of way. He strung his bow and took a quiver of the heavier arrows.

'I'm going to hold them up. Get that thing into the river and be ready when I come running.'

Cathy grabbed her bow. 'Not by yourself; I'm coming with you.'

William instinctively felt a need to protect her. He had always taken on the most dangerous jobs himself in his police career and it was instinctive to do the same now. He shook his head. 'I don't think so; last time we frightened them off because they'd never seen bows before but I think that this time it'll be different. They'll keep coming until some of them are dead or they get through me. It's no place for you.'

She threw him a look that was as eloquent as the words that followed. 'And this is neither the time nor the place for macho bullshit. The two of us have a much better chance of stopping them than just you and you know it, so stop trying to be the big protector and let's go.'

He realised that arguing was going to be a waste of time and in truth was glad of the extra bow. She was still a better shot than he was and he'd never been able to match her rate of fire. As soon as Cathy had a quiver of arrows they moved back along their back trail for about fifty metres; finding a couple of melaleuca trees that afforded them cover and concealment and then waited nervously with bows half drawn.

They could hear the others struggling to get the big, heavy raft into the water but tried to ignore them, concentrating on their back trail. Jimmy's estimate wasn't far off and they soon heard the thud of running footsteps and harsh breathing as a group of tribesmen ran towards them. Significantly now there were no words being spoken, no more excited cries from the pursuers, which led William to believe that they knew exactly where their prey were and now closed for the kill.

William made out two figures in the lead, one slightly in front of the other with a group of ten or so strung back another twenty metres behind them. All of them carried several spears, each with one knocked into woomeras, ready to launch the wickedly tipped spears—similar to Jimmy's new acquisitions—at them.

Even with the obvious intentions of their attackers, William still had the greatest difficulty in pulling back his bow and actually shooting one of the men. He had been a police officer for too long and it was ingrained into him that lethal force was always only a very last resort. Was there something else that he could do now?

Apparently, Cathy didn't feel the same hesitation. As soon as she saw that the closest warrior had seen them and changed his angle of attack towards them, she let fly with her arrow.

At less than twenty metres, she couldn't miss and the heavy, razor tipped missile struck the running man in the chest with enough force to send him back five metres before he crashed to the ground. The arrow had gone almost all the way through him, with the flint head protruding from his back.

William didn't hesitate any longer. He had been working on his marksmanship and took the second of the two leading warriors through the throat, sending the man backwards for several steps before he too bled out in front of them.

Only one other warrior kept coming—an older man with a long grey beard and a fierce face. He stood still over the body of one of the dead men and shouted angrily at William and Cathy before drawing back his spear, deliberately targeting William who stood partially exposed beside the tree.

His arm began to whip forward but he never completed the movement, for Cathy's second arrow hit him right in the centre of his forehead. The flint tip penetrated his skull and dropped him dead on the spot, the woomera and spear falling from his lifeless hands onto the leaf-strewn ground.

William had another arrow nocked and ready as he watched the rest of them. He heard shouts of anger and a lot of waving of weapons from the milling group, but with three of their war party killed before the rest of them could even throw a spear he hoped they wouldn't attack again. Two of them threw their spears but by then he and Cathy were back in the cover of the trees. Neither spear injured them and it seemed that none of their attackers were willing to brave their arrows and close the distance to be sure of their throw. They all drew back uncertainly, waving their spears and boomerangs threateningly but making no further moves to attack again.

William and Cathy slowly moved back a step at a time, bows fully drawn as they shifted their aim from warrior to warrior, all of whom still held back but were obviously building up the courage and anger for another attack.

Cathy looked backwards quickly to see that the raft was in the water and that Jimmy stood at the shore with a spear cocked and ready to throw.

'Now, go now!'

William looked back for only a second and then let an arrow go that he knew would only hit a tree next to the most aggressive looking warrior. His aim was good and he accomplished what he'd intended, for the arrow caused the warrior to think twice about coming forward, for it had only missed his head by inches.

It gave them the opportunity to run to the river and their feet hardly seemed to touch the ground as they raced to join the others. They leapt onto the raft as Mary pushed off and then struggled for balance while they tried to re-draw their bows.

They were half way across the river before the first of their pursuers arrived to throw their spears after them. Several hit their raft and one narrowly missed Jimmy, with the spear point lodging in the raft right next to Ajunda, bringing a shriek of fright from the young girl, but then they were out of range, paddling urgently and laboriously across to the other bank.

A lone saltwater crocodile lifted his head up from the water as it looked at them, but then sank back to the murky bottom, presumably deciding that the strange, noisy floating thing was too much trouble.

When they'd reached the safety of the other side, Jimmy looked back at the pack of angry warriors at the far shore and turned to present his bare backside to his enemy, laughing delightedly at their frustrated anger now that they were safe from their spears. He grinned at William and Cathy and said something excitedly in his own language that was too quick for them to follow.

Mary replied to him and then interpreted. 'Jimmy thinks you two are brave and wonderful and wants to know how many Ngurruku you killed. I also told him to start learning to speak better English because I'm not his personal interpreter!'

William was feeling anything but jubilant. He knew that three warriors were lying dead because he and Cathy had stumbled through time and into their pre-European world. The fact that there had been no choice on this occasion, that it had been a matter of their survival, was almost irrelevant.

It really brought home to him the fact that he and Cathy were going to change history every time they interacted with anyone from this time and place. Three warriors who would have gone on to accomplish whatever had been meant for them to do, were now soon-to-be rotting carcases in the bush. They would father no more children, have no more grandchildren, fight no more battles, make no more artefacts …all because he and Cathy had bows and arrows in a country where archery hadn't yet been seen.

He determined that, unless they could find some way to return to their own time, which seemed damned unlikely, then the next best thing would be that he and Cathy had to go someplace where their effect on the past could be limited. For a moment, the enormity of their situation crashed in on him. How were they going to survive and yet not disrupt the time that they were in? Where could they possibly go to find a safe haven? He shook his head at the seemingly impossible road that lay ahead of them.

His sudden depression apparently showed on his face, for Cathy laid a hand on his arm. 'We had no choice.'

He shook his head sadly. 'I know that but it doesn't change a thing.'

Tears glistened in her eyes and he guiltily realised that he was so immersed in his own feelings that he had ignored hers, that she was feeling the effects of what they had just done the same as he was. He remembered that she had just killed two men to his one and it made him feel idiotic for feeling this way when she was coping so much better, at least on the surface.

'We did what we had to do and we'll keep on doing what he have to do to survive and somehow get through this.' Cathy exclaimed vehemently, shaking away her tears.

William looked at her with a realisation of her inner strength. She was years younger than him, half his size and she'd been ripped from her friends, her family and everything that she knew and loved all because they had stupidly touched an Aboriginal painting. Yet she had a resolute strength that made his self-doubts seem juvenile.

He gave her a hug. 'You're worth your weight in rocking-horse shit; did you know that?'

She giggled. 'Is that an old guy expression?'

'What is a rocking horse?' asked the ever-curious Mary.

'Something that children play on where um, we come from. We're not likely to come across any around here.'

Mary cocked her head to the side, her curiosity clearly

whetted. 'I would like to see this place you come from someday. What is it called?'

Cathy and William shared a look and Cathy struggled for a reply that made any sense. She thought of the Jeannie Gunn book, *We of the Never-never.* 'At the moment we might as well call it 'never-never land.'

Jimmy said something that they didn't catch but it sounded urgent. Mary nodded and looked at the two whites. 'Njimiti says that the Ngurruku will have canoes not too far away and we should get moving. He is right. We must leave. They will never forget us now and one day they will want payback for the men that we have killed.'

CHAPTER THIRTEEN

The other time traveller

They set out again and after an hour of fast jogging. Jimmy led them towards some very rugged gorges surrounded by increasingly dense bush.

Mary had been talking with Jimmy and now she dropped back with William. 'We are going to a place where the Ngurruku will not be able to track us,' she said. 'Njimiti is being very brave because this place is said to be haunted by a white spirit and none of the tribes will go there.'

William was struggling for breath as they jogged along at a ground eating pace. 'Wh… white spirit—like something from your Dreamtime?'

She threw him a thoughtful look. 'You know of our Dreamtime? That is something the people do not talk about. How is it you know of it?'

Puffing and without thinking, he simply replied. 'It's common knowledge in our time.'

He didn't notice that Marinja just stared at him and said nothing as they ran on, while she thought about what he had just said.

Cathy

Cathy was concentrating on maintaining her wind as Mary came alongside of her.

'You and I are friends, yes?' she asked.

'Of course we are.' Cathy panted, completely envious that Mary wasn't even slightly out of breath.

'We are going to share the same man, yes?'

Cathy still hadn't worked that one out, so she hedged by saying. 'Well, maybe… We'll see. Why are you asking?'

'You must tell me the truth about yourself and William. No more stories about never-never land. You must tell me the truth!'

'What do you mean?'

'You are from a different… from another time?'

Cathy nearly fell flat on her face from the shock of Mary's assertion but couldn't lie to her friend. She managed to keep her feet and nodded. 'I promise I'll tell you soon.'

'I really want to know Cathy. I am part of your life now. I deserve to know the truth about you.'

The blonde woman slowed for a moment to a walk, trying to catch her breath. 'Mary, if I tell you the truth, I just don't see how you could possibly believe me!'

The Aboriginal girl touched her arm and looked her in the eyes. 'You tell me. I will know the truth of it.'

Cathy sighed. 'Tonight, okay?'

Mary held her arm. 'It will be good that we have no secrets; we are sisters and will share everything, not only William.' She paused and thought for a moment. 'What is your word for when a man has more than one woman?'

Cathy was glad of the sudden change of subject and chuckled. 'Very lucky or very stupid, take your pick.'

Jimmy led them up a ravine and along a track of sorts made by kangaroos, wallabies and other animals. He stopped where the ravine split into two, with a branch heading off to the left and to the right.

He pointed off to the right-hand folk. 'A white spirit lives up there. We can go no closer but I do not think that the Ngurruku will even come this close to him.'

William's curiosity was aroused at the mention of this 'white spirit', for he remembered that was what Jimmy had at first called them!

He was careful not to mock Jimmy's beliefs but never the less had to raise an eyebrow.

'This spirit can't be as bad as all that, surely.'

Jimmy shrugged. 'My tribe hasn't seen him but Ajunda's tribe has and it must be very bad!'

Ajunda clung to her man's arm, her eyes wide as she stared up the ravine. At the mention of her name, she let fly with a fearful machine gun in the Alawa language that was just different enough to Mary and Jimmy's use of the language to make it impossible for William to understand her.

'What did she say?'

'She says that the spirit killed two people from her tribe. She is very scared.'

William's curiosity was well and truly piqued now. 'Tell me more about this 'white spirit'.'

Mary joined in. 'I think this story must be true. I have heard many people from Ajunda's tribe speak of him. He is all white and is covered in white hair and when he speaks, it is like thunder!'

William frowned. 'Like thunder… like a loud bang?'

Mary said something to Jimmy and Ajunda. Ajunda replied in a fearful rapid-fire of words and Mary nodded.

'Ajunda says that people from her tribe say he has a big stick that makes the thunder, and his thunder can kill you!'

'When was this?' he asked with rising excitement.

He waited until Mary spoke to Ajunda again.

'I think it must be a long time ago.' Said Mary. 'Ajunda speaks of her uncle's uncle who was killed.'

William looked at Cathy and quietly said, 'Thunder stick… you don't think they're talking about a rifle, do you?'

Cathy shook her head. 'It's not very likely. Even if we are in the seventeenth century and a white person has somehow got here then he would have a matchlock rifle or at best a flintlock. I've never even heard of any trace of white people being found in the Top End. Surely the archaeologists would have made a huge deal of it.'

William thought for a few moments and felt excited at a sudden possibility. 'What if we're not the only ones caught in time back here? What if someone else has come back from our time! ' He turned to Jimmy and in their language said. 'Take us to the white spirit. Please, we are not afraid of him, and will protect you all as well.'

Jimmy didn't look in the least convinced but was persuaded by his duty towards William and Cathy. He looked nervously up the right-hand fork. 'Hold little sticks ready. I will take you but white spirit is sure to try and kill me for bringing people to its lair!'

They move warily in single file, with Ajunda clinging so hard to Jimmy's arm that he had difficulty holding his weapons. He spoke angrily to her and she looked close to tears until Mary put an arm around her and threw Jimmy a very dirty look.

About half way along, William spotted a cave high up on the side wall. He felt a jolt of excitement when he spotted what looked like a log barrier blocking the entrance to the cave. The logs were laid on top of each other and trimmed to fit neatly, held in place by uprights that had been driven into the soil between boulders at each side of the mouth of the cave.

'I'm going up there,' William said excitedly. 'Unless I'm very much mistaken, that wall is very definitely not Aboriginal work!'

As he got closer, he could see that the log wall was able to be swung out at one end like a big, heavy gate, allowing one person to squeeze past.

He called out. 'Hello? Anyone there?'

There was no reply and he peered over the barrier and into the dark cave, his eyes widening in shock as they adjusted to the dim light inside the entrance. He realised immediately that he was staring at a rough bush bed made up of a square frame on four legs and with some sort of material stretched across to make a mattress.

On the bed he saw a skeletal figure dressed in rags of clothing, obviously very dead and from the look of the bones of an arm that lay out to the floor, dead for years. The rest of the cave was hidden in darkness.

He turned and called out. 'I need light! Cathy, bring the matches and make a torch please. Then you'd better come up here.'

Ten minutes later, she arrived with Mary in tow and passed over the matches and a bundle of brushes. William lit the torch and then moved past the log wall and into the cave with the others behind him.

Cathy looked down at the skeletal remains. 'The poor man. He died here all alone.'

William knelt and examined the remains of the clothing. The dead man had on a stout leather belt that had survived the ravages of time, with tattered dark coloured trousers still covering the lower body, while a dirty and ragged shirt partly covered the upper torso. A pair of badly worn leather boots adorned the feet. Decay and insects had long since removed any trace of flesh from the remains.

A very long white beard lay across the chest and a mane of long white hair lay scattered around the head, fitting the description of the 'white spirit' nicely.

The skull was massively damaged, with most of the face and the top of the skull missing. Then he found out the cause of the damage.

He had missed it at first in the flickering light from the torch, for it lay on a canvas bag along the inner side of the body, difficult to see by the light of the torch and with only the end of the barrel resting on the bones of the right shoulder.

In his sudden excitement, he completely forgot all about unnecessary swearing. 'Well fuck my brown dog!' William exclaimed. 'It's a bloody three-oh-three!'

Cathy drew a sharp breath. As she and Mary looked on, William gingerly reached over the body and lifted the Lee-Enfield 303 rifle. The story of what had happened was immediately obvious when the thumb bone of the right hand slid from the trigger guard as he lifted the rifle clear.

'Oh shit. The poor bastard blew his own brains out!' William breathed.

Cathy was looking around the cave and let out a little yelp of excitement when she found a leather-bound, tattered notebook. She went out to the entrance so that she could read the contents. After several minutes she looked up with tears in her eyes.

'It's his diary. His name was Edward Williamson and

he was stranded back here in 1959. He thinks that he was stranded here for about ten years before…' She looked with intense sadness at the body and continued. 'Before he was running out of bullets to hunt and protect himself from—in his words—"the blacks". His last entry says…' She held up the notebook into the light and read out the words directly from the book. *'Can't take it any longer, I think I'm going mad with the loneliness. Ammo all gone except for one round and I'll put that one to good use. If someone finds me, give me a good grave and pray for a lost soul.'*

Tears ran down her face as she knelt beside the body and took the skeletal left hand in hers. 'Oh you poor, poor man!' She looked up at William. 'At least we have each other; I can't imagine being stranded all by myself!'

Mary stared at the skeletal remains. 'This is the white spirit?'

Cathy wiped away tears. 'He came back from the future like we did. Not from exactly our time but close.'

William hardly registered that Cathy had just admitted that they were from another time. He was looking at the Lee-Enfield with frustration. The years hadn't been too harsh on it, for the canvas bag had protected it to a large extent from the body's decay and the dry interior of the cave from the weather. There was surface rust on the barrel, magazine and bolt action but the action worked fine as he ejected the empty casing from the old man's final shot. He took out the bolt and reversed the rifle to hold the barrel up to the light as he examined the rifling. The barrel needed a damn good clean out but looked okay. The webbing sling was still in good condition and only needed dusting off.

He opened the butt trap and smiled when he found a half bottle of gun oil and a pull-through, complete with wire brush and cloth wipes. It was apparent that the old guy had looked after the weapon. The oil didn't smell like any gun oil that he was used to and he wondered if it wasn't rendered fat. With a bit of work the rifle looked to be quite usable.

The Lee-Enfield rifles had been introduced to British Commonwealth countries during the 1st World War and were still in service in some parts of the world even in the second decade of the 21st Century. They had been the mainstay of the old British Empire for more than a hundred years. Australian soldiers had used them through two World Wars and they had remained a favourite for Aussie shooters until ammunition began to become hard to find in the 1970s, largely replaced by 308 rounds for serious shooters. They were a rugged, reliable rifle with a heavy round that could kill at a thousand yards in the old measure or more than a kilometre in the new.

The only thing he didn't have for the rifle however, was ammunition. He located a canvas bag with hundreds of used casings and half a dozen empty five-round ammo clips against a wall but there wasn't one complete round.

'Shit, the old guy had some ammo on him when he came back.'

Cathy had been reading again. 'He was a crocodile shooter. He says that he went into a cave and, to quote, "*something bloody odd*" happened to him and he found himself back here like us. He doesn't say where this cave was but I think we can hazard a guess.'

William considered what she said. 'The croc shooting bit makes sense. It was legal to shoot saltwater crocodiles right up until the 70s and the skins were worth big money back then.'

'I have never seen such a thing as this!' remarked Mary, holding up a worn but very serviceable hatchet.

William looked down at the remains. The neatly trimmed logs of the barrier were suddenly explained. 'Thanks Edward, we'll put your axe to damn good use.'

The ground at the bottom of the gully was hard and rocky, but they managed to bury him in a grave about two-foot deep, covering it with large rocks to stop animals digging up the bones. William struggled through a prayer that he made up as he went while they stood over the burial mound. William hoped the old croc shooter's spirit felt a bit better, despite his ineptitude as a minister. A small wooden cross bore the man's name.

Cathy stared at the grave. 'I wonder if someone will find this in the future.'

William shrugged. 'Like you said, there was no record of a white man being found, not in our time at least. Maybe Edward is still under these rocks in the twenty-first century and no one is the wiser.'

The only other salvageable items from the cave were a sheaf knife with a good quality, heavy fourteen-centimetre blade and a well-used sharpening stone. It was a serious weapon and William had no problems imagining Edward skinning out the thick crocodile skins with it. He was chuffed at how much Jimmy was pleased and astonished when the knife was presented to him by Cathy.

He knew that Cathy had made a friend for life when Jimmy went up to her and hugged her and then proudly showed the knife to Ajunda who looked with admiration at her superbly armed man.

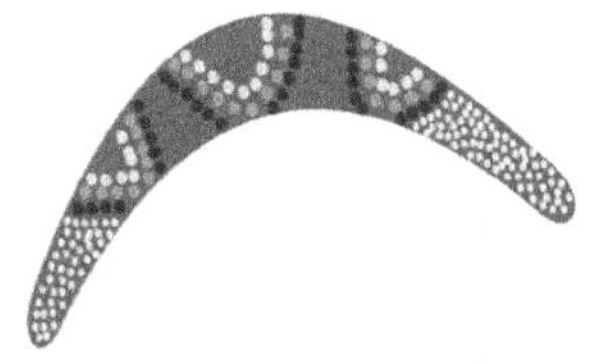

CHAPTER FOURTEEN

Ménage á trois

They made camp that night after climbing out of the ravine, finding a sheltered spot next to a small billabong—although only after checking that there was no resident crocodile in it. There was no further sign of pursuit and William was cautiously optimistic that they had finally shaken off Jimmy's vengeful enemies.

They needed meat so William and Jimmy went off in search of dinner, returning after an hour to find that the three women had been busy.

A small wirra-wirra was at one end of the clearing, around which Ajunda was happily making things comfortable for herself and Jimmy.

William looked curiously at the larger shelter that Cathy and Mary were finishing off, complete with a floor of reeds and a small, smouldering fire at the front.

'What about Mary's place? Why is she helping you and not building hers?'

Cathy and Mary shared a glance and then Cathy gave him a curious look. 'We've decided that it would be uh, better for Mary to sleep in here with us.'

William felt a jolt of disappointment at the prospect of not having Cathy to himself but tried not to show it. 'Why is that? Would she feel safer tonight with us?'

Again, that same glance between the two of them that had him puzzling.

'Just… better,' Cathy mysteriously replied. 'We'll see how it works out, okay?'

He wasn't about to offend Mary by arguing against her staying with them and he was smart enough to let Cathy do what she wanted. Clearly, they were up to something but he knew that he would be the last to find out.

Instead he decided to tackle something over which he actually had some control and retrieved the Lee-Enfield from the canvas bag and set about cleaning and oiling the old weapon. He found a date stamp that showed that it had been manufactured in England in 1941, no doubt put to use against the Germans or Japanese during the war.

The pull-through cleaned out the rifling perfectly. The gun had seen some serious work but it had been lovingly cared for by Edward. Mercifully, there was no rust inside the barrel and the wire brush made short work of the surface rust. Some oil rubbed into the wooden stock made the rifle look almost new. Sadly, it was probably the most advanced weapon in the world at the moment, but for one small deficiency.

He looked ruefully at the bag of casings. 'Shit. This thing would be great to have if only we had some bloody ammo.' He muttered.

Cathy

Cathy came over and sat down beside him, glad that he had something to occupy his mind apart from Mary moving in with them. The last thing that she wanted right now was for him to query why it was happening. How the hell could she answer?

She was nervous and still very unsure of what to do and was even more unsure of what William's reaction was going to be if she went along with Mary's idea. The thought of sharing William both shocked and excited her, particularly in light of the newly explored side to her sexuality. But sharing her man? Such things just weren't done… were they? She'd heard of *threesomes* of course but had never dreamed that she might be in one! This was new territory for her and she had absolutely no idea of what to do or how to do it.

She went over to him with the tattered diary in her hand. 'I've been reading this. Edward never worked out what happened to him. He says on a couple of occasions that he actually thought he was dead and in purgatory, between heaven and hell. He mentions one old Aboriginal who seemed to be tracking him for years and his description of him is sort of like that painting in the cave, the guy with the weird eyes.'

William shrugged. 'It would have been too much to expect him to have the key to us returning to our own time.'

She looked at him for a moment. 'Do you know Will, it'd be kind of, I don't know, boring back there now in a way.'

He looked curiously at her. 'Boring? Are you serious? What about our families?'

She waved her hands in dismissal. 'Oh, I don't mean that I wouldn't go home if I could! My poor mum and dad must be out of their minds with worry and I'd love to finish my studies. It's just that, it's pretty exciting here isn't it? We have to look after ourselves, defend ourselves, do stuff that I never expected to have to do!'

He laughed. 'It's exciting alright, too bloody exciting if you ask me!' He touched the Lee Enfield. 'This would make me feel a darn sight better if we had ammo for it.'

She picked up a spent casing. 'You know, when I was a kid I used to watch my dad reload his own ammunition. He was very good with a two-forty-three target rifle.' She looked at the base where the firing pin had struck the primer. 'His shells were about the same size as these ones. Why can't you reload these?'

He just stared at her for a moment, his mind racing as he considered the difficulties involved. After a while, he shook his head.

'A two-forty-three is a bit smaller than one of these but you're right—they're similar. Unfortunately, your dad probably had a lovely set of scales to weigh the powder, a press, ready-made projectiles, a tin of gun-powder and a nice little box of primers—all of which we lack. We could probably make black powder to fill the cartridge; all we need is sulphur, charcoal and saltpetre. Shit, even if we are in the seventeenth century, they've still been making gunpowder for about five hundred years. Even the projectiles aren't an insurmountable problem if we ever get settled somewhere and have access to a forge of some kind. We could make lead bullets at the very least.'

He took the casing from her and pointed to the indented primer. 'This is the biggie. I don't reckon we would be able to make a decent primer even if we ever find somewhere with a bit more to offer than crocs and bush. I know a fair bit about guns but I'm no bloody genius and unfortunately I'd say we'll need some real bloody genius to get over that little hurdle.'

The rifle was carefully placed into its bag and stowed away. 'Even if I never got to use the bloody thing, I'm going to keep it.' He declared.

Jimmy and Ajunda shared their meal and they sat around the fire for an hour or so while Mary gave English lessons to the young couple.

At one point, Jimmy stared at his new wife for a moment and then turned to Mary. In their own language, he said, 'I have white fella name and you have white fella name. Ajunda should have white fella name too!'

Cathy was good enough with their language to catch the gist of what he was saying. She touched Jimmy lightly on the arm. 'I'm already feeling bad that we call you and Mary by Anglicised names when you have perfectly good names already. It's just laziness on our part and you are both very nice to put up with it. Your pretty wife has a delightful name; she doesn't need a new one.'

Ajunda smiled shyly but then looked imploringly at Cathy. 'New white fella name is a good thing; I starting new life, need new name too!'

Cathy rubbed her chin as she looked back at the girl. Suddenly she smiled back at her. 'Alright then how about we call you June?'

The young girl giggled shyly. 'June is good name. It is almost like Ajunda but so pretty!'

An hour or so later, with the fire burning low, Jimmy and the newly named June left and went to their shelter. Within moments Ajunda's giggling, followed not long after by ardent moans came from that direction.

Cathy

Cathy was still agonising over how she and Mary were going to carry through their half-baked plans. She saw William glancing towards the young couple's wirra-wirra and read the resigned look on his face. The look made her feel at the same time guilty at what he must be thinking and terribly excited at what might lie ahead. She felt terrible that she couldn't just come out with what they intended but knew her only hope was to present him with a *fate accompli* and hope that William wouldn't either die of shock or send Mary packing.

'It's been a long day and I'm a bit knackered,' he said. 'I'm off to bed.'

Mary cocked her head. 'What is "knackered?"'

He managed a rueful smile. 'Tired. We need our sleep.'

Cathy looked nervously at William and took a deep breath. 'You go along. We'll be there in a moment.'

When he had disappeared into the shelter, she turned to Mary, her heart hammering. 'Alright, I agree. Tonight, you can be with William. Go to him now, I'll stay here for a while longer.'

She looked back at Cathy with both surprise and alarm. 'Oh no. You don't understand. I would not know what to do. I have never been with a man!'

'You're a virgin? But you seem to know all about sex!'

'Virgin is not having a man ever? Yes, that is what I am then. I think I am the oldest virgin ever! I know how the dingoes do it and I know how the kangaroos do it; I even know how the goannas do it but I don't know anything about how people do it! I am scared!'

Cathy moved even closer, her look intense as she whispered; 'What do you expect me to do then? I'm willing to share William with you. Can't you sort of just do what comes natural?'

Mary seized her hands and looked urgently at her. 'You must be there with me; you must help me, show me! It is good between the two of us, we both know that. Please help me with making love to William.'

Cathy was torn between the exciting prospect of being actively involved when Mary first made love with William and the fear of how he might reject the arrangement outright.

Mary looked into her eyes. 'At least you have been with a man… Please?'

Cathy took a deep breath, both terrified and excited. 'Oh shit, this is going to be interesting!'

William

William could hear the two women whispering, their voices rising and falling, with Mary's voice sounding almost frightened. Whatever it was that they were discussing, he wished they would finish and come to bed.

Finally, he made out the two of them entering the shelter. It was very dark and the embers of the fire no longer provided any light so he had trouble with who was who.

He felt someone settling next to him and relaxed, ready to sleep now that Cathy was with him. To his dismay however, the other person knelt on the other side of him and he felt her fingers trace up his torso until they found his lips.

Cathy kissed him on the lips and then whispered. 'Honey, I'm afraid you can't go to sleep just yet. Mary and I have something to… discuss with you.'

William felt a hand reach down to touch his manhood; then another hand joined it, the two hands stroking and exploring. There was an immediate and predictable reaction. Before he could say anything, a new pair of lips found his and he realised that he was kissing Mary. Her lips tasted wonderful and she knew how to kiss—remarkably, just like Cathy. After that, he really wasn't completely sure of who did what with whom.

In the long hours of unending pleasure that followed for the three of them, William simply didn't think about Cathy's stricture for him to be careful and Cathy's joy and pleasure at the union of the three of them was such that she simply didn't care as he and Mary made love with her. It was a long time before the three of them eventually got to a well sated sleep.

He awakened first the next morning and sat up on the mat, remembering the events of the previous evening in a daze. He looked to find Mary and Cathy, both naked and in each other's arms as they slept.

He stood up and tied on the loincloth that had long since replaced his shorts. His movement woke Cathy, who eased herself from Mary's arms and walked out into the morning light with him.

'I'm not complaining mind you, but I don't suppose you'd care to tell me what is going on?' he said.

Cathy pulled him down to her level and kissed him. 'You've got two wives now of course, silly. Two of us to keep happy and two of us to keep you in line!'

Mary chose that moment to also come out of the shelter, making no effort to cover her lovely nakedness.

Cathy went to her and put an arm around her. 'Mary believed right from the start that she should also be your woman. I didn't know what to think for a long time but now I see that it is the way it was meant to be. I love Mary and it just feels right to me, William. You and I are trapped back here in the Dreamtime and God knows what will happen to us or if we'll ever get back home. Mary says that meeting us was like suddenly, everything fell in place for her, that all of her life up until then had been just waiting until we came along.'

Mary looked slightly fearfully at him. 'I want to be with you and Cathy. I want to make love with both of you and I want to have your babies. It was so good last night… please do not tell me that you want to send me away.'

Cathy turned and kissed her on the cheek. 'He's not sending you anywhere.'

William thought of the incredible night the three of them had just had and there was no denying that the sex had been something out of his fantasies. He knew though that the sex by itself wasn't enough and he thought hard about how he felt about Mary as a person.

Up until now he hadn't allowed himself to even think of her in that way. Sure, he'd often stolen looks at her delightful figure but that was it, after all he had a wife in Cathy and he was a strong believer in being faithful to your partner in life. Now however, things had changed radically and with Cathy's obvious approval. He looked at Mary and realised that he felt genuine and strong affection for her, along with more than a healthy dose of physical attraction.

Did he actually love her though as he loved Cathy? It was totally confusing to him that, while loving Cathy, he had such strong emotions towards Mary! He looked into her beautiful, intelligent brown eyes, saw the anxiety on her face and knew that hurting her was the very last thing he would ever want to do to her. With shock, he realised that somehow, love for her had been creeping up on him for a long time and that he had been suppressing it out of his loyalty towards Cathy.

He looked at the two of them, both naked and with

their arms around each other and it suddenly felt as though something incredible had happened to his heart, leaving him feeling very, very good.

His line of thinking had only taken seconds but he saw that his lack of an immediate answer had only deepened Mary's anxiety and had Cathy worried as well.

'I think...' he began and saw the worry deepen in their faces. 'I think that I'm one lucky son of a gun!'

Cathy

Both the women grinned and in her relief Cathy felt a need for some mischief after the worry he'd caused them. She looked seriously at him. 'That's very nice, darling but perhaps we'd best make sure that you're not going to have any hang-ups where we are concerned.'

'What do you mean?'

'Well for instance, is it going to be alright if I do this to Mary?' As she spoke, she reached out and caressed one of Mary's breasts, teasing the nipple into hardness and then taking the nipple into her mouth, as Mary sighed with pleasure.

William watched with mouth agape. 'Uh, yeah sure that's, uh that's fine.'

She released the nipple and smiled. 'Oh good. Now is it going to be alright if Mary and I do this?' With that she locked her lips to Mary's, who smiled widely before her lips were otherwise engaged.

William watched the two women kissing passionately as their hands roamed over each other's bodies. When they finally moved apart, he swallowed hard and mumbled. 'Um, that's definitely okay too.'

Cathy looked down at his suddenly tented loin cloth

and with a straight face, asked, 'Darling, are we in a hurry this morning, or do you think we could go back inside for a while?'

He groaned. 'Oh I think we can definitely spare a little time before we get moving!'

When they eventually re-emerged, they were all glowing with happiness for each other. Cathy looked at William and at Mary and had never been more certain about the rightness of something.

She had an inspired moment and took both of their hands. 'I love you both very dearly. I think we should have our own marriage ceremony right here, right now!'

Jimmy and Junie came out of their shelter just then and he grinned hugely. 'You're in a lot of trouble now Willem!'

William smiled wryly but then turned to the two women of his life. 'Maybe so, but I love you both and I am more than happy to call you both my wife.'

Cathy wiped away a tear and nodded fiercely. 'I feel so very happy … husband.'

Mary kissed first Cathy and then William on the lips. 'I am very happy too husband and sister/wife.'

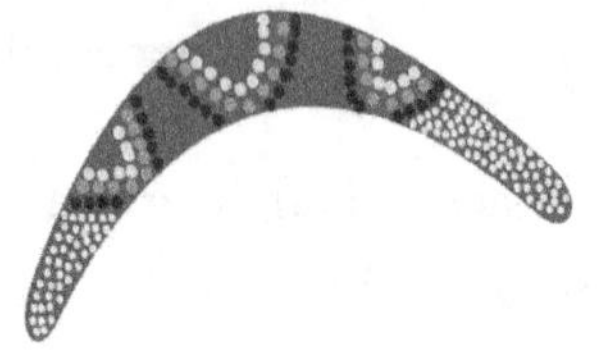

CHAPTER FIFTEEN

Bush lessons

As they moved on, Mary explained to him that they were leaving the ancestral range of her tribe's country and were entering into new territory.

'It has always been this way. Every tribe has their own traditional lands and when a tribe tries to enter some other tribe's country without permission or without paying *sorry goods*, there is war.'

William fingered his bow. 'So we can expect to meet hostiles then?'

She shrugged. 'If we are seen, then I think so. No one likes strangers entering their lands and if we meet one of the local tribes then they might try to kill us. Only related tribes are allowed to move through other tribes' territory unless they want trouble. Why do we have to go this way? If we return to my people's country then it will be much easier for us.'

'Cathy and I—and you now since you're with us— we can't stay here. It's hard to explain but Cathy and I shouldn't be here, in this time. I know that you probably don't understand, but everything that we do here might have some bad effect on the future. I just don't see how we can get back to our own time anyway.'

He saw the flicker of pain on her face as he said this

and hurried on. 'And since Cathy and I have become so close to you, I don't think we would want to if we could … at least not unless we could take you with us. Even if they can get back to Darwin, that was unlikely to be the answer to our problems. If we could meet up with the right people there, it might lead towards an answer for us, but by itself it isn't the whole solution. Somehow, we have to find a place where we can live without changing things too much.'

Mary tilted her head, clearly considering his words. 'So if you change things too much now, then the time that you come from might not be the same.'

William nodded, impressed at her immediate understanding of such an abstract subject, but before he could say anything she went on.

'And if you somehow change it too much back in your time, then you and Cathy might not meet and you might not come back in time.'

That had him frowning in thought. 'It makes my head ache just thinking about it, but essentially, I think that you've got it.'

She stared into space for a moment, her mind obviously still working on it. 'But if you don't come back in time though, then you can't change anything, which means that everything will be the same and you and Cathy will still have to come back to meet with me anyway!'

It was William's turn to stare as he realised what she was talking about. 'Mary, you have just described a thing called a time paradox. You are bloody incredible!'

She grinned. 'I think "a paradox" deserves a big kiss!'

He kissed her tenderly and then looked over at Cathy. 'I wish we could carry out an IQ test on this lady. I have a feeling that she would put me to shame!'

They came to a steep sandstone cliff that ran for miles alongside a clear stream that, over the years, had cut its way through the rock. Jimmy scouted ahead and came back to report some caves that would make a good stop. They walked along a well-worn track at the base of the cliffs until they began to find shallow caves that had been eroded by wind and rain. As they moved along, the caves became progressively deeper and more extensive, many with signs of human habitation, until they found one high up in the cliff that went into the rock face for more than ten metres.

They climbed up a smooth path that had seen thousands of feet before theirs and once inside they discovered thin sandstone walls elaborately and artistically fashioned by wind and rain over the centuries so that in effect there were separate chambers. One branch of the cave went upwards to a small opening near the top of the cliff that provided a look out of the surrounding country.

The floor of the cave complex was perfectly smooth, with deeper depressions that had filled with sand and soil and at several spots they could see where fires had been lit over many generations, leaving streaks of carbon up the walls. They unloaded their bundles and Jimmy took June off to one of the side chambers before announcing that they were going off to hunt for that night's meal.

He held up his newly acquired boomerang. 'I saw some geese back that way. I reckon a big fat one will be bloody good for tucker!' By now, Jimmy was using a combination of his language, with increasingly more English so that both William and Cathy were able to follow him easily as he spoke.

'Keep an eye out for any of your people. These caves

are obviously used a fair bit and I don't want any unwanted visitors.' William said.

Jimmy looked at him, clearly puzzled. 'You all are my people now. Do you mean other people?'

William realised that he had just made a racist generalisation and was suitably abashed. 'I stand corrected mate, I mean keep an eye out for anyone who isn't one of us.'

When Jimmy had gone, William climbed up to the lookout and watched as Jimmy and Ajunda headed back along their trail. Looking around, he tried to spot any tell-tale smoke that might indicate a campfire but there were none. It looked like they had the area to themselves, at least for now.

He glanced down in time to see a large bird taking off near where Jimmy and Ajunda had gone and then made out a rapidly spinning shape that hurtled through the air before taking the goose in mid-flight. It seemed that Jimmy's boomerang worked very well.

They returned an hour later with not one, but two big grey geese. The women quickly gutted the birds and plucked and preserved the precious flight feathers.

Now that her status was settled, William had been working on a bow for Mary and it was almost done. With three bows they were going to need more arrows and the goose feathers were easily the best to use.

Traditionally, geese were cooked by Aboriginal people, feathers and all, wrapped in leaves or in clay and then cooked directly on coals. However, William had other ideas for these geese. He went into the bush with the hand axe and returned some time later with three lengths of green wood—two with forks at the end and a longer, thicker one that was straight but for at one end where it had a ninety-degree bend.

As the others looked on, he planted the two forked lengths into a patch of sand and then moved the small fire to the centre, building it up so that there would be plenty of coals.

Cathy looked on, a smile on her face as she took in the expressions of the others as he spitted and secured the two geese onto the pole and once the coals were right, planted the spit over the two forks.

It wasn't long before the smell of slowly roasting geese filled the cave, fat from the plump birds dripping down onto the coals and causing group salivation anticipation. William and Cathy took turns to slowly rotate the birds until they were cooked to perfection.

Afterwards, Jimmy finished off one last piece of goose and then lay back, groaning and holding his bulging belly. 'I reckon white fella cooking not too bad!'

William and Cathy spent much of the time learning more about the bush from their three companions. They discovered how to take the seeds from cycad trees and to soak them in running water for several days to remove the poisons and then grind them into a flour-like powder. Mixed with fruit and a little fat and then baked on a flat stone, they made delicious and nutritious little cakes.

June showed them how to locate and dig up the roots of a bush, that when baked in the coals, tasted exactly like yams. Mary introduced them to several more types of bush fruit and Jimmy added big fat witchety grubs to their diet, although both William and Cathy insisted on a few minutes in the coals before they would eat them, unlike the other three who delighted in sliding them still wriggling into their mouths.

William and Cathy learned more about the weather and were amazed to learn that these Aboriginal people had much more accurately broken up the year into five distinct seasons, unlike the often inaccurate four that they were used to and certainly more accurate than the 'wet' and 'dry' that most people in the tropics used to delineate the year.

There was the monsoon season which was called Ngurkita, then the end of the rainy season called Kuutula, followed by early part of the dry season called Kuuwula. The full-on dry season was called Kayimun roughly from September to November and then the last season with the earliest onset of the rains was called Malantityi.

They lay up at the caves for several more days while Cathy taught Mary how to use her bow and they topped up their food supply and stock of arrows. Mary had had some previous experience with Cathy's bow and so by the end of the second day, she was hitting her targets consistently at twenty paces.

On the third day, she challenged Jimmy to a contest and was hitting a target made from pandanus leaves every time at thirty paces, while Jimmy could only manage seven hits out of ten with his spears.

'Bloody white fella little spears are cheating if you ask me!' he complained.

Lost hopes

The group left the caves with regret. It had been a good rest in relative comfort and security. William, Cathy and Mary's new three-way marriage had been cemented in more ways than just the wonderful nights under their kangaroo skin blankets and each of them knew with absolute certainty that it was the way it was meant to be.

William had resignedly noted the passing of a very nice tradition during their time at the caves. Cathy had decided that she needed a new top, as the kangaroo skin one that she had been wearing had become stiff with age and irritated her in very sensitive areas. They had several nice furry possum pelts available and she enlisted Mary and Ajunda's aid to show her how to make a much more pliable bikini-style top by stretching and scraping a pelt on a rack and then softening it with a mixture of animal fat and urine until it felt like suede on the inside, with the lovely soft fur on the outside.

Up until then, Mary had been perfectly happy to go bare breasted as she had always done but one look at Cathy's new top and she insisted on wearing one also. When Ajunda followed suit the following day, Jimmy threw accusing looks towards William as though it was his doing!

Cathy had let her hair grow longer and kept it tamed with a wooden comb that he had carved for her. William had to admit that she looked absolutely beautiful with her long blonde hair, tanned skin and possum bikini. He looked at her and an equally beautiful Mary, and realised how incredibly lucky he was.

It would have been easy to stay longer but they knew that they had to keep going. It was now the dry season—almost into *Malantityi*—and most of the rivers were relatively low, making crossings a lot easier.

They came across signs of other people on several occasions, including a recently used camp where the ashes from the fire were still warm. It kept them on the alert but with a couple of cautious detours, they were able to avoid contact with any of the local tribes.

They came to a major river that Cathy thought she recognised as the Adelaide River. There was a rock formation that she said her father had, or would in the future, use to pin-point a deep hole where he always caught barramundi. That meant that they were only a hundred or so kilometres from where Darwin was... or would be.

William had been hoping that they would have been even closer by now. He was becoming anxious to get to Darwin, if for no other reason than to at least know whether the damned place was there or not. They had covered two thirds of the distance and it had taken them a lot longer than he had expected, but at last they were getting close at least.

They were now in an area that would have a significant white population, even going back to the turn of the twentieth century, but there wasn't a sign of an urban landscape or European habitation anywhere. It only confirmed in his mind that they were a lot further back in time than one or two hundred years.

The knowledge that they were at last getting closer to Darwin made them push harder and ten days after crossing the Adelaide River, they came within sight of the coast. They had been labouring up a steep hill and when they reached the top, it was to find that in the distance lay the gleaming waters of Darwin Harbour.

William stood beside Cathy at the crest. Despite the beauty of the harbour, he couldn't help but feel despondent at the vista before them. While he had long ago reconciled himself to the fact that he and Cathy had come back in time, there had always been the hope, however irrational, that it was all some sort of mistake—that Darwin city was where Darwin city had always been and that they would laugh about their error and return to their previous lives... albeit with Mary and each other. Here though, was the final proof.

Cathy took his hand and squeezed it hard. 'It's not there, is it?'

He stared at the wide expanse of Darwin Harbour, glistening in the bright sunlight and without a single sign of habitation anywhere to be seen.

Mary took Cathy's other hand. 'Is this where you come from?'

She sighed and fought against tears. 'It was my home; William came from another place. My mum and dad lived there... or I guess, will live there. My schools, my university, my friends... none of them even exist yet!'

Jimmy's sharp eyes broke their melancholy spell when he peered out towards the horizon and pointed. 'I reckon that's a big bloody canoe out there!'

The others all strained to see but only Ajunda was able to verify her man's sighting at first. 'Trepang boat!' she announced. 'They are coming for trepang.'

'Trepang, that's what you were talking about a while back?' William asked Cathy.

She nodded. 'They used to… I mean they come from what will become the Indonesian islands for them. It's a sort of sea slug and is considered quite a delicacy in Asia. As I understand it, the northern coast of Australia was… *is* one of the best areas in the world for gathering them.'

'What is 'Australia'?' asked Mary.

Cathy looked to see that Jimmy and Ajunda were out of earshot. As yet, the two of them were still ignorant of where the two whites had come from and until William and Cathy worked out how to tell them, they didn't want to confuse them.

Cathy replied. 'In the year 1788, people will come from England… where the English language is spoken, and settle in this land. It eventually became known as Australia. This part of Australia will one day be called the Northern Territory.'

'So do you know what is this year in your um, your map with days and years on it.' Mary's English had been continuing to improve in leaps and bounds and only occasionally did she forget a word.

'Calendar, the word is calendar.' She replied. 'Well, we're not sure of course, but I think that we're in the seventeenth century, maybe the late part of the 1600s. We aren't going to know for sure until we find someone from, well from civilisation.' She cringed at her choice of words. '*Civilisation*. I mean... You know what I mean?'

'So white people like you and William will not come here for many years yet?'

Cathy shook her head. 'I doubt we'll see an Englishman anytime soon. There might be some people from a place called Holland around here though. It just depends on exactly what year we're in.'

Mary took in the information as they all peered out to sea, trying to get a better look at the vessel. Eventually, they could all make out a sea going vessel of some sort but, to William's chagrin, with his older eyes, he was the only one unable to make out any features as the ship slowly came closer. The others were able to make out a single lateen-type red sail and Jimmy even claimed that he could see that there were five people on board.

They began to move off again, determined to arrive at the coast that day if possible. They left the higher elevations and the harbour was no longer visible but William was now anxious to reach the sea. He recognised that he was being bloody racist at the notion, but somehow the thought of contacting people from what he might consider *civilised* cultures was a nice one. He inwardly mocked himself at the thought even so. For all they knew, they might look back on their trip up until now as being peaceful!

'If we get there in time, we'll be able to light a signal fire and maybe attract their attention. Even if they are Indonesians, they must have at least had contact with Europeans.'

Mary gave a note of warning. 'Some of the boat people are not so nice. It is common for people to be taken against their will.'

Cathy looked at her. 'Are you talking about your mother? You mean she was kidnapped?'

'I don't know if it was what you call kidnapped. I think my mother actually loved my father but I'm not too sure how she actually came to be with him. I know that she was taken by my father when she was a young girl about the same age as Ajunda. She stayed with him until I was born and then she left and took me back to our tribe. She told me that the man who is my father was not so bad to her and he let her return to the tribe when she wanted to. I have seen him and I think my mother was right, but other boat people are sometimes very bad. It is common for the boat people to take black women and they are not so good to them. Sometimes they kill us if we try to stop them.'

Ajunda joined in with her limited English. Jimmy had taken to calling her 'Junie' since she had been given the name June and it was beginning to stick with the rest of them. 'My people say that black people go to other land and do much… work?'

William had a terrible feeling that he knew what she meant. He turned to Mary. 'Is Ajunda talking about slavery? Do the Aboriginal people get taken away and made to work for nothing?'

Mary spoke to Ajunda in Alawa. When she turned back to him, her expression was bleak. 'I think that is what Ajunda means. She says that one of her cousin's uncles was captured with a group of other people and they had very heavy… things put on their legs and hands so that they could not run away. She says that her cousin's uncle was too skinny and slipped out of the heavy things and jumped over the side of the boat and got away.'

'My God!' Cathy exclaimed. 'She's talking about chains. People being chained up and taken into slavery!'

William stared in the direction of Darwin Harbour. 'It looks like trepang isn't the only thing these boat people come here for. I guess we can't afford to make any assumptions about a friendly reception when and if we meet up with these guys.'

Cathy was still staring at Ajunda. 'I've never heard of slavery in Australia's history and I'm a history student! This is terrible!'

As soon as Cathy spoke, William thought of the thousands of South Sea Islanders, brought to work on the Australian sugar fields in the 19th and early 20th Century by so-called *black-birders* under very questionable circumstances. He recalled that they had received some sort of payment for their labours, so it might not have been technically slavery … but it was too close to the real thing for anyone who knew about the practice not to feel guilty about it.

'Unfortunately, our history was written by white people, a lot of whom didn't like nasty truths being recorded for posterity. I'm sure there were hundreds, even thousands of shameful things that were done to the Aboriginals once we came to Australia that were simply ignored. Don't forget too, we're in a different time here with a whole different way of thinking. Slavery was still very acceptable and quite common right through to the nineteenth century. Hell, it even still existed in our time in the Middle East and Eastern Europe!'

Cathy shivered in the warm sunlight. 'William, are you sure that we want to contact any of these… boat people? Maybe we're going to be much better off just keeping to ourselves!'

He looked grim. 'I just don't see that we have an alternative, honey. I'm not putting down the way that Mary, Jimmy and Junie live. Hell, I can think of worse ways to live than as a hunter-gatherer but in the long term, it just wouldn't work for us. If it isn't the Ngurruku tribe that want to kill us—and they will certainly want payback after what's happened—it would be some other tribe who thinks we're evil or spirits or something like that and that it would be the smart thing to just stick spears through us and be done with it. We're not going to be able to fight off every attack with our bows and sooner or later, one of us is going to be killed.'

Mary took Cathy's hand. 'We are going to be alright, Cathy. We will look after each other and no one will hurt us while we look for our new home.'

Cathy stared at her. 'Home… that sounds like such a nice word but will we ever be able to find it?'

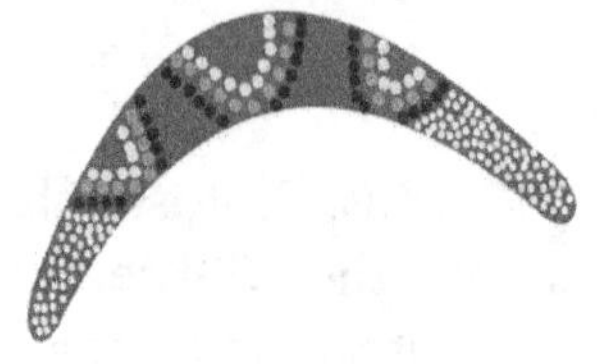

Darwin arrival

Cathy

It was around noon on the following day when they finally reached the harbour. Cathy took the lead now and led the way unerringly through the bush to a series of low, sandstone cliffs that overlooked the water.

She stood at the edge of the cliff and stared down at the small beach a few metres below them and then back to a spot a short distance away. Her eyes were misty as she looked around. 'We are at Fannie Bay. My mum and dad will live just over there, about a hundred metres in that direction. This'll be the hottest property suburb in Darwin one day.'

She pointed to the right. 'That will be the Darwin Sailing Club and the Trailer Boat Club and over there behind us will be the Fannie Bay Gaol. My primary school is about a kilometre away and my high school just beyond that.' She looked around at the wild bush. 'This is so weird!'

William could see what a great spot this was. On his first night in Darwin he had taken Laura to the Darwin Sailing Club for a sunset dinner and it had been a very good night, the views out over the harbour nothing short of spectacular. 'Your mum and dad's place must be worth a fair bit then.'

She nodded. 'Mum and dad bought the place about a year before Cyclone Tracey for I think about a hundred grand. They have, will have, a half-acre block and when we… when we left it was worth a couple of million easily.' She sighed. 'They're pretty well-off anyway and they often told me that they couldn't wait for me to marry and have kids so that they could spoil their grandchildren rotten. I guess that's not going to happen now either.'

She was grateful to feel both William and Mary's arm suddenly around her as she looked around in melancholy.

They camped close to the water at a spot that Cathy swore would one day be the start of Ross Smith Avenue. 'This is where Sir Ross Smith first touched down in Australia when he flew the first flight from England to Australia.'

Mary's head snapped up at that. 'A man flew… like a bird?'

She managed a laugh. 'Well sort of, but in a big metal bird machine.'

William saw the sceptical look on Mary's face and guessed that Cathy was going to have to explain all about aviation before Mary was satisfied. Her curiosity was just about insatiable, particularly with regards to the 21st Century.

He interrupted while he could still get a word in. 'Our first priority is where we set up our camp. Unless we get really lucky, we're probably going to be here for quite some time. I'm not going to allow us to be vulnerable again like when the Ngurruku were chasing us. We'll need a better and more defensible spot to set up. Jimmy and I will see about something good for supper and scout a place out while we're away.'

Cathy pointed off to the headland a short way along to the east. 'Try along there. It's East Point Reserve, or it will be, and I think I remember hearing that the military hollowed out and extended existing caves there during World War Two to use as storage for ammunition and such for their big guns. It might be okay for us.'

He nodded. 'Sounds good but be careful while we're away; we don't know if the local Aboriginals even know that we're here and how they'll react when they find out.'

Jimmy looked seriously at him. 'They know we are here. They just don't know what to make of us yet.'

William

The approach to the headland that Cathy had recommended was almost completely blocked off by a large expanse of swamp. William and Jimmy only went a few paces into the swamp before the distinctive barking of a couple of very big crocodiles made them decide very quickly to find another way in to the headland. They found that only a narrow strip along the shoreline allowed them to get past the swamp and onto higher ground.

They explored for an hour before William found the entrance to a cave in a small outcrop of granite in the centre of a rocky field. The cave only went in for twenty paces but led off to a slightly larger chamber that smelled of the ocean but was pitch black inside. It took only a few minutes to fashion a torch but everything was a bit damp from sea spray and it took considerably longer for his ferrocerium rod to get a small fire going to light it.

With the reed torch crackling, they could make out that the inner chamber was just part of a network leading off again to several more chambers that eventually led them to a narrow opening in the cliff face overlooking the ocean.

The caves themselves were dry aside from where rain and sea spray had invaded the outer chamber but they knew that they had found their base.

William spotted a big golden snapper in the shoals on the way back to near where Cathy and the others waited and even though it took two arrows to get it, he was inordinately proud of his first fish with the bow.

They discovered that the women had been busy in their absence, with a big woven basket of oysters that they had pried from the sea rocks to supply an entrée to his snapper. They were delicious and the smell of the slowly cooking fish ensuring that they were more than ready when it was dragged from the coals.

William told them about the cave and the approaches to the area.

Cathy nodded. 'That'd be right. I remember that there was a big swamp that had to be drained when I was a little kid before they turned the whole area into a big lake and tourist resort. It became a bit of a joke that every night, some of the locals would poop in the lake so that there were big brown floaties in the water in the morning for the tourists to find.'

He laughed. 'I can imagine some of the reactions. I take it that's typical Top End humour at its best. I'm kind of glad that the swamp is still there now though. It'll make it very difficult for anyone with bad ideas to approach us without our knowing. If some of the barking that I heard coming from the swamp is what I think it is, then we're going to have some very mean "watch dogs" to stop anyone approaching us through the swamp. We'll only have to keep watch along the beach strip and seaward. I reckon that we're going to be pretty safe there.'

CHAPTER EIGHTEEN

Base camp

They led the women back to the caves in the early morning. Cathy looked around the area in wonder with grass, low shrubs and bare rock all that could be seen.

'Wow, you know this whole area was turned into a huge gun emplacement complex during the war. I remember enormous concrete bunkers right where we're standing, but I think that the huge naval cannons were sold off for scrap metal. One of the bunkers became a very nice restaurant and the other was used as a World War Two museum. All the tunnels were blocked off but we were told that ammunition bunkers and tunnels ran all the way through the headland.'

There was plenty of material around to build their humpies at the entrance to the caves, for they had no intention of living underground like moles. The caves would be their refuge and storerooms. Torches were made ready to use and showed the full extent of the caves.

William led them through to the small hole at the far end and indicated the ocean beyond. 'We're going to have to start thinking a little more tactically from now on. We can build up a bit of a wall up top so that the cave entrance is easy to defend if we're attacked, but if we're in real trouble at any time and have to escape then we'll need to enlarge this to allow a back door. Then I thought that we'll need to build some sort of boat so that if we need to, then we can get away by sea.'

Cathy looked at him in surprise. 'Is that really necessary? The Ngurruku won't come this far after us; it's as much out of their territory as it is for Jimmy and Mary. Who are you worried about?'

'I'm probably just being paranoid but hearing about these boat people enslaving the locals has got me pretty worried. We already know how potentially dangerous it is around here, at least from the local Aboriginal tribes. Also, from what Junie and Mary tell us, some of these boat people have very little regard for human life and I don't think the fact that we have white skin is going to be any guarantee of safety for you or me either. We need to hope for the best but plan for the worst from them, just to be on the safe side.'

He could see that his pessimism was souring Cathy's enjoyment at being back *home,* even if her home didn't exist here yet. He soon found out that she was determined to make the most of the break from their journey however. The trip from Kakadu had been long and arduous, filled with danger and the need to be almost constantly on the move.

None of them knew how long they would be able to stay here; Cathy insisted on referring to their location as 'East Point', but she wanted some home comforts after months of living as nomads.

They had already made their shelter more substantial than any of the ones they had stayed at on their journey, with four uprights and a real roof of trimmed gum branches and a rear wall. Gaps had been filled in with a mixture of clay and leaves and while a few showers of rain demonstrated where they had missed a gap or two, they were relatively protected from all but the heaviest downpours. A waist-high wall of rocks protected the front of the shelter and the floor had been stamped down and flattened out. A rush bed made for reasonable comfort during the nights but Cathy wasn't satisfied with such basics any longer.

She took Mary and Junie for trips along the coast line and brought back a large collection of drift wood of different shapes and sizes. She presented the haphazard pile of wood to him with a challenging look and an expectant smile.

'This is our furniture Will darling!' she said. 'Would you put it together for us? I think a table so that we're not eating off rocks, some chairs to sit on and a chest to start storing our tools and utensils in, will do to start with. Oh, and of course we need a nice big bed!'

Cathy had started abbreviating his name to 'Will' fairly recently and he liked it. Lately Mary had been doing the same when the three of them were alone. It added to the intimacy that they shared. He held up the hand-axe with a bemused expression. 'I've got an axe and a couple of knives. You don't want much, do you?'

She kissed him on the cheek. 'I'm sure you'll do wonderfully, Will!'

Mary giggled. 'Cathy tells me that sleeping on a bed is a good thing, husband. I am looking forward to finding out what it will be like for the three of us!' She followed this with a lingering kiss on the other side of his bearded cheek.

He stared for moment, looking from one smiling wife to the other and sighed, then nodded. 'I'll get right onto it.'

The results a few days later were a surprise even to him. The three women had been busy making long lengths of cord from pandanus leaf fibre and this enabled him to lash carefully carved bits of driftwood together, making the joints a little firmer still with the use of tree resin. Gradually their furniture took shape. First, he made some basic stools, deciding that chairs were just too hard, but they ended up so sturdy that he realised it was only another step to put a back onto them, so that Cathy got her chairs.

Jimmy helped throughout but was clearly amused at what they were doing. His English was now almost as good as Mary's was and he put it to good use.

'Bloody silly this stuff, I reckon. What's wrong with sitting on the ground to eat? You'll get splinters in your arse sitting on these funny things!'

William threw him a look. 'Jimmy my lad; you'll learn before too long that once a woman gets an idea into her head, by far the best thing is just to go with it. Resistance is futile!'

Jimmy pumped his chest out. 'Junie doesn't boss me around like those two boss you around. I'm the boss in my family!'

That got a laugh. 'You just go on believing that, mate. Anyway, you've only got one woman to deal with!'

That brought a look of sincere sympathy. 'Yeah, you're in trouble all right!'

'Well, it does have its compensations.' William said with a wry smile.

The table was easy after that, with four sturdy uprights, four smaller framing pieces to anchor them, bracing timber and then shaved crosspieces to make the table top. The chest was the most difficult and many pieces of driftwood were converted to firewood before William managed to make a roughly rectangular box with a lid that more or less closed properly.

Cathy stood looking at the finished product and raised an eyebrow at the peculiarly shaped chest. 'I didn't know that you had such an artistic streak. This would make Picasso feel proud!'

The bed was in the final analysis the easiest to make. William made a large rectangular base that sat a foot off the ground and onto this frame the women tied a huge patchwork of kangaroo hides, supported them with a lattice of pandanus cord. William gingerly tried his weight on the bed and was delighted that he didn't fall straight through to the floor.

Both of his women were watching as he tested the bed and he felt a hot thrill when Cathy slid an arm around Mary's waist and murmured. 'I hope you're feeling fit tonight, because we're going to give the bed a real test later on!'

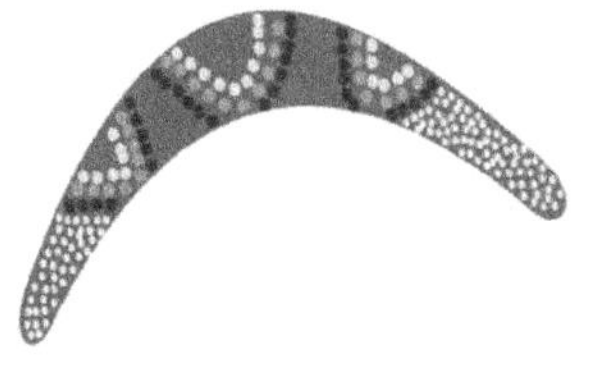

Friendly neighbours

They had been there for two weeks before they had visitors. It was a cool morning when Jimmy staggered out of the smaller shelter where he and Junie lived, and called out. 'Hey William, you'd better get out here!'

It was only just dawn and William was bleary eyed but when he stepped out of his shelter but woke up very quickly. There, in front of their two shelters, only twenty paces away, were twelve Aboriginal warriors standing in a pack, all armed with spears, woomeras, boomerangs and fighting clubs.

William was about to dive back in for his bow when he checked himself. It suddenly dawned on him that the Aboriginals weren't attacking them in any way; none of their weapons were aimed at them and their spears were not yet placed in the throwing sticks ready to hurl. Their demeanour was aggressive, but it was not immediately threatening.

Jimmy came to stand beside him, while the three women stood behind them. William looked back and noted that Cathy and Mary had drawn the same conclusion as he had and did not have their bows ready to use, but saw with approval they were now strung and within easy reach behind them.

One of the oldest of the warriors, grey beard down to his waist and numerous black-ridged scars across his chest, called out in a rapid blast of Alawa that William caught none of.

He realised that Jimmy was nervous in the presence of warriors from another tribe. He reminded himself that his friend was young and only just initiated as a warrior. It must be daunting for him to suddenly confront a group like this.

He looked at Jimmy and tried to reassure him. 'It's okay mate, as long as we all stay calm, we're going to be okay. What did he say?'

Jimmy was grateful for his big white friend's calm confidence. 'He asks what are we doing on their land and why do you have white skin. Their language is a little bit different but not too much.'

'Tell them that we're friends. We do not mean any harm and only want to live here for a short time. Tell them that we have white skin because we come from across the sea.'

Jimmy looked at him with a challenge in his expression. 'You come from this place, same as me. I'm not silly bugger mate, I listen to you talk with Mary and Cathy. I know where you come from. I can't tell them you come from across the sea because that wouldn't be the truth.'

William felt like an idiot for not taking Jimmy into his confidence much sooner. By now he knew that Jimmy was open minded and intelligent enough to learn the whole story. He'd been meaning to do it for weeks but the right opportunity just hadn't presented itself.

'I'm sorry I haven't told you everything about us Jimmy. I should have known better and we will tell you and Junie everything, but these people won't understand how we came to be here. My people, the English come from across the sea and that is how my family came here originally, so it's not telling something that's not the truth … not really.'

Jimmy seemed to be considering the argument that would allow him to tell a partial truth and not offend his ancestors with a lie. He finally nodded, turning back to the elder and talked with him for several minutes.

Mary came up close behind William and whispered in his ear. 'I think Jimmy is convincing them. He says we are a new, small tribe but we will not be staying on their land. They are Larrakeyah people and this one is their chief, Gullaway, I think. Gullaway says we are wrong to be on their land without asking permission and Jimmy says we will give them a gift to… to make sorry.'

She listened some more and then went on. 'Gullaway says maybe we can stay but he wants to see the sorry gift.'

William looked around. 'We don't have anything to give them that we don't need!'

Cathy ducked back into the shelter and came back with his Rolex. 'What about this? It doesn't work any longer but it looks very impressive.'

He groaned. 'That was a gift from my mum and dad. It's worth four grand! What about the car keys? They're no bloody use either.'

She looked sympathetically at him. 'Don't you think that it would demean our gift if it's worthless to us? At least your lovely watch will be put to good use this way and if it wins us some new friends, it'll be worth it, won't it?'

He took it off of her with a sigh and passed it to Jimmy. 'Tell Gullaway that this is a very special um, bracelet from over the sea. Tell him that it is the only one of its kind and is very valuable.'

Jimmy looked at the watch and then at him. 'I can give him one of my spears instead.'

William smiled in appreciation. 'Nah, the bloody thing will never work again anyway so he might as well have it.'

The old Aboriginal accepted the Rolex from Jimmy and listened to what he said and then looked over at William. He held the watch up and looked at it, shook it, then bit it and looked at it again. The other warriors crowded around him, all looking at the shining stainless steel and glass in fascination. Finally, the old man broke into a huge grin and nodded vigorously, letting out a torrent of very happy sounding dialect that needed no translating.

William sighed again and murmured. 'Bloody hell, I hope the damned thing doesn't show up in an archaeological dig sometime in the future; there'll some very puzzled people if it does!'

A much happier group of warriors headed back along the shore and away from their camp.

Jimmy walked back to his group. 'He says we are friends of Larrakeyah people now and we can stay. Their camp is along the beach and he says we can visit.'

They did so the following day and were obviously expected, for their reception was one of universally friendly curiosity from the fifty or so men, women and children who made up the small tribe.

They decided to leave the three bows back at the camp and William carried one of Jimmy's spears, just for appearances, while the three women were unarmed, carrying only digging sticks and bark dishes for collecting food in. They wanted the Larrakeyah to accept them as nothing out of the ordinary, apart from their skin colour.

The last thing that they wanted was for their new friends to wonder at their peculiar weapons or the fact that their women were usually armed and just as dangerous as the two men.

Only Junie seemed completely happy with the situation, for even though both Cathy and Mary had tried to convince her to try out a bow, the timid young girl was adamant that she was more than happy in her role as a traditional Aboriginal wife to Jimmy. Both Cathy and the independently minded Mary chaffed at their relegation as 'just women' but realised the wisdom of maintaining the charade.

Gullaway came up to them as they approached, proudly displaying the Rolex, which now hung from a leather cord around his neck. He gave William and then Jimmy both big hugs, which was less than a pleasure at least for William for it had obviously been quite some time since the old fellow had last bathed.

CHAPTER TWENTY

The Kadijah Man

William looked on with amusement as Mary, Cathy and Junie were quickly surrounded by a mob of excited women, who led them off to sit around a smouldering fire under the shade of a big gum tree. It appeared that visits by strangers were a rare thing in their lives and they were determined to get enough material from the light skinned Mary and the white skinned and yellow haired Cathy to last them through many campfires.

William and Jimmy were Gullaway's guests of honour and sat on either side of him at the men's fire where they spent the next few hours describing their journey from Arnhem Land to the coast.

The senior Larrakeyah warriors who sat around the fire were all impressed, especially when Jimmy described how they had escaped from the Ngurruku who had pursued them. As part of their effort to appear as ordinary as possible, they had decided to gloss over Cathy's role in the short battle with the Ngurruku. As a result they looked at William with something close to awe during the telling of their escape at the river. The fact that bows and arrows had been used instead of spears was also omitted from the tale.

William muttered to Jimmy at that point. 'Cathy is going to kill me if she hears that you've given me all the credit for that business!'

Jimmy grinned and looked back innocently. 'Hey William, you told me that I can't say all the truth so you're going to have to "suck it up".'

William raised his eyebrows. 'Where the hell did you learn that phrase?'

'From Cathy. It's a good saying, isn't it?'

A goanna had been cooking slowly under coals and sand while they talked and it was finally dragged out, cut up and shared between the senior men and their two guests. William had grown fond of the taste of goanna meat during their journey and was enjoying a front leg when suddenly the whole camp went very quiet. Conversation died off in an instant and everyone looking in the same direction.

William saw a thick-set, pot-bellied man enter the camp and was immediately struck by the thought that there was something familiar about him.

He saw that there was fear on all of the warriors' faces as they looked at the new arrival. Then it struck him why the man looked so familiar.

He wore a coat of kangaroo skins and his arms and face where decorated with multi-coloured designs, but it was his eyes that finally made the connection click into place. The man's eyes were… They were insane. They bulged as he looked around him and almost seemed to radiate.

It was the figure from the cave. It was him! He felt a surge of excitement at the thought that perhaps this man might be the key to them returning to their own time!

He looked over at Cathy and saw that she had made the same connection. He saw that she sat frozen on the log that she sat on, her eyes locked on the new arrival just as his had been.

His voice shook as he turned to Jimmy. 'Who is this guy?'

Jimmy looked more scared than William had ever seen him. 'He is Kadijah Man. Bad medicine man!'

'What the fuck is he doing here?' he whispered.

Jimmy shook his head. 'Kadijah men go where they want. Sometimes they cure people if they are sick, sometimes they kill if they do not like someone. They have much magic!'

The medicine man stood in the centre of the camp and looked around. His eyes settled on William and he shivered at the malevolent smile that the man directed towards him.

He walked slowly towards them and William saw that all the Larrakeyah people were as immobile as statues, all with the same look of fear as he approached. To William's amazement, the man walked unflinchingly straight through the hot coals of the camp fire to stand immediately in front of him, no sign of pain on his face as though he had just walked through mildly warm sand.

He stood looking down at William and then spoke in language, but so slowly that William had no trouble understanding him, which worried him even more as the man obviously knew that he had a limited understanding.

'You are the man from the Dreaming that-will-be. I have been waiting for you.'

For a moment, William gaped at him like a fish out of water. He knew!

Finally, he found his voice. 'Sorry friend, you're mistaken. We're strangers from across the sea.'

That same malevolent smile came back. 'I do not think so. I knew that you and the yellow hair girl were who I needed. I brought you back!'

A shiver ran down William's spine and sweat appeared on his forehead. What the fuck was going on? He suddenly realised that all the other men had disappeared like smoke from around the fire, that he and Jimmy were suddenly alone in front of the strange, kangaroo skin clad man and even Jimmy was cringing.

William tried denial again, his throat dry. 'Like I said, you're mistaken.'

The chilling laugh that came out was frightening. 'No, I am not. I know exactly who you are because I am responsible for you being here!'

William thought desperately and finally nodded. Perhaps he would undo what he had done to them! 'Alright, I admit who we are. I don't know why you've done this … what ever it is to us, but surely, we can come to some sort of agreement. If you brought us here like you say, then could you send us back to our time also?'

The suggestion seemed to surprise the man and he was speechless for a moment before suddenly erupting into laughter. 'Send you back? You think I would send you back after all the trouble I have gone to in bringing you here and the months I have wasted searching for you?'

William's heart was hammering. He counted himself a brave person and had in the past confronted all sorts of dangerous situations without flinching but something about this strange man sent shivers up his spine and threatened to turn it to water!

He forced himself to sound a lot calmer than he felt. 'Why the hell not … and if you can send us, there is one other person I want to go back with us!'

The laughter ended as suddenly as it had appeared and was replaced by a look of contempt. 'You are a fool if you think I would undo the great magic I have created in bringing you from the Dreaming.'

He appeared to consider what William had said even so. Apparently, William had piqued his 'professional' curiosity.

'Even if I wanted to, it would take too much of my magic to reverse my spell. The two of you are going to enhance my powers, not drain them! Now enough of this foolishness, where is my yellow haired girl?'

He looked around and spied Cathy, sitting like a rabbit in a spotlight. 'Ah, there she is!' He walked back through the glowing coals again directly towards Cathy and the other women, most of who shrank away and disappeared behind the closest cover. Only Cathy and Mary remained, even Junie shivering off to the side, averting her eyes from the Kadijah Man.

He stopped in front of Cathy and nodded with a look of satisfaction on his face. 'I am Asigi, I am your master. Come with me.'

William had followed the strange man over and heard what he said to his wife. The sense of stunned confusion and fear dissipated in a moment as deep anger replaced it.

'Pig's arse you are!' William said. 'Fuck off you dick-wad. She's not going anywhere with you!'

His defiance might have been in English but the meaning was clear. Asigi turned back to him, laughing in his face. 'It cost me a lot to bring the two of you back from the Dreaming. Do you really think that I am not going to use you both now? The two of you—mostly the girl—will make me the most powerful Kadijah Man of all time. Don't even think about defying me.'

'You can't just march in here and do what you want.

I won't let you! And these people won't let you either!'

Now Asigi laughed again. He looked around at the cringing warriors. 'You say the most humorous things! Do you mean these nothings? None of them will lift a finger to stop me. They know that if I wish to, I can kill them with a single look! I am taking the two of you with me. You cannot stop me.'

'Like fuck I can't!' William roared. He took two steps towards Asigi and the Kadijah Man brought his hand up and blew a fine white powder into William's face.

William took an involuntary breath before he could stop himself and immediately felt his knees turn to rubber and he collapsed like a rag doll to the ground. He was conscious still but suddenly unable to move, only able to watch as Asigi turned confidently back towards a terrified Cathy.

He looked down at her abdomen and nodded, smiling to himself. 'Come woman, your man's blood and the fruit from your womb will make me all powerful in this land. Come with me now!'

Cathy
Cathy knew that she had never been so terrified in her life. Something about his man reeked of pure evil, turning her legs to jelly and catching her frozen breath in her chest, her heart hammering.

Somehow, she found the ability to speak. 'No. What have you done to my husband? I'm not going anywhere with you!'

He leaned closer and stared with his mad eyes deeply into hers. 'I am your master. You will obey me in all things. Stop this foolish resistance!'

Cathy was utterly unable to look away from his eyes; she felt her will dissipating like mist in the morning sun. She told herself that she could break away from his stare but couldn't do it. He beckoned her to stand and she felt herself standing up even though she wanted to stay right where she was more than anything she had ever wanted!

Asigi

Asigi watched as the girl moved to follow him. He had mesmerized stronger wills than hers in the past. He nodded in satisfaction and looked towards the cowering elders, indicating William's helpless form. 'Bring this one to my camp. Tie him up and leave him at my fire and then go!'

He watched with satisfaction as four frightened men moved to pick William up. He looked once more to ensure that Cathy was following him like a sleepwalker and then stepped out to leave the tribe of terrified Larrakeyah behind.

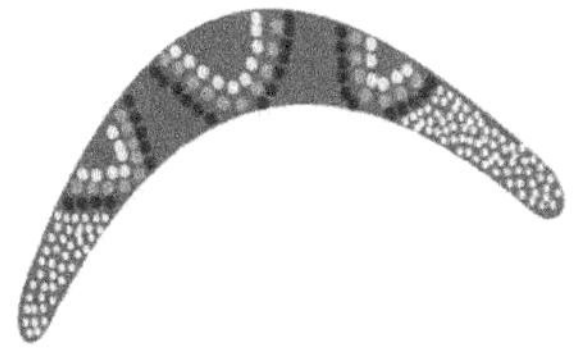

Close escape

Mary

Mary had lived with an ambivalent feeling towards Kadijah Men all of her life. On one level, she knew that they were a necessary part of tribal life. They knew more about the way the body worked than anyone else and used their magic and knowledge of bush medicine very effectively, when they wanted to. There was no doubt that they could cure people and she had seen them save many worthy lives over the years.

However, there was the other side of them that she hated. She had watched as the visiting medicine men came and went from her tribe as though they owned everything and everyone, taking food where they wanted, using women when they wanted to, demanding fear and obedience from everyone.

She had witnessed on a number of occasions when some person, usually a young man, would defy a Kadijah Man when his woman was taken or when a member of his family was cursed. The result was always the same. The Kadijah Man would look at the offender and would point his death bone. Within a month, the person was always dead, wasting away from a sickness that was beyond anyone's ability to cure.

The thought had always been with her that these people died simply because they thought they had to die, that since they believed so utterly in the power of the Kadijah Men and that since the death bone had been pointed at them, all was lost and only dying remained.

She had gone so far as to try to help the victim of a Kadijah Man on more than one occasion, trying to convince the hapless victims that if they wanted to live, then they would. She argued with them, she yelled at them, she forced them to eat food and drink water, all to no avail. To her frustration and to the amusement of the Kadijah Men who she had tried to defy, the victim always, always died whatever she tried to do to save them.

It was only because she was a lowly female that no retribution had been levelled against her. She was below the contempt of the all-powerful medicine men and anyway, her attempts to save their victims only reinforced how futile it was to defy them.

Now though, this Asigi was going to take Cathy and William from her. That was not to be borne.

Asigi started to turn his head as he heard a movement behind him and only just caught sight of the length of red-gum branch that smashed into the side of his head.

Cathy

Cathy was in a dream in one moment, following someone as though through a fog and only vaguely aware of her surroundings. Suddenly, the fog just disappeared and she snapped awake. She stared at the Kadijah Man lying on the ground with blood seeping from a head wound and Mary standing over him with a long piece of timber in her hands, her chest heaving and her hands shaking as she looked down at him.

'What's happening? What's going on?' she asked.

Mary just stared back at her for a few moments. 'I did it! I hit the bastard!'

The four warriors who held William dropped him as everyone in the tribe stared at the unconscious Kadijah Man in disbelief.

Gullaway was shaking as he walked up to them. 'You must go. You will bring a curse our whole tribe if you stay. Go now!'

Mary lifted the wood high above her shoulders. 'Not before I finish him!'

The old warrior moved with surprising speed and snatched the wood from her hands. 'No! It is enough what you have done. If you kill him then his spirit will be the death of us all!'

Mary looked heatedly at him. 'He's just a man—an evil man! If I kill him then he can't hurt anyone!'

Gullaway shook his head, his expression bleak. 'Go or you will be our enemy and we will kill you. Go now and you are still our friends and perhaps we can help each other one day.'

Cathy put a hand on Mary's arm. 'Let's just go. Let's just get away from this evil piece of shit.'

Cathy was intensely relieved when William was able to walk for himself after half an hour. Up until then, she had struggled under his considerable weight as Jimmy and the other two helped her get him away from the insane Kadijah Man. They had been carrying him for almost a kilometre and were almost exhausted by the time he slowly climbed out his fugue and began walking for himself.

They stopped under the shade of a leafy gum tree while he re-gathered his wits.

'How are you feeling?' she asked worriedly.

He shook his head. 'It was the damnedest thing. I could hear and see everything but it took everything I had just to keep breathing! I don't know what that bloody powder was but it was powerful shit!'

Cathy shivered as she remembered her own reaction to the man. 'He might be the key to us returning home but I don't ever want to see him again! He terrifies me.'

William shook his head. 'He's never going to let us go back. If he's the only chance we've got then that's the end of it. For better or worse, we're stuck here.'

Cathy knew he was right. She was thinking about his words when she became aware of Mary suddenly looking at her with bright eyes.

'What is it?'

Mary's eyes went from her face to her abdomen. 'The Kadijah Man. He says that you carry a child. They know about such things. Is it true?'

Cathy stopped and stared at her as Asigi's words came back to her too. At the time, she hadn't given it a thought in her terror of the man, but now his words crashed home. The uninhibited sex life that the three of them had been enjoying was certainly the way for it to have happened! Their love making was intense and completely uninhibited. She suddenly thought about how many times William could have made her pregnant. Then she mentally kicked herself when she realised that her period was way overdue.

She wasn't sure of how she felt about it. She was both shocked at the thought of bringing a child into this crazy world and elated that she might have a new life inside of her!

She looked from Mary to William, a stunned look on her face. 'I hate the bastard but I think that he could be right. I think I'm pregnant!'

William went pale under his tanned skin. 'Oh shit … I mean that's wonderful but … a baby now?' Then he had another unsettling thought and murmured; 'Crap and twins run in my family too!'

Cathy looked into his eyes. 'I don't care if we have quintuplets. I'm thrilled to be pregnant and look out anyone who isn't as happy about it as I am!

Cathy only now became aware that Jimmy had hardly spoken since they'd left the Larrakeyah camp. Now we stood with Junie at his side, his eyes on the ground.

'What's wrong Jimmy?' she asked.

He continued to look at the ground. 'I did nothing to stop him. I was too scared. Only Marinja had the courage to defend you. I am ashamed.'

She put a hand on his shoulder. 'That bastard terrified me more than I've ever been scared in my life and did it just by looking at me. I can certainly understand the effect he must have on the rest of you!'

There was a look of stark determination on his face. 'Thank you for your understanding but it will not happen again! I will not let you down ever again!'

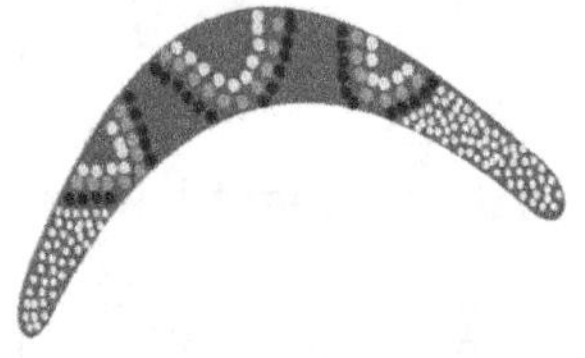

CHAPTER TWENTY-TWO

Asigi's hunt

Asigi

Asigi regained consciousness to find himself in a deserted camp. The Larrakeyah had all gone and he knew that they would travel far and fast to avoid being the focus of his wrath. For a moment, he contemplated following them and teaching them a lesson for befriending the wrong people but decided that they weren't worth the effort just yet. They would wait. His priority was the two whites.

He had known that the yellow haired girl was with child from the moment he looked at her and it was just as he had foreseen. He would rip her unborn child from her body and he would perform the most powerful magic of his life, using the body of the child and the blood of its parents to power the spell. The life forces from an unborn infant and the two parents from the future would release almost limitless magical energy to him.

His teacher had taught him the time trap spell and claimed to have also brought a person back from the Dreaming, although he admitted that he had failed to subsequently find whoever it was that he had brought back in time. Asigi had never known whether or not to believe his teacher and had only half expected the summoning incantation to actually work.

His teacher was long dead now, only bones in the lonely grave Asigi had left him in after he had buried his stone axe in his skull. It was a shame really, for his old teacher would have had to acknowledge him as his superior when he saw that he had succeeded in bringing back not one but two from the Dreaming!

It had been necessary for Asigi to kill him though. When his teacher realised that Asigi was going to be as powerful as he was, Asigi was sure that the old man would have killed him if he'd had the chance.

To bring the two back from where they were, it had been necessary for him to use the lives of two children to power the spell that he sent forward into the Dreaming. The children's disappearance from their tribe had caused him a lot of trouble, for the tribe knew that it was him who had taken them. Only the direst threats had averted their anger and payback. He had made it very clear that not only would the two families die if they sought retribution against him, but their entire tribe with them. It had cost him one of his most valuable resources after that, for, from that day forward the tribe had always avoided him, cutting off one of his easiest sources of food and women. It had been worth it though.

He had lingered in the area of the ancient rock for many months, waiting for his Dreaming trap to be triggered and it had been a source of incredible frustration when he'd need to go elsewhere to confront a rival. The rival Kadijah Man had thought his magic was equal to his own and had learned how wrong he was in the ultimate way. The diversion however, had meant that by the time he got back to the rock, the two whites had already left the area and he had lost track of them as they made their way back to the coast. Now he needed to get his hands on them, to get them again into his power.

He was at a loss as to who had struck him. Surely no tribal member would dare to defy him like that! He shook his head. No. It was just impossible. Then who? He remembered the light skinned woman sitting next to his yellow haired one. She hadn't seemed as afraid of him as the rest of them.

Asigi had a phenomenal memory and he now recreated the image of the girl. He remembered that she had a digging stick and he pictured it. Yes, the tribal design was one he knew. She was from near where he had created the Dreaming trap. The fact that the light skinned girl was with the two whites explained much about how they had survived and made their way all the way to the coast.

Now to lose them again was madly frustrating. He had to find them, but for all of his skill as a user of magic, he had almost no skills in the bush. He would need trackers and now that that the Larrakeyah had run off like frightened dingoes he would have to find others.

There was a tribe on the other side of the harbour. The Wulagi tribe feared him sufficiently that they would do what he wanted. They were at least ten days' walk away, but subduing the two whites was apparently going to be a little more difficult that he had envisaged. He would need their trackers and their warriors. He set off in their direction.

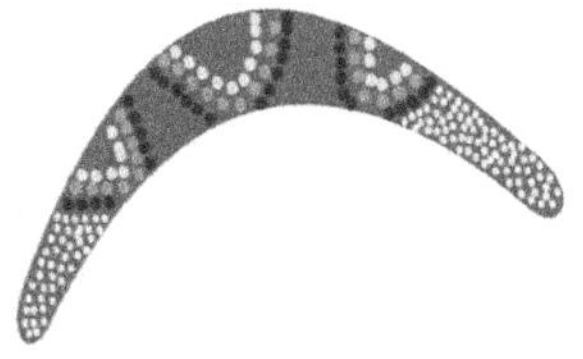

CHAPTER TWENTY-THREE

The Boat People

William

The first thing they did on arriving back at the East Point camp was to begin reinforcing their defences. It had shaken William at how easily the Kadijah Man had overcome him and then put Cathy under some kind of hypnotic compulsion and he was determined that he wouldn't get close enough to them for a repeat performance.

He had a very strong feeling that they hadn't seen the last of Asigi. If he had indeed been the one who somehow brought them back through time then his powers, his magic was obviously very real and, even without his magic, there was no guarantee that the next time he came for them, he would be alone.

None of the others had been able to shed light on the powder that had been blown into his face with such immediate effect.

Junie just shrugged her slim shoulders. 'Kadijah have many powers, many potions and many powders. We are so lucky to escape from that one!'

Her reply gave him a thought. It appeared certain that this Asigi wasn't willing to help them return to the future and according to what he said, he was the most powerful witch doctor around! What if he was lying though? Could there be someone else like him who could use 'magic' to get them back?

He addressed the three of them. 'Do you know if there are other, eh Kadijah men who can do magic like this Asigi does?'

Jimmy and his wife looked blank but Mary thought about it before replying. She knew that William was thinking about returning to his time. The thought scared her because even if he and Cathy wanted to take her with them so that they could stay together, it might not be possible and she might be left behind! The thought filled her with a sick, empty feeling but she loved William and Cathy and so had to tell him the truth.

'There are other Kadijah men around. I have seen maybe five or six of them in my years so there are not many. I think that Asigi must be a very powerful one though. I have never heard of any of them using strong magic like he has. Maybe though … maybe there is one who could help you, I just do not know.'

William guessed that their chances of finding a Kadijah man who knew how to reverse what Asigi had done were somewhere between zilch and zero. The fact didn't change much in his thinking though, for he had already given up on the 21st Century and he knew that Cathy felt the same way. As nice it would be to return to their time and to take Mary with them, they just had to be realists. They simply had to play the cards that had been dealt them.

They first built up the rock wall so that it surrounded three sides of their shelter and now rose to shoulder height, but left narrow gaps to allow them to use their bows if they needed them. They had plentiful arrows but Mary and Cathy checked over each one to ensure that the arrowheads were all firmly in place and the flight feathers all straight. Spare bowstrings were prepared and attached to the sides of their quivers.

The rear of the shelter was at the cave mouth and they now opened a gap there to allow them an easy way out if they had to retreat that way. The exit at the other end of the caves was now open, with only a few easily moved rocks concealing it from the outside.

He couldn't stop thinking about Cathy being pregnant and felt seven kinds of fool for his thoughtlessness in their lovemaking, allowing his libido to replace common sense despite Cathy's earlier words to him. He felt helpless now at the thought that if she was pregnant, and it appeared that she was increasingly sure that she was, then they were going to have to consider the future and safety of their child.

At least some hard work would take his mind off their predicament. William took the hand axe and cleared all of the vegetation from the area around their shelter to deprive any cover to attackers. After hours of hot work in the heat and humidity, he achieved an effect that made the area around their camp like a lunar landscape for a hundred meters in any direction.

All the while, they built up their supplies of dried meat and smoked fish in case they had to flee. Food in the area was plentiful with wallabies, kangaroos and goannas providing meat, while the shoreline proved a cornucopia of sea food of all descriptions, from oysters to big mud crabs to delicious ocean fish. Jimmy made a fishing spear and quickly proved his prowess in bringing home large snapper, huge parrot fish with big bucked teeth that looked like they could take off your fingers and an enormous jewfish that took them three days to fillet and smoke.

Next, William turned his attention to a boat of some kind. His knowledge of boat building had just about been exhausted in making the rafts during their journey. He had sailed recreationally in Melbourne's Port Phillip Bay in various small sailing craft and was a fair hand at boat handling and coastal navigation but had never been involved in making a vessel. He knew that something much more substantial and sea-worthy than a raft was going to be needed if they had to head out into Darwin Harbour with its unpredictable weather and huge tides.

Jimmy was of no help, for his tribe made bark canoes and dugouts for crossing rivers but he had no experience with the open sea, while Mary and Junie didn't even have that knowledge, for boat building had been a strictly male only domain within their tribes.

The solution, when it sailed into the harbour one sunny day, was a tragic one for most of those involved.

He looked up as Junie came running towards him, her face alive with excitement. He knew that she had been collecting fresh oysters from rocks at the water's edge. The oysters and woven collection basket she'd had were apparently forgotten.

Junie's English was very good by now but in her excitement, she reverted to speaking very rapidly in her native tongue.

He only caught a part of what she said until she saw his blank expression and realised her mistake. 'Trepang boat is coming, it is heading this way!' She pointed. Her excitement was contagious and everyone raced to the cliff-tops.

The trepang boat, which Cathy had pointed out was called a *prau* was still half a mile away and was only moving slowly with the very light wind but was still heading in their general direction and would reach East Point within another ten minutes or so.

William knew that it was unlikely that the people on the boat would have seen them yet and was thinking about a signal fire to attract their attention when another boat edged around the distant headland and also turned in their direction.

It was immediately apparent that this was a much bigger vessel, almost twice the size of the first prau and with a lateen sail that was huge in comparison to that on the smaller boat. It was closing the gap between it and the other prau rapidly.

The light breeze shouldn't have allowed it to go that much faster even with the bigger sail but the reason for their greater speed became obvious when they made out three long oars on each side of the bigger boat that propelled the big prau swiftly through the calm water.

'Shit! It's some sort of galleon with bloody great oars. They're chasing these guys. That big bugger's going to run this first boat down!' William announced.

Cathy looked from one boat to the other. 'They might just be both going to the same place.'

The first prau was now close enough to make out the panic taking place on board. There were only six crew members and they all held a variety of weapons as they stared back in fear at their pursuers, with several of them arguing with each other in loud and anguished voices.

William looked back at Cathy. 'Oh they're going to the same place alright; I just wouldn't want to be this first lot when they meet up.'

Mary stared with a thoughtful frown at the first boat

and then spoke up with urgency in her voice. 'We must help them.'

William took note of her concerned expression and considered. There was going to be a much bigger crew on the galleon and they were probably all going to be armed. He doubted that their three long bows and Jimmy's spears were going to make up the difference but it galled him to just sit back and watch.

He calculated roughly where the first prau was headed and made a decision. 'We can get where they're going before they reach it. I reckon they're going to land about where you said the sailing club is going to be. We can wait in the scrub and see if we can make a difference if and when those other blokes attack.'

They all wanted to help the smaller prau, and even Junie tried to argue when Jimmy told her that she had to stay behind.

Jimmy was having none of her arguments though. 'No, you go get bush medicine ready and wait for us. You'll be best damned bush nurse if we need you, right?'

She went up to him and whispered in his ear and then backed away smiling shyly.

Jimmy looked around with a huge grin on his face. 'Junie tells me to make sure I come back in one piece because she is going to have baby!'

William glanced quickly at Cathy, wondering how to keep her and their baby out of harm's way.

She was too quick for him and caught his look. 'Forget it buster, this baby isn't going to stop me fighting. It's going to make me fight harder if I need to!'

He led the way from their camp, mumbling under his breath about mind-reading women.

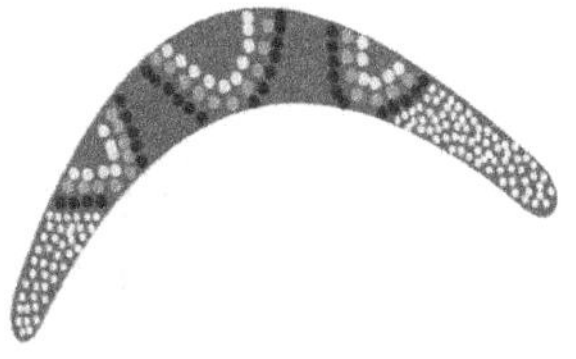

CHAPTER TWENTY-FOUR

To the rescue

They had to run most of the way to beat the prau and the tide was almost fully in, with the water almost to the high water mark by the time that they arrived at Fannie Bay. They could see that the smaller prau was only just going to make the beach before the larger vessel closed on it.

The pursuing vessel was close enough now for William to make out more than a dozen armed crewmembers on the big, galleon style ship. What sent a shiver down his spine however was a large, ornate cannon with intricate designs on the bronze barrel, the bore at least three inches in diameter, mounted on a swivel and pointing out over the bow of the vessel. There was a fierce looking Asian man aiming along the muzzle, a burning piece of rope in his hand and a look of gleeful anticipation on his face.

The smaller vessel finally ran aground onto the soft sand and the crewmembers scrambled to jump off onto the beach, with only one older man holding back. They were still too slow.

The cannon went off with a roar that left their ears ringing. They could only look on in horror as a rain of metal, glass and stones crashed into the tightly packed crew, flinging them in a tangle of bloody limbs off the front of the boat and onto the sand.

Gleeful laughter came from the bigger vessel as it came to a stop with back-oars just short of the beach. Half a dozen piratical figures jumped down into the shallow water and waded ashore armed with wicked short machete-like swords and wave-bladed daggers as they strolled victoriously towards the fallen crew of the prau.

From their concealment only metres away, William could see that some of the crew were still, at least for the time being, alive if badly wounded. It was clear that once the others reached them, they would not stay that way for much longer.

He looked at the big boat. The cannon now pointed up to the sky, smoke still issuing from its muzzle but thankfully out of action at least for now. Other crewmembers milled around the bow, jubilantly watching as their comrades walked up to finish off their victims.

William looked to each side of him. Cathy and Mary both had their bows drawn and Jimmy was ready with a spear. He waited until the first of the pirates raised his sword to chop into the neck of the wounded man at his feet. Then William released his arrow.

Two other arrows and a spear followed and suddenly there were only two of the pirates on their feet; two others clearly dead with arrows through their chests, one with an arrow in his stomach and one with Jimmy's spear transfixing his body so that he was leaning backwards onto the sand, the barbed point holding him up at he looked down, clearly astonished at the spear shaft protruding from him.

The remaining two recovered from their shock in moments and spotted them, screaming a war cry and running at them with their swords held high.

Cathy had always been quickest with her bow and her second arrow got the leading man in the face, the arrow slicing through his left eye and into his brain. The second pirate closed on William, who only just managed to side step the descending blade. He grabbed a hold of the sword arm and used the man's momentum to pivot towards his assailant.

William had been studying karate for five years, having previously practiced judo since he was in his teens. He loved martial arts and was very good at them, finding the more aggressive karate more satisfying than the essentially defensive judo. He had been about to graduate from his first Dan black belt to second Dan and without false modesty, knew that he had been one of the better exponents of karate in his *dojo*, often matching up successfully against even fourth and fifth Dan opponents.

The most heavily stressed rule of karate, one that was drummed into all the students time after time by the Sensei was that, unlike when the martial art had been originally developed in Japan to be used by otherwise unarmed warriors against Samurai in war, karate was now simply a sport and should never, ever be used outside of a dojo.

William was pretty damned confident however, that when that rule had been formulated, no one had given consideration to the possibility of having a pirate attacking them with a sword, with every intention of killing him.

Now, he used all of his strength and technique in a series of blows that would have had him instantly expelled from his dojo and probably thrown into jail back in his own time. The pirate had more than likely never heard of karate and so didn't know that it was a Japanese martial art that broke his arm, burst his right kidney and then finally broke his neck in three brutal blows that took William less than three seconds to deliver.

There had hardly been the time or occasion for him to tell the others about his karate in the perilous trek over the past months and so none of them had been prepared for what he had just done. Only Cathy recognised his skill for what it was from when they had talked about themselves to each other in the very early days.

'Bloody hell William, I had no idea you were that good!'

Her words only added to his distress as he stood panting, both from the explosive exertion and the emotion of what he had just done, while the others stood looking at him in amazement.

The only sounds for a moment were the feeble cries of two of the wounded pirates on the sand. Then, there was a flurry of activity on the big prau as the cannoneer ran to his weapon and tried to reload. Two others brought up big, heavy crossbows and fired hurriedly at them but Cathy put an arrow into one of the crossbowmen's shoulder and the other cowered behind the gunwales of the ship as Mary's arrows sought him out.

Two more quick arrows, one of which clipped his ear on the way through, quickly dissuaded the cannoneer from trying to use his weapon again. They watched the oars plunge urgently into the water, dragging the big boat back out into deeper water until it could turn around and move out of range of their arrows and spears. The cannon was essentially an oversized blunderbuss, and had a lethal but very short range. William felt a wave of relief, for now that the boat had backed off, they were out of the range of its murderous blast.

He stepped out into the open as the vessel moved further away. A crossbow fired a bolt that landed well short of where he stood. It was apparent that the pirate's crossbows lacked the range of their bows and so both he and Cathy sent two more arrows that thudded into the side of the prau, causing them to again use the oars urgently to get further away from them.

William could clearly make out an enormously fat man with a long drooping moustache and goatee beard, dressed in a bright red sarong, open leather vest and with a red bandana around his head. The man was looking at William, the hate in his gaze palpable.

Cathy came to stand beside him and he muttered, 'Oh great, now I've got another enemy that wants my guts for garters!'

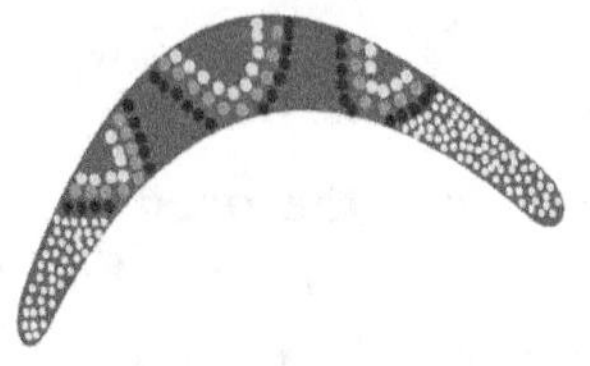

CHAPTER TWENTY-FIVE

Mary meets her brother

The prau had just lost almost half of its crew and William was fairly confident that they wouldn't return, at least for now. The other two pirates had by now died. Despite his bravado, it was obvious that Jimmy was feeling slightly squeamish when he had to force his spear through his victim's body to retrieve the weapon.

They went to the fallen crew to find that only two of them still lived. Both were young men in their twenties; one had a bloody shoulder where shrapnel had lacerated the flesh and the other had less serious wounds to his scalp that, while bleeding profusely, did not appear life threatening.

William and Cathy used strips from the ever-dwindling remnants of their twenty-first century clothing that they had carried with them to bind up the wounds. Cathy looked over to see Mary standing, just staring over the front of the prau. She finished bandaging the man's scalp wound and went over to her.

Unlike the taller girl, Cathy had to stand on her tiptoes to see over the side of the vessel but then drew back in horror as she saw that the older man who had been at the back of his crew had clearly taken the brunt of the cannon's blast. His back and the back of his head was a mass of gore. Cathy felt a wave of nausea as she looked at the man. He lay partially on his side unmoving, his eyes staring blankly at nothing.

Mary still hadn't moved. She just stared at the dead man. Cathy touched her arm. 'Are you alright?'

She stared for just a moment longer and then turned to her with tears in her eyes. 'This is my father.'

Cathy looked at her, momentarily lost for words. William waded through the shallow water and climbed into the vessel. He stepped over a dugout canoe that was stowed mid-ships and then went to the man and felt for a pulse, knowing it was a useless exercise.

Mary had climbed in and knelt beside the man.

'Are you sure it's your dad Mary?' asked Cathy as she looked on.

She nodded. 'Yes. He has not been to see me for years but… it is him.'

'Are you okay, sweetheart?' William asked.

Her eyes glistened with tears but she held them back. 'I am alright. It is just a shock to find him like this. I did not know him very well but I think he was a good man. You know, I do not even know his name! My mother just referred to him when she talked of him as "your father".'

They carried the body from the prau and laid it on the beach. The injured crewman with the shoulder wound was fully conscious and sitting up. He took one look at the dead man and let out a wail of distress, crawling over to the body and sobbing, his one good hand stroking the dead man's face.

Mary knew that many of the boat people could speak various languages of the tribes that they traded with. She squatted beside him and spoke to him in her language now. 'This is your… chief?'

He obviously understood and looked at her, his features numb and the tears still flowing freely. 'This is Goruku… my father.'

Mary abruptly sat back into the sand, staring at him.

Even though the big prau had disappeared back out towards the Arafura Sea, William was far from confident it would not return. There was no way of knowing if there was another vessel nearby who could bolster their numbers to allow them to come back for some vengeance. He decided that they needed to move the prau and conceal it somehow and the sooner the better. An ebbing tide was their enemy for, unless they could re-float the prau quickly, it was going to be stranded high and dry on the sand until the next high tide.

The second crewman had regained consciousness by the time they decided that they should leave and Mary informed them what they intended to do. She had succeeded in learning their names. Her newly discovered brother was Goruluku… she had yet to disclose to him their shared parentage, while the other man was Opaki.

Goruluku grimaced, holding his shoulder, but shook his head as soon as she told him. 'No, boat is too heavy; it must be next tide!'

William looked worriedly out to sea but realised that they had little choice at the moment. He'd already put his shoulder to the heavy prau and hadn't been able to even budge it. He knew that even with Jimmy and the two women to help, it was still beyond them without some more water under the keel, and neither of the surviving crewmen was yet in a state to help, especially Goruluku with his shoulder injury.

He looked around at the corpses still strewn around the beach. 'Okay I guess we need to give these people a burial.'

Opaki went over to one of the dead pirates and spat on his corpse. 'Not with these animals. They hunt us down and kill any of us that they find simply because we come from a different island and are of a different religion! They call us infidels and say we cannot gather trepang and pearls because they are all theirs! No. They cannot be buried with our comrades!'

William could understand how he felt. He had once attended the funeral of a friend and colleague who had been killed in a shoot-out with a couple of drug dealers in Melbourne. His friend had managed to also kill one of the bad guys before he succumbed to his wounds but William had been at the time outraged when he discovered that the drug dealer was being buried only metres away in the same cemetery.

They gathered the weapons from the four pirates and now had four of the short swords and the same number of the wave bladed knives, which Cathy advised were called a *kris*. They also located several gold and a number of silver coins in the dead pirates' leather purses as well as a couple of pieces of gold and silver jewellery that they also removed from the dead men.

Both William and Cathy were at first reluctant to take from the corpses, which had the rest of them mystified.

Clearly puzzled, Goruluku looked at William and in his halting Alawa said, 'You would bury their gold and silver with them? You must be very rich to do such a thing!'

That brought a wry smile to William's face. 'We don't have any money at all.'

'Then why don't you want to take what was theirs? You know that if they had won this battle they would have stripped us all naked and taken even our clothing, as well as the prau and everything in it. It is the way of the world— to the winners of the fight, go the spoils.'

William thought about it and realised that if they were going to try and establish themselves in this time and deal with people like these boat people, then it seemed likely that they were going to need money to do so. He still felt guilty about robbing the dead but saw that it was just plain dumb to do otherwise.

'You're right of course, and we can certainly use some capital I guess.'

In the prau, Cathy had discovered a bolt of brightly coloured and beautifully patterned cotton, showing tropical birds against a background of palms. She cried out in delight and held it up for the others to see. 'Oh this is beautiful!'

Goruluku

Goruluku was extremely curious about the white man and woman. He had been a little shocked to find them with the Aboriginals and was very curious to find out their story. He knew that they were very different from the white people he had ever met and the differences were intriguing. He knew that he would get the story eventually.

Now he watched as the white girl discovered the bolt of cloth. He saw her obvious delight and nodded. 'It is made by the women of our village. My father brings the cloth for trade. There will be no trading now this trip. You can have.'

Cathy was over the moon. 'Thank you so much. I can't wait to get rid of these smelly skins!'

She looked at Mary, who was also looking at the bolt of cloth in delight. 'We are going to be so busy tonight!'

William came over when Goruluku took a big metal shovel from the prau awkwardly tried to begin digging his father's grave.

'Give your shoulder a rest. I'll take care of this.

William dug nice deep graves for all of the dead, with the pirates all consigned to a communal pit while Goruluku and Okapi's crew mates all received individual graves. No one said much as the dead were all laid to rest and then William backed off to give Goruluku and his friend time alone.

Mary

Mary watched as Goruluku stood in silence with his head bowed over his father's grave. She came to stand beside him, unsure of what to say or how to act. She looked at him nervously. The discovery that she had a half-brother was a shock, but one that she quickly realised was the best kind of shock to receive.

She had always felt alone in the world up until she had met William and Cathy, with only Jimmy's friendship to cling to. Now though, she felt a powerful emotion that she had never expected to experience—sorrow, and empathy for the grieving of a brother! She longed to share the grieving with him even though she had barely known her father, but was fearful of how to go about revealing their relationship, especially now that Goruluku was in such pain.

She took a deep breath; it was too much to keep inside of her. 'There is something I must tell you…'

He looked up from the grave and smiled sadly. 'You do

not need to. I see our father in your eyes and in your face. He told me that I had a sister in this land. I just did not expect to meet her on the day of our father's death!'

He stared back down at the grave in quiet contemplation but then looked down at Mary's hand that had slipped into his as they stood silently side by side.

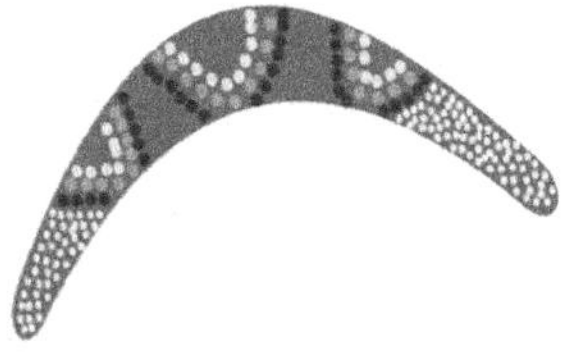

CHAPTER TWENTY-SIX

The truth comes out

They camped on the beach that night. Jimmy had brought back Junie, who seemed thrilled to be able to provide some bush poultices to Goruluku's shoulder. Opaki's scalp wounds had proved as superficial as they had hoped and he helped Jimmy in catching some big mud crabs that proved a filling meal as they sat around a small fire.

Opaki found a kindred spirit in Jimmy, both of them with the same quick sense of humour and a ready smile. The two quickly became friends during the evening, while Goruluku spent most of the time in quiet conversation with Mary.

In general conversation and out of courtesy for their new friends they were all speaking in the Alawa language, but whenever Jimmy, Mary or Junie spoke directly to William or Cathy, they occasionally did so in English. This had both the seamen obviously perplexed.

'What is this language you speak to this big man and his woman?' Goruluku asked his sister. 'I have met other Balanda like them but what they say is nothing like this.'

Balanda was the term that his people used for a pale skinned stranger. Mary knew better than to say too much at this point but had to set him straight on one point at least. 'William is my man too. Cathy and I are both his wives.'

He blinked in surprise. 'This is allowed?'

She smiled dreamily. 'Oh yes, it is allowed in… in our tribe and it is wonderful!'

'You have a tribe… with white people and with people like the rest of you?'

William had been listening in. 'What you see here is the extent of our "tribe", but to answer your question, Cathy and I speak a language called "English". Your sister, Jimmy and Junie have learned to speak it from us.'

Goruluku nodded at that. 'I have heard of your English. We have met traders from the… the Netherlands? They speak of the English but they are not your friends I think.' He paused, clearly taking the time to think. 'Also there are other white people who come in great ships from a distant place called Portugal. They have been coming to our island for many years but I think that they do not like the English either.'

Cathy joined in the conversation, always keen to contribute with her knowledge of history in the region. 'That doesn't surprise me. The people from the Netherlands, the Dutch saw the English as competitors for their spice trade, and as it turned out with good reason. From memory, the Portuguese were mainly in the islands as missionaries, so if they don't like the English it's probably on religious grounds.'

'That all rings a bell with me too.' Said William. 'Shit it's been a while since I read about this stuff, but I don't think it's that long since Henry the Eighth split from the Catholic Church, and there is still a heated battle going on in England between the Catholics and the Church of

England. I'm not surprised that England wouldn't be the flavour of the month with the Portuguese. After all they are as fiercely Catholic as the French or the Spanish.'

Mary was watching her brother as Cathy and William spoke. Because she was aware of their incredible story, she knew that they were both speaking of the distant pass, her time. In their enthusiasm to speak, they were forgetting that little fact and she wondered if he had picked up on the same mistakes in their words that she had.

She quickly jumped in to divert her brother's attention in case he had. 'If these Dutch people do not like my William and Cathy then I do not like them! From now on you must only trade with the English!'

Goruluku grinned at that. 'You sound just like my other little sister; she is always trying to boss me around too!'

Mary's eyebrows shot up. 'I have a sister?'

'Her name is Manissa and she thinks that she can tell me what do to all the time!'

Mary looked wistfully at him. 'I want to meet my sister too!'

The high tide on the next day was a spring tide, which allowed the group to shove the heavy wooden boat back into Fannie Bay. Opaki was quite alright with his minor head wound but Goruluku still had only limited use of one arm, so William provided his inexpert assistance, but between the three of them they were finally able to get the sail up and a light south-easterly breeze helped them to sail back around East Point to where the swamp drained out into the sea.

They found a small creek with sufficient overhanging foliage to partially conceal the prau and then cut more branches so that it was invisible until you got right up to it. Before disembarking, William pointed to a huge black cauldron that sat low in the bilges of the vessel.

'What's that thing for? It looks like something I used to see in cartoons when I was a kid when the cannibals cooked up missionaries! Not that I'd blame them,' he laughed.

Then he saw that the allusion was completely lost on Goruluku. 'Sorry, that's a sort of joke. What is it?'

'It is a trepang pot. We cook trepang and then smoke it before we take it to sell.'

'Do you get much money for the trepang?'

Goruluku shrugged. 'Yes and also for pearls and other things if we find them, but it depends on the quality, quantity and the market. Just one but sometimes two trips each year is enough for our island to trade with other islands and with the yellow people who come down from the great land to the north.'

'Do you mean the Chinese? You trade with the Chinese?' William asked.

The idea excited him for it meant that Goruluku's people in effect had contact with almost the entire East if they dealt with Chinese traders. Between the islanders, the Chinese, the Dutch and the Portuguese, he and Cathy would be able to get an accurate picture of the world in which they now lived… if they ever got off the coast of Australia.

He was more than ever determined to avoid contaminating the future somehow and now with the prau, it looked like it would be possible to perhaps go to one of the islands of the Indonesian Archipelago. At least off the Australian mainland there was surely less chance of their doing something that made them suddenly cease to exist in the future.

Goruluku nodded. 'Yes, Chinese is what my father calls them. They sometimes call at our island and we get very good things from them in exchange for trepang, pearls, turtle shell and also some of the things that we make and grow.'

'Goruluku, do you think it might be possible for us to come back with you to your island? This land is very dangerous for us at the moment. If we could come on your prau it would be a very good thing for us.'

He frowned, and was quiet for a moment, then nodded. 'I think so. My father is... was one of the council that decides things and I will now take his place on the council so they must listen to me and when I tell them all of how you saved our lives. I am sure that they will accept you all.'

He thought for a moment longer and then smiled. 'I will look forward to seeing my other sister's face when I bring Mary home with me!'

'Goruluku...' William paused. 'Look, I don't mean any disrespect but your name doesn't roll very easily off my tongue.'

A smile appeared. 'My sister has told me of how you like to re-name people! You can call me Luku. It is what my sister back home already calls me anyway.'

'Thanks Luku, so where is your island then?'

'Luku' went to a small tightly closed locker at the rear of the prau and pulled out a rolled-up piece of parchment. William's eyes grew wide when he saw that it was a nautical chart.

Luku laid the parchment out on a bench. The map was crude by modern standards but had a compass marked and clearly showed the Northern coast of Australia, Papua New Guinea and the majority of the Indonesian islands.

William's eyes fixated onto a small piece of writing on the bottom left hand corner of the map and his pulse quickened. 'Did your father make this map?' he asked.

'No. He traded it from one of the Dutch captains. It was very expensive and I do not think that the man from the Netherlands was supposed to sell it to us.'

'How long ago was that?'

'Only last year. Why?'

William pointed to the writing. 'That has the year 1650 written. Do you know if that was the year that your father bought the map?'

Luku nodded. 'I was not in the cabin with my father but he told me that the captain copied the map from one in his cabin. I remember that the ink was still damp when my father showed it to me.' He pointed to a tiny speck at almost the eastern-most edge of the archipelago. 'There is Adonara Island; that is my home. My father did this map on the back.' Now he flipped the parchment over to show a detailed map of the island itself. It was small, angular and narrow in places and from indications on the map was covered with mountains.

Luku pointed to a spot near one of the largest bays. 'Here is my village. We are the Paji people, with villages all along the coast and here.' He pointed to one of the apparently mountainous areas, 'Here are the Damon people. Sometimes we have to fight with them, for they want our much more fertile coastal land. These Portugal people talk to the Damon and I think they do their religion now sometimes. We still follow the old religion of our forefathers but sometimes people come and tell us that we must pray to their prophet Mohammed. We do not get on so well with these people either.'

'Tell me about your religion—if it's alright for you to do so?'

'We pray to many gods. There is a god who brings our boats home safely and brings fish to our nets; a god who guards our loved ones; a god who looks after our harvests; a god who brings in the storms and the rains and a god who is the chief god of all the others. We obey the rules that have been handed down to us and respect our gods and they protect and look after us.'

To William, Luku's religion sounded almost like the old Norse pagan religion, with a god for just about every facet of life or even like the Hindus with their multiple gods. He wasn't a very religious person himself but from what he knew of the Hindi religion, which he knew was the oldest major religion in the world, there could not be too much wrong with it if it had been working so well for so many for so long! If a similar type of religion worked for Luku's people, then it sounded just fine and he could understand their refusal to be converted to Islam.

William was trying to get a good grasp of the situation. It could be the answer to their problems of remaining on the Australian mainland. Their whole futures could depend on the viability of them going there. In many ways, he could see that it would be an ideal solution both now and possibly into the future. The fact that this Adonara was so small and being almost on the eastern edge of the archipelago, was so remote from the bigger parts of Indonesia... that might work in their favour in terms of a bit of privacy and avoiding interference from others. He realised that, unless he and Cathy lived like hermits in a cave, it was inevitable that they were going to change the world around them and therefore the future in some way. If they could make their home on a tiny island at the edge of the thousands of islands that made up Indonesia, that change might at least be minimised. The fact that the Dutch, Portuguese and Chinese all called there might be good, or not so good for them. Only time would tell.

'So, this council rules your island?' William asked.

Luku made a non-committal gesture. 'Mostly it does. There is a new Raja; Foramma is his name, but he lives on Flores Island and we do not see much of him. Mostly the Council makes all the decisions.'

'So why did the people in the big prau try to kill you?'

'That was Muluk. He is a big chief from Malacca and is one of those who tell us to pray to their Mohammed. We will not change our gods and so they try to kill us and stop us from trading.'

They took the chart and all returned to the camp on East Point. The three women sent Jimmy and William off for timber and then built another shelter for Luku and Opaki, still behind the protection of the rock wall.

Luku's shoulder still hurt and Junie fussed over him that afternoon, eventually giving him a drink that she and Mary made from plants in the swamp. After that, he slept through the day and well into the evening.

While Luku slept, William laid out the chart for the rest of them to see and explained his thoughts about moving. Mary was fascinated with the larger map of the whole area but more particularly with the detailed map of Adonara Island.

'This is where my father and brother come from; this is where my sister is!'

Cathy took her hand. 'It's like you have two homes—one here in Australia and one there on that island.'

Mary nodded excitedly. 'I want to go there very much!'

William was still pensively studying the chart. In some ways, it would be so much simpler to try and make a home right where they were. At least here, they knew the land and who their enemies were. If he thought there was a real possibility that they would find a way back to their own time by staying, he wouldn't have considered leaving. He just couldn't see how it would be possible though. It was feasible that they might possibly avoid mucking up the future too much if they stayed, but he knew that it was unlikely. Moving off-shore would simplify the problem of changing the future for the Northern Territory and Australia as a whole, but could bring on a whole raft of other issues.

It was obviously a complicated situation on Adonara Island: two different ethnic groups on a tiny little island, other visitors from surrounding islands—and at least three religions and the Portuguese to compound the issue. At least one advantage of being in Australia lay in the fact that it was so big and so theoretically at least, they could keep on the move to avoid the many pitfalls and dangers that staying here meant. The island where Luku and Opaki came from was infinitely smaller and trouble could possibly be a lot harder to avoid. Would they be able to live in such a small and complex environment?

Luku

It was dark before Luku woke up and after he had eaten he came over and sat down near where William, Mary and Cathy talked.

'My shoulder is feeling much better. I think Junie's medicine must be very good.'

Mary smiled at him. 'I'm happy for you, brother.'

He returned the smile but then it faded and he looked at the three of them. 'I know that you are good people. You saved my life and Opaki's when you did not have to. Mary did not know then that I was her brother and you all put yourselves at risk for us and have made an enemy of Muluk.' He paused. 'So I want to know why you are hiding the truth from me.'

'What do you mean?' asked Mary.

He looked at Cathy. 'You said that the Dutch "saw" the English as an enemy and then you said that you "remembered" that the Portugal people came as missionaries.' He turned to William. 'You also talked about things as though it had happened. My sister tried to take my mind from your words but I know what I heard. You spoke as if these things happened in the past.'

He looked from Cathy to William now. 'Also you are both too big and too healthy. I have never seen anyone with nice teeth like yours and you both have strange little marks in the same spots on your shoulders. Lastly, I saw when you used your hands to kill that last Macassar man. I have never seen anyone fight like that. I do not understand and would like you to tell me the truth please.'

Luku knew that he was close to the truth when both the whites went red in the face. His sister touched the big white man on the arm. 'Tell him.' She said.

William

William wasn't surprised in the least at Luku's powers of observation and perceptiveness, given who his sister was. Brains obviously ran in the family. All of his astute observations were spot on and it had never occurred to him that they would stand out like that.

They'd managed to look after their teeth since coming back by using small twigs from the ti-tree bush, which made excellent toothbrushes and even left a nice taste in their mouths. Dental hygiene was almost unheard in the seventeenth century though, and most people in this time would have been lucky to have a full set of teeth past their teens. Even Luku and Opaki, as young as they were, had gaps where rotten teeth had been pulled out.

Luku had also spotted their inoculation marks that must have looked strange and out of place in an age where immunity to such things as smallpox, typhoid and tetanus were unheard of.

So too their physical shape. In a time where people probably died of old age in their fifties, he and Cathy were in perfect health from their life styles back home and from the overall environment back in the twenty-first century with all the advances in medicine and health that came with their time. He was a big bloke to start with, touching just on six foot four inches in an age where only a very few men reached anywhere near that height. Lastly their constant exercise, combined with their lean, healthy diet since coming back in time ensured that they were in better condition than most.

He let out a breath and looked at Mary's brother. 'If you were to know our truth, then you would know that telling others will put our lives at much risk. If people knew the truth about us, I believe they would hunt and capture us, or kill us, just because of who we are. Would you be able to keep our secret?'

Cathy looked worriedly at him. 'Why would they want to kill us?'

He shook his head. 'Just wait and I'll explain.' He looked back at Luku. 'Would you?'

Luku thought for only a moment. 'I owe you my life and this is my sister. I would never put you all in danger. Yes, I will keep your secret.'

'Alright then, so be it; that map was made in the year 1650 according to the Christian calendar. Cathy and I were born about three hundred and fifty years after that map was made. Somehow, we have come back in time… because of an Aboriginal magic man.'

It sounded so simple when he reduced it to a couple of sentences but he realised how improbably it must sound and now he watched Luku stare at him, wide-eyed and his mouth open in shock.

William turned to Cathy. 'We both know a good bit of history; I've always loved it and you're a damn historian. Can you imagine if someone works out that we can predict the future for them?'

She thought about it briefly. 'They would want us for their personal fortune tellers?'

'Except that we wouldn't be guessing like a fortune teller; we would be quoting what we know will take place.'

In a small voice she said, 'I don't know all THAT much about the seventeenth century.'

He let out a short laugh. 'You don't need to. When did the Dutch East India Company come here? How long did they last? When did the English take over their monopolies? When and where did wars break out in Europe through the seventeenth, eighteenth and nineteenth centuries and who won them? Need I go on? We would make Nostradamus look like a rank amateur. Every power-hungry arsehole within a thousand miles will want us for his private pets and if he couldn't have us, he'd make sure we were dead so that no one else could have us either.'

It was Cathy's turn to stare at him. 'Oh my God. You just made me want to find a hole to jump into and never come out!'

Mary looked at both of them with fear in her eyes. 'How can we protect you? You would both be in great danger!'

Luku's just looked stunned. 'You know these things that William said?'

Cathy nodded. 'I'm afraid so.'

He glanced at his sister, then looked squarely into William's eyes. 'You have my most solemn oath; I will keep your secret.'

William took Jimmy and Junie aside the next morning and told him of their intention to go to Luku's home island. Cathy and Mary were as convinced as he was in the wisdom of leaving the Australian mainland if they could, but as much as he valued his friend and his wife, he knew how powerful the attachment to their land was.

To his delight, Jimmy didn't hesitate for even a moment. 'You are my tribe now William. You are my chief and my friend. My home is where you and Cathy and Mary are.'

Junie looked uncertainly at Jimmy but then nodded. 'I belong with my man. I want to come with you to this place too!'

It took a week before Luku's shoulder had healed up enough for him to be able to use his arm and they used the time to ready the prau for a trip back to Adonara Island. It was already well stocked with rice and dried fish, which were the main staples during the short voyages and stacks of green coconuts which supplied their drinking water. To this, they added their substantial stocks of dried and smoked meat supplies.

Luku informed William that the trip usually only took about a week with good winds and no more than three weeks even if they had to constantly tack. The best news from William's point of view was that Adonara was just to the northeast of Timor, which was a virtual stone's throw from the coast of Australia. They would be able to return to the country of their birth whenever they needed to. They had no idea of what lay ahead of them, but the thought that Australia was close was somehow comforting.

They were ready to depart when Luku informed them that they could not leave just yet. 'I have been thinking about our return. With the terrible things that have happened to us, I very much want to return home but we cannot go back to my village with my father and most of our crew dead and our hold empty. We must gather trepang and pearls, as well as turtle shell. Then we can return with our heads held high and the death of my father and my friends will not have all been in vain.'

William was worried about the return of the pirates as well as the Kadijah man, Asigi's return. He knew that neither party was going to just forget about them but at the same time, he knew that his group was very much in Luku's hands.

'How long will it take?'

'If you and Jimmy can help us harvest then there is a rich field of trepang just up the coast and we can set up our smoke house on the other side of this harbour. Opaki is our best pearl diver and if Jimmy can take turtle shells for us then I think we can leave in two months.'

'That's too long! In case you didn't realise, there are bad people out there just itching to kill us!'

Luku shrugged. 'We are here much later in the season than usual so we will have to turn back for home in any case before the south-easterly winds subside but I cannot go back empty handed. Our village is very small and we will be returning without four of our people, which will bring great hardship as well as great heartache. To return without the means for our village to trade and prosper will make things ten times as worse. We have two months before the winds change. We can do it.'

William could see that there was no point in arguing so he gave in with good grace. 'You'd better tell us what to do then.'

They loaded the last of their stores into the prau and brought it around to East Point, tying it securely to rocks near the caves. They would leave in the morning.

CHAPTER TWENTY-SEVEN

Asigi attacks

Asigi

Asigi was tired, hot and very, very angry. When he had arrived at the Wulagi camp, it was to find that he had missed the tribe by mere hours as they moved further around to the other side of the harbour. He caught up with them as they were establishing their new camp and it had taken hours of threats and cajoling to convince the elders to loan him a dozen of their warriors and their best tracker. It was only because he had proven the lethality of his threats in the previous year, when he had pointed the bone at one of them who had offended him, that they finally agreed to his demands. His power was still fresh in all of their minds. The warriors who accompanied him were far from happy but all much too terrified to do anything about it.

Asigi led them back to where the Larrakeyah camp had been twenty-three days after he had left, sure that they would have long since departed the entire area and that he would never locate them. To his relief, the tracker had no trouble in finding their sign. He led them through dense bush and then along the beach until they came to a swamp. Here, he lost the sign for some time, but eventually led Asigi down to the rocky foreshore.

'They went this way. I think there is no other way out and they are still at the end of this headland.'

Asigi strained in the growing darkness to see any sign of his fugitives. There was nothing to be seen and he made a decision. 'We will wait until the morning and then we will attack.'

He looked around at all the warriors, all of who made a point of avoiding eye contact with him. 'Remember; do not kill the white man and do not even think about harming the yellow-haired white girl. Kill any others but leave those two for me, or you will all feel my wrath!'

Junie

Junie woke early to a call of nature. She rolled over to look at her sleeping man and smiled at her good fortune in being chosen by such a good, kind and caring husband. She had not forgotten him from the one time they had met and had never been happier since he had stolen into her wirra-wirra and made her his wife. She reached down and stroked her stomach, imagining the child inside her that she would give to Jimmy.

With the two new boat people, it was crowded inside the walled off area, so she was careful not to wake anyone as she moved quietly out to where they all relieved themselves about a hundred steps away.

The dawn was close but only a soft light appeared to the east as the sun only thought about waking up for another day. She stood for a moment and looked towards the slowly disappearing darkness, thinking that this was going to be such an exciting day. They would harvest the trepang and then leave this land and go on the big canoe to a whole new land! The thought of leaving her family and her tribe so far behind scared her but she loved Jimmy so much!

She squatted down to do her business and was about

to stand up again when a noise caught her attention. It was a low cry of pain and then a muffled curse. She froze, her eyes and ears straining now to find the source of the noise.

She made out a movement in the semi-darkness and then heard a whisper. Finally, she heard the sound of two spears clattering against each other, a sound she had been hearing all of her life and suddenly Junie knew. She rose to her feet and screamed out loudly. 'Wake up! It is an attack! Wake up every one! We are being attacked!'

Jimmy

Jimmy heard his woman's voice even half asleep. He had stirred when she got up to go out and so was not in his usual deep slumber. He leapt to his feet and was out of the shelter with his spears in his hands in seconds. He heard running footsteps from the direction of the cliff and readied a spear in his thrower.

William was suddenly beside him, his bow ready. 'What is it? Was that Junie?'

A spear came out of the darkness and hit the rock wall immediately in front of them. Then came another.

Cathy and Mary appeared, followed by Luku and Opaki, who had swords in their hands. More spears hit the rock barrier and others went overhead to hit their shelter.

Jimmy agonised over his wife. Where was she! Then he had to stop thinking about her for the moment, for the attacking warriors were so close! He watched as William drew back an arrow and let fly. Cathy fired once and then again. Mary let go an arrow and Jimmy threw two spears in quick succession. Cries of agony rang out in the darkness and heavy thuds told the group that some of the warriors were running straight into the rock wall in the dim light.

The defenders all fired arrows and spears as targets became clearer. One big warrior leapt onto the top of the wall but was sent back screaming with Luku's sword in his belly. Another grabbed Luku's arm and tried to drag him over the wall but Opaki slashed the attacker's wrist with his sword, leaving Luku to stare at a severed hand that still gripped his arm.

The warriors suddenly began to retreat, dragging their wounded with them. There were angry shouts from far back that sounded like Asigi's voice. Whatever his threats, they were not enough to make the warriors attack again.

As real light began to filter through to light the camp, the group tried to take stock. None of them were injured but over the wall they could see two dead bodies and blood trails of a number of other wounded warriors.

Suddenly, Jimmy's eyes grew wide as he remembered his wife. 'Junie! Where is my woman?'

They found her near the latrine area. The side of her head was deeply indented where a war club had smashed into it. There was blood that had flowed from her nose and mouth from the blow that had taken her life but her face was strangely peaceful as she lay on her side with one hand cupping her stomach.

There was no breath and no pulse when William checked, and they could all only look to Jimmy in despair. Jimmy's wail tore apart the morning. Mary and Cathy held him, his slim body shaking with his cries of anguish and loss. They stayed with him for several hours and he gradually calmed down, but the lines of deep anger and loss were still etched across his face.

William went to him as he squatted near Junie's covered body. 'There's nothing we can say mate. We all loved Junie and she saved us all.'

Jimmy looked up with red eyes and nodded. He took a sudden deep breath and stood up. 'I know. I know.' He searched around where Junie had been slain, taking very careful note of the footprints of his woman's killer. Once he was satisfied that he would be able to follow this man, he purposefully moved to where a number of spears lay on the grass. He took up three spears and found his woomera. 'I am going for payback.'

William put a hand on his arm. 'Mate, it won't bring her back,' he said, although he understood the impulse.

Jimmy angrily shook off the hand. He looked into William's eyes and there was no compromise. 'It will appease her spirit. Don't follow me. I must do this alone.'

William knew that there would be no stopping his friend. The whites of Jimmy's eyes were now specked with brown and William could see the intense anger that his friend only just managed to keep bottled up. Attempting to interfere with Jimmy now was the very last thing that he would consider. 'Please come back to us, mate. Losing Junie is enough; we can't lose you too.'

Jimmy just nodded and then he was gone.

Asigi

Asigi was furious with his battered band of warriors. The attack would have been almost perfect with surprise and overwhelming odds... until that cursed woman had begun to scream out. He could not believe that he had been deprived of his yellow haired woman with her precious child and her mate. He was so close to achieving all that he strived for. He could not lose out now.

'You are all cowards!' he yelled at his conscripts. 'You

ran like dogs from a handful of defenceless women and boys! You must go back and attack again. Go back or I will curse you all!'

One big warrior stood with a war club in his hands, the end still red with gore. 'I only saw one who was defenceless. The rest fought like demons! You did not tell us that they were behind rocks or that they had little spears and blades that could kill us so quickly!'

The other warriors trembled at his temerity in talking back to the Kadijah Man but mumbled their agreement. Of the twelve attackers, there were only seven still alive, three of those with arrow wounds. Two had been left at the scene of the aborted attack and three others had died during their retreat, including one warrior whose hand had been cut off.

Asigi bit back his fury. He saw that the warrior was shaking with fear of him, as he should and was quite shocked that he was actually talking back to him!

The warrior's voice was shaking when he went on. 'Going back to attack again in the daylight will kill us all. We have already lost too many warriors. It has made our tribe weak enough without losing more. No, we go now.'

Asigi stared back at the warrior. He could see the terror in the man's eyes as he defied him and, for a moment, Asigi was tempted to use all of his powers to make these warriors attack again. He was a realist though and knew that, despite the terror that he invoked in them, on this occasion he would not dissuade them and even if he could insert enough backbone into them for another attack, it would probably be useless.

Where had the whites gotten such weapons? Who were these new friends of theirs? He cursed his misfortune but knew that he was going to need new, stronger allies to gain his prizes.

'Go then like the whipped curs that you are. I don't need you!'

He looked once more in the direction of the whites' camp and cursed loudly, heading in the opposite direction, his mind searching for answers.

Jimmy

Jimmy followed the tracks with ease. He passed three dead warriors on the way but they were not the ones he sought. These were armed with spears and boomerangs, the weapons placed alongside the bodies so that they would be protected during their journey beyond.

He found blood in the tracks as he drew closer, and smiled grimly. They had paid a high price for attacking his people but not yet high enough.

Not too much further on he found a wounded man leaning back against a tree. It was obvious that he was in danger of bleeding to death from the arrow that still transfixed his leg. Jimmy was surprised that he had been left behind. It did not speak well for his comrades.

He was slumped against a tree when Jimmy walked up silently behind him, his spear poised at the man's throat before he realised that he was there. The man waited for death but Jimmy only looked at him. 'The one with the war club—what is he called?'

'Gurrawa. He is Gurrawa.' Jimmy stared silently at the terrified warrior, his hands tensed to send the spear into his throat but then he stood back. 'What tribe are you?'

'Wulagi—but we have no fight with you! The Kadijah Man forced us.'

Jimmy looked at the man's wound. An arrow had

pierced his leg almost in the same place that he had been wounded on the day that he had met William and Cathy. He suddenly reached down and wrenched the arrow out of the man's leg and then took off the cloth headband that Cathy had given him and used it to bandage the wound. 'You will live. Gurrawa will not.'

Jimmy tracked them for another hour before he got close enough to hear their voices ahead of him. They were still moving slowly because of the wounded warriors and he was able to loop around and get ahead of them.

He waited until they crossed a small tidal creek and then stepped out into the open, his spear ready.

'Gurrawa, I am going to kill you!'

The six warriors all stopped in alarm, looking around for other attackers.

Jimmy shook his head. 'I am alone. Gurrawa you killed my woman. She carried my child. Now you must fight me and I will kill you!'

He could see that this man was an experienced warrior and under normal circumstances, Jimmy would not have challenged him. This was anything but normal though and he knew that he would kill this man.

The warrior looked at him with a sneer. 'Go home to your mother's teat little boy, before I take that spear off of you and shove it up your arse!'

Jimmy ignored the insult. 'Are you a coward then that you can only attack an innocent woman in the darkness?'

Gurrawa reddened with anger. He was only armed with his club and boomerang and turned to the man who was next to him. 'Cousin, lend me your spears. I will give them back to you once I have washed them in this fool's blood.'

This was ritual combat and none of the others would

have dreamt of interfering. There were no rules other than that each man had to face the spears of the other until justice was seen to have been done. They stood back while Jimmy and the Wulagi warrior faced off at the distance of ten spear lengths, as was customary, each now armed with three spears and their woomeras.

Jimmy felt a cold anger settle over him as he faced his woman's killer. He really didn't care at that moment if he lived or died as long as this Gurrawa died first. He took deep breaths and relaxed his body, his eyes fixed on the other man's eyes and feet. The eyes told when an enemy was going to throw his spear but his feet had to move before he could actually launch his spear.

Gurrawa looked around at his friends, grinning and telling them how easily he was going to kill this upstart but then with a sudden movement, whipped his head back to take a sight on Jimmy and then shuffled two steps before launching his spear in a blur.

It was a clever thing to do and Jimmy was almost caught by surprise but not enough for him to die. He was so completely focussed, that the spear seemed to be in slow motion as it came at him and he bent his abdomen around the spear as it slid harmlessly past his ribs.

The smirk on the other man's face sent a surge of anger through Jimmy and he cursed himself when he hurried his return spear, putting all of his anger into his arm but not using his brain. The warrior laughed as it flew past him without even having to move.

Both cocked a new spear onto their woomeras and again, the Wulagi man threw first.

Jimmy swayed backwards from the spear that came right at his face and the tail end of the spear shaft struck a glancing blow to his forehead on the way through, raising a weal on his skin but not injuring him.

He took his time with his next spear and aimed at the man's centre.

Even as he threw, it was clear that this Gurrawa had not survived numerous battles by being slow. He moved his torso just at the right moment and grinned back at him, clearly pleased at the ease with which he evaded the spear that sped harmlessly past his body. Then he made a fatal mistake and glanced back at his tribesmen for their approval. He didn't see that Jimmy had immediately taken up his last spear.

The warrior was still reaching for his weapon when Jimmy's final spear plunged through his body at the point just below his rib cage. The wind left him as he crashed back onto the sand and he looked with bewilderment at the spear that pierced him.

'It was my turn!' he croaked.

Jimmy knelt next to him, taking hold of the spear shaft and wiggling it back and forth. 'I don't think we have to wait for our turn in these fights. Does it hurt, woman killer?'

Gurrawa's mouth opened and closed as he struggled for the breath to reply but then a gush of blood spewed from his mouth and he sank back, his last breath wheezing out of his lifeless lips.

Jimmy pushed his spear through the man's body and rinsed it off in the creek while the other Wulagi looked wordlessly on, then he slowly walked over to where Gurrawa's cousin held his war club.

He held out his hand. 'That is mine now. I will bury it with my woman.'

The Wulagi knew that Jimmy was within his rights and

the club was handed over. As Jimmy turned to walk back towards his friends, he stopped and looked at them one last time. 'Your other man is still coming. You should wait for him. I think you are short of warriors now.'

Asigi

Asigi was still pondering where he could get help to capture the two whites when he saw the big, oar driven boat making its way laboriously up the harbour. He immediately knew who it was, having had dealings with Muluk on a number of occasions and finding that he and the Macassan were kindred spirits, both completely without moral scruples and with an utter disregard for the life of anyone who got in their way.

On several occasions, Asigi had kidnapped and delivered young females to the Macassan, to be used and then disposed of or sold as slaves, in exchange for favours and goods from their home. Occasionally, Asigi had arranged for a number of tribal camps to be raided by the Macassans, disposing of some of his enemies for him without having to lift a finger himself.

As a result, he had the best equipped camp on the entire coast in a cave in a secluded little glade beside a trickling stream. By the standards of the tribes and even compared to other Kadijah he was wealthy, with iron pots and utensils for mixing his potions, knives and even a dart gun that he had used on more than one occasion to deliver death to those he had pointed the death bone at, but who were slow to succumb.

He knew where the boat people often made camp at the far end of the harbour. Usually, they had gone back to their home by this time of the year and he wondered what had delayed them so much.

It was dark by the time that he reached their camp; the big fire on the beach was like a beacon to guide him.

Asigi stopped at the edge of the light. 'Muluk I see you!' he called in greeting.

The big Macassan was on his feet in an instant with sword drawn as he tried to make out who it was. 'Asigi, it is you?'

Asigi walked slowly forward, his hands open and empty. 'I am surprised to still see you in this land, Muluk. I thought that you would be taking your leisure at you home, enjoying some of the slaves that I have given you.'

It didn't worry him that Muluk didn't particularly like Asigi. He doubted that the Macassan liked anyone else either! As he had just been reminded him though, he was a good source of income in the form of slaves. He saw him looking into the darkness behind the Kadijah.

'I have sold those last ones and look forward to seeing what young delights that you next bring to me but it appears that you have come empty handed this time.'

Asigi looked around the camp and saw that there were only eight, including Muluk. He began to understand why the Macassans were still here. Their big boat was heavy and relied on the oars in light winds, needing more than he had to propel the vessel.

'I can find more young "guests" for you but I wonder where the rest of your crew is.'

Muluk's face went dark with anger. 'We were ambushed by some huge white bastard with a bow! He and whoever is with him killed six of my crew!'

Asigi knew instantly who Muluk was talking about. He wasn't about to let the Macassan know how important the big white man and his pregnant woman were to him but he began to see how he could use Muluk to get what he needed!

He tried not to sound too interested. 'That is terrible! I'm sure that you were just going about your business when you were ambushed too!'

Muluk picked up a skin of arak and took a long pull. 'Bah! We had cornered a boatful of infidels from Adonara and were about to finish them off when the damned white bastard came out of nowhere and began shooting fucking arrows at us! We were lucky to get away!'

Asigi smiled thinly at him, settling down onto the sand and casually taking a drink of the fiery arak from Muluk's skin. 'What if I could locate this big white bastard and his people for you?'

Muluk shook his head. 'No, I don't have enough men to even row properly and handle the boat as well. I am going to have to go home and hope that the winds are kind to us.'

'What if I can get you some men for the oars, plus a few young guests for your… entertainment? You have the cross bows, the big gun and your swords; you could kill them easily!'

Muluk looked up suspiciously. 'Why would you be so helpful to us?'

He looked casually back at him. 'I would want the big white bastard and his woman, who is also white skinned— and I would want them both alive.'

'What are they to you?'

He had no intention of telling him the truth. 'They have annoyed me. I want them for my enjoyment as I teach them what a silly thing that is to do.'

Muluk looked at him for a moment and then laughed.

'Done and done! Where are we going to get these men for my oars? And the young ones?'

Asigi thought for a moment and then smiled. The Wulagi tribe had failed him badly and cost him his two whites. This would be a fitting punishment for them. 'There is a tribe not too far from here. Recently, they lost many of their warriors and they are ripe for raiding!'

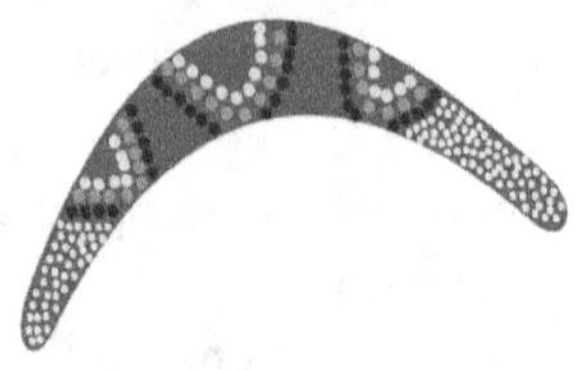

CHAPTER TWENTY-EIGHT

Gathering the harvest

Little was said when Jimmy walked back into the camp. William looked at the war club in his hand and only put a comforting hand on his shoulder and nodded in approval.

There were no dry eyes during the burial the next morning; even Luku and Opaki were misty eyed as they saw how much the girl had meant to them all. When it was over, Jimmy stood for a moment, looking at the grave and then cast his eyes around the bush about them.

William came to stand beside him. 'Thinking about staying here now, mate?'

Jimmy shook his head. 'No William, my woman is gone now and it is time to begin a new life away from these shores. She will always be a part of me and I will never forget her, but her death brings this part of my life to a close. It is time to go.'

William noted that, in keeping with Aboriginal ways, Jimmy didn't use Junie's name, believing that to invoke a dead person's name caused their spirit to be troubled. William was vastly relieved that they would not be losing him from their small family.

It was true that Jimmy would in all likelihood be dead if not for himself and Cathy being in the right place at the right time, but they had saved him only to have him find Junie and then lose her because of the two of them! If not for their presence, Asigi wouldn't have attacked them with his band of warriors and Junie's sacrifice to save them wouldn't have been needed. William looked at his young friend and just hoped that he could somehow repay him for what he had lost, in part due to them.

He placed a hand on his shoulder. 'Mate, you wouldn't believe how honoured I feel that you're going to stay with us.'

Jimmy managed one of his huge grins. 'Hey Willem we're all family, right?'

Jimmy only called him 'Willem' now occasionally as a sort of a joke. It meant that he was beginning to recover a little from Junie's loss. 'Damned right we are!'

Jimmy was thoughtful again for a moment. 'Well, you can make your little brother one of your bows so that I can send those little spears as fast and as far as Mary does! It's not right that she is a better warrior than I am!'

'You're giving up on your spears?'

Jimmy gave a little smile. 'Nah, but I know that the bows are a lot better and will let me get our enemies quicker and from further away. I'll keep my spears for the fun times when they get real close to me!'

Despite the levity of Jimmy's words, William detected the grim resoluteness in his friend and knew that a lot of people who got in Jimmy's way in the future were going to pay for the loss of his wife.

They set out in the prau at neap tide the following morning, sailing diagonally across the harbour, skirting a huge sand bar and reaching a small beach littered with flaky rocks that glittered in the sunlight.

William reached down and picked one up, frowning. 'This looks like bloody mica!'

Cathy laughed. 'That might explain why this place is called Mica Beach! My mum and dad used to bring me here for weekends. A pub will be built just along the beach a bit at Mandorah.'

Mica was a wafer like mineral that would one day be used extensively as a very effective electrical insulator. He weighed the piece of pure mica in his hands, wondering when or if he was ever going to need an insulator again.

Luku and Opaki supervised the construction of a smoke hut on the beach which took the best part of the day and the big iron cauldron was offloaded from the prau and set hanging from a tripod, with stacked timber ready to be lit beneath it.

Next, Luku brought out some long, very thin bladed spears—the blades razor sharp, almost a foot long and no thicker than the thinnest filleting knife. He handed them around. 'You will use these to spear the trepang. It is important to kill them quickly or they will spit out long white threads and after that they are no good to eat. You will be able to skewer ten trepang onto the spear before having to bring them back to the canoe.'

He turned to Cathy and Mary. 'It will be your job to boil each batch of trepang until you see them change colour, no longer. Then take them out of the water and place them in the smoke hut. They must smoke then for a day and they will be ready.'

At first light the next morning, the men set out in the two dugout canoes that were stored in the prau. Luku led them to a sand bar just up the coast and pointed down through the clear seawater to ten to twelve-centimetre long creatures that inched their way slowly along the sand at the bottom. There were thousands of the creatures along the length of the sand bank.

Luku grinned. 'It is harvest time!'

The following days and weeks were exhausting for them all. Gradually, William and Jimmy gained some degree of proficiency with the trepang spears but even so, only brought back half the amount of trepang that Luku and Opaki did. They took it in turns to ferry each load of trepang back to Mica Beach for Cathy and Mary to cook and smoke before packing the finished product into palm leaves.

The prau was once again concealed up a deep creek, prow facing the harbour in case they needed to leave in a hurry, with branches hiding it from view. None of them needed reminding of the presence of the Macassan pirates. William and Luku discussed the possibility of Muluk's return and they agreed to be especially watchful on the harbour.

Their caution was proven justified twice when they spotted the big prau cruising about the harbour, obviously looking for them. On each occasion, the smoke house fires were hastily extinguished and the canoes weighted down with rocks and sunk in shallow water until the prau was clear of the area.

Each night, they carefully packed away the smoked trepang into the hold and then sat around the campfire talking. They also used the time to improve their language skills. Luku and Opaki were both curious to learn English, while William and the others realised how important it was going to be to learn the language of what they hoped would be their new home.

Luku and Opaki spoke a language called Lamaholot, although they explained that the Damon people on their island spoke a related but different language again. William proved to be the least skilled linguist and could only just carry on a conversation in the time they had, while Mary and Cathy were almost fluent in the same time. Jimmy too picked up Lamaholot more quickly than he did thanks to his friendship and constant companionship with Opaki.

William was aware that his aptitude for languages was lacking and he chaffed at being slower than the others to pick up the new language. He was nothing if not persistent though, and reapplied himself to picking up Lamaholot after that with a new determination.

He observed with pleasure that Jimmy was continuing to slowly recover from the loss of Junie. He and Opaki were now good friends and Luku voiced his obvious approval from his point of view as well, as Jimmy developed very quickly into a good trepang gatherer. William had by now made Jimmy a bow and he was almost obsessive in learning how to use it, with Cathy his main instructor. He had been hitting objects with stones and then spears since he was old enough to walk and now he impressed them all by how quickly his well-honed instinct to hit what he was aiming at enabled him to develop into an archer of real talent.

Cathy was of the opinion that Jimmy was throwing himself into anything he could to distract himself from Junie's loss but gradually the 'old Jimmy' with the irrepressible sense of humour began to re-emerge from his mourning.

At the end of five weeks, they had enough dried trepang to almost fill the small hold in the prau. Jimmy had caught a dozen big turtles as well, beheading the unfortunate creatures and then leaving the rotting carcases on anthills where they were efficiently cleaned out of flesh, leaving only the valuable shells to go into the hold.

At Jimmy's insistence, they had eaten the first turtle that he'd caught after his assertion that it would be the most delicious meat they had ever tasted. Only he and Mary had enjoyed the subsequent meal, with the others finding the extremely strong flavour overpowering and unpleasant. Smoked wallaby meat provided the meal for most of them after only a few mouthfuls of the turtle meat.

Neither Jimmy nor Mary were very popular the next day, with the rest of them turning their noses up at the strong smell that emanated from the pores of their skin as they perspired. A very dejected Mary spent her first night in a long time sleeping by herself!

Opaki grinned at them all as they sat around the fire when they had sufficient trepang. 'Now it is my turn. Tomorrow we look for pearls!'

As a Territorian, Cathy was aware that at one time Darwin had been a good source of excellent pearls. An industry had thrived right up to the start of the Second World War, at which time the mainly Japanese pearl divers had found themselves unsurprisingly unwelcomed in Australian waters. There had still been pearling even in the time she had 'left' but by that time, the pearls were all cultivated ones and the industry firmly in the hands of one long time Darwin family.

Opaki led them to two big reefs up one of the three arms that led off Darwin Harbour. He grinned as they dropped the simple stone anchors from the canoes.

'This is my secret spot; I always find pearls here!'

He was right and, over the next four days of continual diving, he brought up thousands of oysters, out of which they found more than thirty big, perfect pearls including two extremely valuable black pearls. They were all heartily sick of eating oysters by the time he'd finished but by the last day, the exhausted group all knew that they had at last finished their work.

When Luku looked at his hold and counted the pearls, he grinned at them all and brought out a large bottle of cloudy liquid, as well as wooden cups for them all.

William sniffed at the vaguely coconut aroma of the liquid and waited until Luku and Opaki both took appreciative sips.

'What is it?' William asked.

Luku took another sip. 'It is arak… very good! Tonight we celebrate, for tomorrow we go home!'

'I've heard of Arak. It's alcoholic isn't it?'

Luku grinned. 'If that means that it makes you feel very good until you fall down and go to sleep then yes, it is alcoholic! It is made from distilled red rice and coconut milk… very good for you!'

William reached across and took the cup from a sighing Cathy. 'Never mind honey, the rest of us will have your share for you!'

She poked her tongue out at him. 'I hope you have a terrible hangover tomorrow Will!'

Mary had one sip and pulled a face before handing her cup over to Jimmy. 'Ugh, how can you drink that?'

Luku took a long sip and hummed as the fiery liquor slid down his throat. 'This is a good batch. How can you not like it?'

CHAPTER TWENTY-NINE

Leaving Australia

Cathy was awake before any of the others and took great pleasure in watching all of the men as they slowly woke up. Luku and Opaki were obviously used to the arak and they weren't too bad, being able to actually function once they were awake, even if they were very careful in their movements.

William woke up with a loud groan of pain and held his head in his hands. 'Oh crap, did someone get the number of the truck that hit me?' He staggered to his feet and walked the ten paces into the water and slowly sat down, staring blankly out to sea.

Cathy awarded Jimmy a ten out of ten for his reaction to the drink. Given his age and the fact that as far as she knew, Aboriginals didn't traditionally use any alcohol, it was unlikely that he had ever tasted anything like Arak before. She remembered how animated it had made him last night, dancing his own private corroboree around the fire and singing loudly and tunelessly for everyone's entertainment. He had been the life of the party.

Now she watched as Jimmy sat up and looked around as though confused as to where he was. Cathy saw the stricken expression on his face as his body began asking him urgent questions about what he had done to it. He staggered to his feet and stared around at them all for a moment, then his eyes went wide and he began dry heaving. He walked on rubbery legs towards the ocean and only just made it before his dry heaves were no longer so dry and William could only look on in horror as Jimmy fed the fish right next to him!

That set off a chain reaction and both Cathy and Mary were soon rolling around in helpless laughter as Jimmy's convulsions set off William's, which set off another round of vomiting by Jimmy, which made William lose the very last of his stomach's contents.

Even Luku and Opaki were laughing at the display and Luku had to wipe tears from his eyes before he commented. 'Do you think I should have warned them about how strong arak is?'

A very fragile crew sailed the prau back to East Point. They had left the bulk of their possessions in the caves and didn't want to simply leave it all behind. Highest on William's list of priorities was the Lee Enfield rifle, which he was determined to keep.

Their camp was undisturbed since their departure with no signs of human visitors, but William knew that it was a matter of when, not if their enemies would return. The prau, even though it was a solid and seaworthy vessel was now fully laden as they added their possessions to the cargo of trepang and turtle shell, with very little freeboard.

Luku saw the way William was looking warily at the distance between the gunwales of the prau and the ocean.

'Don't worry, we won't capsize or get swamped. Just wait and watch.'

He indicated the two dugout canoes that they had been

using for the past weeks. He brought out four long poles that William had been wondering about and called out to Opaki who came over and assisted him as they attached two of the poles to each canoe and then slid the other end through ports on each side of the prau with wooden pins that slotted neatly into place.

William quickly realised what they were doing and marvelled at the ingenuity as their single hulled prau was suddenly transformed into a three hulled trimaran.

'Now we are very stable even with such a heavy cargo. This is the very best time to return home. When we usually sail here, it is in the monsoon season and sometimes our ships are lost in the storms but now the wind is south-easterly and will take us gently home through the calmest seas.'

It was with very mixed feelings that they sailed out of Darwin Harbour and out into the Arafura Sea. For William, Cathy, Mary and Jimmy's part, they were leaving everything that they could relate to behind them and going into a complete unknown. There was very little talk as they cleared the Coburg Peninsular and turned northeast towards the Indonesian islands.

Luku was now the captain and navigator with the death of his father and, like his father and ancestors before them, had always navigated by his knowledge of the sea, the sun and the stars.

When Cathy produced her small compass, he was both overjoyed and awed at the small, modern device that he announced would make their trip so much easier. He looked carefully to where Opaki was talking to Jimmy before whispering. 'This is from your time?'

Cathy nodded. 'Yes but surely there are compasses around in these times aren't there?'

He shrugged. 'The Dutch and the people from Portugal have them but they are very careful to keep them to themselves. I went onto a Dutch ship with my father when he bought the chart and saw theirs, but it was almost as tall as me and very heavy. This is a little miracle!'

He pulled out his map and excitedly studied it while William and Cathy looked on. 'We are very late in the season for selling our trepang. I was going to rely on one of the Chinese merchants to come to our island so that we could sell it but there is a chance that they would not come to our village again until next season.'

He pointed to a larger island to the west of Adonara Island. 'This is Wetar Island; my father went there several times and dealt directly with the warehouses there. He told me that along with Macassar, it is one of the main collection points that the Chinese use before they take the trepang back to their home. With your compass, we can go directly there and maybe get a very good price for everything!'

Opaki came over to see what Luku was talking about and heard his last comments. 'Are you crazy? You have never been to Wetar and it will put at least two weeks onto our journey home. We will never find it!'

Luku glanced down at the compact little prismatic compass and gave him a confident smile. 'Oh yes I will!'

Cathy

Life on the prau, or *tipnol* as Luku explained was the name for their particular type of prau, was far from easy. It was only eight metres long from raised prow to the steering oar, with only rudimentary accommodation for the six of them.

Mary wasn't in the least discomforted with having to share such a limited space with so many others in close proximity, in the tribal life that she was so accustomed to, there was no such thing as privacy. Cathy on the other hand, took some time to become accustomed to using one of the bailing buckets for calls of nature. It was much easier for the men, who just hung out over the side. All the males studiously ensured that they had other things that had to be looked at during these occasions but Cathy still longed for the glorious luxury of her own private bush to go behind. She had long since stopped dreaming of a flushing porcelain toilet; that sort of thinking only led her to remembering everything else from the modern world that she was missing out on. That in turn led her to a fit of melancholy about her home, family and friends that lasted until Mary came over and put an arm around her. Then everything seemed alright again. She realised that as long as she had Mary and William, she had everything she needed.

Most nights, they found sheltered anchorages in the myriad of tiny islands that dotted their route, with only one occasion when they had to sail through the night. None of them slept that night as they all kept watch for hidden reefs waiting to rip the keel out of their vessel. They were all a wreck the next day but slept like the dead on the following night.

Meals were cooked over a brazier, using charcoal as the fuel source and to both Cathy and Mary's pleasant surprise after the first few days at sea, Luku and Opaki insisted on doing all of the cooking. They suspected that this may have been due to Cathy's first effort at fish and rice that the two Paji men could only eat after adding a lot of spices. Nonetheless, both women enjoyed not being expected to do all of the cooking.

Fortunately, the two Paji were considerate of their friends' milder palates and only moderate chilli and spices were added to the meals but even so, the cooling effect of coconut water was very much appreciated by the newcomers to Paji cuisine.

William, Cathy and Mary were afforded the luxury of a semi-private tent right at the front of the boat, but with three others in such close proximity, the small area of privacy was strictly for sleeping only.

They had been at sea for two weeks when William noticed that Cathy and Mary had spent much of the day in whispered and excited conversation. When they retired for the night, he found out why.

They were laying on the thin mattress in their sleeping area. The women had of course been discussing exactly how this would go, so with a thrilled Cathy looking on, Mary rolled over until she was leaning on his chest and smiling down at him.

He had a very good feeling what she was going to say but kept his excitement bottled just for the moment. 'Yes?' he asked.

Mary's smiled broadened. 'I'm going to have a baby too!'

William knew that it was madness for Cathy and Mary to be pregnant with his children given their situation, but he also knew how much he loved the two of them and to have Mary also carrying his child somehow made all of their problems trivial.

<h1 style="text-align:center">CHAPTER THIRTY</h1>

A great deal done

With the gentle south-easterly wind behind them, they skirted Timor to their right and then changed tack to follow a north-easterly course along Timor's long coast. Leaving Alor Island to their port side, Luku navigated their way through a series of small islands and through a short passage until finally they could make out Wetar Island straight ahead of them.

Their map had been both continually consulted and updated during the voyage and now Luku used it to point to a bay on the southern side of the island. 'That is the port of Limar. It is where I hope that we will find the Chinese traders.'

They approached the sheltered bay in the late morning and to Luku's elation they could clearly make out a big fat Chinese junk tied up to the wharf. Even better from their point of view, they were the only prau present as they drifted in on a feathery wind, rope fenders protecting the side of the prau as a local caught their rope and looped it around a wooden bollard.

Cathy insisted that they all wear the new sarongs that she had made for them. It had been years since she'd worn one but they weren't at all uncommon in the very casual Darwin that she'd grown up in, so she was quite adept in making and wearing one. William was the first to admit that it was a heck of a lot more comfortable than the leather loincloth that he had been wearing. So it was that when they climbed from their prau onto the rickety wharf, it almost looked like they were wearing a uniform.

A big warehouse seemed the most logical place to go. They were heading in that direction when an imposing Chinese man dressed in exquisite blue and yellow silks swept out of the entrance to the warehouse and came towards them with two other Chinese in tow, a welcoming, if avaricious smile on his face.

William watched the man's face as he came closer. He saw his gaze pass over Luku and Opaki quickly with a satisfied expression but then he read the confusion when he fixed his gaze on himself and Cathy. William smiled to himself, realising how out of place the two of them were, not that Mary or Jimmy would have been expected sights either.

The man stopped in front of them and looked from Luku to William as though unsure of who to address. In the end, he took the middle ground and threw his arms wide.

In fluent Lamaholot he called out to them. 'Welcome friends! I see that your noble craft is very low in the water—no doubt full of the best quality trepang!' Then, he looked directly at William and repeated what he had said, again fluently, but this time in a language that William recognised at Dutch.

William was impressed. This was obviously a very intelligent multilingual man. No wonder he could afford to wear a fortune in silks! They had already agreed that Luku would conduct all of the negotiations for the sale of their goods and again William observed the slight confusion on the man's face when Luku and not the white man addressed him.

Luku gave the man a polite bow and then said, 'Indeed sir, we have some of the finest trepang I have ever seen, in addition to fine turtle shell and the best quality pearls.'

The man again looked with confusion at William and he guessed that the Chinese merchant hadn't come across a situation of a white man taking second place to an islander. He bolstered William's opinion of him however when he showed that diplomacy was another of his accomplishments. He appeared to immediately adjust to the unusual situation and smiled as he gave a short bow to Luku in return. 'Allow me to introduce myself. I am Wing Lew Fatt. Perhaps you would care to show me your cargo?'

Luku straightened. 'I am Goruluku; I am the Captain of this vessel. Please come on board.'

Wing Lew Fatt stepped into their prau with an ease that told them that he was no stranger to the seas. He spent half an hour inspecting the trepang, probing each wrapped bundle, sniffing and testing until he was happy with both the quality and condition of the sea slugs.

William noted that his two assistants hadn't even come on board the prau. It was obvious that the merchant believed in being hands-on with his business dealings.

Next, Lew Fatt closely inspected the turtle shell, nodding as he traced his fingers over the smooth shells and checking for flaws in the surfaces. Finally, he signalled to his two assistants and in rapid fire Mandarin gave them instructions.

Then he turned to Luku. 'I agree with you sir; these are indeed fine quality goods. My men will do a count if that is agreeable to you while we adjourn to my humble quarters for refreshments.'

He led them to a lavishly furnished reception area equipped with low, brilliantly lacquered tables and plump silk covered cushions. Tea was brought out and both William and Cathy savoured the scent of the delicate beverage served in ultra-thin porcelain cups.

After so many months of hardship, it was so nice to sit in such a comfortable room, surrounded by quality artwork and silks, and sitting on something that was actually soft! William saw that Cathy was enjoying it every bit as much as he was. He saw that the Chinese man seemed to be genuinely pleased at the obvious pleasure they were displaying as they enjoyed the tea and signalled his servant to immediately refill the cups when they had drained them.

It was obvious that his curiosity was killing him as he tried to work out who and what they were but William had dealt with Chinese many times over the years and he knew that good manners were of the greatest importance to Orientals, and would prevent too blunt an enquiry. Instead, he spoke quietly to William, again in Dutch.

When William shrugged with incomprehension, he tried again in a vaguely Spanish sounding language that William guessed to be Portuguese, the only other European language that the Chinaman would expect to encounter in this area.

While this impressed him in finding another language to add to Lew Fatt's impressive list, William could again only shrug. Then he felt a little guilty in prolonging the mystery, which was obviously driving the man to distraction and replied in his halting Lamaholot.

'I don't speak Dutch or Portuguese. I speak English though.'

Lew Fatt stared at him in confusion. 'How can this be? I have heard of the English of course, but never in these waters!'

William thought carefully before replying, keeping the reply as brief as he could. 'We were marooned and Luku here took us onto his vessel.'

The reply only raised more questions. 'Marooned? What ship were you on to be marooned? How did an English ship come to be in this area?'

He really didn't want to have to lie to Lew Fatt. He quite liked the man and it was obvious that he was quite intelligent so he knew it would be too easy to insult him with a glib answer.

The truth however was also out of the question. He figured that inventing a ship that sunk was the likeliest story he could offer. 'We were passengers on a Portuguese ship that was supposed to take us to Jakarta …' he realised that mistake in a hurry and quickly amended his story. 'I mean to Batavia. The ship was sunk and my wife and I were the only survivors. Luku rescued us near where we harvested the trepang.'

He could see from his expression that the man was clearly not swallowing the story in its entirety but there was nothing he could do about that. Fortunately, he was too polite to probe further. 'Then you are very fortunate, you and your charming wife.'

William was tempted to explain about Mary too but he'd already raised enough questions in the man's mind. 'Yes, we were fortunate and now we are partners with Luku and Opaki.'

Luku interjected. 'William has said that we rescued him but in fact it was the other way around. He saved us from pirates. We would be dead now but for him and the others.'

'It is so?' Lew Fatt exclaimed, looking at William with even more interest. 'Then you are both fortunate it seems.'

Just then, the two assistants came into the room and handed Lew Fatt a tablet filled with Chinese characters. The merchant scanned the tablet and then turned to an abacus at his side, his fingers flying over the instrument as he made calculations.

He considered for a moment, glancing at William before turning to Luku. 'I can offer you twenty *sycee* for your trepang and a further five for the turtle shell.'

Luku tried to hide his excitement. It was more than they had ever been paid before and to the best of his knowledge, far above the market value for his trepang. He wasn't sure why the merchant was offering such a premium price but knew that the Chinese *sycee*, which were distinctly stamped silver ingots with a guaranteed content of silver, were a highly sought after currency and would stand them in good stead in any subsequent negotiations with others.

He wasn't about to question the wind-fall and so did not reply but simply produced the bag of pearls, with the two black pearls in a separate wrapped cloth. 'What about these?'

Lew Fatt took his time in examining each pearl, spending the greatest time on the blacks. When he finished, he rested his chin in one hand and thought for some time; then looked directly at William and addressed him.

'I will give you a further twenty sycee for the whites and fifty for the two blacks but there is a condition.'

William guessed from Luku's barely concealed excitement that they were being offered a premium price. He also surmised that at this point, his friend was unsure of how to proceed. He knew that Luku would defer to him if it became necessary in the negotiations with the merchant and so spoke up.

'What is this condition?' He asked.

Lew Fatt looked hard at him. 'It is known that you English are very aggressive in trade. If you and your wife are here then I think it means that many more of your English will come here too. I trade with the islanders, with the Dutch and with the Portuguese but then so do many of my colleagues who come to these waters. I will give you this good price for your things if you agree to give me the exclusive trading rights for all English.'

William almost blurted out that there were no Englishmen around at all, but then reconsidered. It was true that he and Cathy were the only 'English' around at the moment but he had every intention of establishing some sort of permanent presence in these islands and to do that he was going to have to earn a living to prosper. He had nothing to lose by agreeing to Lew Fatt's condition and in the future, perhaps much to gain. At the same time, he very much liked the Chinaman and could see no issues with dealing with him on an exclusive basis in the future. He knew though that he owed the man as much honesty as he could give him, without revealing everything about themselves.

He worded his reply carefully. 'I will guarantee that I will not trade with any other Chinese trader but you, nor will anyone who is with me. It is not possible for me to make such a broad promise on behalf of others that I do not know but I will undertake to recommend you as the merchant of choice for any English that I speak to.'

Lew Fatt considered his reply and then nodded sharply and smiled. 'Agreed. Would you like more tea?'

The Chinese silver ingots filled a small wooden chest that Lew Fatt provided to them. Luku was ecstatic at their newfound wealth. 'This is the most we have ever made on a cargo! Our village is now rich. We can buy whatever we need now!'

William grinned. 'Well I hope it puts them all in a good mood so that they let the four of us all stay then!'

Luku laughed. 'That will not be a problem. No one will want to dispute me when we come back with all of this silver!'

Limar was a busy port with numerous traders offering everything from pots and pans to weapons, to clothing, to food, to jewellery.

Luku ceremoniously handed each one of his friends one of the Chinese sycee ingots with a smile. 'I am going to buy many things that my village needs. Take these and get things for yourselves!'

William saw the glaze appear in Cathy's eyes as she looked at all of the shops in the area and grinned, handing over his ingot to her. 'You two get some nice things while I give Luku a hand. I'd love a nice pair of pants or shorts, but the sarong will do if you can't find some. I wouldn't mind a vest or jacket of some kind, but that's all that I need.'

Cathy weighed the two ingots in her hand and then took Mary's hand. 'Come with me sister-wife—we are going shopping!'

CHAPTER THIRTY-ONE

Asigi and the pirates

Asigi led Muluk and his crew to the Wulagi camp in the middle of the night. The Macassans glided their canoes silently through the still waters and soundlessly kissed onto the sand only metres from where the tribe slept. There were no sentries out and it appeared that they were blissfully unaware of the fate that was about to befall them.

Asigi didn't want to have any survivors spreading the word of his participation in what was about to take place and so stood off in the bush as the Macassans crept into the camp, swords drawn and crossbows cocked and loaded.

A Wulagi elder woke up just in time to realise that he was about to die but managed to get out only a shuddering gasp out as a razor sharp sword plunged into his throat. A woman cried out loudly as she was struck down and suddenly people were running everywhere as the tribe realised that they were under attack. A few warriors took their spears and attempted to fight back but spears were standoff weapons and the Macassans were right amongst them, their swords, cross bows and knives taking a dreadful toll on the small tribe with only a small handful managing to flee into the bush and a wailing, fearful group of captives held down in the centre of the camp with swords at their throats.

Delighted at their easy victory, smiling Macassans walked among the numerous fallen, their swords finishing off the few who lay badly wounded and helpless about the camp. Afterwards, six stunned young warriors were dragged in a state of shock to the canoes and then out to the big prau, where they were chained to an oar bench. Three younger children were locked into Muluk's cabin.

It was only then that Asigi showed his face on the prau, as he was no longer concerned when the six warriors looked with shock and dismay to see him with the destroyers of their tribe. What they knew no longer mattered, for they would not be returning to tell anyone about his role in what had taken place.

It took longer than they would have liked to complete all their purchases in Limar. For her part, Cathy was ecstatic to have another three sets of sarongs with matching shawls and several pairs of beautifully made leather sandals. Mary had caught the shopping spirit as well, proudly parading in her new clothing and wearing footwear for the first time in her life.

William was more than happy with his finely worked leather vest but had to admit that the fine pair of boots done in wonderfully soft kid skin that Cathy surprised him with were a great change from the battered hiking boots that he'd been wearing ever since they had been marooned. They even fit! He looked around at the sandals that everyone else wore but for some silly reason felt so much better in a good, stout pair of boots.

Luku had been busiest of them all and the prau was now sitting almost as low in the water as when they'd arrived laden with the trepang. Fine pottery and metal pans, bolts of cloth, fine needles and razor sharp knives, sacks of rice and sago and rounds of cheese made up most of his purchases but what interested William the most were two dozen bars of iron that now formed the ballast of the prau.

'What's with the iron, Luku? Do you have a blacksmith on Adonara?'

'An ironworker—you call him a blacksmith, yes? Indeed we do. His name is Rantuka and we are very lucky to have him.'

Luku pulled out the *kris* from his belt and held it out so that William could see the incredible workmanship that had gone into the waved blade, with beautiful sea sirens easily discernible on the 20 centimetre length of steel.

'Rantuka is a true craftsman but also an artist. The things that he can do with a bar of iron are wondrous! He is an alchemist with metals and will use some of this iron for ploughs, pots and small utensils. Some though, he will mix with his secret ingredients and turn into good strong swords of steel and fine crossbows with iron bolts for the next time we meet any Macassans!'

Muluk

Muluk wasted four fruitless weeks searching for the whites before his patience had ran out. The six new galleon slaves had at last been trained in use of the oars by means of liberal use of a whip, so the endless patrolling of the harbour hadn't been a complete waste of time but he had had enough.

'Bah! They have gone home! We are wasting our time here. We must leave now before the winds change to the northwest! We leave in the morning!'

Asigi seethed with anger. 'I know that they are here

somewhere! We have a bargain; you must find them for me!'

Muluk laughed. 'You were going to lead me to them, remember? It is your fault that we haven't found them. By now they must be halfway to Adonara; I will get more boats and men and that is where we will go. Then I will wipe them out.'

Asigi

The Kadijah Man thought about threatening the Macassan with his curses but realised that without the absolute belief—like that which the tribes had in his powers—the threat would be wasted on Muluk and in all likelihood would probably end up with himself as fish bait. It seemed likely that his prey had joined up with these boat people from Adonara but he didn't believe that the white man and yellow haired woman had yet gone from these shores. He could almost smell their presence still but he realised that trying to convince Muluk to continue the search was a waste of time.

He had used up much of his magic in bringing them from the Dreaming and yet he knew the rites that could bring him so much more power. He knew that if he could use the blood of the yellow haired girl and that of her baby, augmented with the blood of the white man, he would be able to create such magical power as had never been seen. He absolutely had to get his hands on the two whites and so the only other way to accomplish it would be to go to this island, hope that they did indeed go there and then seize them and use them for his magic.

'Alright then, so be it. I will come with you.'

Muluk looked at him incredulously. 'Why in the seven hells should I take you with me?'

Asigi knew that only one argument would win over the Macassan. 'Because then you will have an ally here who will bring you endless lines of slaves for years to come—instead of an implacable enemy who will make sure that every tribe along the coast believes that you are all demons who should be attacked at every opportunity.'

Muluk

The Macassan's face was completely still for a moment. He realised what a dangerous enemy Asigi would make but at the same time realised how much at his tender mercies he would be away from his magics and on his vessel! As odious as the witch doctor was, he might even be useful to him. He waited until he knew that he had Asigi worried and then he burst into laughter. 'Welcome to my crew!'

With the strong backs of their new oar slaves to propel the big prau, in addition to the huge sail, the prau quickly left the mainland waters behind. Muluk had two fully crewed ships at the shipyard at Sumbah Island where they had been carrying out repairs on their praus and so he set a course to the northwest and with the wind on his port beam, made good speed through the Arafura Sea.

He wasn't aware of the fact that he was weeks ahead of the Adonara prau, who were still back in Darwin Harbour, exactly as Asigi had insisted was the case.

The proud, defiant Paji on Adonara had been a thorn in his side for years. For all of his lack of morals in achieving his aims, Muluk thought of himself as a good Muslim, conveniently forgetting his frequent consumption of arak, the unjustified murder of hundreds of innocents and the small matter of his sexual preference for young and unwilling males and females. He believed very strongly that if he could spread the faith of Islam throughout the islands, then he must surely be a warrior of Allah and as such, was assured of his place in Paradise.

He had made numerous attempts to convince the Paji on Adonara that they should abandon their old, useless gods and follow the one true God, but to no avail. When he had sighted them approaching the north coast of the great land, it had seemed a golden opportunity to destroy the prau belonging to Goruku and his son. Goruku was the loudest voice on his council in defying Islam and he knew with him gone, the Paji were his for the taking.

Now his damned son had escaped him, along with the white bastard and his woman that the Kadijah Man was so hot to get hold of. He was determined that it was the last time that the Paji would defy him. This time, he wouldn't be going to Adonara to convert them however. They'd had their chance to embrace the true religion; now they would all die or fill his slave coffers.

He picked up his two other ships in good time and hastily added some of his best fighters to his vessel, along with more crossbows. The next time that he met the white bastard, he wasn't going to be chased off by their damned bows.

Their six Aboriginal galleon slaves where physically broken and almost useless to him after weeks of back breaking rowing, combined with poor food and endless beatings. He offloaded them to a broker on Sumbah when they had recovered sufficiently for the slave pens. Their futures were not bright ones. Most likely, they would end up in one of the big plantations in the islands but from experience, Muluk knew that the blacks from the mainland never adjusted to life outside of their tribes and never lasted long. As long as he got a few coins for each of them he was happy. It was hardly his fault that their tribe had fallen into such disfavour with the magic man that he wished them all dead. Such was life.

There were six small villages of Paji along the coast of Adonara Island and he planned their attacks to sweep from the most southerly village and then rapidly move up the island until he had destroyed them all.

Muluk now had fifty fighters at his disposal; it was more than the warriors of all of the villages combined and they were all better armed than the Paji would be. Now they would learn the cost of defying Islam! He only prayed that the white man was there as well. No matter his agreement with Asigi, if he could kill the big, arrogant white man then he would be very happy.

Disaster on the island

Luku

Luku was anxious to reach home after so many weeks away. He dreaded returning to his sister with news of the loss of their father but at least he would be able to lessen her grief by bringing her new sister to her. Their mother had passed away years before and he was confident that Manissa would welcome Mary into their family.

He made a last tack that would take them to his island and smiled as the wind filled the sail, taking them swiftly home. He looked at William and Cathy standing at the prow and knew he had been very lucky in meeting them. Not only had they saved himself and Opaki from Muluk, but they had been of great assistance in gathering the trepang. Best of all though, because Wing Lew Fatt believed that William was the first of a new wave of English, they had been given unbelievable exchange for their cargo! He still had half of the silver ingots in the chest and their wealth would enable his people to thrive.

His joyful anticipation of returning home was soon soured. They could smell the smoke long before they came within sight of the ruined and still smouldering villages. Their own village was half way up the coast, but both he and Opaki had friends and relatives in every one of the Paji villages and as they sailed past the burned out remains of the first two, they were already grieving, for it was only too clear what had taken place.

A raid like this hadn't happened in many years, with the Raja's law stopping much of the inter-island warfare that had been commonplace in years gone by. They knew from the old stories of what to expect. The years of relative peace had lulled them into a false sense of security under the reign of the old Raja and now his son. It was obvious though that the Raja hadn't been able to stop these raids and as they neared their own village, both of them braced themselves for what they knew they were going to find.

The prau silently coasted to a stop as the keel slid into the white sand in front of their village. They all stood and just looked for a few moments at the desolation in front of them.

Not one building had survived. Every home was razed to the ground, the metal working hut, which was built from stone, had been wrecked and the big wooden meeting hall was a burnt-out ruin. Dozens of bodies of men, old women and children littered the ground in all directions, gaping cuts in necks and limbs witness to the ferocity of the attackers. A few of the bodies had cross bow bolts sticking out of them and some had clearly been badly burned as they ran from their torched homes.

A deathly quiet reigned over the village. Only the crackle of burning timber and the cries of crows broke the silence.

Luku sank to his knees in the sand beside the body of a young boy. He was a cousin and was only five years old but his head was almost severed from a vicious slash across his young neck.

Finally, Luku stood and he and Opaki wandered about the village, each looking with dread for their own family members. Opaki's cried in anguish when he located his mother and father near the remains of their home. His cries were the only sound to be heard as he held their lifeless bodies to him.

Luku was sure that every female that he found would be Manissa but each time he rolled over a female form, he felt guilty relief that none of them was his sister. He knew that the raiders would have taken some of the younger and prettier women away with them for sale as sex slaves and Manissa was a very beautiful woman, desired by many of the men of his village.

Family honour was ingrained into Luku's way of thinking and he was torn as to whether he would have preferred to find her body or have her live a degrading life as someone's property, even though that very conflict filled him with guilt; after all, it was his sister!

Eventually, it was Jimmy's keen eye that gave himself and Okapi some hope. Jimmy had been wandering around the edge of the village when he spotted some unusual tracks in the soft, sandy soil. He dropped to his haunches and read the sign carefully, then followed the traces through the soil for a number of paces into the dense bush behind the village.

Luku watched him. 'What is it, Jimmy?'

'Some people came this way. I know the sign for the people who did this thing to your village and these do not belong to them. A small number of people came this way. Some of them were helping others. I think that some of your people have escaped.'

Luku and Opaki looked with desperate hope into the

bush in the direction Jimmy indicated. 'Let's go then. They may need our help!'

William put a hand on Luku's arm. 'We should be armed. Some of the bastards that did this might still be around.'

Luku nodded and they quickly grabbed weapons. Jimmy led the way, his eyes reading the tracks with ease. It was obvious that some of the people in the group of escapees were wounded and were being helped by others, although the small amounts of blood that he spotted indicated that the wounds might not be too severe.

They had been gone for half an hour when Luku started looking worried again. 'We are getting very close to Damon territory. They are no friends of ours so we must be on our guard.' His words were soon proved true when sounds of fighting reached them within the next twenty paces. They all readied their weapons as they pushed on.

They broke out of the bush to find two groups of people facing each other across a clearing. Luku looked at the group of men, women and children in one group and joy filled his heart when he saw his sister Manissa. She was standing protectively in front of other women and half a dozen frightened children, while four Paji men stood in front of them all, with swords out and ready to fight.

Facing them were a dozen short, stocky men, also armed with swords, their faces fierce and angry. One of their number lay wounded on the ground with a sword slash to his abdomen.

Both groups turned to look as they rushed through the clearing and joined the Paji. William, Cathy, Mary and Jimmy all stood behind the Paji men, their arrows pointed at the others, while Luku and Opaki joined their kinsmen.

Luku saw that Rantuka, their metal worker was one of them. He proudly saw that the man held his sword ready, his eyes firmly on the other group. 'These are Damon, what do they want?' Luku called out to him.

The relief in Rantuka's face as he saw Luku and Opaki, armed with swords and with armed friends with them was unmistakable. He looked with disgust at the other group. 'They knew that we have been raided by the Macassans. They know we have almost been wiped out and now they want to finish the job.'

One of the opposing group called out. 'This is our territory. You know that you cannot be here!'

Rantuka called back angrily. 'We need sanctuary from the Macassans. You know we mean no harm!'

The Damon man laughed cruelly. 'You will get no sanctuary from us. You are finished on this island and your land will be ours now! If you do not leave, then we will kill you all.'

Luku rose to the threat and spat back. 'We will not be so easy to kill. Back off and let us go in peace or you will discover that my friends' bows will end your miserable lives very quickly.'

The Damon spokesman looked warily at William and the others, clearly unsure of what to make of the big white man, but from the look on his face, recognising the threat of the long bows. He lowered his sword and spat on the ground. 'Leave then, but you *are* finished on this island. If you remain, then we will raid and kill you all. Do not think that these bows will help you then either— our friends the Portuguese have weapons that will help us to kill you easily!'

The Damon collected the wounded man and backed

off, leaving the Paji to breathe sighs of relief.

Luku gathered his sister into his arms. 'Manissa you are safe! It is a miracle!'

She hugged him hard. 'It was terrible. We had no warning of them and then they were burning and killing us. We could not fight them. There were too many and they were killing everyone, so we ran away.'

'Thank the Gods that you did or you would be dead or slaves by now!'

She kissed his cheek. 'I knew you would find me, brother!'

He felt a glow of warmth. 'I am so happy that we got back in time but it was not me who found you. It was Jimmy!'

Manissa looked for the first time at the four newcomers. 'Who are they?'

'These are our friends from the great southern land. This big fellow is William and his wives Cathy and Mary.' Each of them nodded as they were introduced. 'And this is Jimmy who read your tracks and led us to you!'

Manissa stared at Jimmy in fascination and whispered to her brother. 'His skin is so black and he is so beautiful! He really saved us?'

Luku nodded. 'If he hadn't led us here, then the Damon might have killed you all!'

He smiled to himself at the way his sister was staring at Jimmy and guessed that Jimmy might be in trouble. His people had a relaxed attitude to relationships between the young men and women of their tribe, although there were strict limits as to how far young lovers could go before marriage. His sister was old enough and bold enough to set her sights on a man and he already admired Jimmy, so had no objections if Manissa found him to her liking. 'There is more, Manissa,' he said, nodding in Mary's direction again. 'You know how father spoke of his daughter in the great land to the South? I would like to formally introduce you to your sister—Mary.'

The two women looked uncertainly at each other. 'It is true?' asked Manissa.

Mary nodded nervously. 'I never really got to know… our father but it is true.'

After the terrible events that had happened to her village, Luku was pleased to see that his sister had found a tiny vestige of her humour returning. Even though it knew it meant trouble for him, he had to hide his grin when Manissa finally broke into a smile. 'Oh sister, have I got lots of things to tell you about Luku!'

Survivor's choices

They returned to what was left of their village and William, Cathy and Mary pitched in to help with the wounded while the others gathered up the fallen. They built four big funeral pyres on the beach from salvaged timbers from the burnt homes and the piles of driftwood along the foreshore. When the dead were finally laid onto the pyres, there were none of the holy men of the village who had survived and so both Rantuka and Luku called out prayers to their gods as the dead lay amid the roaring flames.

The departing Macassans had thrown burning torches onto two praus that had been drawn up on the beach but in their haste to move onto the next village, had failed to realise that neither of the fires had taken hold on the sea dampened wood of the vessels.

It was a shocked and saddened group who sat around a fire that night. Luku and Opaki talked about all that had happened during the voyage to Australia as well as what the future held for all of them. Manissa and Rantuka listened to their tale thoughtfully and said little at first. William, Cathy, Mary and Jimmy tried to stay at the edges of the conversation, knowing how profoundly the islanders had been affected by the disaster that had fallen upon them.

The practically minded Manissa was the first to see the central issue that confronted them and decided to speak up. 'We cannot stay here,' she stated. 'If the Macassans don't come back, then the Damon will attack us anyway. We have to leave. If the Damon attack us with the Portuguese helping them, then we are doomed and we know that the Portuguese hate us for refusing to follow their god on the cross.'

Some of the others argued against leaving the only home they had ever known but Rantuka agreed with Manissa. 'She is right. We have to find another island—one where the Macassans will not find us and where there are no Damon to plague us.'

William finally had his say. He had already discussed finding another island with Luku and Manissa during the day, for it had seemed obvious that staying here was just not an option. He brought out Luku's chart and pointed to a tiny island several hundred miles to the north. 'What about this place?'

Luku and Rantuka peered at the chart. 'That is Damar,' said Luku, 'I think my father went there sometimes for spices, for much grows wild there. He brought back cloves, coffee and nutmeg and spoke of establishing a trading post there, for we cannot grow those things on Adonara.'

Rantuka nodded. 'I have heard him speak of it. I don't think anyone lives there. It may be too small to support a village.'

William looked at him. 'Is it too small to support a group our size?'

Rantuka

Rantuka looked at the imposing white man. Luku had told him of everything he had done for them and spoke in tones of complete admiration. Rantuka and Luku were now the two most senior members of their village but he knew that if they were going to start a new life elsewhere then the old ways were ended. He had no desire to lead the remaining few who were left of their people and Luku was too young.

He sensed in William that he was a natural leader and more importantly, he seemed to be a good man. That was what his people needed right now and he was happy to defer to him. 'I think so, but I'm not sure about how much good water is there. We can go and look though and perhaps, if it is not the place for us, then we could look elsewhere.'

William looked around. 'I suggest we go to all of your other villages first and gather up any other survivors, as well as anything that we can salvage to start afresh. We're going to need these two praus and possibly a few more if there are any.'

Luku and Rantuka nodded. The two shared a look and came to an unspoken agreement. Rantuka looked at William. 'Tell us what we need to do.'

Their village had been one of the luckier ones in terms of survivors. They went to each ravaged village and the story of butchery and loss was the same in each. It soon became apparent that the Macassans had specifically targeted elders, presumably with the aim to take away any decision-making capacity in the survivors, while many young women and children were simply missing and presumed to be bound for the slave markets. In most villages, almost all of the males of fighting age had been killed. The Macassans were clearly trying to ensure that there would be no raids of reprisal against them.

In all, they only located another fifty Paji from all of the other villages. Funeral fires burned all along the coastline, blackening the skies for days as dozens of families disappeared in the ashes.

A number of the survivors spoke of the strange looking black man who had accompanied the Macassan raiders—a man who had looked carefully around in every village they went to and asked everyone if they had seen any people with white skin. Of course no one had, for William and his friends had still been enroute, but the description the people gave of the man caused the four of them to all look at each other in disquiet. Asigi was still after them and was now in the islands.

They salvaged another three praus—one of them a bigger, two-mast vessel that Luku informed them was called a *padewakang*. On hearing this, Cathy promptly named the vessel the 'Paddy Wacker'.

It was more than a week before they were ready to leave. Most of that time was spent in dealing with injuries and in loading food and everything that they could carry into their small fleet. Rantuka had been able to salvage most of his metal working equipment from the ruins of his forge. It was going be so sorely needed when they re-established.

A short, slightly built but nevertheless imposing apothecary from one of the other villages had saved most of his herbs, chemicals, minerals and medicines due to the fact that he had long ago built a cellar underneath his home in which he kept it all. His dwelling had been burnt to the ground but to his vast relief his precious horde were untouched.

He was instrumental in caring for the numerous wounded and quickly proved that he was a master of his trade, dispensing medicines and herbs that saved many lives as well as showing a depth of knowledge in treating injuries, particularly burns. Many of their wounded had suffered varying degrees of burns and his salves were almost miraculous in easing the pain of many. As busy as he was though, he spent much of his time looking at William and Cathy in fascinated speculation.

Several surviving carpenters were able to bring aboard their axes, adzes, saws and drills. All were going to be very important when they established their new home. A very large proportion of the time however, was spent in endless debate that often descended into outright argument, for not all wanted to leave their island and even less were happy to have a big, strange white man taking command.

William's attitude to the issue was that he was willing to provide leadership to this small group of grief ridden survivors if they wanted him to. His training as a police officer had taught him how to lead, and he had a natural tendency to always step forward in any case. He was not however, willing to try and force his leadership on these people. He said nothing as others argued against his leadership and he thought someone else would surely be elected until first Luku, then his sister and then Rantuka all spoke strongly for his leadership.

William's chief opponent was a huge Paji from what had been the largest of their villages and the one that had suffered the most losses. His name was Pelang and he had been the son of one of the councillors who ruled the Paji. Up until now he had led a privileged and pampered life and saw no reason not to rebuild the villages where they had always stood—with him as the new Chief Councillor, naturally.

Another survivor from the same village quietly informed Rantuka that Pelang had been the first to flee when the attack started and had even been the cause of an elderly woman's death when he pushed her over in his haste to get away. The woman had still been struggling to get up when a Macassan's sword had slain her.

Pelang was the tallest islander that William had met and his heavily muscled body gave testament to his pampered and well-fed life. Few liked his blustering, bullying ways and on hearing of his cowardice during the attack, William and Luku had even less time for him. To make matters worse and without any encouragement whatsoever, Pelang somehow got the idea that Manissa would make a wonderful wife when he took over as Chief Councillor.

Despite being generally disliked however, Pelang had a persuasive and commanding tongue and during the week had swayed almost half the survivors to his way of thinking. He was relying on the fact that most people are resistant to change, particularly change in the magnitude that William was advocating and he convinced many that the Macassans would never return and that the Damon could be persuaded to leave them alone if they were spoken to by someone with such commanding powers of diplomacy as he possessed.

William knew that to stay meant disaster and probable annihilation for the Paji and yet he felt strongly that the Paji should decide their own fate. He could only give his opinion. Then it was up to them to decide. Come what may, he was determined that at least the four of them would still leave and guessed that Luku and his sister and probably Opaki would stay with them as well.

Pelang brought himself unstuck on the seventh day

after the raids when he went up to Manissa, who was sitting on a fallen coconut trunk and in conversation with Jimmy. William had noticed her obvious attraction to his young Aboriginal friend since she'd first laid eyes on him and it was obvious that she enjoyed his company. William thought it could only be good for Jimmy and only hoped that he was sufficiently recovered from Junie's death. It was just as obvious though, that Jimmy was dazzled by the exotic beauty of Luku's sister and clearly didn't know how to handle her attentions.

He was watching when Pelang went over to the two of them, his fists clenched and his whole attitude wrong from William's point of view. He wandered over a little closer as Pelang confronted his friend.

'Get away from her, blackie!' the big Paji hissed. 'The likes of you have no business with my woman! I am going to be the Chief Councillor and she is going to be my wife!'

Jimmy leapt to his feet, his anger immediate. Pelang was at least twice Jimmy's size but that made no difference as he stood up to him.

'She is not yours or anyone else's woman and I'll speak to her as much as I want! Get away from us!'

Pelang sneered and pushed Jimmy hard in the chest, sending him back several feet. 'You're cheeky for little black runt. I'll say who she can talk to and it will certainly not be someone like you! Now go away before I beat you for your insolence!'

Jimmy stepped right up to him. 'I've heard about you. You are the coward who ran away and left his villagers to die!'

Pelang's face went deep red, with both shame and anger in equal proportions. He swung his fist and caught Jimmy in the side of his head before he could react. The blow sent him crashing to the ground, only semi-conscious. Pelang followed this up by kicking him viciously in the abdomen. He was about to stomp on Jimmy's head when Manissa threw herself at him.

'Leave him alone, you monster!'

Pelang seized her wrist and pulled her hard to him. 'You are my woman and you will do as I tell you!'

She responded by spitting into his face. 'Do you really believe that I will ever be your woman? Never in a million years!'

William rushed over now but was too late to stop the man slapping Manissa's head, but not too slow to stop him slapping her once more when he dropped a large, heavy hand onto his shoulder.

'Let the lady go!' ordered William, his face a mask of anger.

Pelang turned and sneered. 'Oh the big white man who thinks he's in charge! I'll teach you who is in charge here!'

He released Manissa but swung his ham-like fist at William's head, confident in the power of his blow to drop William as he had Jimmy. His fist never made contact.

William saw the telegraphed punch from the moment Pelang began it and easily swayed aside. Then he delivered a karate blow called a *nukite* or 'spear hand' that sank into Pelang's abdomen with enough force to drive the wind instantly from the big Paji's diaphragm. He had only used half the force that the blow called for, as the spear hand was designed to be lethal, but William had no intention of killing Pelang; he had done enough killing lately. As it was, Pelang sank to the ground white faced and wheezing, struggling for breath and staring wide eyed up at the big white man.

William and Manissa were both helping Jimmy to his feet when they realised that they were surrounded by a large group of Paji, all of whom were pointing with delight at the grey faced, wheezing Pelang and laughing gleefully at his downfall. That was the end of Pelang's support base. Most of those who could now see him for what he was wanted nothing more to do with him.

That night, Luku and Rantuka called for a vote, nominating William as Chief Councillor. Only five people did not vote for him and to his embarrassment he was surrounded by a multitude of Paji, all trying to shake his hand, pat his back or hug him.

Manissa

Afterwards, Manissa broke away from the throng of excited Paji when she saw Jimmy sitting to the side and looking on. She looked down on him and felt a strange and very nice feeling inside of herself as she looked at the dark skinned but beautiful new arrival who had come into her life. 'You did not speak the truth back there, you know.'

She knew that Jimmy was embarrassed at being knocked down so easily in front of her, but now he looked at her with a frown. 'I always speak the truth! What did I say that was untrue?'

She looked calmly at him and smiled. 'You said that I am not anyone's woman. That is not true.'

Jimmy waited for her to continue but she just walked off then with the smile still firmly in place and leaving him perplexed and floundering behind her.

CHAPTER THIRTY-FOUR

A new home found

They sailed with the next morning's outgoing tide. In the end, only four stayed behind with Pelang and watched with obvious trepidation as the praus left. Many had tried to convince them to come, but Pelang had made exorbitant promises to his small band of followers and they were gullible enough to believe him.

William had a huge dislike for Pelang but didn't like leaving him behind, not out of concern for his welfare, but for concern for their own. 'He knows where we are going and he's going to be very keen to pass that information on to anyone who wants to know. I don't like it.'

'What choice did we have—aside from tying him up and dragging him with us?'

'I know there wasn't a real choice. Maybe I shouldn't have pulled my blow like I did. I've got a nasty feeling that we're going to regret leaving him at our backs.'

Cathy had watched William drop Pelang with one hit. 'You pulled it?' She asked with surprise.

William shrugged. 'Yeah.' He sighed.

She thought for a moment. 'Well we're just going to have to make sure that we can't be attacked and massacred like these poor people were. Out next home is going to also have to be our castle!'

He had a sudden thought as a memory from a military history lesson at army boot camp came back to him. The instructors had been talking about the most efficient and effective forms of quickly built fortifications from ancient times and he remembered that one example had stood out as far superior to all others. 'Maybe not our castle, but at least our fort. And you know, I think I know just what it should look like too!'

Asigi

Asigi was so angry with Muluk that he wasn't game to even speak to him for days. He'd known that the two whites were still on his home shores and was cursing the fact that he hadn't somehow forced the Macassan to stay until they'd located them. Now, he had come all the way to these ridiculous islands with the Macassans, watched as they'd happily slaughtered whole villages and with not so much as a sign of his whites. And the most galling part was that he was still very much reliant on them and it would only take a word from Muluk to have his throat cut and his body thrown over the side. He'd had to bite his tongue and play a diplomatic role that was anathema to him.

'I need to go home to continue my search for the two whites. I'll make it worth your while to have one of your boats take me.'

In truth, Muluk couldn't wait to get rid of the loathsome Aboriginal man. Still, he wasn't going to make it too easy for him. 'Perhaps I can arrange it but the winds have changed and it will be very hard for one of my praus to fight against the wind and the seas on the way back to your land. You will have to make it very profitable to me.'

'Fine, fine I'll find ten slaves...' he looked up

meaningfully. 'Ten young slaves for you, but we will have to go further inland to get them this time.'

Muluk felt a stirring of excitement and gave thought to which of his men he could rely on to bring the slaves back to him untouched… until he got to them. He finally decided on one of his lieutenants, one completely lacking any imagination and who was totally afraid of him. Yes, he would do. 'Alright then but make sure that you deliver!'

Jimmy

They sighted Damar Island after five days at sea. It was so small that even with the chart it had taken days of searching before they finally found it. Jimmy had hated every moment of the journey. Manissa's comment about having a man was eating at him even though he knew that it was irrational. After all, he was just a skinny black warrior and she was just so impossibly lovely and unattainable for someone like him.

He still missed Junie and in the short time that they'd had together he had come to love her. Junie had been so good with him and he knew that they would have been very happy together but now she was gone and as much as he mourned her passing, he kept having these thoughts about Manissa. Luku's sister was just so captivating, that sometimes Jimmy thought he would go crazy with the silly thoughts that he had about her. No matter how hard he tried, he couldn't stop the thoughts and now to find out that she had someone else was driving him crazy.

He even pulled Luku aside and, trying to sound as though it was of no real interest to him and tried to get to the truth of it by the use of guile, which didn't at all come naturally to him, but he felt was justified on this occasion. 'Hey Luku, so we are getting close now, eh?'

Luku looked broodingly at the chart. 'Maybe we are… if I can ever find this damned place.'

Jimmy nodded and put a supporting hand on his shoulder. 'If anyone can find it then you can. We are so lucky to have you and your sister with us.'

Luku looked up at the mention of Manissa. 'My sister, what's she got to do with finding the island?'

'Oh nothing really I suppose… I just mean she will be happy too when she… and her man can settle down.'

Luku looked up from the chart in surprise. 'Manissa has a man? Why wasn't I told about it? I am her brother!'

Jimmy looked at him in frustration. 'You don't know who it is either then?'

The Paji looked worriedly at Jimmy for a moment and then felt a huge relief when he realised what was going on. He hid his smile carefully; if Manissa was playing games with Jimmy then it wasn't his place to spoil her fun, at least not so soon.

'I'm sure that she'll let us all know who the lucky guy is when she's ready to do so.'

Jimmy glowered and looked away in disgust. 'Oh yeah. Great. I can't wait.'

William

As they approached the island, they could see that it was almost completely covered in dense forests. There was a high peak in the middle of the island that looked like it might have been a volcano in the not-so-distant past.

Looking at the peak brought another bad thought to mind and William looked urgently at Cathy. 'Bloody hell, I just remembered! Isn't Krakatoa around here somewhere? When the hell is it going to blow? I sure as hell don't want us to set up a new home only to have it blown to atoms when that big bastard goes up!'

She thought for a moment with a frown but then visibly relaxed. 'It blew… blows in the 1880's, I think, something like that… and anyway, I'm pretty sure that it's way over Sumatra way. I think we've got at least two hundred years up our sleeves. Just as well too, because when it blows, it's going to be the biggest explosion the world has ever seen.'

The fact that they had foreknowledge of the Krakatoa eruption brought on a whole line of thought, one that William hadn't yet considered. But now that he did, he realised it might be absolutely vital into the future. 'If we're going to be staying, and it looks like we don't have much of a say in the matter, then that's the sort of thing we're going to have to write down.' He looked at her swelling belly. 'At least with forewarning about that sort of thing our descendants will have a bloody big advantage in years to come.'

Up until this moment, Cathy had never given thought to what might transpire into the future beyond given birth to her and William's child and bringing it and any other children up in safety and security. Now though, she had a vision of children and grandchildren and then their children who would one day span the years right through until her own time in the twenty-first century. It was a mind opening moment that rocked her to her heels.

One of her purchases in Wetar had been reams of parchment, ink and quills to write with. She had bought it all simply because she missed writing but now her face lit up at William's suggestion. 'You are absolutely right! I'm going to start making a record of everything from history that I can think of! You should do the same before it all slips from our minds. We'll make it into a big book that we can hand on!'

He embraced her sudden enthusiasm. 'We'll make it a priority then and we'll do it together so that we can jog each other's memories. I'm sure that we would be able to fill in lots of gaps in each other's knowledge and we would want to make this thing as accurate as we can.' He frowned then. 'We're going to have to figure out some way to protect the information though. Only our family must ever know about our "predictions".'

The small fleet sailed right around the small island. William estimated that it was only about twenty kilometres long and not quite that in width. It was small as far as islands went, but he was hopeful it would be big enough for them. They called into several likely looking bays, all of which fell short of their requirements in one way or the other, before arriving in a small but well protected cove on the southern side of the island to anchor in. At first glance, it looked alright, with good protection from the monsoons and plenty of room for their fleet plus a beautiful, white sandy beach that almost called out to them.

William, Cathy, Mary and Jimmy were aboard the larger prau, along with Luku and Manissa. It was late afternoon and they stood in a group, watching the sun sinking down behind the big peak and leaving the rest of the island in deepening darkness.

Mary and Cathy each took one of William's hands. He looked at them each in turn. 'Well it looks like we might be home at last.'

The island was becoming just a mass of blackness in

front of them as the sun disappeared. Cathy touched her belly. 'Oh I hope it is, and I hope it's going to be a happy home for us all!'

Mary was also starting to show now and she too touched her belly. 'It will be. This is where we really start our tribe!'

William was anxious to find out if the island could sustain their small community. He decided to take Cathy and Mary, plus Luku, his sister, and Jimmy ashore. They landed at first light by canoe, all armed in case of trouble and with the six praus full of anxious Paji looking on. In the light of the new day, they were able to see features that had been hidden in the failing light of the previous evening and they reinforced the impression that cove might be ideal for their purposes. Two headlands provided shelter from the winds from the north and northwest, which was where the monsoons would come from and the beach shelved quickly, which would enable the praus to be brought in close to the shore.

The strip of sand that made up the beach was narrow and crowded in by huge coconut palms laden with fruit, while dense forest lay just beyond them with enormous hardwood trees towering into the sky. It was immediately obvious that they were not going to be short of building materials if the rest of the island ticked all of their boxes.

'Alright, let's split up into pairs.' William said. 'Our main priority is fresh water and plenty of it.' He caught Manissa looking at Jimmy and smiled to himself. 'Jimmy you go with Manissa, Mary with Luku and Cathy and I will go off in that direction.' He said, pointing to the right of the beach.

Manissa

Manissa looked back at Jimmy as she moved to the left and raised an eyebrow. 'Well are you going to come with me, or do you want me to go all alone into the forest?'

Jimmy had been sulking around Manissa all morning, his usual cheerfulness buried under his insecurities over her. He wasn't about to let her go into unknown territory without his protection though and followed her into the forest.

Luku had chided his sister earlier for giving Jimmy such a hard time. 'Put the poor boy out of his misery, Manissa. For goodness sake, he's a damn wreck at the moment!'

Manissa had looked fondly over to where Jimmy sat morosely and sighed. 'I suppose I should, but it's been such fun watching him for the past week!'

'You are a cruel woman, sister! I feel sorry for Jimmy already!'

Now, as they worked their way through the forest, Manissa moved closer to him. 'So, have you guessed who my man is yet Jimmy?'

He glowered at her. 'No I haven't and I don't really want to know either!'

'Why not?' she asked, wide eyed.

'Why not?' he exploded. 'Why would I want to know about some other guy that's going to get you?'

She stopped and turned to face him. It was time to end his suffering. 'It's you silly. You're my man.'

He gaped at her in astonishment. 'Me? I'm your man?'

She grinned, adoring the dawning realisation and delight in his brown eyes. 'Uh-huh. So, are you going to kiss me?'

Hardly believing his good fortune, he took her into

his arms and their lips met and stayed together for long minutes.

It was only when both of them began to feel like taking it much further than kissing, did Manissa break away from him. 'Can you wait? Can you wait until we are married Jimmy? I've never been with a man and I want to be your wife before you become my first.'

He had never expected to find love again after losing Junie and now Jimmy felt emotion swelling in his eyes. 'I'll wait a year if I have to. Although I think I might shrivel up and die if it is that long!'

Finally, they remembered why they were in the jungle and continued their explorations. When they returned, hand in hand and with pure happiness written on their faces, everyone was grinning. Luku came up to him and shook his hand. 'Welcome to my family Jimmy. I am so happy that from now on, my sister is going to have someone else to pick on aside from me!'

Mary had gone with Luku looking for water and they had been totally successful. They'd located a stream coming down off the mountain that fed into a small but deep pond before continuing down to the sea. In addition, they had located a spring bubbling up from the earth and the water was sweet and clear.

In his explorations with Cathy, William had used a sword to dig down into the soil and found it to be dark, rich and loamy, full of organics and capable of growing great crops. They found cloves, nutmeg, pepper trees, cocoa bushes, cashews and even coffee growing wild in clearings throughout the forest. It was clearly a highly fertile and productive island and he was amazed that it wasn't inhabited. Then, they found the burnt out ruins of a small village and it became clear why it wasn't. At some point of time, probably more than twenty years ago, judging by the size of trees that had grown up through the remains of old homes, the island had been raided.

They found skeletal remains scattered here and there, poking up through the vegetation that had almost buried them over the years. It looked to have been a village of perhaps thirty to forty people at one time but they were long gone.

Someone, perhaps Macassans or some other enemy, had wiped the small community out, leaving the island vacant until their arrival.

CHAPTER THIRTY-FIVE

Building the fort

The rest of the Paji finally came ashore. After consultation with Luku, Rantuka and some of the other Paji, William had identified a likely place to build their new home against one of the headlands, which fell away with steep cliffs to the sea. He was thinking strategically and with the steep headland against their backs they could build a defensive settlement that would overlook and command the cove.

While all of their stores and equipment was being offloaded, William took Cathy, Jimmy, Luku and Mary aside. Manissa was included in the group when Jimmy insisted that his future wife should know all of his secrets.

William unrolled a parchment that he had been working on and laid it out on a flat rock. 'We can't afford to simply build a new village like the one on Adonara now that we're here.' He looked directly at Luku and Manissa. 'Sooner or later, the Macassans or some other enemy are going to find us and what happened to your people on Adonara cannot ever be allowed to happen again. That's why we are going to build our new home here with protection and self-defence as the main priorities.'

'This is what I have in mind.' He pointed to the charcoal drawing that he had made on the parchment. They all studied it. The drawing showed four high walls set in a perfect square with towers on each side of the square spanning a gateway. There was a deep ditch marked in front of each wall and long spiked poles were drawn in at the bottom of the ditches.

The inside of the square was marked with homes set in neat, perfectly straight lines with a large, central square shown next to a bigger building in the centre of the whole thing.

Luku nodded his approval. 'It's a very strong looking fort. I like it!'

Cathy was still studying the drawing. There was something very familiar about it and suddenly it came to her. 'It's a Roman fort, isn't it?'

He was proud of his wife. 'Very good! I thought that I was the only one who knew what a Roman fort looked like. I learned about them during my time in the army.'

She grinned. 'I knew that staying awake during lectures on ancient civilisations would pay off one day!'

Manissa queried them both. 'What is a Roman?'

Cathy answered. 'They're people. They were an empire based in Europe. They ruled a big part of the world for about a thousand years until they basically fell apart in about 500AD. They were very aggressive and conquered lots and lots of countries while they expanded their empire. Wherever they went, they always built forts as bases and to provide security against their enemies. Every one of their forts was essentially the same and they looked pretty much just like this one will!'

'Well, not quite.' William amended. 'I did this drawing before I realised that we had this headland to build up against with nice steep cliffs to stop anyone from attacking us from the rear. Not much will change except that some of the headland will now form one of the walls and it'll be a bit more rectangular and larger than the Romans used to build. We're going to have to fit everyone inside with their own homes and little yards plus room for any new arrivals that we get. The Romans used to fit a thousand men into one of their forts so I reckon we can all fit in quite nicely with room to spare.'

He flipped the parchment over and used some charcoal to quickly sketch out what he meant, adding a tower on top of the headland that would look out to sea.

Manissa was deep in thought. She looked around and saw that no one else felt the confusion that she was experiencing. 'How do you know these things?' she turned to her brother. 'We have never heard of "Romans" before, so why aren't you as surprised to hear about them as I am?'

Luku looked a little embarrassed. 'Because I already know that William and Cathy don't come from here and they know lots of things that you and I couldn't possibly know. I just assume that these "Romans" are one of those things.'

'Not from around here... So where are they from?'

Jimmy took her hand and sighed. 'You're not going to believe this, but it's true...'

William was anxious to start their fort as soon as possible. Rantuka introduced him to Teronga and Lemala, who were the two carpenters. William showed them the drawings and explained what had to be done.

Teronga was the slightly older of the two, a stoutly built short man with arms that bulged with muscle from many years of sawing, chopping and hammering. He looked long and hard at the drawings, looking from the original which had more detail, to the quick sketch on the back and finally nodded.

'It can be done but we are going to have to cut a lot of trees down and I'm going to need many strong backs to help get it done.'

Lemala was in his late twenties and deferred to Teronga but nodded his agreement. 'It will be a wonderful thing! I wish we had lived in something like this back on Adonara!'

Luku spoke up. 'Everyone will pitch in. I for one won't sleep well until we are behind these walls.'

The two carpenters took charge of work parties and everyone, William and Cathy included, followed their orders as they selected trees to cut down from the surrounding forest. For weeks, the sound of axes and saws could be heard as huge hardwood trees were cut down and then laboriously sliced into manageable quarters using big, two-man saws over a very long, deep saw pit.

William volunteered on most days to work on the bottom of the sawpit. It was the hardest and dirtiest of the work and at the end of each day he was utterly exhausted and covered head to toe in sawdust.

The site for their fort had been cleared and excavated by another work party and deep holes were dug to take anchoring posts that would provide the strength to the sides of the fort. Blocks and tackle from all of the praus and lots and lots of manpower dragged the big posts into position. A sturdy wooden derrick was built on top of the bluff behind the fort and it was used to inch the huge, heavy posts into the upright, with teams of straining workers pulling thick ropes to keep the posts under control. Eventually, each post dropped with deep thuds into their six feet deep holes and then, thousands of rocks were used to fill up the holes and rammed down hard.

The apothecary's name was Wuringa. He was an affable, slightly built, short little man in his fifties. Because of his medicines and medical knowledge and being so instrumental in helping to treat the wounded, plus the fact that he was of such slight build that he wouldn't have been of much physical help anyway, he had not been required to do any of the manual labour that the others happily contributed to, but had been exploring their island, usually with either Cathy or Mary in tow for his protection.

William soon got to know him and struck up a quick friendship. He quickly realised that Wuringa was possessed of a very sharp intellect and a broad general knowledge beyond his medicines and herbs. Of all the Paji, he was the only person to have heard of Romans. It turned out that Wuringa had attended university for five years in Amsterdam after being befriended by one of the Dutch traders, who paid for his education and travel after Wuringa had cured the trader's wife of yellow fever, usually a killer in these times.

In conversation William had come to see that, notwithstanding their own 21st Century educations, after them, Wuringa was the most educated and knowledgeable person in their group, with a general knowledge of the 17th Century world that William and Cathy both milked ruthlessly. William felt strongly that they needed to know as much about the time they had been cast into as possible. Reading about it in school so long ago was no substitute for hearing first hand from someone with Wuringa's experience and intelligence. The difficulty in doing so was to get Wuringa talking about Holland and Europe without giving away their circumstances. It wasn't that easy though and William was beginning to think the Wuringa was seeing through their explanations of where they came from. It appeared that he knew enough about seventeenth century England and had even met Englishmen during his time on the Continent, to know that the two of them were far from typical 'Englanders', as the Dutch called them.

At last, William had been able to confirm the exact date though, and they now both knew that the date was, by Wuringa's reckoning, June 5th, 1651. They began keeping their own calendar from then on.

Even Mary, who soaked up information like a sponge, soon realised what a font of information he was from his time in Holland. It wasn't all one-way traffic however, for Mary knew things from her tribal existence that sometimes made Wuringa's eyes pop.

The little man was fascinated to see a Roman fort, even if it was slightly different from the originals, come to life. He stood watching the anchor posts being dropped into position and then the rocks rammed down to keep them in place.

He looked over at William and shook his head. 'It will never stay upright. You don't realise how strong the forces of nature can be here. The first monsoonal wind that comes along will have your whole fort leaning over like a drunk in an alley. If we get a cyclone then we will be lucky to have two sticks still together. You need concrete.'

Even considering Wuringa's exposure to learning, William was surprised and a little worried that the man knew of the existence of concrete. To the best of his knowledge, concrete was a nineteenth century invention, so how did Wuringa know about it? William had also been worried however at how stable the anchoring posts would be, as the rest of the fort would only be as strong as they were, but he hadn't been able to come up with a solution to make them anymore solid. But concrete? He snorted, 'I'd love to have some concrete but I doubt we're going to get any around here!'

Wuringa smiled. 'Ah, you know about concrete too! I thought I would surprise you for once. Never mind. Well I happen to know how to make it. You're making a Roman fort so we'll use Roman concrete.'

Now William was intrigued. 'Roman concrete?'

'Yes of course, what other kind is there? I read about it in Amsterdam. The Romans used a substance that they called concrete in most of their constructions. It was incredibly durable and effective. I saw an old Roman bridge while I was studying and the spans were still as strong as the day they were put there. I've had a good look around our little paradise. That big lump in the middle of the island was an active volcano not too long ago. I've found deep pits of compacted volcanic ash near the base of the mountain and I've also found limestone deposits. That's all that I need to make concrete. Give me half a dozen men and I'll make concrete for you that will last a thousand years!'

It was a no brainer as far as William was concerned. 'How long will you need?'

Wuringa thought about it. 'We've got to dig up the ash and mine enough limestone; then we have to build an oven to roast the limestone in, crush the burnt limestone and then mix it together. Give me two weeks and I'll have it ready.'

'Done. We'll use the time to cut up the rest of the timber. If you can produce real concrete, I'll bloody kiss you!'

'Ugh, please don't. Although, one of your pretty wives on the other hand…'

William laughed and clapped him on the back. 'If you make the concrete, *both* of my wives will kiss you!'

The next morning Wuringa disappeared into the interior of the island with a dozen volunteers to assist him, wheel barrows, picks, shovels and axes in hand. They took with them four of the huge barrels that had been used for water storage on the larger of the praus, the Paddy Wacker. The rest of them returned to the never-ending job of felling trees and cutting timber.

Everyone remaining, even the bigger children, worked as if their lives depended on it to get all of the remaining timber cut and sawed. There was no lack of enthusiasm in any of them, for after what they had gone through on Adonara, they all knew that the fort was all that might stop them from one day being annihilated.

William still put in long hours at the bottom of the sawpit but was increasingly being pulled out to solve disputes between some of the Paji. Without a Council to go to with their issues, they were all turning to William to settle matters.

Tempers were fraying with the work load placed upon them all and most were still in mourning for slain family members, so it didn't take much to turn trivial matters into sometimes violent confrontations. All of the male Paji wore the wave bladed kris daggers and twice they were pulled during disputes and only William's size and authority prevented bloodshed.

They finally reached a day when all the timber that they needed for their new home had been cut and sawn. There was no sign of Wuringa or his team yet and so, at Cathy's suggestion, William decided that everyone deserved a day off.

Skins of arak appeared as if by magic, fires were lit along the beach and food was soon sizzling in coals and on flat iron pans. The mood was immeasurably lighter than it had been and then, just as they were all about to begin eating and drinking, Wuringa and his men appeared out of the trees with barrels full of white powder carried between them.

William went to them and looked into the barrels. 'It almost looks like flour.' He remarked.

Wuringa grinned. 'If you baked this flour into a loaf you wouldn't like the bread very much!'

William looked at the small man. He appeared exhausted, his face gaunt, and he'd lost weight—with not much to lose in the first place.

'You've done well and right on the knocker for your two weeks. Thank you Wuringa. If this stuff works like you think it will, our fort is going to be just about impregnable.'

Wuringa accepted a skin of arak from one of the Paji. He took a long drink of the fiery liquor and let out a sigh of pleasure. 'I've been drinking water for fourteen days. This is so nice. Remind me to never become a Moslem!'

Cathy and Mary joined them. William had cued them to Wuringa's promised reward and the little man was suddenly being kissed on both cheeks by the two women at once. He beamed with pleasure and looked at William. 'You need anything else done, just ask!'

There were a few sore heads the following morning and for once, Teronga had trouble in motivating his workers, but by mid-morning the barrels of concrete powder were wrestled into position at the anchor posts. Once the powder was tipped into each hole and pounded down so that it filled every space between the rocks, water was added. A few last-minute adjustments to ensure that the thick, quarter tree trunks were perfectly straight and then they were tied off to see if Wuringa's concrete would do its job.

The little apothecary tried to act completely confident but his frequent trips to each post hole was evidence that he was as nervous as the rest of them. The white sludge in the holes set with painful slowness but after twelve hours in the hot tropical sun, they could all see that it was going to work. By sunset, the concrete had completely set and Wuringa proved the point by taking an adze and ramming it down onto one of the postholes, only to have it bounce back with a loud ringing sound. Everyone was jubilant except for Rantuka, who found that he had an adze to put a new edge onto.

From then on, the fort began to take shape in earnest. With the huge and rock-solid anchor points to work from, it was a simple matter of brawn and trade knowledge for Teronga and Lemala to erect the framework for the walls and then to begin attaching the pre-cut timbers that would make up the most important part of the outer defences of the fort.

William watched the two carpenters at work and realised how lucky they had been to have them as they trimmed thick pieces of dowel and then drilled corresponding holes to fasten the timbers immovably onto the wall without a nail or piece of rope being used. By the end of the fifth day, the walls of the fort were complete.

Next came the towers, and Teronga and Lemala were everywhere, directing workers where each piece of carefully prepared timber had to go before they personally hammered each dowel into place. In three more days, the watch-towers on the walls were built. Sentries went up into the towers for the first time that night and were able to patrol the walkways that ran along the walls from one tower to the next. The tower on the bluff behind the fort was last to be built and accessed by a stout ladder. From now on, no one would approach them by land or sea without them knowing.

The thickly reinforced gates were next and everyone worked tirelessly, all realising that with this last effort, their fort would be truly secure at last. When the big main gate was pulled closed and the thick crossbar slid into its place, everyone thought it was high time for another celebration—with corresponding hangovers the next morning.

CHAPTER THIRTY-SIX

Jimmy gets married

Work continued ceaselessly for weeks and then months. A deep ditch was dug around the three exposed sides of the fort and spikes embedded into the outward facing slopes, with even bigger sharpened stakes all along the top. Anyone who tried to go through the ditch was not going to be a happy camper.

Sanitation had been a chief concern for William and Cathy, considering that their community members were going to all be living in a relatively enclosed space. The accumulation of sewerage and waste could quickly become a health risk for them all, with diseases like typhoid possible unless they did things properly right from the start.

Once again, William took a page out of the ancient Romans' fort-building manual. First, they built a communal toilet block complete with men's and women's sections, with real wooden seats and with a wooden channel running behind them, leading out to a deep and covered pit that was dug well clear of the fort for the purpose.

William then described how an aqueduct worked and was surprised that it provoked so much good-natured humour among the Paji. As it turned out they were far from strangers in transporting water and they located some big stands of bamboo and cut down the thickest of them. These were split down the middle and hollowed out before being attached to a system of trestles running from the spring, down a slight slope to the toilet block. They ran a branch off of this bamboo aqueduct that led off to a deep, stone lined hole dug right in the middle of the fort for their drinking water.

It took a lot of fine-tuning but in the end, they all had the exquisite luxury of self-flushing toilets! Cathy refused to leave the first time she used the new facility and sat with a blissful smile on her face for more than ten minutes until a woman with more urgent needs chased her off.

As a final touch, William arranged for the beaches to be scoured for sponges. He recalled reading of how entire centuries of Roman soldiers were often struck down by dysentery because they all shared the same sponges. Everyone was given their own sponge to use in place of toilet paper with instructions on the importance of keeping the sponges clean between uses. To the Paji, who were used to communal latrines and dung pits, with a leaf to wipe themselves, this was all a wonderful step forward.

Up until now, everyone had been camping out under rattan tents and there had been few complaints as they all watched their fort taking shape. There was an enormous communal pride in what they were achieving and even though everyone had been stoic throughout with their Spartan living conditions, there was widespread relief when houses were finally being built.

William knew where he wanted the houses to go in the interests of tactical efficiency in the event that they had to move within the fort with speed in case of an emergency situation, but he had no idea what the Paji would want in terms of construction, size or layout. A group of women, with Cathy, Mary and Manissa prominent among them, told the carpenters what they wanted.

Unlike their former homes on Adonara, which had been built on bamboo stilts six feet off the ground, their new homes had to be radically different. They finally arrived at a square, four room design, with a bathing and laundry area, two sleeping rooms and a common room. When Cathy informed them that this room should be called a 'lounge room' the idea caught on quickly. The Paji women scoffed at Cathy's suggested of a kitchen under the main roof and so firepits with clay ovens were attached to the rear of each home under a sloping timber shelter. Homes went up quickly after that and gradually family groups all began making furniture and then moving into their new homes.

Manissa had hinted very strongly to Jimmy that she wanted a home ready to move into before their marriage took place. By now, he was desperate to tie the knot with the beautiful and exotic Paji and so he shamelessly bribed Teronga to jump him up the list and build his home early on. William helped him make furniture but this time with guidance and occasional assistance from Teronga, so the results were significantly better than the driftwood furniture of their first effort.

Finally, the home was finished and Manissa gave her new home the tick of approval. Then she shocked William by asking him to marry them!

'I can't marry anyone! I'm not the captain of a damned boat and I'm certainly not a priest!'

'It doesn't matter. In my village the holy man would marry us but there are no holy men left and no one else in the village is any more qualified than you are. Jimmy and I both agree that we want you to do it.'

Luku wasn't any help to him. 'Strictly speaking, you are the head of our community now, so you're more qualified to marry my sister off than anyone—and the sooner, the better.'

Manissa threw him a nasty look for that comment but he ignored her and just grinned. 'Hey sister, I'm on your side!'

She threw him a well-practiced nasty look, but turned back to William. 'Will you do it? Will you marry us?'

'Of course I will and it will be an honour, besides, I reckon Jimmy would be sharpening his spears for me if I didn't.'

The wedding ceremony was unique, with elements taken from Paji, Aboriginal and the odd non-religious Australian wedding that he'd attended,. Jimmy kept insisting that he would have been happy just to kidnap Manissa and run off into the forest for their honeymoon. This plan was met with a fairly unsurprising lack of enthusiasm on the part of the intended bride, so Jimmy had had to sit back stoically as virtually everyone but he planned for his big day.

William felt completely out his depth when he finally conducted the ceremony but everyone else agreed that it was a fine wedding and even Jimmy was pleased with the short but beautiful ceremony that had been concocted.

As he and Manissa stood up from the wedding feast afterwards, William gave him a fierce hug. 'My friend, Manissa is a fine girl and I know that you're going to be very happy. I've a feeling that there is a certain woman up in the spirit world looking down on you with a big grin too!'

Jimmy choked up a bit at the reminder of Junie but then Manissa came and took his hand.

'Come husband, it is time for you to teach me things that only a married woman can learn!'

He looked briefly up to the heavens as if for Junie's approval, and then put an arm around his woman. Cheers and ribald advice followed them as they disappeared into their home.

By their choice, the house that was built for William, Cathy and Mary was the last to be completed. It was in the centre of the fort and William explained that in Roman times it would have been called the 'principia' and housed the Roman legate or general, serving as both his dwelling and a command centre. By necessity, it was the biggest of all the buildings, for with similar uses in mind it would include living quarters for the three of them—with two more very soon to be added to their family—and a meeting place for the whole community.

William was becoming busier and busier with the running of their small community and had been worried that he wouldn't be able to put in the time to build nice furniture for Cathy and Mary. He needn't have worried, for the trio were so popular with all of the Paji that on the day that 'the big house', as it was referred to, was finished the three of them were presented with a full ensemble of furniture, including cots for the two soon-to-arrive babies. They were all deeply touched by the gesture and moved into their home with relief after so many months of sleeping in a tent.

By Cathy and Mary's estimation, they now only had a month before Cathy was due to give birth and perhaps a month beyond that for Mary's baby. Both heavily pregnant women settled with pure bliss into the beautifully carved and deeply padded chairs that had been made for them.

William had kept the Lee Enfield rifle hidden ever since arriving at the island. None of the Paji with the exception of Luku and Manissa knew where they were from and it was too much to expect the rest of the community to accept the fact that they were from the future as readily as Luku and his sister had. Explaining the rifle would be just about impossible without revealing all and was sure to arouse a lot of questions, so he waited until they moved into the big house before fetching it from where he'd kept it hidden and carried it in its canvas bag—as well as the bag of empty casings—to the house under the cover of encroaching darkness.

Rantuka's new smithy was adjacent to the big house and he was working late on another of the dozen cross bows that he'd been making at Luku's request, when he noticed William walk past.

'William, can I have a word?'

He inwardly cursed at being sprung but stopped. 'What can I do for you, mate?'

Rantuka smiled at the term 'mate'. Everyone was getting used to the strange words that William used. He walked over, eyeing the long bag curiously. 'I've almost used up all the iron that Luku gave me and was wondering if we could do a run to Wetar to buy more. I know we could use more rice and a host of other things too. We could take the big prau and be there and back in a week.'

A few days previously William had been looking at one of their praus and it had brought a memory of one of the occasions when he and a few of his mates had gone sailing on Port Phillip Bay, out of Melbourne. The memory had very quickly sent him running to retrieve his carefully hidden mobile phone. He inserted the battery and to his relief saw that it was still at a quarter charge.

When he opened the phone and brought up the photo gallery he grinned widely as he checked back through his photos. There he was with his police mates, standing on the foredeck of their sloop, with at least six other yachts in the background, all of them clearly showing how their sails were rigged!

He quickly found pen and parchment and began drawing the images on his phone. From the images, he come up with a few fairly revolutionary ideas, based on Western yacht rigging that should make all of the praus much faster and able to sail closer to the wind. Luku and a few others were now helping him with the project on the Paddy Wacker and it wasn't too far off being ready.

Hitching up both the rifle bag and the sack of casings to hold them more securely, he nodded. 'Sure, I'll have a word with Luku in the morning. We're doing some alterations to the rigging on the big boat, so maybe not tomorrow but we should be able to leave by Wednesday.'

There was a sudden tinkling sound and William could only look down in dismay as two of the empty casings spilled from their bag onto the ground.

Before he could react, Rantuka had scooped up the two casings and made to hand them back to William when he had a second look. He examined them closely. 'What are these?'

William reddened. He hated lying and especially to a friend. He pondered how to answer without being too untruthful.

'It is a bullet casing for a rifle, a very new kind.'

The metal worker continued to examine the two casings. 'It is brass but so fine and perfectly round! How was this done? It is amazing! I could not make anything so fine as this. I can't even see where the join is where they made such a perfect tube out of the brass!' He thought for a moment. 'I have heard of the muskets that the Dutch and the Portuguese use. Is a rifle like one of those?'

William knew that the casings were mass-produced on lathes. It was technology that was a long way off from the seventeenth century and to compare a matchlock musket to the Lee Enfield .303 was like comparing a pebble to a mountain.

He looked at Rantuka and considered his options. He liked the man a lot. He had been a steady and dependable ally since the day they'd met and William judged that, with the possible exception of Wuringa, Rantuka was the most likely not to freak out if he learned the truth about he and Cathy.

He opened his mouth to tell him the truth when none other than Wuringa came out of the shadows and looked eagerly at the rifle bag in William's hand. 'Ah, you've finally decided to bring it out of hiding! I've been waiting with great anticipation to find out all about it!'

William's look of consternation must have been too obvious and he gave a short laugh. 'Oh, come on! You can't just hide something under a pile of timber and not expect someone as curious as me not to find it! It's some sort of new weapon isn't it? I've played with it a number of times but for the life of me I can't see how it was made or how it works.'

William sighed. The cat was clearly out of the bag, so

the Lee Enfield might as well come out too. He nodded towards Rantuka's smithy. 'Can we at least go somewhere a little more private before I tell you about it?'

A very curious Rantuka lit a lamp as William pulled the big Lee Enfield from its bag, while Wuringa looked on with a big grin at the prospect of at last learning one of the big white man's secrets.

William held it up and worked the bolt action, explaining how the bullet was loaded into the chamber and then the trigger released the firing pin to detonate the bullet. 'This is probably—no, it is definitely—the most advanced firearm in the world at the moment. It fires a bullet for about a mile and holds five rounds in the magazine here, so whoever is using it can fire further and more rapidly than any other weapon in existence.'

He looked at the two men with a hopeful look. 'I don't suppose that the two of you could keep this a secret?'

The little apothecary was practically dancing with eagerness. 'Oh of course we won't tell anyone about your secret but I want to see it in action!'

Now William shook his head ruefully. 'I wish I could, but these empty shell casings were the ammunition. I don't have any others, so I can't use it.'

'Why don't you fix these up and then use them?' asked a puzzled Wuringa.

William explained the difficulties involved, the chief one of these being primers to detonate the powder.

Wuringa picked up a casing and sniffed at it. Then he handed the casing to Rantuka and pointed to the primer at its base. 'Can you make these little metal cups?'

The metal worker took a slim metal pick and eased the primer cap out of the casing. He looked closely at it.

'Mine might not be quite so fine as these but I can see how it would work to send a big spark into the casing. I could make them out of copper so that it is soft and the "firing pin" thing could hit it properly. 'He pointed to where the crimped end of the cap had been spread out by the detonation of the primer. 'That will be the trickiest bit because I would have to make the top a bit weaker than the rest of it so that the charge can escape. Maybe I could put just a tiny hole on the inside. Yes, I think I could do it.'

Wuringa nodded in satisfaction and looked back at William. 'So you only need a projectile, some gun powder and something to go into the little caps that Rantuka makes?'

William looked back with a warily hopeful expression. 'Yes, but the gun powder would have to be extremely fine grained and we'd still have the big issue of a primer.'

Wuringa waved a hand dismissively. 'Bah, I've can make gunpowder in my sleep and I know how to make at least three different substances that will go "bang" if they get hit.' He thought about it and then smiled happily. 'I have some mercury and I have some nitric acid. Those two always get excited when they are combined! Leave it with us William, I think we can get your rifle banging away happily!'

Rantuka nodded his agreement. 'Give me a drawing of what shape you want the… the projectile. I can make them from lead but I've only got a little bit of it. If you're going to Wetar, see if you can find some more for me.'

CHAPTER THIRTY-SEVEN

The trading mission, a close escape

The prospect of having the Lee Enfield back in action filled William with eager anticipation and he quickly told Cathy and Mary of his plans to return to Wetar for, among the other needed items, lead for his bullets.

Cathy smiled at his enthusiasm. 'Big boys and their toys! Alright but don't be away for too long; this big lad of yours is kicking like hell lately so I'd say he's about to make his entrance to the world.'

William looked down worriedly. 'I can't go then!' Then he looked up with a silly grin. 'You think it's a boy?'

She laughed. 'Of course you can still go. I'm sure there's plenty of time if you're only going to be away for a week, and anything as big and rambunctious as this baby is, has just got to be a boy!'

Mary put an arm around her. If anything, Mary was even bigger than Cathy was but looked beautiful with her pregnancy. 'Don't worry, we'll look after each other and there are two very experienced midwives here. We'll be just fine.'

He looked worriedly from one of his women to the other, torn between his eagerness to go and his sense of duty to stay. He knew that his presence on the trip wasn't essential. Luku and Opaki could get everything that they needed without him there, but he wanted to be able to really evaluate the sail modifications on the big prau first hand. He still felt distinctly guilty when he allowed his women to insist that he go. 'If you're sure then…'

Cathy kissed him on the cheek. 'Bring me and Mary something nice—and some more really nice material... maybe some of Lew Fatt's silk?'

Luku and Opaki were over the moon with the way the big prau now handled. It was still rigged with its original big lateen sail as a mainsail and a slightly smaller one on the foremast but now also had two foresails running from a newly installed bow-spit up to the forward mast. One of them was a smaller jib which was instrumental in allowing them to sail close to the wind, while the other which had taken a lot of work from the Paji women, was a much larger genoa, which could generate incredible energy from the wind.

The final modification to the round-hulled prau was the installation of two larboards. These were big wooden plates fitted on swivels on each side of the vessel, each of which could be lowered into the water, depending on which tack they were on, to provide stability and steerage when close to the wind. William wondered what the reaction of the first Dutch ship that they met would be, for he had remembered about the larboards from pictures of old Dutch sailing vessels. Where before, the Paddy Wacker had been able to make perhaps six knots in a good breeze, it now made closer to ten or even twelve and they could now sail within two points of the wind, immeasurably closer than before.

The success of their modifications to the traditional rig made them all determined to do similar with the rest of their fleet. William cautioned them that once they were within sight of other vessels, or near to Wetar itself, all the new rigging and sails had to disappear. A big, almost comical figure head of sea nymph had been therefore made to fit onto the bow spit, disguising its real purpose and covers made to be thrown over the larboards. Their fleet's improved sailing capacity would be kept to their advantage for as long as possible.

To their disappointment, Wing Lew Fatt was not at his warehouse, having left weeks before to return to China to conduct his business. William still managed to purchase two large bolts of beautifully woven and dyed cloth that he knew would keep him in the good books with his wives, who he knew were intending to start up a cottage industry with the Paji women.

Luku and Opaki traded some of Rantuka's excellent ironware including excess knives and swords. Such was their quality that they only had to spend a few of the silver ingots and were able to load the Paddy Wacker with everything they were after, including good quality iron bars and, more importantly from William's perspective, bars of lead. As a bonus, William located an apothecary shop and, remembering Wuringa's plans for making his percussion caps, was able to purchase a glass flask of mercury.

Their departure was delayed by four days when a Macassan vessel came into Wetar. William didn't want them following them back to Damar, so he kept a low profile and Luku and Opaki made last minute purchases and trades for the sake of appearances and carried out maintenance on their vessel that didn't need doing at all.

The wooden dock was crowded on this visit and so they were tied up two vessels out, with a Sumatran vessel between them and the wharf. This proved fortunate when the Macassans became curious about their boat. The Paddy Wacker was the only vessel as big as their six-oar galleon and two of the Macassans came to stand on the dock, checking them out thoroughly.

William was in the forward cabin, out of sight when one of the Macassans called out. 'Hey! You in the big boat! Where are you from?'

Luku sauntered to the rail. 'Why do you want to know?'

The man sneered. 'Because you look like Adonara infidels; I thought we wiped you scum out!'

Luku looked to the side where Opaki held a crossbow just below the side rail, his expression dark with rage and eagerness to fire. Luku had to control his own temper as well. Too much was at stake to let their thirst for vengeance jeopardise their surviving community.

He forced himself to remain calm and called back. 'Where is that? We are from Timor!'

The Macassan looked suspiciously at him for a few moments and then slowly turned away. 'Are you indeed? Well then, have a nice trip home, won't you? Maybe we'll see you out there somewhere.'

William waited until they were out of sight and stood with Luku and Opaki. 'He knows.'

Luku nodded. 'He probably recognised our boat. I've no doubt that he was one of the murderers who raided us.'

William thought for a moment. 'We can't afford to let them find us on the way back. I wish now that we'd brought more crew but they need every hand back home.' He looked up at the descending sun and then at the state of the tide.

'How do you feel about a bit of night sailing?'

Luku brought the precious prismatic compass out of his belt pouch. 'With the stars and with this, I can sail us out of here on the blackest night in the middle of a storm if I need to!'

William looked again at the tide. It was almost at full tide and would begin to run out again in about two hours. The old wooden wharf was probably past its use by date but had the advantage of being in nice deep water. The fact that they were outboard of the Sumatran vessel made it even better. He looked up at the sky and was grateful to see a few clouds, which might help them by hiding the light of the moon.

'We'll leave with the last of the outgoing tide. I reckon that'll make it close to midnight and we should be able to slip away without those bastards noticing. Even if they do see us leave, there won't be enough water for them to chase us.'

The plan worked, but only to a degree. They quietly slipped free of the Sumatran vessel without even waking the crew on board. The outgoing tide caught them nicely and they drifted clear until they could run up the big lateen sail, which caught the light evening breeze and glided the Paddy Wacker silently through the still waters and towards the open sea.

They were almost clear of the bay when they heard urgent voices behind them, then shouts and the splashing of many oars.

William squeezed his eyes closed in frustration when he realised what the Macassans were doing. They were using canoes or ship's boats to pull the big galleon free of the sand and into deeper water, with the galleon's oars adding to their power. For a moment, he was hopeful that the Macassan plan wouldn't work, that they were too firmly aground but knew it was wishful thinking. The galleon had been on the outer edge of a group of moored vessels and he knew all too well that they were going to be pursuing them very soon.

They had one hope and that was to get their full complement of sails rigged and out so that they would have enough sail power to outdistance the oar-powered galleon. The bogus figurehead had been removed before they left and so Luku stayed on the tiller while William and Opaki urgently pulled out the jib and genoa, tying them on and then hoisting first the jib and then its big brother up to the foremast.

They could hear the sound of oars hitting the water at what ancient mariners would have considered ramming speed, and the Macassan galleon was clearly getting closer and closer.

Then, Paddy Wacker suddenly felt like a big old warhorse hitting the gallop as the wind caught the genoa. They went from two or three knots to close to ten in a matter of moments and William had to race to drop the portside larboard as their boat heeled dangerously on that side. They raced away in the darkness, sea spray covering the three of them as their wonderful big boat left the Macassans far in their wake, cries of frustration drifting faintly to them on the wind.

Daylight saw the Paddy Wacker clear of both land and pursuing Macassans. The winds had picked up as the day gradually became warmer and they had to take down the genoa. It was nice to be racing home at the boat's enhanced speed, but not worth blowing out the big sail or snapping the foremast.

Luku had spent an exhausting night on the big tiller and was grateful to be relieved by Opaki. Twice during the night he'd veered suddenly when his well-honed senses picked up the sound of shoaling waters, but his superb seamanship had seen them safely through the hazards and now on course for Damar.

William sat next to him as he worked the aches out of his shoulders from holding the tiller for so long. 'I don't want to be in a position where we have to run from those bastards again. When we get back, I'm going to work with Rantuka and see if we can't come up with some artillery for our fleet. It's obvious that they knew exactly who we were and I doubt they wanted to catch up with us for a social chat. Next time that happens, we're going to have a little surprise for them.'

Luku's eyes lit up. He remembered all too well the cannon that had killed his father and most of their crew. 'Artillery is cannon, yes? Oh I think I'm going to like that just fine!'

CHAPTER THIRTY-EIGHT

The rifle and the baby

They sailed into Damar around noon two days later and were dropping the stone anchor when William saw that only Mary was coming down to the beach to greet him. He immediately felt a sense of panic. He dropped over the side and went up to her; fear written all over his face.

'It's Cathy, isn't it? Is she alright? What's wrong? I shouldn't have gone away, should I? Is it bad? Mary please tell me!'

Mary had been standing and waiting for him to take a breath. Now she put a hand on his arm and gave him a smile of joy. 'She's fine, husband. She is sore and tired after a very long night, but now you should come to the house and meet your fine new son!'

William stared down at the tiny little creature in his arms with tears of wonder in his eyes. There were also tears, but of joy, in Cathy's eyes as she looked at her husband with their son.

'I want to call him William—William Charles,' she said tiredly. 'It's Mary's idea really, but I want to start a tradition of the first-born male of our line being named for you and the first born female named for me. One day, William and Cathy Wasley are going to walk up to my mum and dad in Darwin and introduce themselves.'

He was feeling choked with emotion. He looked down at his son through a filter of tears. 'Welcome to the world, William!'

William stayed with his wives until young William had been fed and was sound asleep, before heading off to see how Wuringa and Rantuka had been doing.

They were pleased with both the lead ingots and the flask of mercury that he gave them. 'Come and see our progress!' Rantuka invited him.

The smithy had made a special workbench just for this project, screened off from public view. He drew a curtain aside and there on the bench lay a row of conical shaped bullets. William picked one up and turned it around in his fingers. It was exactly like the drawing he'd done and, to the best of his memory, just like a real .303 bullet.

Rantuka grinned at the big man's obvious approval. 'I was just going to make them from lead but I have some antimony set aside so I've made them with an alloy of both. They are much harder than just lead and easier to work with. I have also made a tool to crimp the casings onto the bullet once we have filled them with powder and placed the caps in them.'

Wuringa jumped in. 'The mercury that you have brought me is wonderful because I have used up my supply, but look what I have!' He opened a small wooden box and carefully lifted out one of a dozen very small copper capsules, each an almost perfect match for the original primer caps. 'I've combined the mercury with nitric acid and ethyl alcohol. It is wonderfully explosive!' He handed one of the caps to Rantuka, who set it into a vice and then poised above it with a small hammer and tiny metal spike.

Rantuka placed the spike carefully in position and then

gave it a gentle tap with the hammer. A woman walking past the smithy gave a shriek of alarm as there was a sudden sharp crack as the little cap detonated, with a small flame burning briefly against the bottom of the vice.

The metal worker grinned. 'The first time I did that I nearly shit myself!'

Wuringa cackled at the success of the demonstration and then brought out a small wooden keg, opening the lid to reveal that it was completely filled with fine, black powder.

'I've seen the gunpowder that the Dutch use and always thought it was too course to be truly effective, so your proviso that it had to be fine was wonderful. I've mixed the sulphur, saltpetre and charcoal, then I've wet it and set it into cakes, then ground it to a powder, soaked it again but with alcohol this time. Then when it was once more dry I've ground it again but very, very fine. You should be able to get a really good bang out of this stuff!'

William was over the moon. 'When can we try them out?'

Rantuka shrugged. 'I can put together a dozen of your bullets by tomorrow and just need more caps from Wuringa to make more.'

Wuringa nodded. 'I'll get right onto them now that I've got more mercury.' He looked up at William. 'Don't forget though, we all get to have a go with the rifle!' He waited until William nodded his agreement and then added. 'And then you can tell the two of us all the wonderful secrets about yourself and your lovely blonde wife!'

William just stood and thought about it. The circle of insiders was getting bigger and bigger. 'I'll tell you what, finish off my ammo and we'll go for a little sail on Paddy

Wacker. Then maybe we'll have a little, very private chat. Fair enough?'

Wuringa reached out and shook his hand. 'We have a pact!'

William grinned ruefully. 'Yeah well, you're both going to have to earn it, because I have another project for the two of you after this one, and it's a doozy!'

He left them wondering just for the moment, for the next project he had in mind was potentially a complete game-changer.

Both Cathy and Mary were less than pleased at being left behind when William, Luku and Jimmy took Wuringa and Rantuka out on the Paddy Wacker the next afternoon. Opaki had been a little hurt to be informed that he had to stay ashore as well and at the last minute William made the decision to include the young Paji in their select group as well. This pleased Jimmy immensely as he and Opaki were very good friends and Opaki was a regular visitor to Jimmy and Manissa's home.

They sailed around to the uninhabited side of the island, dropping anchor about two hundred metres from the shore and then Jimmy and Opaki went ashore in a canoe and placed a dozen coconuts in a line along the beach before paddling back out eagerly to the Paddy Wacker.

William took the wooden box of cartridges and loaded three ammunition clips with rounds before inserting one of them down through the open breech and into the magazine.

He worked the bolt to send a round into the firing chamber and then looked around nervously. 'Shit, I'm as nervous as a new recruit back at Puckapunyal!'

The others just looked at him strangely, not a clue what he was talking about. He wound the sling around his left arm and then adjusted the rear sight to the distance, took off the safety catch and brought the old Lee Enfield up to his shoulder, sighting carefully. He hadn't used a .303 for many years but remembered its kick and so pulled it in hard to his shoulder as he sighted carefully on the left most coconut on the beach. He breathed in, let out half of a breath out and then slowly squeezed the trigger.

There was a very loud boom and white smoke billowed from the muzzle of the rifle. Everyone but him jumped about two feet into the air. William looked anxiously through the clearing smoke and with chagrin realised that his coconut still sat mockingly on the sand.

'Dammit, the sights must be out.' Was his lame excuse.

This time he used the high railing along the side of the vessel to steady his aim. Once more he slowly squeezed the trigger to the same loud boom, the same cloud of smoke and worst of all, the same mocking coconut. He could almost see it smiling back at him!

He adjusted the sights and took his time and the third shot was a treat. He grinned with elation to see his coconut lying about ten feet back on the sand, burst open like a ripe watermelon.

Jimmy, who had picked up some of William's more unfortunate phrases, summed up for everyone. 'Well, fuck my brown dog!'

Grinning like a kid with a new toy, William brought the rifle back up. Two more rapid shots followed, then he reloaded and fired three times more. Three more coconuts flew into the air with two near misses where he hadn't been able to see properly through the smoke.

He put a fresh clip of rounds into the rifle and handed the Lee Enfield to Jimmy. 'Have a go, buddy.'

Jimmy gingerly took the heavy rifle. William showed him how to hold it and warned him about the recoil, then worked the action for him. Jimmy aimed awkwardly as he'd seen William do and then suddenly closed his eyes and jerked hard on the trigger, despite William's instructions to squeeze it gently.

The Lee Enfield went off with its usual report. The bullet went high over the island and Jimmy suddenly flew backwards, shock on his face and the rifle flying through the air until William caught it.

Jimmy looked up in pain, rubbing his aching shoulder. 'That bloody thing tried to kill me!'

William couldn't stop laughing. 'Shit mate, I think you just set a new record for bad marksmanship. You just missed a whole bloody island!'

When he stopped laughing, William turned to Wuringa and Rantuka. 'You two are bloody geniuses! Well done!'

Wuringa looked longingly at the rifle. 'I would love to fire it but I think it would break every bone in my body!' He paused and thought for a moment. 'I think I know how to improve the gunpowder so that it doesn't smoke so much. Let me think about it.'

Opaki and Rantuka both fired the weapon and handed it back on both occasions with respect for William's marksmanship and gratitude that it was he would have to fire the shoulder bruising brute!

Afterwards, William sat with them and told them the entire story from the day that he and Cathy had met on Obiri Rock. Even Jimmy hadn't heard it all and not a word was spoken until he finished.

William let them digest all that he'd told them. Then, he looked from one to the other. 'Cathy and I would be in a lot of danger if you spread this about, but more than that, our whole community would also be endangered. I'm sure that we are going to have our share of enemies over the years— it comes with these times I guess—but I can promise you all that it will be ten times worse if people out there know that there are two people from the future on Damar.'

He paused before continuing. 'This rifle is going to be a big asset to us. It'll enable me to stop an enemy way before they can get to us and I've got other ideas that should make us too hard a nut to crack for anyone. We have to be smart about it though and maybe we'll have to be fairly ruthless at times too to protect our secrets. You were almost wiped out once but if we can keep our advantages to ourselves then I reckon that the Damarese will be a force to be reckoned with in years to come.'

Wuringa nodded soberly. 'I knew that you had secrets but I had no idea that they were this big! I see that you have thought this through though and you are quite correct. We must hide our advances and never use them to show how wonderful we are. Instead, if we are very sneaky and very lucky, we will build a society on Damar… and perhaps on other islands too, that will ensure our health, wealth and happiness.'

The community grows

Mary went into labour a week later. By her and Cathy's calculations, she was several weeks early and so everyone was worried. Cathy was thankfully on her feet by then and was able to assist the midwife who came in for the delivery. Mary had never known the meaning of pain until her contractions started. Holding her hand to comfort her, Cathy had to remind herself that Mary was probably still only about nineteen years old, which might have been older than when a lot of Aboriginal girls began to have children in these times, but it was still young!

William was a complete wreck as he waited outside with Jimmy, Luku and Opaki. Every time that Mary screamed, he would be on his feet, staring in anguish at the house until one of the others calmed him down all over again. He had wanted to be in the room for the delivery but one look at his shaking hands and white face had resulted in him being ordered from the delivery room.

Young William had come into the world after only a blessedly short two hours of labour but Mary took more than five hours and still the baby would not come. Wuringa finally came to the rescue, delivering a potion of his own design for Mary to sip on between contractions and finally, after almost seven hours, the babies came.

Afterwards a shell-shocked William recalled that twins tended to run in his family, with cousins who were twins and his own father a twin. The hindsight wasn't any help to him though when he walked into the bedroom to see two perfect little babies, a boy and a girl, nursing at Mary's breasts.

William thought that he must surely be the luckiest man alive as he was allowed to pick up the babies one at a time. Henry Goruku Wasley was a few minutes older than his sister Lillian Marinja, but both were perfectly healthy and equipped with very sound lungs when they began announcing their arrival to the community.

There had been several other births by this time. Their small community was growing and William was approached by a group of Paji including Wuringa and Rantuka not long after the twins were born, with a suggestion that it was time to formalise their community with a new Council.

William agreed immediately, realising that it was a move way overdue and he made it clear that all positions were to be open, including that of Council Chief. Having an election had occurred to him on a couple of occasions but they'd always seemed to have too much happening. Now there was a respite from their usual hectic rush to get things done and he convened a meeting in the room of the big house, The double doors had to be left open when almost every person in the community wanted to attend. He called for nominations and seconders for the Council and was humbled to be the first to be nominated by Luku, with a dozen people vying to be his seconder, no other nominations and then a universal show of hands to re-elect him as the Chief Councillor.

Both Cathy and Mary were nominated but declined. They had discussed the possibility of being nominated with William and both had told him that they didn't want it to appear that their family was dominating the new council. They justified their refusals by stating that they were too busy being new mothers as well as having several other projects that were occupying their time.

Six others were duly elected, including both Jimmy and his wife Manissa. She wasn't the only woman elected, as two others of the more astute and outspoken Paji women were also included. William liked the mix of genders in the new council. He was sure that it would make for some interesting meetings if Manissa or the other two ladies got worked up over an issue. Rantuka was also elected onto the council along with Wuringa, which pleased him even more.

William called the first session of the new council to order and said, 'Right, this place needs a name next. You people are the Paji from Adonara but now that we are here, perhaps it's time that we should put the past behind us. Rantuka has suggested that we should all think of ourselves as Damarese from now on. I think our home here needs a new name as well. I'm open to suggestions.'

There was silence for a moment and then someone from the back of the hall called out; 'This place fills me with hope! Call it 'Newhope''.'

There was silence for a moment as everyone digested the name and then grins started to appear and a buzz of conversation grew while the name was discussed. Finally, the Council endorsed the new name for their town and the community applauded and shouted their approval. William waited until the noise quietened down and then he gave them a vision of what he, along with not only Cathy and Mary, but Jimmy, Manissa, Luku, Wuringa and Rantuka had come up with for how they saw that their community should develop. Some of the ideas were quite radical to what the Paji were used to but in the debate that followed, almost all of the council and most of those listening in became enthusiastic at the model that William suggested.

It had been Cathy who remembered the concept of how a Jewish Kibbutz worked in Israel after that state had been established and had suggested it in their earlier brain storming sessions. They used this basic idea of community socialism and came up with their own, hopefully improved version.

Once he realised that there was general consensus for the model, William addressed them all. 'We will all be working for the common good. Every member of our community will be able to carry out their own trade and earn their own wealth, with all the help that the rest of us can provide. If Rantuka or Luku or Jimmy or myself makes a thousand coins of profit, then we will keep eight hundred of them but one hundred will go into the public coffers for community works and a further one hundred will go into our welfare chest. That will apply to everyone at the same ratio.'

He waited for that to sink in before continuing. 'We will never however, have the very rich and the very poor in our community.'

Jimmy spoke up. 'That's how it works in my tribe ... my old tribe. No one was ever hungry and everyone looked after everyone else.'

William gave him a nod at the reminder of how things

were always shared where he came from. He was continually amazed at how much Jimmy had developed since he'd met him and was rather proud at the thought that he was one of the ones responsible for that development. Of course the biggest influence by far was his new wife!

He continued. 'Our welfare chest will be used for anyone in hardship, too injured to work, too old or for any other legitimate reason that they can't support themselves.' This brought nods of approval from some of the older people in the crowd.

'I want to expand our fleet and to arm it. We will never again be at the mercy of the Macassans or anyone else. We will be a trading community and this will commence as soon as our fleet is ready, with another trip to the mainland for trepang and other goods. Everyone who comes with us will get an equal share of the profits.'

One man who William knew as Onguku—the leather worker—put up his hand. 'Rantuka, with his wonderful iron and steel will be able to earn much more than I can with my leather. Are you saying that if he earns a thousand coins, he has to put in two hundred of them, but if I earn a hundred coins then I only have to put in twenty?'

Rantuka answered 'Yes that is so, although I don't want you to take my two hundred and spend it on arak, Onguku!'

There was a wave of laughter at this, for the leather worker was well known to be partial to arak. He took the jibe good-naturedly and grinned ruefully as he sat back down.

'Are there any other questions?' William asked.

Olanna, one of the two females who had just been elected onto the council spoke up. She was a widow whose husband and one young son had been killed in the raid.

William knew that she had been a power-house during the move from Adonara and the construction of the fort. 'There are not many of us. How are we going to do all of these things that you say with so few people? I do not even see how we could fight off the Macassans as we are now.'

William nodded. 'Good point. The answer is that we probably don't have enough people here right now. What I propose is that we start looking for others who want to make a new start in life, who don't want to live under someone's thumb. I'll be surprised if there aren't a lot of people amongst these thousands of islands who'll jump at the chance to join a free, equal society.'

Olanna spoke up again. 'If you get Moslem people here then they will want us all to become Moslems like them. That is what made the Macassans attack us in the first place.'

This had been discussed at length beforehand and so Luku answered her. 'We agree. So at first, we are only going to allow people here who follow the old gods like we do, or the Christian God like William and Cathy do. We will also let the Hindu people and the Buddhist and the Jewish people join us, but no one, including ourselves will be allowed to try and push his or her religion on anyone else. Once we are really established, we will open our island to people of the Moslem faith also but only on the condition that they follow our rules.'

A new type of cannon

Work on re-rigging their fleet took several more weeks. By then, the monsoons were upon them with a vengeance and so the praus had to be drawn up on the beach until the weather abated.

William put the time to good use with the help of Rantuka and Wuringa. He was determined to have an offensive capability on the praus. He remembered seeing a documentary on an English vessel called 'Warrior', which, among a host of other maritime advances, had a revolutionary new type of cannon that had virtually made every other warship on the seas obsolete overnight.

With that in mind, he outlined the concept of a breach-loading rifled cannon to the two Paji, using the Lee Enfield as an example. 'What you needed to do is to make a bigger version of this. The rifling doesn't need to be this good and the breach can be more basic, as long as it seals tightly for firing.' He held up one of the .303 rounds. 'Use this as your template for the ammunition. Just make them bigger and obviously of the same size as the bore of the gun.'

Rantuka scratched his head. 'I've got plenty of copper and tin so I can make bronze casings but I could never make them as precise as these are.'

'They don't really need to be. We only need them to be a uniform size and strong enough to contain the charge when it goes off, so that the projectile flies out the other end. Then, as long as the barrel and breach are strong enough so that the whole thing doesn't blow up in our faces, we'll be laughing.'

That had been weeks ago and the two Paji had been locked away in Rantuka's shop ever since. William had only needed to make the occasional suggestion as the two geniuses worked long and dedicated hours. Now, the prototype gun was ready for testing.

The gun looked not unlike a small conventional cannon at first glance. It was mounted on a wooden carriage on wheels and wasn't all that impressive to look at. Only a round swivel base beneath it and a graduated slide beside it distinguished it from any other gun carriage. At only two inches at the mouth, it had a much smaller bore than a ship's cannon of the time, so to a casual observer it looked like a small signal gun that you might find on any man-of-war.

Rantuka had come up with a fairly simple breach mechanism that opened at the top on a thick hinge and then locked down into place with two clamps. Such was the quality of his steel work that the breach was almost impossible to see until it had been opened up. The rifling in the barrel had been his biggest problem and even though he managed to cast the barrel with a very rudimentary copy of the inside of the Lee Enfield, he had then had to spend many hours with long, hard wire brushes smoothing out all of the imperfections inside the metre and a half long barrel.

Wuringa's contributions had been significant. He had given Rantuka some minerals from his collection that had been used in the casting of the gun to make the steel harder and stronger. Then when Rantuka had completed twenty of the twenty millimetre shell casings, Wuringa's genius had really come to the fore. William had requested a projectile that would explode on impact with timber. His reasoning was that a solid projectile would just pass through most timber ships, leaving a hole and little other damage. With this in mind, Wuringa had designed a hollow shell head with two compartments. The larger compartment contained black powder and the much smaller, and slightly modified version of the mercury compound that he used in the primer caps for the .303 ammunition.

They went down to the beach in front of the fort for the big trial. Every person in Newhope lined the shore as they set the gun up at one end of the beach, while a big wooden target was erected at the far end, about four hundred metres away. William had no idea what sort of trajectory the shell would have—or its range—but figured that if they could hit an enemy at even fifty metres, they would still outrange any contemporary weapons. He needn't have been concerned.

Wuringa and Rantuka both insisted on being there during the firing of their creation so William had a sturdy wooden shelter built a few metres from the gun. He would have let one of them fire it for the first time, but if it blew up when they test fired, at least he hoped to save his two resident geniuses. William sighted on the far target, allowing for a slight drop over the distance and wound up the elevation just a fraction before opening the breach and loading in one of the shells. They had designed a simple spring -loaded trigger mechanism that would release a metal spike to strike the shell base.

Now, he cocked the striker back and took hold of the lanyard attached to the trigger. Every eye was on him as he checked the alignment of the barrel one last time and then pulled on the lanyard.

The weapon went off with a sound like ten of the .303 rounds at once. There was only a small cloud of white smoke, proof that Wuringa's improved black powder worked. When the smoke cleared, William looked down the beach at the target. It had been a hit, obviously striking the target, because the explosive shell had virtually disintegrated the entire timber structure.

Wuringa and Rantuka did a little dance of joy with each other, jumping around on the sand, while the whole crowd along the foreshore were laughing and shouting out their acclamations at the demonstration of their community's sudden new military strength. William was amazed at the gun's performance. He had fully expected the round to hit the sand somewhere along the beach before the target but not only had it flown true, it had hardly dropped in its trajectory. He wondered what the range of the gun was going to be.

With the new gun and the Lee Enfield, William was now confident of their ability to defend themselves at sea, and Rantuka and Wuringa could start work on a Mark II model for use in the fort. There was finally a break in the weather and so it was time to return to Australia for trepang.

CHAPTER FORTY-ONE

Allies

Both Cathy and Mary wanted to come on the voyage but both were realistic enough to know that it just wasn't practical. Not only did they have the three babies to care for that they were not prepared to hand off to nannies, but Cathy had commenced school classes where she was teaching anyone who was interested the 'three Rs'. All the children were attending and a number of the women.

She was also teaching English, so not only were her students learning to read and write. They were also learning to do so in her language as well as their own. Cathy was looking to the future and reasoned that if their community all learned English as a second language then they would be better placed in years to come. When Wuringa learned about the English lessons, he became her first adult male student.

She intended to add geography and history lessons in the future but was going to have to put a lot of thought into the curriculum for history. It wouldn't do to teach her students things that hadn't happened yet!

Mary assisted in the English lessons but was also working on her literacy skills and her quick mind soon made her Cathy's equal in arithmetic. Her handwriting quickly improved and it didn't surprise Cathy in the least when Mary picked up very basic algebra easily as well, which was as far as her knowledge of the subject extended to. Books of any kind would be on the shopping list when she next went to Wetar.

The two of them had also set up a cloth making industry. Olanna had made the suggestion that they should be able to increase cloth production dramatically if they organised it more. Cathy put her mind to the problem and soon realised that if one team loomed, one team spun, one team weaved and one team coloured and decorated, they should be able to set up a virtual production line. Using spinners and looms brought from Adonara and raw cotton that was found growing wild on the slopes on their mountain, production began. Dye was made from a variety of berries and from shellfish. The Paji women had been making their own cloth for many generations, so they remained the experts, but Cathy and Mary organised it in a way that meant they could make much more than they needed. It would be a valuable export for the future, just as would be the cloves, nutmeg, pepper trees, cocoa, cashews and coffee that were now being grown in small but expanding plantations.

They decided on taking Paddy Wacker and two smaller praus for the voyage, with a crew of ten for the bigger vessel and six for each of the others. He was tempted to stay behind with his wives and children but he quickly rid himself of the selfish thought. There were unknown challenges in returning to Australia, the Macassans and Asigi chief among them, and he was not about to delegate the journey to Luku or anyone else. A leader had to lead. He realised that it would leave the fort relatively undermanned while they were away but William was completely confident in their fortifications, along with the dozens of crossbows that Rantuka had made to keep everyone safe until they returned.

The night before they left was one that William would long remember, with both Cathy and Mary determined to exhaust him. Neither of the two women was shy in caressing each other as well as him during their lovemaking and seeing the two of them doing wickedly delightful things to each other drove him to heights of virility he never dreamed he was capable of. When he eventually got to sleep, it was with a tired but very happy smile on his face.

The north-westerly wind drove them towards Australia at a very good speed. The new sails on the smaller praus were even more effective than on Paddy Wacker, so they found that they had to have the canoes permanently deployed as outriggers during the voyage so that the fast little vessels didn't threaten to capsize with each tack. With all three vessels running down wind at around twelve knots, Luku stated confidently that nothing on the seas would be able to out sail them now.

They cleared Timor and turned south for the northern coast of Australia, still making good time, when they realised that they were fast catching up to two other praus headed in the same direction. The jibs and genoas came down immediately and all three praus quickly had figureheads fitted. They were now actually slower than the two in front of them for the outrigger canoes slowed them without the extra power of their foresails.

To their surprise, the other two praus half lowered their sails and only drifted along, obviously waiting for them to catch up to them. There were tense moments until Luku announced that he knew the two praus. They were not Macassan, but from Ambelu Island, a tiny island hundreds of miles North of Damar. Luku told them that he and his father had previously teamed up with them in trepang expeditions, sharing their resources and working harmoniously for months at a time. Most importantly, the people of Ambelu were all Buddhists and like the Paji, had resisted the onset of Islam.

Smiling faces awaited them as they drew closer. A short but well-muscled man in his thirties called out to them. 'Goruluku, you devil; only you would be cheeky enough to try and beat me to the trepang! Where is your father? Is he having a little nap while you do all the work?'

Luku felt a moment of sadness at the reminder of his father but called back. 'Lakabella, you rogue, don't tell me that I'm going to have to put up with you again this year!' He manoeuvred the Paddy Wacker alongside the small prau and they lashed the two vessels together. The seas were calm enough to do so safely and the man called Lakabella climbed aboard, followed by the captain of the second prau.

'Do you remember Sohoya? He was a crewman on my boat last year and now he is the captain!' said Lakabella.

Luku took the other's arm in a traditional greeting. 'It is good to see that you have prospered and advanced yourself, Sohoya.'

The man's face fell. 'It is only because half of our village was wiped out by Macassans. I am just the most qualified man left alive who can do the job.'

Luku looked from one to the other. 'I sense that fate has brought us together like this. We no longer live on Adonara, for we were also raided by those animals and almost wiped out. They also killed my father Goruku and most of the crew of our prau in the great southern mainland.

Lakabella spat over the side. 'I only live for the day that I can pay those Macassan bastards back with my sword!'

Jimmy had come aboard from another of their praus and introductions were made all around. The two Ambeluans looked with great curiosity at Jimmy and more particularly at William when he was introduced as the Chief Councillor of their island.

Luku then had a quiet conversation with William. 'I believe that these people would be a wonderful addition to Newhope. They are a good, honest and hard-working people. I trust them and do not believe they would betray us.'

William nodded. 'Well I certainly trust your judgement. Go for it.'

Luku went back to Lakabella and Sohoya. 'I have much to tell you. We have moved to Damar and are building a wonderful new community there. In the next months I will tell you all about it and then perhaps you might want to bring all of your people and join us.'

Lakabella looked soberly back at him. 'We knew that you were no longer on Adonara, for we called there on our way. I know that you will not be happy to hear it, but Damon now live where your village was. When we called there, all we found of your people were five rotting bodies hanging from trees.'

Listening in, William found it hard to feel pity for who those five would have been. Pelang had obviously failed in his attempt to appease the Damon. He only felt sorry for the four gullible dupes who had remained behind with him.

He noted as Lakabella looked at the new cannon which was mounted near the prow on its carriage, its small barrel clearing the front of the prau by inches. 'I will particularly look forward to hearing about this funny little cannon that you have here.' He said to Luku.

Luku laughed. 'When you see what this gun will do to the first Macassans that we meet, you will not think it is so funny!'

They cast off from each other and set their sails again. So as not to out-distance their new companions, the Damar vessels left their foresails in their bags, although the bogus figureheads were all removed in case the improved sails were needed quickly, much to the puzzlement of the Ambeluans. This was the longest leg of the trip south and entailed staying at sea overnight. The lanterns of the other vessels were a comfort to them all as they crossed the Arafura Sea in darkness.

With the aid of the stars and the compass, Luku led them unerringly to Darwin Harbour and they all beached at Fannie Bay and set up camp. That night, they sat around a big campfire. Including the new additions to their company, there were now thirty-four of them. Old friendships were renewed among the crews and both Lakabella and Sohoya listened with great interest as Luku and William told them all about their home on Damar.

When the tale had been told, Lakabella was quiet for a long moment and then looked at Luku. 'You said earlier that the fates brought us together at this time. I think you are correct. We follow the teachings of Amida Buddha, who tells us never to harm another living thing. We try to live by his teachings but now we know that we cannot turn the other cheek to these Macassans or we will cease to exist.'

He glanced at Sohoya, who nodded in encouragement. 'You seem to have a plan for the future, a wonderful plan, and when we return home I will encourage my people to join with yours.'

Early the next morning, they sailed to Mica Beach and set up their smoke huts and cauldrons. Both groups had favourite grounds for harvesting trepang and it quickly became a contest between them to see who would bring back the greatest haul each day. The cauldrons were constantly on the boil and the smoke houses burned through tons of wood in the weeks and months that followed.

Jimmy ecstatically swapped his sarong for a loincloth and took a team to hunt for turtles, while others sought out sandalwood, pine and ironwood. Opaki took three other divers and began to amass a good haul of pearls and pearl shell. They worked from sunrise to sunset, day after day. Only monsoonal storms gave then respite from their labours but slowly and steadily the holds in all the praus became full.

William had been alert every day for any sign of Asigi, half expecting another attack at any time. It was during one of their respites during a period of heavy rain when William and Jimmy crossed over to East Point that they received news of the magic man.

Their old camp at East Point was virtually the same as they had left it, with their rough driftwood furniture still there, untouched so far by white ants. Jimmy was paying homage at Junie's grave when Gullaway and a small group of Larrakeyah walked into their camp. The old Larrakeyah chief still proudly wore his Rolex around his neck and embraced the two of them with gusto. William returned the hug, trying not to react to Gullaway's striking body odour. He apparently still hadn't bathed since the last time they'd met.

A fire was lit and a wallaby haunch miraculously appeared and was thrown into the coals. William had become accustomed to spicy Paji cuisine since moving to Damar but the plain, unadorned taste of wallaby on coals brought back happy memories to him.

During the evening, the subject of Asigi inevitably came up. Gullaway brightened immediately. 'He is bad fella now. Asigi took boat people to bush tribe—the Worrigee mob. Those boat people kill lots of Worrigee and take young people with them back to their boats, but Asigi was seen with them. Now Asigi is outcast and other Kadijah say his magic is no good. If we see Asigi now, we will kill him dead!'

'Has he been seen since?'

Gullaway shrugged. 'Maybe, maybe not; some people say that Asigi go away on boat with boat people. We hunt him but have not found him so maybe they are right.'

William considered the information. If Asigi had come back here but then returned to the Indonesian islands, then Cathy and young William were once again in danger—not to mention anyone else who might get in their way—and yet, he still had faith in the fortifications they had built.

Talk turned to trade and Gullaway proved very amenable to his people hunting turtle in return for steel knives and axes. The Larrakeyah were skilful hands with their big, heavy dugout canoes and arrangements were made for deliveries over to Mica Beach.

Two weeks later, they arrived with a huge amount of turtle shell. William made a mental note to limit the amount that they harvested in subsequent years. He most definitely did not want to contribute to endangering the species for the future. As it was, the praus were all now fully loaded. Even the Paddy Wacker was sitting low in the water and all outriggers were set for the trip to Wetar.

Lakabella and Sohoya had by now been introduced to the new sail configuration and with their marine savvy minds, were immediately sold on the innovation to their praus. As a precaution against having sails blown out by wind gusts, Paddy Wacker carried sufficient spare sailcloth to equip the two Ambelu praus and there had been plenty of time for their crews to learn how to properly use them.

The north-westerlies had abated and the south-easterly winds replaced them. It was time to head home.

CHAPTER FORTY-TWO

A battle at sea

They all saw the wisdom of returning in convoy, with the slowest, the Paddy Wacker, in the van. The first leg to Timor was uneventful and they were anticipating their arrival in Wetar when they were ambushed by the Macassans. With five vessels they had thought themselves to be too big a group to tackle, even for the Macassans, but it soon became apparent that the Moslem pirates were becoming much more aggressive.

Three big oared galleons and another four-sail powered praus came from behind Alor Island and caught them neatly with the wind at their backs as they attacked. It was obvious that they had been lying in wait for trepang-laden boats coming north to ambush and to relieve them of their cargoes. They had probably done the same thing many times before and had undoubtedly taken untold wealth in stolen goods as well as killing a lot of innocent seafarers in the process. It was extremely unlikely however, that they had ever before had their prey turn into the wind and set course directly towards them.

Both Lakabella and Sohoya had been initially shocked at the tactics that William had proposed in the event that they were attacked. It had only been an explanation of the capabilities of the cannon—and with the production of the dozen cross bows and the two long bows on board their vessels—that they felt confident enough agree to fight and not flee if attacked.

The Macassan.

The chief of the Macassan fleet was a man by the name of Waiwera. He was a very rich, utterly merciless Macassan with more than a hundred fighters in his fleet. He had been preying on the 'little islanders' as he called them, for years and had grown stronger and richer with each raiding season.

He watched with momentary confusion as the infidels turn towards, and not away from them. He shrugged. Their strange sails and the fact that they could sail so close to the wind was perplexing but he wasn't unduly perturbed by such things. Perhaps they saw the inevitable futility of fleeing from them and were coming to surrender.

He laughed at the thought. Surrender might shorten their suffering but not change the ultimate result. They were all dead men and their little fleet was his!

William

William opened fire at what he estimated to be five hundred metres. After Rantuka and Wuringa, he was the most knowledgeable with the new cannon and elected to be the one to fire it. The pitching motion of the Paddy Wacker caused his first shot to go way over the head of the leading galleon and the second to plunge into the sea just in front of the vessel. With his third shell though, he waited until the Paddy Wacker was just cresting a wave before pulling the lanyard.

The galleon was still more than four hundred metres distant and to the Macassan vessels around it, it must have seemed like something on board had suddenly exploded. The shell struck the big galleon right at the prow. The shell that Wuringa had invented, detonated on impact and the resultant explosion disintegrated the entire front of the galleon.

He could imagine the dismay of the other Macassans. To them the galleon would have seemed to nose dive straight down into the ocean in front of them.

Soon, only timber and a couple of floundering survivors were seen where the war galleon had been only moments before.

William reloaded another shell into the breach block and sighted on the big galleon slightly behind it. He wasn't particularly proud of the way that he felt at the moment, as he knew that he was committing cold murder. The Macassans didn't have a prayer against his cannon but they had decided their own fate when they attacked. He knew with a cold and utter certainty that none of this enemy could be allowed to survive to spread the word of their new capabilities.

The next shell hit mid-ships of the turning vessel and this time there was a huge fire. Perhaps where the shell had struck, there were inflammables on board the boat, but the result was the same.

The final galleon immediately backed off but the four smaller praus pressed their attack. The cannon sank two more before they closed and then he picked up the Lee Enfield when it was too close to use their main armament. Then the Macassans learnt what a .303 could do at less than a hundred metres. Four helmsmen died in six shots and then three more clips of .303 decimated the remaining crews.

Long bows and cross bows then sent a shower of death onto the survivors until the praus were all adrift, empty of living crew.

The last galleon was fleeing; the unfortunate slaves at the oars lashed mercilessly as Waiwera looked back in terror at his worst nightmare come true. A gasp of shock escaped his throat as he realised that the biggest prau had turned into the wind again and was heeling sharply as it began to pursue him. His eight oarsmen were almost exhausted already but the oar-master beat them unmercifully to get more out of them.

It was in vain and Waiwera looked on in panic as the strangely rigged prau closed relentlessly on him.

William saw a big cannon being hurriedly manhandled to the stern of the galleon by four Macassans. He didn't want to use his own big gun but equally didn't want the bloody great cannon firing back at them either.

He brought up the Lee Enfield and fired twice in quick succession. Two of the Macassans dropped dead to the deck and the barrel of the cannon fell with them; the remaining two crewmen appeared to instantly lose interest in the relocating the cannon.

Now Luku brought the Paddy Wacker alongside and cross bows zipped through the air from both directions. The Lee Enfield roared four more times with four more dead the result. Then, a grappling hook drew the vessels together and William dropped the Lee Enfield and took up his sword as they boarded the galleon. As he followed Luku aboard the enemy craft, he reflected briefly that he would have never thought in a million years that one day he would be leaping onto a pirate ship with a sword in hand and yet now he was, followed by another five of the Paji, all intent on vengeance.

The inexplicable loss of their whole fleet and then the devastating toll that the booming rifle had inflicted on them had clearly taken the heart out of the Macassans. Eight exhausted galleon slaves were still chained to their oars and looked on, but only seven Macassans were still on their feet and, even though they slightly outnumbered the Paji, they still held their ground.

William rushed them. He discovered that his martial arts training had provided just the skills he now needed and his sword was a blur as it knocked aside a Macassan's sword and then ripped across his throat. Luku and another Paji were still firing their cross bows, while Jimmy let loose three more arrows with great effect.

Soon, only the Macassan captain was still on his feet, but instead of continuing to fight, he dropped the sword to the deck and held his hands out in submission.

'Please; have mercy!' he cried.

William only hesitated for a moment. This man would have wiped their whole fleet out if he could have, and in any case, there could be no survivors. He lunged forward with the sword and took the Macassan through the throat. A spray of blood fountained out and he dropped to the deck.

William was still staring down at him when he realised that two of their praus had by now drawn alongside. Their assistance was no longer required but when Lakabella boarded a few minutes later he let out a cry of joy. The eight galleon slaves, all locked into the rowing benches, took one look at him and they were suddenly laughing and crying just as much as he was.

He looked at William. 'These are my people. They were captured when we were raided and I never thought I'd see them again!'

William was at a loss of what to do with the galleon. The captains from Newhope and their new allies realised that the captured praus were an easy decision—they would add to the Damar fleet. But they had no use for a big lumbering galleon that needed eight oarsmen to make it half-way practical to sail.

William went into the big cabin at the stern. It clearly belonged to the recently deceased captain. His eyes fell with interest on several charts. He unrolled one and found it to be much more comprehensive than Luku's. He rolled them up to take them with them and then spotted a chest that was wedged under the bed along one wall. It was locked but his thick sword blade easily convinced it to open. His face lit up with a big grin. The chest was filled to the brim with coins!

He closed the lid and searched the rest of the cabin. The only other item of interest was a sword. It was twice the length of the short swords used by the islanders and clearly of European manufacture. The word 'Toledo' was inscribed near the hilt and William drew the blade fully out of the scabbard. The sword was perfectly balanced and a thing of beauty. He had a new sword.

He carried the charts, chest and sword up to the others and opened the chest to show the gleaming gold and silver coins that completely filled it.

'It looks like this trip is in profit already!'

The triumphant crews from the two praus, crowded around to examine the coins. There was a good amount of Chinese sycee, as well as large silver coins, marked *stuiver* with different amounts from twelve to forty-eight and others marked '8 real', with the word *Espan* stamped into them. The gold coins looked to be roughly made in comparison to the silver ones but had a lovely weight. They were marked with a thick cross and the word *doblon*. William stared at the coins. He realised that he was looking at 'pieces of 8' and 'gold doubloons'. He remembered stories of his childhood of Treasure Island and Blackbeard the Pirate. This was the stuff of so many stories from his own childhood and now he had a whole chest of them!

All present discussed the galleon and no one saw any use in keeping it. The galleons were only used by Macassans and possessing one could only be interpreted in one way. It had to go. About half a ton of trepang and any useful items and equipment, including the cannon and all of the weapons were removed and then a pair of axemen went down to the bilges. They scampered back onto the Paddy Wacker ten minutes later, their feet wet as the big galleon settled rapidly into the sea. It was gone within minutes.

The big prau was now sitting very low in the water with the extra weight, and William hoped that they didn't hit any rough weather or they could be in trouble. The cannon went into the bilges for safe keeping until they returned to Damar. William was sure that Rantuka would be able to put all of the lovely bronze to good use.

Their four new praus went with skeleton crews back to Newhope. Lakabella watched them go from on board the big prau and then glanced at William.

'I cannot say that the violence that I have seen today does not go against the tenets of my faith and yet I know that it had to be done. I never imagined that the Macassans could be defeated so easily. With your weapons, you could control this whole region!'

William shook his head. 'That's the last thing that I want to do. These Macassans had to all die so that our secrets remain just that—our secrets, but we only keep them so that we can be strong to live in security and without fear. We are not and will never be interested in conquering or subjugating anyone else. We just want to be left in peace.'

Lakabella looked at him for a moment and then smiled. 'That is what I hoped you would say. When I return home, I will be arguing very strongly to unite our people with yours. Then those four praus will come in very handy when we move to Damar!'

CHAPTER FORTY-THREE

Successful trading

They made Wetar three days later and their arrival caused a stir. Luku glided the Paddy Wacker alongside the wharf and William saw three separate parties of silk-clad Chinese waiting there. He smiled when he saw Wing Lew Fatt, and when he stepped off the prau, he went straight up to him.

Much to the consternation of the other parties of Chinese, Lew Fatt greeted him like a long-lost son. 'Ah, my mysterious Englishman. I see that you have found new vessels, and all of them sitting so wonderfully low in the water!' The others joined them and he waved the way to his warehouse. 'Come, let us get more comfortable and we can talk with a little more privacy.'

Including Lakabella and Sohoya, there were ten in Lew Fatt's office on this occasion. The Chinaman waited until tea had been served and the sighed. 'You have no idea how happy I am to see you with praus presumably full of cargo. We have only had three praus come in this season and they were all Macassans. My warehouse is almost empty and we have heard that all of the praus are being taken by pirates. I was beginning to despair of getting any trepang this year!'

William offered a slight smile. 'I don't think that's going to be a problem for a while. Those particular pirates have… gone elsewhere.'

Lew Fatt had fully noted that William was no longer deferring to Luku. The big white man was now clearly in charge and it was also clear that the Paji captain was perfectly happy with the situation.

'Is that so? Can I take it that these Macassans are unlikely to return from this "elsewhere"?'

'You can most certainly take it that way.' William answered.

Lew Fatt fingered his moustache. 'Ah... that is very interesting to hear.' He called out and a much younger Chinese man came in. Lew Fatt had a rapid conversation with him in Mandarin and then turned back to William as the man left. 'That is my most worthy eldest son. I now trust him to assess your cargoes if that is agreeable to you.'

William smiled again. 'He'd best take lots of assistants with him because there is a lot to assess!'

Lew Fatt rang a small bell and food and more tea was brought in for everyone. It was several hours before the son returned and handed a slate board filled with characters to his father, along with a few brief words in Mandarin. The Chinese merchant looked down at the rows of writing with a look of consternation. Then he began working his abacus and after about ten minutes he took on a pained look before looking up at William.

'You have too much for me to handle by myself. Please return tomorrow while I discuss with one of my colleagues the sharing of your bountiful cargoes. I believe that I can achieve a satisfactory price for you by sending some of your trepang to my homeport and some with my colleague to his. This will avoid flooding the market and driving down the value of your trepang. I will of course take the remainder of your cargo myself. You have been very busy this year!'

William and the others nodded. 'Fine, we'll see you in the morning then.'

Lew Fatt looked at William with a measured look. 'One of the Macassan praus that called in here was a big galleon. My son tells me that the cannon from that vessel now rests in your bilge. Now I am sure that I will never see those particular Macassans again!'

William was sure that the sharp-eyed son would have seen their cannon as well as the Macassan one. He wondered what the Chinaman would make of it. He pulled out a bag of pearls from his jacket and handed them over as well.

'Like I said, those particular pirates are no longer going to be a problem.'

Lew Fatt nodded knowingly and then peeked into the bag of pearls and grinned. 'I knew that we were going to be wonderful friends!'

They left a week later with all of their vessels loaded with a huge assortment of goods including the entire stock from three metal merchants that now sat with the cannon in the bilges of the Paddy Wacker. Lakabella and Sohoya left with an agreeable share of the Chinese silver ingots and assured them that they would be seeing them again very soon. The balance of what Lew Fatt had paid them, along with the chest of coins from the Macassan meant that their little community was suddenly very wealthy.

They had one scare on the way home when a very big ship appeared on the horizon and began to come their way. It was utterly unlike any prau, with big square sails that were visible even at that distance. William assumed that it was a Dutch East Indiaman and knew enough about the aggressive Dutch of the seventeenth century to know that they wanted to steer well clear of them on the high seas.

Some of Cathy's earlier subjects in her history degree, before she'd settled on Australian history as the focus for her degree, had been general European history. It had been too broad a subject to her mind and she had opted to concentrate on what had happened in Australia. Her parents however, had a very thorough knowledge of European history, which she had absorbed in her younger years, so she still remembered most of the highlights and many of the dates from those times. Now Cathy reminded him of some of the politics of the times that they were in. Oliver Cromwell and his Roundheads had deposed and subsequently decapitated Charles I about thirty years before and had just about handed power back to his son Charles II. Cathy recalled that with an ineffectual Charles II in power, a Dutch fleet had sailed right up the Thames and had bombarded the depleted English fleet before towing half of it back to Holland.

They were unlikely to get too friendly a reception from a Dutch vessel and even with their innovative gun, William would hardly take on a European ship with multiple cannons on board. Rantuka's cannon would no doubt outrange any gun that the Dutch had but if they managed to get close enough, they would be in real trouble. They turned down wind and to their relief the big genoas pulled their fleet beyond sight of the Dutchman.

As they pulled into the bay at Damar a day later, it was gratifying to see that the four new praus had already been fitted with bowsprits in preparation for their new sails. William and Luku had already discussed a couple of other innovations for all of their present fleet as well as working on plans to start their own ship building yard right there on Damar.

With their new-found wealth, it was time to invest more heavily in their future and the smaller praus—and even the Paddy Wacker—were not going to be sufficient if they were going to become the financial powerhouse that William envisaged that their community could one day become.

CHAPTER FORTY-FOUR

New arrivals

William received a wonderful welcome from Cathy and Mary and spent much of the first two days with his three children in his arms. They were beautiful, chubby and happy babies who stared up wonderingly at the huge man who held them so lovingly while making inane sounds.

No one had been idle in the past couple of months, with the school going really well, fine cotton being produced by the ladies' cooperative and the first crop of pepper and cloves already harvested and ready for sale.

Rantuka and Wuringa led him smilingly to their newest creation and pulled off the canvas cover with a flourish. As successful as Mark 1 had been, it had one serious drawback in its recoil, with the need to drag it back into position and re-sight after each shot. It still had four times the rate of fire of any contemporary cannon but Rantuka had come up with the idea of making springs for a recoil dampening mechanism.

Once again, the man's genius had come through. William looked down at the squat weapon and saw immediately where Rantuka had forged two large springs and four smaller ones, sitting alongside the breach mechanism on each side. He had also modified his breach block to open and lock down more easily.

Rantuka grinned as he saw William's eyes roving lovingly over the weapon. 'I hope that you have brought me a lot of lovely iron because I've used up all of mine making this.'

William ran his hands over the cannon. It was a thing of stark beauty and reminded him of a smaller version of a twentieth century Bofors gun or even a recoilless rifle. 'Have you test fired it yet?'

Wuringa gave a big smile. 'Of course! I sent a shell so far out into the harbour that we could only just see the splash!'

They hadn't finished offloading the fleet yet and Rantuka's metal was right on the bottom so it would be the last to come off.

'Mate, you're going to wet yourself when you see how much I've got for you. Not just iron too; I've got copper, lead, antimony and even some blue stuff that the bloke on Wetar swears is good for hardening iron.'

Rantuka laughed. 'It's probably clay! The next time you go to buy metal, I'm coming with you!'

William shrugged. 'Well he did look pretty happy to offload it to me.' Then he had a thought and grinned. 'You're going to love the bloody great bronze cannon I've got for you though!'

Wuringa became thoughtful at the mention of the cannon and then, he looked up. 'Didn't you say that you wanted to keep our weapons a secret?'

'Sure,' William replied. 'I don't want to start a bloody arms race around here. It's one thing us having them, but if this technology becomes common knowledge then history will get turned on its head, with automatic weapons and artillery pieces way before their time. We're going to have to protect our advances from anyone else at all costs.'

Wuringa nodded. 'That is what I was thinking also. So why don't you put this bronze cannon up here on the wall? If we have to fire at someone then we can let them think it is that cannon that is firing at them.'

Rantuka chuckled. 'I don't really need the bronze and I think it is a good idea. I can even get Teronga to make me a big fancy carriage for the gun so that it will look more impressive than it really is. If we get any strangers here then we can conceal our real weapons and let them see something they'd expect us to have.'

William grinned at them. 'You two are devious buggers... I love it! We'll take Mark One back off the Paddy Wacker and bring it up here as well. We might as well have double the firepower if we need it and then we can put this one back on the boat when we leave again.'

Two days later, Lakabella sailed into their bay. He had with him, aside from a crew of four, two older men and one old woman and introduced them as the three surviving members of the Ambelu Council. The three gave a traditional Buddhist greeting with their hands high in front of their faces as they bowed.

The oldest was a dignified old man by the name of Darellu with his brother in law Bingellu and his wife Castaja. All three looked up in surprise and curiosity at the high walls of the fort.

'We have talked at length about coming here. Most of our village thinks it is a good idea but want Darellu, Bingellu and Castaja to see for themselves before we decide. I am also very curious.' said Lakabella.

William respectfully shook the hands of each in turn.

'You are welcome. Come into Newhope and we'll show you around.'

A second toilet block had been added since he'd left and, at Cathy's instigation, this new one included enclosed showers. No one had ever heard of such a thing of course but it had very quickly become extremely popular, with line-ups both morning and night to use the showers.

The three visiting elders looked through the toilet block and said little. They were shown where everyone collected their water, given a tour of a couple of homes and then the big house and still only talked among themselves.

Then, they were given a tour of the fortification itself, walking along the walkways between the sentry towers and then taking note of the big brass cannon that now sat on a huge, elevated gun carriage overlooking the bay. Their two real guns were concealed under canvas at opposite ends of the wall.

At the end of the tour, they all sat in the meeting hall of the big house with Newhope's Council. At last, Darellu addressed them. 'You have built a wonderful thing here for your people. I see that you are protected against the predators and you have wonderful ideas such as the place you go to shit and then wash.'

William grinned at the old man's turn of phrase but waited for him to finish.

'Your houses are strange but I can see that people could live in them in comfort,' the old man said. Now he looked directly at William with his rheumy eyes. 'I want to know why you would let us come here to live with you.'

The other two elders nodded, waiting for his answer. He knew that his answer had to be completely truthful. He dearly wanted the Ambeluns to add to their community but had enough respect for the council elders not to give them a convenient or trite answer. 'We would welcome you because Luku and others say that you are good people and I feel that you would accept the new ways that we are offering. We would welcome you because we are few and need more people who think the way that we do, to be truly strong as we build a future.'

William put an arm around his wife. 'And we would welcome you because enough people have suffered from the Macassans and here you would never have to fear from them again.'

Darellu looked from one to the other. Then, tears suddenly came to his eyes. 'It is done then; my people will come.'

Afterwards, Cathy asked Lakabella the reason for Darellu's tears.

'Darellu has already said that he will not leave his home. He will stay to be buried with his wife. Bingellu and Castaja will also stay, so they know that by this decision they are sending their people and loved ones away from them.'

CHAPTER FORTY-FIVE

The Dutch East India Company

Six praus, including the Paddy Wacker, went back to Ambelu. William opted to stay to spend time with his wives and children. Little William was by now trying very hard to walk and his half-brother and sister followed his efforts with great interest to see if it was an activity worth pursuing.

Henry and Lillian were of a slightly darker complexion than their blonde haired and blue eyed brother and yet the three of them were inseparable. If one laughed, they all laughed; if one cried there was a cacophony of noise; and as William soon found out when he was left to look after his children, they all did other less pleasant things at the same time as well! It was a wonderful interlude of family time and peace. Nights with Cathy and Mary were such that William found himself smiling during the day just thinking about the night before, which inevitably led to the next night being just as interesting.

The peaceful hiatus was too good to last of course and one day, when they were expecting the fleet to come back from Ambelu, they had a much bigger visitor instead. It was a Dutch East Indiaman, probably the same one that they had seen on their way back from Wetar. The lookout on the bluff had given Newhope good warning of its approach and everyone came inside the fort, the remaining praus drawn up onto the beach and the gates shut.

William watched it drop anchor in the middle of the bay, a big orange, white and blue flag flying from the stern and a flag with a big red lion on a background of yellow tied to the foremast. To William's eye, the ship was ungainly and ugly despite the ornate woodwork that adorned the upper works of the hull. It had a very high prow and stern with semi-enclosed areas at each end. The middle of the ship was much lower. He guessed that it was around sixty metres long and probably ten or so metres wide. Two big mainmasts supported large and smaller cross trees, with a much smaller third mast back at the stern.

Most ominous to him were the nine gun-ports along the side facing the fort and he could make out four more at the stern and two up forward. If there were an equal number of guns along the port side, that meant that the ship carried twenty-four guns. So far, there were no guns run out but he had no doubt that it wouldn't take them long to do so. Hundreds of seamen swarmed around the vessel as a ship's boat was lowered to the water and then an elaborately dressed officer stepped from a ladder into the boat and it was rowed ashore.

The big rowboat ran onto the sand then a dozen armed marines formed a protective screen before the officer stepped onto the beach. William had a good look at the arms that the men were carrying. They looked to be matchlock muskets, hopeless compared to the Lee Enfield but still capable of throwing a big ball of lead very fast. The officer was armed only with a sword.

William waited above the main gate in one of the towers along with Wuringa. He had on his new Toledo sword as well as his best clothing of ornate sarong, waist coat and boots. All along the ramparts of the wall, men and women crouched with crossbows ready, while Cathy, Mary and Jimmy had their long bows at hand, as did he. The Lee Enfield was in its bag at his feet but William dearly didn't want to have to use it.

He watched as the Dutch shore party drew up into two neat ranks and then marched with the officer in the lead towards him. He wasn't about to just open the gate and invite him in so he waited until they came to a halt in front of the gate and called down.

'Can I help you gentlemen?'

The officer looked up with surprise to be addressed by a white man where he expected natives. He called something out in Dutch but William didn't understand a word aside from 'Englander'.

Wuringa translated. 'He wants to know what an Englishman is doing on a Dutch island.'

William doubted that even a 17th Century English person would understand much of his twenty-first century English—or the other way around—but obviously some of the words sounded English enough to the officer.

'Tell him that this is a privately-owned island and belongs to no country.'

Wuringa replied and then gave William the man's reply. 'He says that all of these islands belong to the VOC and that we are trespassing.'

William laughed. 'Bullshit! The Dutch East India Company had trading rights to the East Indies but only have territorial claim to Jakarta... or rather Batavia as it's now called. Tell him… no bugger it, I'm going down to talk to him. You up for it?'

William knew that he was taking a big chance by opening the gate but was gambling on the fact that the officer would be 'a gentleman' who might respond to him if he acted like one as well. Yelling back and forth from the wall wasn't the way to go about it. Just to be on the safe side, he quietly told everyone to be ready with the bows and cross-bows if they tried to force their way inside. Even a dozen Dutch marines wouldn't last long against a dozen crossbows and three long bows fired from almost point-blank range.

He waved cheerily to the officer and then pantomimed coming down to talk to him. The big door creaked open just enough to let him out, followed by Wuringa.

He walked up to the man and made a short bow, as he assumed people did in these times and then held out his hand. 'Hello there! I am William Wasley. And you are?'

The man just stared at him for a moment, taking in his beautifully decorated pure silk vest and sarong and then resting his eyes for a moment on the Toledo sword hanging at his waist. He measured William for a moment and then suddenly smiled and shook his hand. 'Willem Van Der Veldt Mynheer!' Then, in broken English, he added. 'At you service sir!'

William laughed with delight. 'Two Williams!'

The officer said something in Dutch, which Wuringa translated. 'He says that the Stadholder in the Netherlands is also named William. He also asks if we are going to stand in the sun all day or are you going to invite him inside our fort.'

It was a hot day and William could see that the officer

and all of the marines were suffering in their hot uniforms. 'Tell my friend Willem that of course he is invited inside and that we will bring shade and cool drink out for his men.'

The Dutchman smiled, recognising the ploy to keep his men out of the fort. He bowed graciously and snapped an order to a midshipman standing behind him.

Paji women carried out rattan shelters and coconut juice cooled in the stream that ran into their fort to the waiting marines and sailors, while the Dutch officer walked with William to the big house.

His eyes were constantly moving as they walked along. William smiled when the man looked back and upwards, his eyes lingering on the big brass cannon pointed at his ship. Part of the ruse with the cannon was the high pile of black painted coconuts sitting beside it. From a distance they looked convincingly like big, dangerous cannon balls.

The Dutchman took in the first-class workmanship that Teronga and Lemala had put into building the big house. They sat in comfortable and richly cushioned chairs used for the council meetings and Cathy brought out one of the bottles of Madeira that William had purchased on Wetar.

William introduced Cathy to the officer and the man was instantly enchanted by her blonde beauty and lovely smile. He leapt to his feet and bowed low as he kissed her hand, with an elaborate burst of Dutch that Wuringa translated.

'Lieutenant Van Der Veldt is entranced to meet such a vision of loveliness so far from civilisation and swears that he is forever your servant.'

Cathy had little experience with such elaborate manners but pictured in her mind Vivien Leigh in *Gone with the Wind*, another of her favourite old movies. 'Well I declare! Please tell this charming gentleman how pleasant it is to meet someone so sophisticated and genteel.' She even managed a southern accent.

William was struggling to keep a straight face but knew that there was vital business to discuss. He looked at Wuringa. 'Please inform Lieutenant Van Der Veldt that while we consider this to be a privately owned island, we will be more than happy to trade our spices with the VOC at very favourable terms.'

The VOC Officer's ears pricked up at the two magic words, 'trade' and 'spices'. He waited until Wuringa had translated and then tried to look serious and even threatening when he replied.

Wuringa listened for a moment and then turned to William and Cathy. 'The Lieutenant says that while it might be possible to conduct trade with us. He demands an assurance that you have not claimed this island for England. He says that if you have, then he would have to inform his captain, who would consider it an act of war and would then attack this fort.'

There was no need for subterfuge in his reply and William held his hand over his heart, looking the man straight in the eye. 'I give you my word that this will never be English Territory!' He wasn't lying either; after all, he wasn't about to give anything away to the bloody Poms!

Mary then came in. She had recognised the smoothly diplomatic way that William and Cathy were handling the Dutch officer and heard her cue when trade was mentioned. She carried in a large woven basket filled to the brim with peppercorns and handed them to her husband with a quiet word. 'Give him a present of these. I think he will be a happy man then!'

William looked with gratitude at her and was about to introduce her also as his wife but then realised it might not be smart. So far, the Dutchman thought that he and Cathy were a wonderful upright English couple; his moral standards might not stretch to polygamy!

From the way that the Dutchman was eagerly eyeing the pepper, William guessed that it had considerable value and by giving it to him as a gift, the man wouldn't have to share it with anyone on his ship.

'Please accept this as a gift and a taste of the many spices that this island produces. If you would care to call back in several months' time, we will have completed a full harvest and will have much more to trade.'

Wuringa translated as he handed the heavy basket over and the Lieutenant was suitably impressed.

They finished the Madeira and the man stood up and again kissed Cathy's hand, then bowed to them all with a friendly final word. Wuringa translated again. 'The Lieutenant says that he will pass his recommendation to his captain that this island should be considered neutral in terms of its sovereignty and that when they next call here they can look forward to trading with us.'

They escorted him back to the gate but he paused and pointed up to the brass cannon and spoke to Wuringa with a little laugh. 'The Lieutenant wishes to point out that perhaps if we are serious about defending this fort, then we should invest in some modern iron cannon such as they have on their ship.'

William tried to look gratified and at the same time keep a straight face at the suggestion. 'Please tell Lieutenant Van Der Veldt that we appreciate his advice and will make enquiries about modernising our defences.'

They waited until the ship's boat was well away before Cathy nudged him. 'You're such a bullshit artist when you put your mind to it!'

'What about you… Scarlet O'Hara!'

The ship, which they could now see was called 'Eendracht', pulled its anchor about an hour later and departed.

William sighed resignedly as he watched the big vessel leave. 'Bugger it, now I'm going to have to learn Dutch too!'

CHAPTER FORTY-SIX

Bonding a community

The Ambeluans arrived on the following day. In addition to the six vessels that they had sent, another eight came back with more than one hundred and twenty people on board. Lakabella saw the surprise on the faces of the reception committee and looked abashed.

'I'm sorry there are so many,' he said. 'These are not all from Ambelu; there are only seventy of us. After I arrived home, three praus came to our island from Kepalauan Gerong to seek refuge from a fleet of Macassans lead by a man named Muluk. They follow the old gods as your people do and Muluk has sworn to hunt them down and kill them. I thought it would be alright for them to come.' He gestured towards a slim man wearing a blue sarong and headband. 'That is Arkiang, he is their leader.'

William's head was swimming. He had no idea how they were going to accommodate so many new arrivals but knew that if they were in fact genuine refugees, then they would just have to do it somehow. They had very early on decided on a policy of conservation of the timber on the island, with three trees planted for every one cut down, but the hard wood trees took many, many years to grow and building homes for so many new arrivals was going to use up a lot of trees.

There was room inside the fort for probably another hundred homes if necessary but there were going to have to be new amenities blocks built, with more waterways and more effluent pits dug. The council would have to think long and hard about it, but it gave him a headache just imagining the logistical problems that they now faced. The mention of Muluk sent a shiver down his spine. He could still recall the man's malevolent look that day on the beach and then learning that he had been responsible for the massacre on Adonara made him only too aware of how dangerous an enemy he was.

He called a meeting of their committee for that evening and invited representatives from both the Ambeluans and the Kepalauans. In the meantime, the beach became a swarm of humanity as tents sprang up and cooking fires were built. The proximity of the fort leant a feeling of security to the new arrivals. The big walls that they could get behind in short order allowing traumatised refugees some peace of mind for the first time in months.

The Paji people worked their way through the new arrivals, providing help and food where it was required and occasionally renewing friendships, particularly with the people from Kepalauan, who some knew through religious festivals over the years. A delegation of three came from both groups of the new arrivals. William made introductions of all the council members, as well as of Cathy and Mary and then he asked Arkiang and Lakabella to provide a summary of each of their peoples' resources and abilities.

It was going to be a mammoth effort to house so many and he had no intention of dropping the task into Teronga and Lemala's laps to do it all themselves. The council was relieved to learn that the Kepalauans had five carpenters among them and the Ambeluans another three. In addition, the committee was delighted to learn that two of the Kepalauans were ship builders and one a master stone mason.

On learning of the latter, William immediately arranged for the man to be assigned five young apprentices. He knew that their wooden fortress was only a relatively short-term home and sooner or later, they were going to have expand into something more solid and enduring. He was absolutely certain that masonry would be a huge part of it.

They were also gaining two more metal workers to work with Rantuka, another apothecary to assist Wuringa and more than a score of skilled weavers who would add to their cloth production. Both communities also had fishermen, trepangers and pearl divers among them. If they could manage to meld these three different communities into one people then they were going to be well set for the future.

Finally, William explained the basic philosophy of their community—with only a few eyebrows raised, but no arguments in regard to the twenty percent of earnings that went into the public coffers. It was discussed by the members of the existing Council and all agreed that they had to power to increase their numbers without recourse to a further vote, given the circumstances. The Council grew by six by the end of the evening and then the arak came out. By the end of the night, most of the council members felt like they had been best friends with the others for years.

William and Cathy were well into completing the work on their family history book that was to be handed down to future generations. They realised that they were in a unique position to enable their descendants to have a forewarning and exclusive insight to many of the events of history as they unfolded. They hoped that this would help their family in the centuries to come to maintain a safe but prosperous mini-nation amidst the turmoil of the times leading up to the twenty-first century, allowing them to arrange alliances and forge friendships based on the fore-knowledge that they were able to provide to them.

They realised that there were gaps in their shared knowledge of history but between them, they were fairly confident that they were arming their future family with enough knowledge to keep them safe in turbulent times. They would know with the benefit of William and Cathy's hindsight of the dangers of Napoleon, Hitler, Tojo, Stalin and all of the megalomaniacs that threatened civilisation in these years. There was a special warning about the Japanese who would infest these islands in the Second World War, with a strong recommendation for temporary relocation to Australia until the conflict was over. The attacks on Darwin were mentioned to alert them to what would happen in February 1942 when the Japanese attacked the Australian mainland for the first time and recommended Brisbane as their best haven during the Second World War.

Then, they went one step further and laid out for their descendants a timetable of inventions, developments and trends for the next four hundred years. They were arming their family in years to come with the knowledge of what was going to be invented, where and by whom and of the implications of those inventions.

Their descendants were going to know well in advance of the industrial revolution that started in England in the nineteenth century. They were going to know what to invest in, which companies were going to be successful and safe for family money. They would be ready for medical breakthroughs and would be able maximise the benefits from them as well as assisting in their development.

William took special delight in his notations about the development of computers in the twentieth century. A couple of struggling young eggheads working out of a garage with revolutionary ideas about making use of a weird idea called 'the internet' and the development of personal computers were going to be very gratified to find ready backers and investors for their fledgling companies.

The opening page of this substantial, leather bound book of parchment however bore an entreaty and warning to their descendants.

'To all of our beloved descendants,

You will know by word of mouth from your mothers and fathers that I, William Wasley and my first wife, Cathy Johnson, come from a future time, from the year 2018. We hope that the words contained in this book will enable our family in generations to come to grow, to prosper and to be safe.

Each generation of our family will have a leader, or perhaps a family committee of leaders. You will decide. Keep this book, this absolutely unique history of what will be, safe and hidden from all but a precious few. Know that, should knowledge of the book ever reach the ears of others, then those in power or those who thirst for power will do anything, kill anyone, to gain possession of this family tome.

Use the knowledge that we lay down for you wisely and

cleverly. Keep yourselves in the background, never becoming so powerful or rich that others will want to take what you have or become suspicious of how you have attained it. Use history for the benefit of our family as we have outlined it to the best of our knowledge. We stress USE IT, but never, EVER try to consciously change it. It is inevitable that you will all change how things would have been if we had never come back in time. It will be a fine line at times and we trust to your wisdom to maintain the balance. Change history too much though, and there is no way to know what the result will be.

Maintain a Democratic community; look after the welfare of our people. Make health, education and prosperity a priority for all.

Cathy, Mary and I will not try and rule from the grave, despite what it may sound like in this missive. We believe and hope that you, our sons and daughters, grandchildren, great-grandchildren and all who follow us will grow to be the wise, clever, honourable people that we dream of.

Use this book with our love. One day, give our love to those that Cathy and I left behind in the twenty-first century. We have given thought to the right time for Cathy's parents in Darwin and mine in Melbourne to be informed. To ensure that you are believed and that there is no doubt that we are gone from their time, please wait for exactly one year from the date of our disappearance from the twenty-first century. Go to them on February 23rd, 2019.'

They both signed the note and then so did Mary.

CHAPTER FORTY-SEVEN

The pirates locate them

Muluk

Muluk was not a happy man. He had been frustrated when the remnants of three different communities had somehow escaped from his clutches, depriving him of gold and slaves each time and allowing infidels to carry on their heathen ways without the wisdom of Mohammed to guide them.

He was worried as well. An entire Macassan fleet had simply disappeared while taking Trepang gatherers returning from the Southern land. One lone survivor had been found near to death and before dying, the man had spoken of a white demon who slaughtered the entire crew of his ship single handed.

Muluk dismissed the story, but memories of the white bastard who had killed his men on the beach that day made him wonder. The medicine man Asigi was still annoyingly with him and he constantly nagged at him to pursue the unsettling white man and his woman. He'd thought to have the black man's throat cut many times but held off, for now at least. Besides, Asigi had very handily disposed of one of his overly ambitious lieutenants for him with a powder in the man's coffee. It had been amusing to watch his former friend contorting on the floor while Asigi's powder tore up his guts. It was a salutary lesson for the rest of his men that it was the price of trying to usurp his authority and steal crews away from him.

They were in need of repairs to the fleet, as well as supplies and some rest, and so had called into Batavia, which since the Dutch had taken over, was the biggest city in all of the islands. He now had fifteen praus in his fleet and more than two hundred men, all of them with gold and silver in their pockets from their crusade against the infidels that they had been raiding. He had no doubt that the inns and whorehouses of Batavia were going to be very happy to relieve them of a large proportion of it before they departed.

Once he arranged for his repairs and supplies, Muluk was intending to head to the slave pens to see if there were any tasty little replacements for his present sleeping companions but first, he had a huge thirst that needed to be slaked. He found a slightly upmarket inn that he knew had good ale and even better arak as well as very good food, and settled in with some of his now thoroughly subservient and respectful lieutenants in a booth near a group of Dutch sailors.

He had a tankard of ale in one hand and a tankard of arak in the other and was just settling in when he overheard one of the sailors speak of the 'beautiful blonde wife' living with her English husband on a tiny little island.

Muluk could be very affable when he put his mind to it and he was charm itself as he had a round of ale brought to the whole table of sailors. 'So, my fine seamen, perhaps you have met with my very good English friend and his wife! I have been trying to find them to pay them back the gold that they lent to me but they moved from their island and

I have not been able to find them!'

One of the Dutchmen was a petty officer. He took one look at Muluk and doubted very much that the reason for the Macassan's need to find the Englishman was to pay him gold. He eyed the heavy purse that hung from Muluk's sash. 'My lieutenant is very taken with these people and he would be very angry if I revealed the location of his friends. I could get into a lot of trouble.'

Muluk had observed the direction of the sailor's eyes and placed an eight *real* coin on the table in front of him.

The petty officer eyed the coin greedily but shook his head. 'My friends would get into trouble as well.'

Muluk cursed under his breath but place four more of the pieces of eight onto the table. 'I'll want to know the exact location of their island.'

The petty officer scooped the coins up and smiled. 'Do you have a chart?'

William

Work was a lot easier this time with so many extra hands, both skilled and unskilled. In a deliberate move, homes for all three communities were intermingled to encourage them to begin to grow together and not as separate groups within the fort. Even though the Buddhist Ambeluans followed a radically different philosophy to the multi-god following beliefs of both the Adonaran and Kepalauans, theirs was none the less a philosophy of acceptance and peace and so there were remarkably few disputes as families moved into the new homes that sprang up.

Two new amenities blocks had to be built and the system of aqueducts expanded and strengthened to provide water not only to them but also to the extra water cisterns that were put in. Cathy had a light bulb moment and convinced Teronga and Lemala of the value of guttering on the homes surrounding the cisterns.

They had a nice shower of rain on the very night that the bamboo guttering was finished and Teronga stood watching the water flow into the cisterns, scratching his head. 'Why hasn't anyone thought of this before?'

Rantuka

Rantuka was very happy to have two additional metal workers to help with his workload. He organised for his smithy to be expanded considerably, with an extra forge and bellows and with apprentices appointed as well. There was a constant demand for metal implements and tools. In addition, William had stressed to him the importance of their expanded numbers being able to defend themselves, so crossbows and swords were constantly being turned out.

As much as he welcomed the extra hands, Rantuka wasn't ready however to completely take his new colleagues completely into his confidence and so established a new and separate workshop attached to his house where he continued work in improving the first cannon as well as working on Mark III. He was trying to incorporate a magazine feed so that three rounds could be fired without reloading the breech. He was also building up a stock of shells with Wuringa's assistance, storing the growing inventory of ordinance in a purpose built cellar near the base of the wall.

He was putting in long arduous hours but didn't complain and had found the time to court one of the Kepaluan widows, who was looking for a new man just as he was a new wife.

The community's sentry roster was also expanded, much to the relief of the few Paji men who had been putting in very long hours up on the walls and now there was a constant rotation of sentries between the towers. Spices were beginning to flow into their storehouses.

In the rich Damar volcanic soil and with such a high rainfall, the new plantations were exploding with growth. Whole teams of women harvested and prepared the many spices, all of them carefully packed and stored for sale, while rolls of beautifully printed cotton went into storage huts built for it. A sturdy wharf was also completed, extending a hundred metres out into the bay. Now their praus could easily tie up before loading and unloading.

Numerous trips were made to Wetar and livestock was brought back. The Council recognised the uselessness of having chests full of gold and silver sitting doing nothing in the strong room, and luxuries began to appear. A store was established and the Damarese were able to purchase such things as fragrant soap, haberdashery, household implements and food items.

Mary brilliantly designed a system of credit that was established so that purchases were offset against shares of profit from their community's trade. Purchases where recorded on parchment, with a limit to how much any family could buy. Cathy watched her sister-wife in awe as she visualised and then implemented the system. One day, she would tell her that she had effectively just invented 'credit cards' hundreds of years early!

Everyone pitched in and all worked for the common good. Gradually, the three peoples were all merging into one; more and more of the Kepalauans and Ambeluans were already following the example of the Paji and were referring to themselves as Damarese.

Inspired by memories of yachts mooring in front of her parents' home in Darwin, Cathy suggested that mooring points should be put in around the bay so that the praus would no longer need to be drawn up onto the beach, other than when their hulls needed cleaning. Now she could look out into the beautiful tropical sunset to see the praus all sitting peacefully at rest around the bay. It reminded her so much of the view out over Fannie Bay that tears often came to her eyes.

William, Cathy and Mary were putting in long hours with their community but couldn't remember being happier. Young William, Henry and Lillian were thriving and shooting up and both women were walking around with rapidly swelling tummies from their second pregnancies.

William thought back to such a short period before, when he and Cathy had found themselves stranded at Obiri Rock with almost nothing. Now, they had a home, a family and were part of a wonderfully dynamic and happy community. Sometimes he almost felt a need to pinch himself to ensure that it wasn't all a dream.

When the Eendracht arrived back at Damar, the Dutch were duly impressed at being able to tie up in deep water at the end of the sturdy wharf with several metres of water under their keel. On this occasion, almost the entire officer compliment came ashore and William, Cathy and Mary—in a less obvious role—hosted them to a huge feast in the meeting hall.

Lieutenant Van Der Veldt was amazed at how much they had grown in such a short time, with rows of neat new homes everywhere he looked and busy people in every direction. He commented on it and William shrugged. 'We offer refuge to anyone who needs it. Lately there has been a lot of them.'

William pragmatically recognised the fact that the Dutch were going to dominate the East Indies to a large extent right up to World War II. The English would take over much of their trade in the late eighteenth century but these were the people who he and his people were going to have to deal with for a long, long time.

As Cathy reminded him too, the Dutch and the English had fought a series of wars in the seventeenth century, with the Dutch the victors in several of them. That being the case, he knew that he had to go to great pains to stress the island's absolute neutrality, for there was no question that they had to be very good friends with them.

He knew how much gold and silver they had in their coffers and he guessed that it probably would have made every man, woman and child on Damar very wealthy back in his time. They were constantly sending fleets of praus now back to Australia and Wing Lew Fatt was getting very rich in their trading, as were they. They could afford therefore to be generous in their trading terms with the VOC.

Thanks to Wuringa, William's Dutch was now passable and he and Cathy were able to converse with the captain of the Eendracht and his officers. He was fascinated to learn from Captain Cornelis Buysera that he had taken over command of the Eendracht from Dirck Hartogh. William still remembered from his school history lessons that Hartogh was one of the earliest explorers of Australia. The captain seemed happy to accept Lieutenant Van der Veldt's verdict of their neutrality, much to William's relief.

During the meal that evening, a team of volunteers brought steaming platters of pork and fish, rice and vegetable, oysters and clams and then mangoes and shredded coconut out in a seamlessly continuous stream of food.

William completely exhausted his Madeira during the meal but the Dutch were impressed by the ale that one of the Kepalauans had been brewing up and so by the end of the evening their Dutch friends left full of lovely food and lots and lots of ale.

A slightly hungover purser arrived the next morning and negotiated for almost half a tonne of spices and ten bolts of cotton. He must have thought that he was robbing them compared to what he had to pay at other ports but at the end of the day there was another very large chest full of Dutch Guilders to add to their strong-room.

Lieutenant Van der Veldt came to see them on the morning of the ship's departure. He had been a constant visitor during the few days that the Eendracht was with them, and a friendship had developed with William and Cathy at first and then with Mary as well when he finally realised that William was married to both beautiful women. His initial sense of shock was quickly replaced by envy and admiration when he saw how much the three of them loved each other.

He sat with William at the front of the big house. It was obvious that something was weighing on his mind. Finally, he made up his mind and spoke. 'Do you know of a man called Muluk?'

That bought all of William's attention. 'Unfortunately, yes I do. How do you know the name?'

Willem was troubled. 'This may be nothing, but one

of my sailors has come to me in the last week. There is a petty officer on our ship who has suddenly come into more money that he would normally earn in a year. The sailor claims that he took the money from this Muluk person in return for revealing this island's location. For this, he was paid five pieces of eight that should have been shared, but he kept it all to himself.'

'Do you know when this transaction was supposed to have taken place?'

'It was in Batavia three weeks ago. Is this Muluk your enemy?'

'Yes, I'm afraid that he is.'

The Dutchman glanced up at the bronze cannon that still sat on the ramparts guarding their bay.

'Your fort is very good but if this man attacks you, he has many men. You really should get more cannons you know, William. I can put you in touch with some very good people in Batavia if you like.'

The dilemma of lying to a friend again plagued him but William realised that there was simply no way that he could reveal their true offensive strength to the Dutch. It allowed him time in any case to consider the new threat from Muluk as he worked out what he could say.

'Thank you for the warning about Muluk. Forewarned is forearmed, as they say, and your idea about the cannon is appreciated, Willem. We intend to visit Batavia very soon and I will see what is available. Do you suggest any particular cannon?'

'I can recommend thirty-two pounders.' He looked guiltily around and then added. 'If you can arrange for Drakes, which are made by your English, they are very, very good—perhaps even better than ours!'

William appreciated his friend's candour and felt even more guilty at the thought that even the best English cannon was a popgun compared to theirs. He deliberately changed the subject and pursued an issue that had been worrying him. 'We have money here that we would like to bank. I assume that there are banking establishments in Batavia?'

Willem's face brightened. 'Oh yes indeed.' He paused as if considering how he could continue and then hastily blurted out his next statement. 'In fact, I have been giving some thought to going into commerce in Batavia myself. I have built up some capital and the First Netherlands Bank of Batavia might offer me a junior partnership if I were to...' he looked with guilt at William. 'If I were to bring a substantial new client to the bank.'

William looked at the man and considered. They had an awful lot of gold and silver coins now in their strong room, quite aside from what had been put aside in the community funds. It was more than enough to tempt altogether too many thieves and pirates and too much not to put to better use. Wuringa had sorted out all of the various types of coin and by his rough estimate they had more than the equivalent of two hundred thousand guilders. He had always been able to rely on his sense of judgement of a person. It had stood him in good stead during his police days and now he instinctively trusted Willem as an honourable and honest person and made a decision on the spot.

'How much would a hundred thousand guilders impress them?'

Willem swallowed hard. 'I think that would impress them a lot. You have that much here?'

'It isn't all in guilders but yes, we actually have a bit more than that.' Now he looked Willem in the eye. 'I'd like to make you our agent in Batavia. You can bank our money, hopefully at a good interest rate against a line of credit from the bank.'

He could see that Willem was seriously considering the offer and so went on. 'We are expanding our operation here and expect our trade to continue to grow. We will be buying and selling constantly so you'd be kept busy as our agent. I don't mind that you work for the VOC or the bank as well, but I would want to know that you have our interests here as your priority. How would you feel about that?'

The Dutchman looked at him curiously. 'How would you know that I wouldn't just take your guilders and go home to the Netherlands? A hundred thousand guilders would make me a very rich man back home.'

William nodded as he considered the possibility. 'You could I suppose, but I think that you are an honourable man. Throw in with us and I'll make you rich anyway. You'll be working for a percentage of every transaction, but if you were to take our money and run, then you'd just be a thief for the rest of your life.'

The Dutchman suddenly grinned. 'Well I hate thieves, so I guess that would only leave me one option!'

William held out his hand. 'Welcome to the company, Willem.'

The Dutchman shook his hand firmly. 'What is the name of this company anyway?'

'One of your first tasks for us will be to register our new company name.' He thought for a moment. 'I think "The Damar Trading Company" fits the bill.'

Willem nodded. 'I like it.' Then he looked curiously at William again. 'What about this Muluk person though? Aren't you worried that he'll come here with all of his men and wipe you out?'

'I'll let you in on a little secret, Willem. We're not quite as unprepared as that big old gun up there would suggest. If Muluk comes here, he's got a hell of a fight on his hands.'

William's calm confidence puzzled his friend. 'Do you already have other big guns or something that I don't know about? I don't understand.'

He put a hand on the Dutch officer's shoulder. 'Mate, there will be lots of things about us that you'll have trouble understanding until you get to know us a lot better but trust me on this, if Muluk comes here, he won't leave again.'

CHAPTER FORTY-EIGHT

The attack on the fort

Muluk

The Macassan was looking forward to this. Finding the tiny island hadn't been easy even with the directions that the Dutch sailor had supplied, but now they were finally approaching it. He had sent praus out over the whole area and one finally came back to his base in the Malaccas with the news he had been hoping for.

From the Dutch petty officer, he'd learned that this white man had built himself a fort of some kind and even had a large and ancient bronze cannon. This would pose a problem but not one that would worry him. He wasn't about to go climbing assault ladders himself and so simply set about recruiting more fighters to attack the fort and to be cannon fodder. He realised that he might have to knock down a wall or a gate though and bought two big new cannon of his own that would fire an iron ball for almost two hundred paces. Let's see the white man's cannon compete with that!

He had spies in Batavia who informed him that one of the big VOC ships was visiting the island at the moment. He wished that the informant had told him about it earlier or he could have just followed the square-rigger. As it was, he knew that he would need to wait until the Dutch left.

He was quite happy to tackle a bronze cannon but not the firepower on one of their ships.

By inviting another, lesser Macassan chief, his fleet had now grown to twenty praus and almost four hundred fighters. He moved the fleet to Kabaena Island so that the Dutch would have to sail past on their way back to Batavia. Then, it was just a matter of waiting. The white man in his little fort wouldn't stand a chance.

As soon as the Eendracht left, Newhope's preparations for war went into overdrive. Traditionally, island women protected the children and livestock during warfare but William guessed that they were going to need as many triggers on cross-bows as they could muster. By including able-bodied women as well as all the men who could use one of Rantuka's cross-bows, William had a hundred and twenty defenders. In addition, there were forty others who would act as couriers, water carriers and if needed, stretcher-bearers. The very old and the very young, including his four-year-old children would all go to a reinforced and sandbagged home at the very rear of the fort, the safest place in the event of an attack.

Young William had protested long and loudly about this state of affairs. It particularly caused a storm when, after what he thought was a very reasonable request, his father informed him that; 'No, he couldn't have his own sword to chop the bad man's head off.'

Cathy and Mary were five months pregnant by now but had flatly refused his suggestion that they shouldn't be up on the wall when and if the Macassans attacked. Together with mid-wives, they had however, set up a sort of hospital in the meeting room of the big house, with masses of prepared, clean bandages ready to use and lots of kettles full of water ready for the boil. Wuringa offered to take charge of the hospital and had listened carefully and grimly when Cathy explained to him the concept of *triage* and about the use of pressure bandages and tourniquets. Both she and William gave them all first aid lessons from their 21st Century training, but they hoped it would never be needed. The issue made William determined that when this was over, he was going to find some decent doctors to come to Damar.

There were now enough cross bows to arm them all and Rantuka and his new associates had turned out thirty iron bolts for each one. Every day saw groups of twenty people up on the walls, practising with their weapons by firing down at targets outside the wall at different ranges. With their advantage of height, the Damarese were becoming more and more proficient with the weapons and the cocking arm that Rantuka had designed and incorporated in them enabled even the youngest and slimmest defenders to pull back the steel cord and fire at a rate of two bolts a minute. White washed rocks were placed at careful intervals so that everyone would know when the attackers were within cross bow range.

William wanted the attackers to bunch together to provide his defenders with easier targets, so to accomplish this, he had asked the metal workers to turn out hundreds of wicked, metal caltrops by welding long nails together so that when dropped, they always landed with a sharp iron spike sticking up and waiting for someone to step onto. These were sown into the sand to the left and right of the beach, leaving only a narrow gap for attackers to come at them.

They had a full load of ammunition for the Lee Enfield and when Rantuka and Wuringa finished the upgrade of the first gun and then finally finished the Mark III, they were able to mount all three of their secret weapons on swivelled mountings at three points of the wall. William would operate the first cannon with Jimmy assisting and Luku and Opaki the second.

When William decided to give the Damarese a demonstration of Mark III, it solved two problems. Even though everyone was grimly determined to fight for their new home, he could see fear in many faces. They had all suffered recent and traumatic experiences from the Macassans—almost all of them having lost loved ones to the merciless pirates—and it was natural that they were nervous at the prospect of being attacked by them once more, notwithstanding the fort that now protected them.

The other issue William had been worried about was the effect that the booming weapons would have on the defenders, who at best had only ever heard a musket being fired before. He didn't want his people dropping their crossbows in fright when the big guns started firing. To solve the problem, William had a big raft taken into the bay and moored about three hundred metres out, and then invited everyone up onto the walls to watch.

Rantuka had claimed the right to operate Mark III himself, after spending so much time and using so much genius to create the first repeating cannon in history. The council had wanted to christen the three weapons 'The Rantuka', Marks I, II and III, but their creator declined the honour and insisted instead that they simply be called the 'Damar guns'. Now, as everyone looked on, he carefully inserted the big clip containing three shells into the top of the weapon and then sighted carefully into the bay.

Normally, the gun had two operators—a loader and an aimer or firer—but today, Rantuka waved Teronga away and did both jobs himself. He wasn't all that sure that the weapon would work as advertised and didn't want to endanger his friend unnecessarily.

He looked back at William and smiled a little nervously. 'Now I know how you felt when your women were about to have their babies!'

Fingers went into all ears as he pulled back the cocking action and then reached for the trigger. The gun boomed. Fire belched from the muzzle and the big gun jumped in its mounting. Then, it boomed again—and then again, as Rantuka continued to aim and pull the trigger. There was silence in the aftermath, but then when everyone looked out to see that the raft had ceased to exist, a huge cheer went up. Their morale problem was solved and Rantuka's grin was wider than a Cheshire cat's.

Asigi

Asigi could almost feel the two whites in his power. He had already made plans with Muluk to be allowed the use of one of his praus to take his captives back to his land. He realised that by now, the woman would have given birth, so a small amount of the potency of his magic would now be lost but he would have the two adults and also their child! He could only hope that by now she was with child again.

When he saw how many boats and men that Muluk was assembling for the attack, he realised that a lot of their fighters were going to be killed in the battle to come. So when Muluk arranged the order in which the praus would land and attack the fort, staying on his big galleon well to the rear, Asigi decided that this would be a good place for himself as well.

Their lookouts on the headland at Kabaena Island watched the Dutch VOC ship sail past and ran down to inform Muluk. The biggest armada of Macassan ships ever to be assembled emerged from their hidden anchorage and set course for Damar as soon as the big sailing ship had passed.

VOC Ship

The lookout in the crow's-nest on top of the main mast of the Eendracht was conscientious about his duties and proud of his excellent eyesight. He constantly looked ahead for any hidden reefs that could tear the belly out of their great ship but also looked further afield for other dangers such as pirates or even the dreaded English ships. Now, he carried out a full circle in the crow's-nest and, as he came to the rear view, frowned to see in the distance a mass of vessels swarming out from the lee of an island in their wake.

He called out loudly. 'Look out! Ships abaft!'

Lieutenant Van der Veldt was the officer of the watch and immediately threw the telescope to his eye. He made out the Macassan fleet immediately and knew exactly what it meant. A cold feeling of dread ran through him as he realised that his friends were in the most dreadful danger.

Captain Buysera came to the quarterdeck. 'Report please, Lieutenant!'

Willem saluted. 'Yes, sir. There is a very large fleet of Macassan vessels on their way to Damar. They must have been hiding behind that island that we passed a while back.

I make out about twenty praus.'

His captain studied him. 'You're sure that's where they are headed?'

'Yes, sir. It will be that Muluk that we heard about. He has a vendetta against Mynheer and Mevrouw Wasley.'

A smile appeared. 'You like your English friends, don't you?'

Willem reddened a little. 'They are fine people sir and their new community on Damar is a wonderful example of what hard working and enterprising people can accomplish out here and as we know; they are the source of excellent quality spices at a very good price for the company!'

The captain gazed back at in the direction of Damar and thought for a moment. 'Lieutenant I'm not about to fight a whole fleet of Macassans for your friends.'

Willem had expected the decision. Their vessel was the most powerful in the region but could be swamped and taken by so many Macassans. 'Sir, with your permission, I would like to take the pinnace back with a crew. I realise that we will be too late to assist them but we may be able to offer some aid to any survivors.'

The captain looked at him soberly. 'If these pirates capture you then you will be either killed along with the crew or at best held for ransom. I can't take the risk. I'm sorry.'

Willem felt a desperate need to help William, Cathy and Mary. 'Just a small crew of volunteers, sir. I give my word that we will turn around at the first sign of a Macassan ship heading our way.'

Cornelis Buysera was a humane man and he too had been taken by the slightly strange but likeable English couple. 'Alright then. But strictly volunteers only!'

Willem saluted and then raced down the stairway to find his volunteers.

Muluk

Muluk chose dawn to attack. He would be attacking with the sun coming up from behind him and straight into the faces of those in the fort. His men were eager to attack, almost salivating at the thought of the dozens of young women and girls awaiting them and of the vast hoard of gold and silver that Muluk had assured them was in the fort. They loved nothing better than killing and to do it in the name of Allah was to ensure their place in Paradise.

Three of his big galleons led the fleet, their big oars churning the calm waters as they headed straight into the bay. A line of smaller praus followed them, five in each of three tiers of fierce pirates and then his own and his fellow chief's galleons at the rear.

Muluk's prau was still to enter the bay and he watched as his galleons drew closer and closer to the unsuspecting fools in the fort. He could make out the fort now. It was bigger than he had expected and the walls looked high and solid, but once he landed his cannon they would be reduced to kindling in short order.

There was no movement in the fort, no lights and no cries of alarm. They had caught them napping! He felt his blood race at the prospect of easy slaughter and called to his oar master. 'Faster, man—get those dogs to put their backs into it!' He eased his sword in its scabbard, anticipating the exciting feeling as he sank it into someone's guts.

There was a loud boom from ahead and he smiled at the thought of their bronze cannon finally waking up and throwing their balls at them. It would do them little good today. Then, before that thought had finished, he frowned to see the middle galleon suddenly explode. There was another loud boom and then another and the second of his galleons seemed to disintegrate, leaving nothing but a hole on the water and flaming wreckage.

He struggled to come to terms with what he was seeing. The damned white man had to have other cannon as well! He was full of battle rage now. It would still do them no good. 'Attack them! Kill the infidels!' he screamed.

His third galleon finally reached the beach and he felt a huge relief for this was the one with the cannon on board. 'Let's see how they liked a taste of their own medicine!'

There were more booms from the fort and he watched praus being blown out of the water. What sort of cannons were these? A moment of doubt sent a quaver through his guts, but now he only wanted to kill. So what if a few of his fighters were dying? All the more gold for him!

'Attack!' he screamed again. 'Attack and kill them all!'

William

William fired one last shot and had the satisfaction of seeing another prau disappear in a shower of water and splinters. He ceded his position to Jimmy and picked up the Lee Enfield.

'Try and take out those praus at the back, mate. I'm going to give these blokes on the beach some grief.'

Jimmy grinned as he moved back to the firer's position. 'It's about time! You've been having all the fun!'

William slid a round into the breech of the .303 and looked for targets on the beach. They'd taken out probably half of the praus and even as he looked, two more blew up and then Jimmy, who fired and at almost point-blank range for the big guns, couldn't fail to miss another.

Newhope was winning but there were still hundreds of Macassans heading towards them. William looked to where one of the first galleons had run up on the beach. He'd been unable to hit it with the big gun because of the angle and now he saw that the forecastle on the vessel was swarming with Macassans as they wrestled with two huge cannons. There was a boom from one of them and suddenly an almost perfectly round hole appeared in the wall of the fort to his left. He couldn't see what damage the ball had done inside but he wasn't going to allow the cannon to fire again.

The sunlight was now in his eyes but it also had the effect of highlighting the Macassans with the sun right at their backs. William saw that the other cannon was about to fire and sighted on a man with a burning match. It wasn't a difficult shot. The Lee Enfield spoke and the Macassan went flying back with most of his head missing.

He worked the action and fired on the person who leapt to pick up the match. His third shot took out the person trying to reload the first cannon. He fired twice more and quickly reloaded, leaving the forecastle of the vessel empty of living people.

Luku was on that side and he had seen the threat. His gun blew the front of the galleon off and the two cannon crashed down onto the sand, barrels first.

William switched to the crews of smaller praus that were now coming ashore. He used another clip and then another. The Lee Enfield's barrel was growing hot now but he couldn't afford to let it cool.

Dead Macassans dropped one after another as William fired on them from less than a hundred metres. Another clip gone and he slid more rounds into the magazine. He worked a round into the breech and pulled the trigger. Misfire!

He tried to eject the round but the action wouldn't work. It was too hot. Macassans were now swarming ashore, screaming loudly as they ran at them. Many carried ladders and others waved swords. A few stopped to fire crossbows but the range was too great. Only a few of their bolts even made the wall.

Suddenly, those on the left and right began to scream with pain and not blood lust. The caltrops were working and William smiled grimly as Macassans rolled in the sand trying to pull the vicious barbs from their thinly sandaled or bare feet.

Those in the centre were now at the first white stone marker and the Macassans from the flanks moved to follow them.

William dropped the Lee Enfield and took up his long bow. Cathy was on one side and Mary on the other. Jimmy blew up a big galleon right at the back and then took up his bow as well and joined them.

The attackers were at the second white rock. 'Fire!' William yelled.

A hundred and twenty crossbows and four longbows fired at the same time. Macassans dropped, screaming, to the sand, some with four or five bolts in them. The crossbows went quiet as they were reloaded but the four of them fired again and again with the longbows, rarely missing.

Now, there were less than forty Macassans left but they had reached the ditch. More screams came from below as they found the spikes and stakes. Only one ladder hit against the wall and the first Macassan who climbed it fell back with a crossbow bolt right between his eyes, but four more gained a footing on the walkway.

William ran towards them but quickly saw that his help was not needed, as iron bolts thickened the air and each of the pirates dropped with multiple quarrels in them. Another full volley of the cross bows annihilated those few still alive in the ditch and now Macassans were running back towards their praus.

William suddenly heard a scream from behind him. Asigi seemed to have materialised out of thin air and was pulling at a screaming Cathy's arm. He was trying to stare into her eyes but she was struggling madly against him. He yelled at her. 'You are mine! I am your master. Come with me!'

William dropped his bow and drew his sword to stride quickly towards the evil Aboriginal man. Asigi saw him coming and laughed maniacally. 'No, you can't stop me now! I've got her. She's mine and she is with child again! I will be so powerful, so pow...'

That was as far as he got, for William swung the Toledo blade in a flat arc and took Asigi's head clean off in one very neat blow. The head hit the parapet with a wet thud. Asigi's eyes looked up in fixed and final shock as his body hit the boards beside his head, his neck a fountain of blood.

William looked down at the headless corpse with mixed feelings. One the one hand there was a vast relief that the person who wanted to use them for some sort of occult ritual was never going to bother them again. The other side of the coin, but one he was able to quickly shrug off, was that he had just killed the one person who could have sent them back to their time. The thought was surprisingly easy to dismiss. This was now their time, here and now with their family and friends. The satisfaction he was feeling was quickly interrupted however, when Mary sudden called to him. 'William, one is getting away! It is Muluk!'

'Damn it, we can't let him get away!' William ran back to the cannon and then cursed in dismay to see that there were no more shells. He looked out into the bay and saw Muluk's galleon backing oars frantically. The distinctive Macassan was visible at the stern as he screamed at his rowers to get him away.

William picked up the rifle and tried to free the bolt but it was seized still. He looked towards Rantuka's gun but the man looked back helplessly. 'I am sorry William, I fired them all.'

He was turning towards their last hope, Luku's gun at the far end of the wall, when Luku fired off his last shell.

The galleon had turned and had almost reached the entrance to their bay, the range at least five hundred metres. They defenders on the wall held their breaths and could all hear the shell as it tore through the air. Then the stern of the galleon simply disappeared as the shell hit. Virtually everyone on the ramparts let out a yell of joy as the last galleon was sunk by the incredible shot but then the noise died off as one survivor, still recognisable because of his bright red vest, surfaced from the water beside the wreckage of his prau and clung to a spar.

William was not about to let Muluk escape death. He had brought so much death and destruction to the islands that there was no way that he was going to be allowed to escape the noose at the very least.

He looked around for Luku, meaning to send him

out with a boat to capture the Macassan, when a sigh of satisfaction ran along the wall. He turned back to see a circle of sharks, attracted to the hundreds of dead bodies in the water. He felt pity for the Macassan as he watched him spinning in utter terror as the sharks drew closer. He closed his eyes as the pirate chieftain disappeared under the water with a last scream of terror that reached them on the walls.

Luku stood with a serene smile on his face as the water finally calmed, with a visible cloud of red where Muluk had died. 'That was for you, Father!'

VOC

Lieutenant Van Der Veldt approached the entrance to the bay with trepidation. He had ordered the sail dropped and they were under oars as they nosed gingerly into the bay, ready to turn and run at the first sign of Macassans. They had heard a long series of explosions as they got closer but then only sudden silence. He dreaded what it might mean. They cleared the headland and Willem let out an exclamation of shock at the sight that was before him.

Where he had expected a whole bay full of Macassan praus and rampaging pirates, the bay was instead covered with floating wreckage with dozens and dozens of bodies floating face down amid the wreckage. He could see more wreckage on the beach, with bits and pieces of shattered praus littering the shore while more wreckage sat in the shallows. The sands were littered with more bodies that led all the way up to the fort and then, he realised that there were people moving about outside the walls.

They rowed into the beach and Willem stepped ashore through water red with blood. His sword was in his hand but he only saw dead Macassans wherever he looked. He saw William directing a group of people who were collecting bodies and piling them to one side, while more people were emerging from the fort to carry on the same task. There seemed to be simply hundreds of dead Macassans.

He walked up to William. 'How on earth... how did you... what happened to them?'

William allowed himself a grim smile. 'Like I said, there's a bit more to us than meets the eye, mate. You'll get used to it once you know us better.'

It took days to collect all of the dead and burn them in a series of fires along the beach. Sharks took care of some of the corpses in the water but there were too many even for their voracious appetites and the rest had to be laboriously hooked and dragged ashore in boats before they could be cremated. None of the Damarese shed a tear for the Macassan dead, all remembering the funeral fires for their own dead.

The William and the Council had been wonderfully surprised to learn that their own casualties had been extremely light. Four men and one woman had been struck by crossbow bolts and Wuringa and his willing nursing volunteers had managed to save all five. Miraculously, they had just fought a major battle against a numerically superior enemy and they had not lost one person.

Willem had caused them a worry when he'd spotted Rantuka's Mark III before it could be hidden away. He stared at the strange looking gun and turned to William. 'What is that thing?'

William took on a pained, hopeful look. 'Would you believe a modified Drake?'

Willem watched as a cover was hastily thrown over the weapon. He considered William's answer and then smiled a little. There were so many mysteries surrounding his big English friend and this was perhaps one of the most intriguing, for there was no way that the big bronze gun had won such a victory for them and this was no 'modified Drake' hiding under the cover.

He glanced along the wall and saw to other suspiciously covered objects of about the same dimensions. It was obvious that William was in possession of some fearsome firepower that had reduced an entire fleet of Macassans to kindling. His first thought was that as a Dutch officer, his duty was to carry the news of these weapons to The Company. Then, the thought came to him that with William's sense of honour, of which he had become very much aware, and with their deepening friendship, he could afford to trust William implicitly.

'Would you like me to believe that it is a modified Drake?' Willem asked.

'That'd be really good!'

Willem pursed his lips and nodded sagely. 'I'd heard that they are very good.' Then he looked earnestly at his friend. 'Just don't ever fire that "Drake" at my people please?'

William clapped him on the back. 'Hey, we're mates aren't we? Why would I ever do a thing like that?'

The Dutchman and his crew stayed with them for a month until Eendracht returned for them. Willian sensed that the Dutch Lieutenant was going to be an integral part of their continued successes, so during that time, Willem was admitted into the small circle of people who knew the truth about them. After waiting in vain for them to tell him the punch line to the joke and getting only serious looks in return, he eventually came to believe their impossible story. He liked William, Cathy and Mary very much but not only that, he felt that his future prosperity was very much tied to them also. He would keep their secret.

When Captain Buysera questioned him as to how the Englishman and his community had survived the attack by the Macassans unscathed, Willem had felt terrible at bending the truth to his superior, but consoled himself that he really didn't know all the details yet himself! 'Sir to the best of my knowledge, one of their ships in the middle of the fleet was filled with gunpowder and exploded just as they came into the bay. It just blew them all up!'

The captain looked at him for a few moments over lowered eyelids, and then seemed to make a decision and nodded. 'Will you make an entry to that effect in the ship's log?'

Willem only hesitated for a moment. Once he entered his concocted story into the ship's log and signed it, his fiction became, for the intents and purposes of the VOC, fact. If it ever came out what really happened, his reputation would be ruined. Knowing what he now knew about his 'English' friends though, there was no alternative.

'Yes, of course Captain,' he said. 'It is what happened, after all!'

'That will do for my report then, but you are really going to have to learn to lie better if you want to become a banker, Lieutenant! I have no idea what really happened here but the fact remains that there are now a lot less pirates to interfere with our trade. That will make The Company directors very happy—and if they are happy, then I am happy.'

CHAPTER FORTY-NINE

Doctors, teachers and an ending

This time, Mary beat Cathy in the motherhood stakes, giving birth to a lovely girl who was named Maria, another sweet girl who became her namesake and was called Cathy, into the world.

Newhope now had a doctor who had been trained in both Amsterdam and London. They had lured him through an agent in London, by offering more money than he ever dreamed of earning. He supervised the births, but wasn't required to assist, with the midwives having none of his well-intentioned but superfluous advice as they brought the newest members of their community into the world.

During his first few months on Damar, the doctor often wondered at the wisdom of coming to the island. None more so than when Cathy sat him down and patiently but adamantly tried to convince him against well-established practices such as the use of leeches and bleeding! He knew better of course but quickly learned not to try and put such well-founded principals into practice, for his supply of leeches disappeared at an alarming rate. It was frustrating for him and inexplicable that his patients seemed to recover more quickly without being bled.

They had other strange practices too, such as their insistence that everyone in the community cleaned their teeth every day! It was a silly idea of course but also confusing as to how he was only rarely called upon to pull teeth. Then again, he became lost when Cathy referred to things called 'bacteria' that were supposedly the cause of infections and insisted on strange practices like boiling bandages before use and using vinegar to clean cuts and wounds. Once again though, it all seemed to work, making him feel very insecure at times. As silly at it sounded, it was almost like Cathy knew more about medicine than he did. He was being very well paid though and gradually he began to adopt some of their outlandish ideas, just to get along with them.

Four young teachers were employed as well. Two were young Dutch women from Batavia who had been sold as bonded servants to repay debts against their respective families. It wasn't an unusual event for the times, with hundreds of daughters and sons sold off every year to save their families from debtor's prison and bankruptcy. It was simply a part of the times that they lived in.

The two miserable girls had fully expected to spend the next ten years, which was the term of their bondage, as menial servants or perhaps even prostitutes, which was the fate of so many young women in their situation. They were both gratified and puzzled when their contracts were purchased by a really nice English man and his wife and when they arrived on the island they discover that bondage simply did not exist there and that they were now completely free, the monies paid to those holding their families' debts simply forgotten. Not only that, but they would be earning real money, money that would eventually enable them to build up a dowry so that they could one day marry, something they had given up thoughts of when their parents had sold them off. To their further astonishment, they were informed that if they wanted to, they could even return to their families if they wished to at any time. It was very confusing for them for a time but both agreed that staying with their benefactors, at least for a reasonable period, seemed a very good idea.

There was also a male and female teacher who had come out from England. The man was a gentleman, the fifth son of a baronet who would never inherit his father's title, or for that matter get one penny from his estate aside from the money that had been given to him to enable him to, as his father had put it, *'Go to the Indies and make your fortune, my lad'*.

The English woman, from a respectable merchant family in Dover, had been left penniless and stranded in Batavia when the family who she was travelling with as nanny to their child had all been struck down with typhoid. Abigail had miraculously escaped the disease despite nursing her charges throughout their illness. After the funerals, she had been at wit's end of how she would survive and so the offer to come to this island paradise to put her own excellent education to use had seemed like a gift from God. She and the two Dutch women quickly became close friends.

They were all extremely surprised when they were presented with the syllabus, to find that all of the children on the island, as well as a few adults who were keen to improve themselves, were to be taught literacy, basic mathematics, history and geography, as well as the English and Dutch languages but not a single word of Latin.

It was all very odd and unheard of for 'village people'—their usual term for island natives—to receive exactly the same educational opportunities as anyone else.

A program was set up for the brightest students to also study commerce, while a scholarship fund was set aside for the very best to go away to university in either the Netherlands or England.

They had one problem with the two English teachers right from the start and one that they had fully expected. Their contemporary English was of the times, naturally, but to William and Cathy—and to Jimmy and Mary who had learned their English from them—the new arrivals' English was archaic and very hard at times to understand.

It wasn't just their pronunciations either. As their employers, the two English teachers conversed mainly with William and Cathy but it took both of them a long time to come to terms with some of their terminologies.

Wuringa was observed by the male teacher and William was quite offended when he was referred to as an *arsworm*. It was much later that he learned that this term referred to a short person! So too, it surprised William that *a haberdasher of nouns and pronouns* was their own way of referring to their new profession as teachers. One of their phrases that stuck though was that of *nipperkin*. This became the commonly used term thereafter for a pint of wine or beer!

The two from England had just as much trouble with William and Cathy's English and it was months before they all learned how to get around the idiosyncrasies of their respective use of their language. William's frequent use of Aussie slang didn't help either so he quickly learned to tone it down when conversing with them. William and

Cathy explained away their own strange pronunciations by telling the two that they had been travelling for many years and that their English had become 'tainted'.

Willem left the VOC and secured his partnership with the bank. On one of his visits to the island he fell instantly in love with Abigail. The attraction was mutual and just as Abigail was settling into her role, Willem whisked her off for a wedding and honeymoon. None of them begrudged Willem his happiness. Another teacher would be easy to procure but Willem was proving to be invaluable to them.

One service he offered to a very grateful William was to take his measurements to his tailor in Batavia, returning on his next trip with a complete wardrobe of Western clothing.   William had enjoyed the freedom and cool comfort of wearing a sarong after so long in an animal skin loincloth but it felt wonderful to put on a pair of trousers again.

Already, Willem had invested their money in some very profitable ventures that were returning excellent profits. Every time he called at the island he took back another chest of coins from their own trading for further investment. His commissions were making him a wealthy man.

William and Cathy were working hard on their secret history, which continued to grow, as well as some carefully considered and timely advice to future generations, but that wasn't all that they were going to leave for their descendants. They carefully selected gold doubloons and pieces of eight in the very best condition and wrapped and stored them away with instructions for their eventual distribution in several hundred years when the coins where truly rare.

One day, their descendants, when their turn came, would be able to present pristine pirate coinage worth millions of dollars to some very bemused numismatists.

The population of Newhope continued to grow as the years rolled on. With their enlightened health practices, they had a higher life expectancy than anywhere in the region, as well as most places anywhere in the world at that time and with their prosperity and security came a population boom. They soon outgrew the fort and carefully planned homes sprung up all over the island, all with indoor plumbing of course!

Jimmy and Manissa had three children and they were constant companions to the children of their friends. With their children growing and in good care, William, Cathy and Mary began to travel more, with several trips back to Australia, mainly for nostalgic reasons but more particularly to Batavia with increasing frequency. The Dutch society in Batavia soon began to look forward to their visits, for the sight of a finely dressed William with a beautiful woman on each arm never failed to get tongues wagging and imaginations soaring.

As Willem's wife and confidant, Abigail was now one of the tight group who knew where Damar's font of knowledge came from. She gave birth to several children in the next years and to their delight, she insisted on them being educated back on Damar when they became old enough.

By the time that William was in his sixties, the Damar Trading Company was extremely rich. By that time, The Damar Trading Company had so many shares in 'De Verenigde Oostindische Compagnie'—or the VOC as it was usually referred to—that, if they'd cared to, they could have nominated someone to take a seat of the *Board of Nine*! Keeping in mind the time when the fortunes of the VOC would wane in the region and those of the British East India Company would flourish, the Dutch VOC shares had a sell-by date firmly set in their company's books.

Being a prominent member of the VOC Board was the last thing that William wanted in any case. He knew that the future security of Damar lay in discrete financial strength combined with covert military capabilities. It would be disastrous in the long term to become known as a regional powerhouse… financially or militarily.

Rantuka's apprentices were already turning out advanced weaponry, including fully functional replicas of the Lee Enfield for their protection, but the whole island realised the utmost importance of maintaining the secrecy of their strength. The combined populations of three different island groups had bonded beyond any of their dreams. The entire population of Damarese thought it a lovely joke that they had all this wonderful money and powerful weapons that the rest of the world didn't know a thing about. They all knew though, that to maintain their splendid standard of living in comparison to what they had known and to keep the security from hostile outsiders that their wonderful weapons provided, it was vital to keep their secrets very much to themselves. These were facts of life that were impressed on every new Damarese that was born and every new immigrant to their community.

Damar ships became common between the islands and their growing dimensions and distinctive designs, always being tweaked by William, made them stand out from the vessels of any of the other islands in the region. This was despite their innovative sail patterns being emulated widely by others in the area who recognised how much better the Damarese vessels sailed.

Rantuka came up with a ship's cannon for their vessels that were the epitome of his genius. He took the Damar Gun and worked out how to fit them inside the false casing of a big brass cannon so that to a casual observer, the Damarese ships looked to be armed with antiquated cannon and nothing more.

After four Macassan and three Sumatran pirate ships tried to take some of the Damar ships at sea and all seven vessels simply disappeared without trace, the word spread that ships from Damar were bad news and should be avoided at all costs.

William, Henry and Lillian all attended universities— the former two at Oxford, and Lillian in a more gender friendly Amsterdam-based institution. With their studies completed, they returned home and took up management positions in the company; followed in due course by their younger siblings.

'Young William' came to be referred to simply as 'William' and his father—to his horror—one day heard himself being referred to by one of the Damarese as 'the old man'.

A VOC ship called in one day and an elegantly dressed gentleman was introduced to them as the renowned portrait painter, Barent Fabritus. William looked at his beautiful wives and his fine family and realised that there was one more gift that they could leave for the future. They dressed in their best clothing and their family had to sit through many hours as Barent did a portrait of them. Even though he was well paid for the commission, he still insisted that it was his finest work. When they viewed the finished product, Cathy burst into tears. She and William were clearly recognisable from their younger selves and she knew that one day her mother would look at the painting and recognise her immediately. After they all admired the realistic and lifelike painting for a few weeks, it went into the family vault to better preserve it for the years to come, with instructions for its eventual delivery together with letters that they each penned.

William died in his ninetieth year. He woke up one morning to find himself short of breath, but still insisted on carrying on with his busy schedule for the day. His heart gave out just after having a quiet lunch with his wives. Cathy and Mary, along with five children, twenty grandchildren and six great-grandchildren attended his internment at the foot of the mountain. All of his friends and a good portion of the population of Damar were there as well.

Afterwards, Cathy and Mary strolled slowly arm in arm to their home overlooking the bay. They went to the balcony and looked out. It was full of shipping, the port that now filled the cove had formed from the simple beginning of one wharf and was bustling with activity, the sun bright and shining on their creation. They looked to where the old fort had stood. With their potential enemies knowing better than to try and attack them, it had been pulled down long since and the timbers used for homes and public buildings, including the little row of shops that now stood in front of the homes that had formerly been contained within the fort's protection. Cathy took pride in looking at the little row of shops. There was a general store, a butcher, a bakery, a haberdashery and an apothecary shop where Wuringa's successors now operated. The area was landscaped and included public picnic areas and even a toilet block. As far as she knew, it was the first dedicated shopping arcade in the world!

The years had been kind to them both and they were still attractive women with a deep bond for each other and mutual pride in the love that they had shared with a wonderful man.

Cathy squeezed Mary's hand. Proud tears leaked from her eyes. 'We haven't done too badly have we?'

Back to the present day

The monsoons were being nice to them and it was on a fine February day in the year 2019 when the sleek, hundred and twenty foot luxury yacht glided alongside the main wharf at Darwin Harbour. Lines were thrown and tied off and a young couple stepped down the gang plank and went to a waiting white Range Rover.

The man was in his twenties, tall and well-built with neatly trimmed black hair, an olive complexion, hazel eyes and a strong jaw. He was dressed expensively but modestly in tan trousers and a blue, open necked shirt suited to the Darwin heat. A stainless-steel Rolex watch adorned his left wrist. Wearing the watches had become a family tradition ever since the company in Switzerland began making them.

His female companion was a stunning looking girl, only a few years younger. They were brother and sister. She wore a beautiful blue and gold silk dress that demurely but elegantly showed off her lovely figure. She was shorter than her brother and where his hair was raven black, hers was a light gold in colour, cut stylishly short. She wore a string of black pearls around her neck. Most people who saw them assumed that they were costume jewellery. They were not.

The man accepted the keys from a smiling cousin waiting at the car. His cousin clapped him on the back and then hugged the girl. 'You're so lucky to be the ones. We're bloody envious of you both. We've all been dreaming of this day for generations!'

The man grinned. 'I know how you feel. We've been anticipating this day since the day our parents told us what we'd have to do today.' He looked anxiously at his cousin. 'How are they?'

His cousin waved away his concerns. Their family had been established in Darwin for more than a hundred years and a network of concerned cousins had been keeping a discrete eye on Cathy's parents ever since that fateful day exactly one year before.

They had in fact been very surreptitiously watching the family for many years before that as well, but with the strictest limitations on any contacts with the Johnson family. One of the cousins had actually watched Cathy board the mini bus with her friends from university that day, while another had been absolutely thrilled to have William come into his Hertz Office to hire a Jeep Cherokee from him. It had taken all of his willpower to act normally with him, but immediately photocopied the rental agreement so that he had an 'autograph' from the most famous of all Wasleys!

The whole extended Wasley clan, consisting now of numerous related families with a number of 'old Darwin' surnames, were all well off and very close to each other. All felt it was a privilege to be able to keep an eye on Cathy's parents since the disappearance and even had counsellors on retainer and ready to step in had Judith and Peter Johnson appeared in any real mental danger from the loss of their beloved daughter.

'They're fine. Still a bit sad I think but they've both returned to work.' He tossed over another set of keys. 'This is to the place next door to them. We bought it a few years back and it's been unoccupied ever since but it's been cleaned up ready for you and the fridge is full… so is the wine cellar.'

The man grinned. 'Good on ya, mate. Some beers in the fridge too, I hope!'

'Does the Pope shit in the woods?'

'I don't think that's the saying.' He laughed and then looked at the girl. 'Shall we?'

It was only fifteen minutes to Fannie Bay. They stopped in front of the Johnson house and both looked at each other as they readied themselves for what was to come.

Judith Johnson heard the doorbell and called out to her husband Peter. 'Dear, would you see who that is, please?' She waited but there was no reply and chuckled to herself. When her husband buried himself in his work, he was oblivious to the world.

She got up and opened the door to a lovely young couple standing with a quite strange expression on their faces. There was something about the girl that made her frown but then her manners came to the fore.

'Can I help you?'

The man spoke. 'Mrs Johnson, my name is William Wasley and this is my sister Cathy. Can we come in and speak to you and to your husband?'

Judith Johnson frowned again. 'May I ask what you'd like to speak to us about?'

He looked reassuringly at her. 'If we can come in then we'll explain everything to you both.'

She stared at him. 'William Wasley was the name of the person who disappeared on the same day that our daughter did a year ago.'

The young blonde girl put a hand softly on her arm. 'Please… we will explain it all to you.'

Professor Peter Johnson came out after his wife's repeated calls, to find her sitting opposite to two young people in their lounge room.

She looked up at him. 'Dear, this man says his name is the same as the person who disappeared with our daughter. He tells me that this young lady is his sister, and that her name is Cathy.'

He stood and stared levelly at William for a moment and then went to a thick folder in the bookcase. He opened it and brought it back to show a newspaper clipping showing photographs of William Wasley that had been published in the N.T. News after the disappearance.

'No. He's not. I guess that he could be his son at a pinch but this is William Wasley.'

William swallowed hard. 'I'm not his son sir, but I am related. I am his great, great, great, great, great, great grandson and this is my sister. Both of you are our great grandparents five times removed.'

Peter Johnson was a highly intelligent man and no person's fool. 'Are you trying to mock us on today of all days? This isn't an episode of *Doctor Who*. This is the real world!'

Cathy Wasley stood up and with great care, withdrew an object from her valise. She unwrapped it delicately and then walked two paces to present it to the Johnsons.

There were tears threatening to spill from her eyes as she addressed them. 'This is a gift to you from your daughter and her husband. We have been waiting a long, long time to give it to you. We have been instructed to give it to you on the anniversary of the day that your daughter disappeared along with William Wasley.'

The couple stared at the painting in front of them. They saw a family portrait of three adults and five children posing in front of a background of palm trees and blue sea. Judith focussed on the middle-aged woman in the portrait and suddenly cried out, her hand flying to her mouth and tears spilling from her eyes.

'That's my Cathy!'

Peter Johnson looked hard at the portrait and locked onto the signature at the bottom. It was clearly legible. He grabbed his computer tablet and quickly entered the painter's name.

'This is utter nonsense. It's some sort of fraud attempt! Barent Fabritus died in 1697! What are you two trying to pull?'

Cathy had tears flowing down her face by now. She reached into the valise again and brought out a thick parchment envelope. There was another in the valise that they had to take on to Melbourne to another set of parents.

'Please read this. I believe that it will answer everything.'

Judith Johnson stared at the tears on the young woman's face for a moment and then took the envelope. It was sealed with wax. She broke the seal and took out a sheaf of parchment pages. One glance at the handwriting and she knew who had written it. It began 'Dear Mum and Dad...'

She bit her lip and handed the thick letter to her husband with a shaking hand. 'It's from our Cathy!'

Cathy Wasley went to her many-times removed grandmother and put an arm around her shoulders as the distraught woman began to cry, just as she was.

Peter began to read, and then a stunned look came onto his face. He went pale and almost fell back into a chair as he began to read it out to his wife.

It was hours later that Cathy's parents finally led the young couple from their home. They opened their front door to let them out and stopped in confusion to see more than fifty people standing in front of their home, all of them looking anxiously and lovingly towards them.

William turned to the Johnsons. 'These are our cousins. Every one of them are your descendants.'

Judith looked around. There were people of all ages in front of them and it was hard to believe that so many people could be their descendants. She spotted a couple of babies held in their mother's arms and her eyes suddenly gleamed. 'Oh wonderful! At last I've got grandchildren to spoil!'

End